# THE
# GLASS
# SPARE

LAUREN DeSTEFANO

# THE GLASS SPARE

BALZER + BRAY
*An Imprint of HarperCollinsPublishers*

Balzer + Bray is an imprint of HarperCollins Publishers.

The Glass Spare

Typography by Jenna Stempel

ISBN 978-0-06-249128-2 (trade ed.)
ISBN 978-0-06-279741-4 (special edition)

17 18 19 20 21   PC/LSCH   10 9 8 7 6 5 4 3 2 1

First Edition

*For Aprilynne, who takes ideas and turns them into gold*

AT THE HEART
OF ALL BEAUTY LIES
SOMETHING INHUMAN.
–ALBERT CAMUS

# PROLOGUE

On the morning Wil was born, the queen ordered that sheets be hung across every window of the castle. It was an old superstition from her wanderer's upbringing, to keep fragile spirits from being lured off by the beautiful song of death. It was a song that only the queen could hear, calling sweetly in the rustle of the October leaves—for it had come to take her away as well.

In her efforts to have a daughter, the queen had given the king three sons, and it was against the advisement of the king's finest doctors that she have a fourth child at all. The queen knew this child could well kill her.

Wil came out bloody and white, with purple veins marbling her cheeks, and no promises that she would live. She didn't cry as her brothers had, but the most peculiar thing about her was the birthmark that lay between the spread of her ribs. It was a clean white line, as though someone had cut her open, torn out her heart, and returned it.

The king had always been fearless, but he feared her. When his sons were born, they had been perfect dolls of boys. But in this child's eyes, he saw something very much unlike his other children. Something that did not belong to this world at all.

Wil would be the last spare. For days after her birth, both mother and child lay in the shadow of sheets that hung over the windows, curled up small together in the wealth of blankets damp with sweat. But they did not die, despite what the doctors had murmured.

On many nights in Wil's childhood, the queen would hold her and rock her to sleep, and she would whisper, "Death itself is no match for you. The day you were born, it shrank away in fear."

# ONE

You're wind. You're everywhere.

Rawhide bag slung across her chest, Wil pushed into the crowd.

She went past the storefronts and cafes, straight to the vendors whose carts lined the Port Capital's edge. The Port Capital ended where the sidewalk was hemmed by a low stone wall. Just over its edge, the ocean's waves were some ten feet below, slapping against the stone and then rolling back into their depths.

She loved it here; she loved that her footsteps on the cobbles became a part of the city's hard beating pulse. In the Port Capital, she was not the princess who had never left her kingdom. She could carry herself as though the sea was an old friend, as though she'd been everywhere and seen it all. Anyone might believe it.

The Port Capital was the finest trading center the world had to offer: a city made of stone and geometric oak beams, twelve-paned windows that glistened like tiny pieces of sun. It sat on the edge of a restless sea that tumbled and rolled right into the open mouth of the sky.

But venturing into its shadows carried its own feeling of dread—no matter how many times she had done it.

Gerdie frequently employed her to run these errands; he might go himself, if he weren't so perpetually lost in the throes of his genius. He was quite good at scaling the stone wall. But, as it was, sunlight hadn't touched him for days.

He would be at the castle now, maddened with purpose, the glow of his cauldron tracing the bags under his blue eyes, his monocle gleaming. He would be muttering, whispering, pleading with the elements he manipulated.

The materials he needed for these endeavors always seemed to lead her to the underground market. Still, being the sister of an alchemist prodigy had its advantages. One of her favorite of his creations was sheathed to her thigh: a slender dagger with a cruel crescent arch. At a glance, its floral etchings were purely decorative, but with one clockwise twist of the hilt, the pin-size holes in those etchings would well with sleep serum. The instant blood was drawn, the fight would be over.

She also wore a pair of his old boots that came to her knees. He wouldn't miss them. They were too small for him now, and a childhood spent at the mercy of Gray Fever meant none of his shoes had gotten much wear. The fever was a vicious illness that embedded into the spinal cord. If its victims lived at all, they were often left paralyzed. Gerdie had been bedbound for months at a time, and rarely well enough to be allowed outside.

The clock tower had just chimed noon, and by now, everything unloaded from shipping crates would be for sale in shops and in the vendors' market.

Everything.

As usual, she'd chosen the least assuming outfit she could find for a journey into the Port Capital. It was a blue dress, without the frill and fanfare of most things her mother had tailored for her. At the collar was a simple beaded floral pattern in the typical Northern fashion, whose threading was beginning to wear. Unremarkable. All this added to her invisibility quite nicely, Wil thought. Invisibility in plain sight was her finest skill, forged over a lifetime as the third spare in the royal line.

She stopped at a vendor selling hunks of glittering stone affixed to cheap metal chains. "From the famed mountain palace of the Southern Isles," the vendor was shouting in Nearsh, to whoever would listen.

A fake accent, Wil knew, just like the stones. Nearsh was the language of Arrod, but because Northern Arrod was the trading hub of the world, it was adopted by nomads and ports around the world.

The woman was well dressed, in a crisp red tunic and matching trousers that belled at the ankles, ruffled with pristine black lace. Something like the outfits displayed in the store-fronts here, which meant it was purchased here. Probably an indication that she would pack up her wares and phony accent and be gone by the time next week's import ships departed; Wil had seen it dozens of times before.

A young boy and girl sat at her feet, peering at passersby under the slats in the cart. The children were equally pristine and dressed in a matching green dress and vest set, respectively. They caught Wil's eyes, and their casual interest in the crowd took on a new purpose. The vendor glanced at her too. "Fancy a necklace for those lovely collarbones of yours?" she asked.

"I'm looking for something shinier," Wil said, cautious. The children were still watching her. She extended her index finger and gave three quick taps to the strap of her bag. An innocent enough gesture, unless her suspicions were correct.

The girl crawled out from under the cart. "Were you look-ing for sterling chains instead?" she asked. Her accent sounded Eastern.

Wil raised her chin in a nod.

The underground vendors loved to send the girls to hook their customers. Young orphan girls with ribbons in their hair, or elegant young women with soft faces and sweet smiles, all to mask the sinister depths of their trade.

The boy moved as though he wanted to stand. The ven-dor cast the boy a look, though, and it rooted him. The vendor likely wasn't any relation to them—just a lackey—but the boy was clearly the girl's brother. It wasn't merely their resemblance Wil noticed but the way the boy looked at the girl. Like letting her go off alone was the same as casting a gem into the sea.

Owen looked at her that way.

For her part, the little girl was unafraid. She gave Wil a smile that didn't reach her steely eyes. "My father makes the finest jewelry you'll find anywhere in the world," she said. "Follow me."

The girl walked with purpose, her twin braids gleaming in the hot August sun. She moved expertly through the crowd without touching any of the passersby, Wil at her heels.

Arrod was an ancient kingdom, and many of its buildings were hundreds of years old, outfitted for electricity but otherwise untouched. Beyond the bustle at the docks, where shadows of tall stone buildings stamped out the sun in their alleyways, it was like stepping into a cartographer's old map: blanched bone white by sun, the windows dark and blank, no indication that time had changed a single stroke of ink.

Here was where the wealth of Northern Arrod receded into disrepair. Twenty years earlier, a storm had flooded the Port Capital, and its outskirts had never recovered. Towering stone buildings with dark oak trim were left to the elements. Wil thought they were beautiful, and the tragedy of their abandon made them even more so.

But she knew better than to mention renovations to her father; a king had no time to deal with the poor, she'd heard him say many times. Not with territories to conquer and leaders to reason with. Not with the reins of the world in his fists.

A laundry line hung between two windows, pinioned by tiny tattered dresses.

The little girl led Wil down the alleyway under the laundry line, and they came to a stop at a metal door. The dagger at Wil's thigh felt more present at the sight of it. Metal doors. She hated those. They were much harder to escape if things got ugly. And in the forgotten outskirts of the Port Capital, things did tend to get ugly.

She began to clench her fists, but thought better of it and quickly slackened her hands. Best to use her small stature and unremarkable face to her advantage, to play the part of a defenseless girl off on a fool's errand.

*You're wind. You're everywhere.*

The little girl knocked three times, paused, then knocked twice more. After several beats, the door yawned open. The girl slipped past the man who had opened it, into the darkness that swallowed her immediately.

The man was tall. He had boulders for muscles, marred by veins. His mere presence was a warning. He took in the sight of Wil, expressionless.

*Gerdie had better appreciate this.*

"Powders or metals?" His voice was a rasp.

Doing her best to sound deadpan, Wil replied, "Powders. Tallim."

Tallim was a paralytic when boiled, highly illegal, and

difficult to smuggle because of its strong scent. And, unfortunately, this meant the underground market could only obtain it in small quantities. Wil would cheerfully haul a ton of the stuff in a burlap sack all the way back to the palace for her brother if it meant never having to go through the ordeal of getting it again.

The man studied her. Not much to see, he must have been thinking. Just a girl, with eyes as dark as a moonless night, and long tangled hair to match. On her head was a pair of orange data goggles—a common tourist trinket. No visible weapons. Not much by way of height—even Gerdie, whose growth had been stunted by his many bouts of illness, towered over her. And he certainly wouldn't think she was at all related to the Royal House of Heidle—those princes with their aquamarine eyes and blond hair, just like the king and queen.

The man moved aside to let her in, as she'd suspected he would.

The room was small, its windows boarded up from the inside—as were many of the windows here.

There was a single gas lantern hanging from the ceiling. Four children sat on the floor, measuring minerals from unmarked tins beside an empty shipping crate. Orphans, most likely, sold and traded like the goods they handled. The children held each spoonful up to the dim light, inspecting it, making sure they had not been dealt fillers like sand or sugar, before packaging them into neat little pine boxes.

On the other side of the unfurnished room, a man sat in

the darkness, sorting through various bits and gears—precious metals molded and disguised to look like old machine parts. They would have to be melted down, probably diluted with something cheap to add bulk and get a higher price.

Wil recognized the tallim immediately. It was the pile of foul green granules that smelled like sewage and bonfire. The children hadn't gotten around to sorting it yet. It was in an open container at their feet.

The man sorting the metals was thin, and he appeared frail. Indebted to the dealer, perhaps, and maybe even the father to one of these children. He was emaciated, his cheekbones cutting sharp dunes in his face. He didn't look like much of a threat, but Wil kept him in her periphery. She stood with her back to the wall. *See everything. Be everywhere.*

The smell of this place was overwhelming. Must and chemicals and sweaty skin. Without air circulation of any kind, the heat was unrelenting.

"It's a thousand geldstuk," the muscular man said.

There wasn't much room to haggle, Wil knew. It was on the low end of what she'd paid before. "All I have is eight hundred." Her voice was toneless. Paying asking price was what a wealthy girl would do—a girl worth following home, worth targeting for ransom.

The man advanced on her, pinning her with one arm against the wall. Wil's eyes flickered to the hollow below his throat. The jugular notch. A hidden vulnerable spot amid a fleshy sea of muscle.

He leaned so close that his breath grazed her lips. "The price is a thousand." He was looking at her mouth, her chest, and then, at last, her eyes. "But we can work something out."

Owen's voice filled her head. *Only instigate a fight you can win.*

The man was thrice her size, easily. But Wil had the element of surprise on her side. He wouldn't be expecting much push-back from a small thing like her.

In the shadows beyond the reach of the lantern, the little girl had moved to stand beside the man dealing with the metals. Despite the bravado she'd put forth in the streets, she seemed frightened now, in this confined room. And there was something else in that fear, Wil noticed. What was it? Expectancy?

Her throat went dry. What had this girl seen this man do to other potential customers?

The man grinned at Wil. The dagger was beginning to feel more and more necessary. The only law in the outskirts was barter. There were no uniformed kingsmen patrolling these cracked roads. A cry for help was the same as an alarm signaling the arrival of easy prey.

"Five minutes with you seems worth the two hundred geldstuk you owe me," the man said.

Wil hadn't expected this to be easy, but she had hoped. Mostly, the underground vendors tried to swindle her with diluted wares, or packets of dyed sugar. Sometimes they pretended to be feeble or blind to earn her trust. Wil favored that lot of crooks. At least their stares didn't seep through her skin like canmar poison, rotting her from the inside once it got into the blood. She felt sick. But her senses heightened.

If this was how the man wanted it to be, she had no choice. The last time she had agreed to pay full price, the vendor, an old woman feigning feebleness, suspected she was a child of Arrod's famed wealth and tried to follow her home. Three of her lackeys had melted out of the alleyway and joined her; Wil escaped the four of them and was nearly shot for her trouble.

"Please," she whispered. "All I have is eight hundred. I can come back in a week with the rest." She curled a loose fist against her mouth, her eyes flitting nervously downward.

The man traced a wisp of dark hair that had fallen loose from her clumsy ponytail. The touch radiated deep into her stomach, churning an uneasy tide.

He smiled.

Wil's fist tightened, and in a single sweep, she threw her full weight into her arm and slammed the side of her fist to the man's nose.

The cartilage snapped.

He staggered back, dazed, choking up a mouthful of thick blood.

But it didn't render him unconscious. He would overcome his shock in seconds. Wil rushed past him, to the tin of tallim, and a discarded cloth to serve as a lid. She got a lungful of granules for her effort, and her eyes filled with tears from the sting of the next painful breath.

She sensed the man coming at her a moment before she whirled to face him. He managed to get out a slurred obscenity, but his gruff voice was fading. There was a dagger in his hand now, its blade small against his enormous fist. He lunged at her and she arched back and then to the left, out of the way of his blade's path. She grasped the knob of the metal door, tallim spilling out as she jostled the tin.

Locked. Why did the doors always have to be locked? There was a window; she'd seen it when she first assessed the room. It was boarded up from the inside, but she'd be able to fit through if she could loose one of the planks. There had to be something she could use to pry it away. She looked to the tools the metal-worker was using.

The man came at her again, and she twirled around him as though in a dance, making him dizzy when he spun to follow her movement.

She'd hoped her blow would stupefy him long enough for her to get away, but he seemed to be regaining himself.

She reached for her dagger an instant before he reached for her throat. She was just able to twist the hilt. The crescent arch slashed his bicep, drawing a crimson line. He grunted and stumbled forward faster than Wil could evade him. He had her on her back, her wrists pinned, the breath gone from her lungs.

The tin hit the ground hard, scattering the tallim across the floor, the granules falling through the cracks in the rotted wooden floor.

*No.* Some distant part of her, fighting to breathe, knew that all this would be for nothing if she lost them.

But no time to worry about that. The man landed a punch to her jaw that filled her vision with gleaming metallic stars. Then her own gasps for air fell silent because his hand was clenched around her throat, cutting off her ragged attempts to breathe, making her lungs swell and burn. The stars in her vision multiplied and turned black. Her dagger had fallen into the endless dark at her periphery. His blood and saliva dripped onto her mouth.

She felt her mind going dull, her body drifting like thin swirls of sand in the ocean's shallows.

She rocked her hips, twisting until she was able to draw her legs up between his solid arms, and with the last of her waning strength, she kicked his chin. It knocked him back just enough for her to slither out from under him, gasping. She struggled to her hands and knees and commanded herself to breathe.

As the stars cleared away, behind the hulking figure of the man who was already rising to his feet, Wil saw daylight. The door. Somehow it was open.

Her ears were ringing from the punch. She didn't know if she could trust what she was seeing. She didn't know if she was truly on her feet at all, or if this was some dream as she lay unconscious by the spilled tallim.

But then she heard a voice saying, "Go! He'll kill you!"

The little girl. Wil saw three of the girl's tiny silhouette in the doorframe before she blinked and they shifted back into one.

At last, the sleep serum took effect and the man fell to his stomach, his eyes glazed. Wil hoped it was a dream serum, and that the dream was an ugly one. In mixing his serums, her brother often infused them with photographs of things that could influence dreams. He was the only one in the world who could do it, Owen had said. And Owen would know—he'd seen the entire world and met its top alchemists. It was their family's secret that Gerdie was the boy prodigy who surpassed them all.

Wil recovered her dagger, as well as the man's, and began hastily scooping the tallim back into the tin. It burned her hands like hot coals. She did hate the powders especially—always some horror to them.

"Go," the little girl pleaded. "He won't be out long."

Still a bit unsteady, Wil rose to her feet. Her knees were shaking. Adrenaline filled her like bees in her veins. As her lungs reacquainted themselves with the concept of breathing, she forced the fear away.

She stopped in the doorway to look at the little girl. "Go back to your brother," she said. "He'll be worried about you. Here." She pressed the hilt of the man's dagger into her palm. "If he comes back for you, stab his kidney. Do you know where that is?" She pointed to her own lower back in gesture. "Won't matter how much bigger than you he is." Next, she pressed the thousand geldstuk in the girl's hand. More than enough for two passengers to board a ship bound anywhere.

The girl gave something like a smile. And then they were both gone. The girl, to the Port Capital, and Wil, to the line of familiar trees that were rustling on a summer breeze, waving her on as she ran home.

Her head was filled with wind and gleaming stars, but she didn't allow herself to rest until the city was well out of sight.

The first time she'd been to the Port Capital, she had been six years old. She wasn't supposed to leave the castle walls, but she had begged her brother. As heir, Owen could do whatever he wanted, and he had relented.

Immediately, she'd been in love with the gentle chaos of it. The people everywhere. The smells of food and sea and perfumes fighting to be the thing that enticed her.

Owen had been fifteen, his shoulders already haughty, his chin ever canted in the assured wisdom of a someday king. "Look," he'd whispered to her as she clutched his hand. "This kingdom is ours. All of it."

They weren't dressed like royalty then. They'd made themselves unremarkable so that they'd be safe; their shared royal blood was their secret, and the idea had made Wil smug, excited, invincible.

He hoisted her onto his shoulders so that she could see everything at once, and the ocean shimmering on and on where the city stopped. She could see it all. "You're not human," he'd said. "You're wind. Remember that. You're everywhere."

# TWO

By the time Wil made it back from the Port Capital, her cheek was throbbing from the punch, but her vision had at last stopped tunneling.

There would be bruises. She would have to use the jar of concealer that sat among the assortment of glass bottles and brushes on her dressing table. She did this for her mother's sake: played the part of a princess, with unmarred skin and no desires beyond comportment and calligraphy. The queen had resigned herself to Owen's wanderlust, but Wil was precious to her.

Wil, the child who looked the least like her mother, was the one who most mirrored her own wanderer's spirit. Wil's restlessness could take her anywhere. Her beating heart longed for the sea that reached for her like fingers. It whispered promises to her as she slept. And one day she would succumb. The world would swallow her like a kite fluttering up into the sky.

Even though the queen didn't speak of this fear, Wil knew it. She tried to hide her restlessness. She escaped the castle in secret, climbing the notches in the stone wall in the shadows where the ivy and brambles grew thick. The guards couldn't be trusted to keep quiet about her comings and goings, and so she'd developed a skill for evading them.

There was a new rotation of guards when Wil reached the castle's looming stone wall. Odd. That shouldn't happen until the evening.

She lowered her data goggles over her eyes. They were one orange-tinted glass pane that covered both eyes, making the world look as though it were sunset. According to the time in the lower right lens, she had been gone for three hours, but her instructors wouldn't betray her absence, afraid to admit to the queen that they had yet again lost track of their peripatetic charge.

The wall was fourteen yards high. Not nearly as tall as the castle looming within its perimeter, but high enough to obscure it from view of anyone passing by. The castle was nestled in the heart of a thick wood, broken only by trickling streams and small valleys, through which troupes of wanderers would often pass. The queen opened the windows when they did, letting their shanty songs fill the somber walls.

Skirting the guards, Wil began to climb the wall. Halfway up, she reached for an overhead stone and sucked in a breath at the sudden pain in her ribs. She paused to let the feeling subside, and then she moved again. Again, the pain returned, making her lightheaded. She tried to recall the details of her skirmish with the underground vendor. There was some vague recollection of a fist or a knee hitting that spot, but it had been when her body was too starved for oxygen for her to concentrate on anything but escape.

By the time she reached the top of the wall, the pain was radiating down to the balls of her feet. Tears were welling in her eyes.

She sat on the wide ledge of the wall for a long while, her hands pressed on the stones before her, breathing deep, testing the varying levels of pain as her chest moved. Only a bruise, she hoped. Not a break. A break would be harder to conceal. Wil kept most of her ventures a secret from her mother, but her father finding out about this errand would be the greater risk.

The king saw Gerdie's prowess for alchemy early on. But Gerdie kept most of his weapons a secret. If enough of them were produced, they would end the world, he'd said.

In their father's hands they would, at least.

To distract herself from the pain, Wil focused on a purple spawnling that had built its nest in a tangle of ivy, and the speckled violet eggs it had laid.

As she focused on the eggs, the goggles groaned and squeaked until at last the data appeared on one of the lenses:

*Spawnling eggs. Indigenous to the North.*

Wil blinked hard, prompting the data to scroll like a page turning.

*. . . can have a vocabulary of five hundred words, and live up to one hundred years . . .*

"Come down, Monster," a voice called, and the data dissolved as she looked away from the nest.

She peered over the edge.

Owen. The fringe of his blond hair glowed in the hot August sun. "And are those my goggles?"

Wil raised them up to sit at the crown of her head. She was forever pilfering things from his chamber. She couldn't help herself; he had been nearly everywhere and brought back the world in tiny bits and pieces, neatly arranged in drawers and wedged between his books.

"You're back!" she said, smiling. "How was Southern Arrod? When did your train get in?" She envied her brother for the fact that he had ridden on several trains now, and she'd only seen them at a distance from the castle's wall: lumbering black things whose rails glowed with blue electric light.

Owen narrowed his eyes at her. No doubt he was scrutinizing the outline of the tin showing through her bag, wondering what she'd gotten herself into. "I returned hours ago. Several poor instructors are off looking for you, you know."

He was waiting for her to descend. She forced herself to

move, and her core trembled at the pain. She kept her face turned away from him and gritted her teeth.

Owen's gaze fell to the faint purple burns on her hands as soon as she set foot on the ground. "Tallim for Gerdie," she explained, smoothing her hands on her skirt. "Nightmare stuff to handle."

The beaded floral arrangement at her collar had torn, and now several of the beads had fallen away, shining like colorful insects in the grass at her feet.

Again she smiled, if only to get that worried look off his face. It didn't work. Owen had taught her everything he knew about the world. What she was allowed to see of it, at least. But that look he gave her was an immovable rock in a churning stream.

"I saw workmen bringing a cement mixer this morning." Wil changed the subject. "The guards let them in at the gate."

"Nothing gets by you, does it?" His grin revealed a row of pristine white teeth. But Wil knew how to look closely. She saw that his eyes were too bright today. He was burdened.

He began pacing back toward the castle, and Wil knew to follow at his heels. The castle yard had ears. Though Baren was not much for wit or charm, he had a way of being everywhere. He materialized from shadowy places. His siblings didn't include him in their unshakable trio, and so he'd learned to listen for the murmurings he wasn't meant to hear.

Owen said nothing as they breezed up the stairwell and

through the channels of stone and oak that led to his chamber.

Owen's chamber was a stark source of brightness after the gloomy stone hallway. His wall was lined with books—so many that a track ladder was required to reach the second-story shelves. He had an insatiable desire to learn everything he could about the world and its people and its things. Even the windowsill had become a shelf, housing trinkets of his travels that caught the sunlight.

Wil sat in the chair at his desk, relishing in the relief the stillness did to ease the pain in her ribs. After Owen had closed the heavy wooden doors of his antechamber, she said, "Why are the workmen here for you?"

He fell onto the corner of his bed, his body at once a heap of bones. "Papa is building a house for me in the eastern field."

"Why do you get a house?" Wil said. His chamber was already twice the size of her own.

"Because my twenty-fifth birthday is this month," Owen said. "Papa thinks it's long past time for me to choose a wife, and my condition was that I wanted out of the castle."

Wil considered this, scrutinizing the worry that began to ebb through her at her brother's announcement; their father favored Owen, but more than that, he needed him. Owen was always the one tasked with handling foreign relations, always being sent off to be the king's eyes and ears in the world. That had always been more pressing than Owen marrying and producing an heir. No. If their father wanted Owen to marry, it had to be part of some strategy.

Owen's grim face confirmed her fear.

"He needs you to marry for an alliance." She rolled the chair across the floor until she reached him, the sound of wheels against oak making a loud scrape in the grand space. Her scuffed boots were toe-to-toe with his of pristine polished leather. She lowered her voice. "That's it, isn't it? Why do we need an alliance, Owen?"

Owen stood and retrieved a massive atlas from his desk. It fell onto his bed with a heavy sound, and he opened to a map of the Southern Isles. He rested his finger on the mountains of Cannolay, which sat in the largest of the cluster of tiny islands there. Cannolay was the Southern Isles' capital city, which housed King Zinil of the Royal House of Raisius in what was lauded to be the world's most extravagant palace. Vendors sold hunks of the mountain that led up to the palace, or what they claimed to be—in cheap jewelry settings.

"You remember Gerdie's Gray Fever," Owen said. "Mother sent for Cannolay's finest healers, and they saved him when our own doctors couldn't."

Her jaw tightened at the memory of that awful fever. She had been five years old, Gerdie six, but the memory was vivid. The choked gasps and bloody cloths. The castle darkened by the covered windows.

Already in the first six years of his life, Gerdie had long been displaying signs that his brain was a thing of spectacular

exception. Though they were only a year apart, he had far surpassed Wil in all their remedial work and he'd proven to have a
mind for the chemistry of things. He was like their father that
way; he found old sciences more reliable than new technologies;
he preferred methods that were ancient and true over machines
that broke down. The king had done away with the training
cauldron and commissioned a proper one to be forged just for
Gerdie. There was none other in the world, especially as the
demand for alchemy had dwindled in the last several decades as
digital technology fueled by wind and water began to take over.

Throughout his childhood, Gerdie hardly left the laboratory even as Wil whined and pleaded for him to come outside.

He had been occasionally troubled by little things like
fevers that came and went, and he was always the last to recover
when all the royal children fell ill with seasonal flus and colds.
Then, one day, the Gray Fever came all at once and interrupted
his plans, turning his extremities ashen and his face red, pulling
him into a fitful sleep that lasted for weeks without reprieve.
Wil had sat at the foot of his bed, worrying over all the thoughts
that were trapped in his skull. She could feel her brother slipping away from himself, the Gray Fever taking all the things he
would have gone on to become.

Thanks to the Lavean remedies of the South, he lived, and
Wil had kept vigil over every relapse that would plague him over
the years. And with each one, the same fear moved through her
blood anew: that her brother had swindled death, and it would
be back to collect him.

Yes. She knew about the Southern Isles and their miracle plants very well.

She stared at the page. "Is there talk of going to war with the Southern Isles?" she said, puzzled and pondering. She considered the new rotation of guards—was her father bracing for an attack? "I haven't seen any of their ships among the imports for several weeks. The South is refusing to barter with us, isn't it? Why?" It was no great loss, tradewise. Arrod had never dealt much with the Southern Isles, other than for the infrequent shipment of satins, or dried plants that only grew in its tropical climate, but even so, the absence had not gone unnoticed by Wil. Few things did.

"Because Papa wants to acquire their territory, the way our kingdom acquired Southern Arrod a hundred years ago," Owen said. "The Southern Isles have the resources, but they aren't wealthy like the North. Papa believes that if the two kingdoms can join, they can form an unstoppable alliance. King Zinil disagrees. He refuses to give over any of his islands, and he's cutting off the rest of the world in defiance."

The atlas sat open, the ink that traced the isles gleaming in a sunbeam. "If Papa acquired the Southern Isles, it would become part of our kingdom?"

"Yes," Owen said. "All the islands would become the Cumulative Southernmost Arrod. You can appreciate King Zinil's hesitation."

Wil raised her eyes to her brother. "Surely there's something between all and nothing."

Owen smiled at her. "Try not to worry on it so much. Nothing has happened yet; it's all talk. These sorts of things can take years."

Frowning, she turned the page to see a bright spread of the South's indigenous flora. "Will your bride be from the South, then?"

"I imagine Papa will invite the world's leaders to my party. And tell me I'm free to pick."

Owen wasn't free to do anything these days, Wil knew. She hated to see her brother like this. Trapped. A someday king, bowing to the whims of their father.

He tapped her nose, shattering her troubled expression. "Don't think on it too much, Monster. These aren't your problems to sort. You're fifteen."

She hated when her brother pointed out her age, as though it should matter. By fifteen he had seen far more of the world and carried far more responsibilities than she would be trusted with. She sighed, frustrated, and the motion made her cringe in pain.

"Are you going to tell me what trouble you've gotten yourself into?" Owen asked, closing the atlas.

"It's nothing," Wil said. "Just danced with a vendor a bit."

Owen opened his mouth to speak, but the floor shuddered with the force of a small explosion. A boom thundered the castle.

Wil closed her eyes in a long grimace. "I'd better go make

sure Gerdie hasn't just killed himself," she said, standing, grateful for the diversion.

"Hey." Owen's voice stopped her as she reached the doorway. She spun to face him. "You have to be careful out there, Monster," he said.

She smiled at that.

She left Owen's chamber and breezed through the servants' kitchen, down the narrow corridor that led to a tiny wooden door barely higher than her head. The red bulb above the door was lit, which meant that her brother was not to be disturbed.

This light didn't apply to Wil.

The smell of charred air and melted steel hit her even before she'd begun to descend the crumbling steps that led into the basement.

She found her brother standing in a smoggy rectangle of light that streamed in from the only window. He was staring into his cauldron, so deep in his concentration that he flinched when Wil touched him.

She laughed. "What were you trying to make?"

"Flexible armor," he said.

"What would you do with flexible armor?" Wil asked. She peered into the cauldron. He tugged her arm, reeling her a step back from the smoke.

"You've seen knights' armor," he said. "Imagine if it had all that durability, plus the flexibility of leather."

Wil raised a brow. "Papa asked for this?"

"No, this was purely my own idea," he said, proudly raising his shoulders. "I do get those on occasion. But Papa was rather anxious to see if I could pull it off."

With her thumb, Wil wiped at the condensation on his monocle; though he was nearly blind in his left eye even with the lens, it did provide just enough improvement to help his acuity when he worked. It was held in place by brown leather straps that wrapped around his head like a claw. The dull bronze hue of the leather complemented the metal braces that held his legs steady. Remnants of where the Gray Fever had ravaged him. He was a boy who by the looks of it had arrived in the world before he was finished being assembled.

He blinked at Wil as though waking from a trance. "Did you get it?"

She unlashed the bag from her shoulder and set it on the table. "Yes, I think most of it survived." She extracted the tin of granules, the smell burning her throat as she unwound the cloth. "What do you need it for this time?"

"Bullets." His voice trailed. He was watching the strain on her face when she breathed. He had not missed the fading burns on her hands. "High winds, Wil. What exactly happened out there?"

"It's no big deal."

He nodded to the bench that lined the wall. It had been there for hundreds of years, one of the few pieces of furniture he hadn't hauled down the steps himself. Not that he ever used it—the idea of being still hardly ever occurred to him. "Sit," he ordered.

Wil obliged. Sweat beaded her brow.

Gerdie stood in a beam of light, assessing her as though she were something he'd just extracted from the smoke with a pair of tongs. Bruises were beginning to blossom on her cheek, around her throat. The sight of them awoke him from his frenzy, and for the moment he was not a maddened genius but a boy again, with round cheeks and worried eyes. Her injuries told him the story. The vendor had tried to strangle the life out of her.

He knelt before her, braces creaking like rusty gears, and brushed the tips of his fingers over her left ribs.

Wil choked on a scream of pain. Gerdie jerked back. He saw the way her eyes darkened, the way she gasped as she regained herself. "There's a break," he said.

"No." Wil shook her head. "Just sore. I'm fine."

Gerdie ignored her. "I should have gone with you."

Wil did enjoy when he snuck away with her into the Port Capital. The way the cogs of his mind turned in such places, the flashes in his eyes as he analyzed the mills that churned the water to harness electricity. The way he caught all the little imperceptible pieces that made a city live.

But bringing him into the slums was a bad idea. He had a soft heart under all that genius frenzy. He would have been trying to rescue all the orphans, or stopping to buy enough cheese and bread to feed a small village and then trying to do just that.

Wil eased her back against the wall and closed her eyes. It was nice to be home, at least, where no one was trying to kill her. "Did you see the cement mixers this morning?"

When she opened her eyes again, Gerdie was handing her a mortar of green mush. The cool tangy smell of mintlemint leaves ground with water and serlot oil filled the space. The usual concoction he mixed to ease the pain when she came home broken.

She raised it to her lips and took a tentative sip. Swallowing didn't hurt, at least.

"Owen told me about the wedding this morning," Gerdie said, sitting beside her. His eyes stared through the floor as he considered. "I don't know what Papa is planning for this war, but I don't like it." He looked at Wil. "He can't know that you've been smuggling in supplies for me. I don't want him to find out about the bullets I've been working on."

"You still haven't told me what they'll do."

"Once it gets past the skin, the tallim has a magnetic pull toward the spinal fluid," Gerdie said. "If I can get these bullets right, they'll seek out the spine and dissolve into it. Should incapacitate the target for several hours."

His voice lowered to a whisper, even though there was no one to hear them in the basement—not even Baren could have eavesdropped through the heavy door that guarded this space. "I've been working on something for Papa for months now." He took Wil's arm and steered her toward his shelf of bottles and boxes and powders.

He took a small wooden box and held it up. Wil looked curiously at it. It was small, crude, wholly unremarkable. He opened it to reveal a metal orb, small enough to fit in the palm of her hand. It was smooth and black, and when Wil leaned forward to inspect it, she could see her own reflection in its surface.

Then, before she could touch it, Gerdie closed the box and placed it back on the shelf, carefully camouflaging it among his things. "There's enough accelerant and shrapnel in there to set a city on fire," he said. "I call it darklead. It's a fusion of metals and gunpowder, mostly. Without alchemy, it wouldn't be possible to condense so much matter into such a small space."

Wil took a step back from the shelf, as though the mere explanation might cause the thing to detonate.

"Why didn't you tell me?" She thought of all the hours her brother spent laboring alone in his lab, the gait of his somnambulated daze when he hadn't slept. These things were so typical of him, she hadn't thought anything unusual was troubling him. But she knew with certainty that their father had forced his hand on this. Her brother loved making weapons, loved perfecting them, creating something that had never before existed. But he didn't have it in his heart to destroy a city, no matter that his brain was capable of creating such a thing. Not even one in an enemy kingdom.

"It wasn't safe to tell you," Gerdie said. His eyes were serious. "Papa can't find out I've told you."

"You know that your secrets are safe with me."

"I'm the only one who knows how it works," Gerdie said. "Papa has seen it, but he wouldn't be able to use it without me."

Wil looked to the smoking cauldron, dread stirring within her stomach. If this war came to fruition, Gerdie's hand would be forced. He would be their father's weapon. All of them would be.

# THREE

On the evening of Owen's twenty-fifth birthday, the castle grounds were filled with life and strangers.

Wil sat on the wall where she could see the kingdom entering the gate and carrying all manner of grandiose things.

She also noted more guards standing along the wall's perimeter. Yesterday, she had narrowly evaded one on her way into the city, unable to predict the new tumult of their rotations.

Beside her, Gerdie was struggling to position his left leg before him. His bones always gave him trouble when the weather was humid.

"Oh, Gerdie, look," Wil gasped. "Is that a mermaid fountain? It is! It's so gloriously tacky."

"Wonderful," he muttered. "We'd better go before someone sees the king's failure spying on the heir's glorious party."

Wil's head snapped to him. "Are you still sulking about that? Papa sent me away, too, you know. To buy perfume, no less."

"The less you are seen by the kingdom, the more he can use you as a spy," Gerdie reminded her. "He doesn't want anyone to see *me* because he's ashamed of me."

"Hey." She inched in front of him and stared until he met her gaze. They looked nothing alike, save for the sharpness of their chins. But they were part of a set just the same. "Do not welcome Papa into your head. You know better."

Her brows were drawn, jaw set. This was the way she had looked at him when they were small, and he whispered on his sickbed that he was dying. He had said it only once, and she had hit him. Sometimes he could still feel the spot on his arm pulsing when she glared at him.

It hadn't been the last time his sister would bruise him. She was a ruthless sparring opponent, always a move ahead, always at his back before he could follow. But when they were on the same side of a fight, they worked in effortless tandem, as though they were limbs of a shared mind. With the exception of Owen's training sessions, Gerdie had never been in a fight that didn't involve his sister; peril of any sort only seemed to find him when she was present.

Gerdie didn't want to admit it—he was awful with emotions—but her solidarity made him feel better.

He looked past her shoulder, to the parade of brass

instruments and carts of imported food being wheeled in through the gate. "We should go," was all he said.

Though Wil was the one who climbed the stone wall a dozen times a day to escape her instructors, and was always the fastest of her siblings, today she could just barely keep up with her brother as they descended the outer wall, he was so eager to get away.

Gerdie watched her place one foot gingerly on the ground before the other. "It's been two weeks," he said. "Is that rib still hurting?"

"The mintlemint leaves have been helping." She charged forward, brushing off his concern. "Come on. I heard some chatter in the Port Capital that there were some wanderers headed east of the river."

"When did you go back to the Port Capital?" Gerdie asked, keeping pace beside her. "You made an enemy when you stole that tallim. You should be avoiding the city until at least next month, when the vendors leave with the exports."

"I didn't want to steal it," Wil said. "I am not the one who chose to do things the hard way. Anyway, he's probably forgotten all about me by now."

"Didn't you also set two of his slaves free?"

In the waning sunlight, Wil answered him with a wicked smile. Gerdie laughed, despite everything. "You just can't resist causing trouble, can you?"

"I don't cause it. It just . . . seems to find me."

They trudged through nearly a mile of woods before they heard the sounds of distant song. Wil grabbed Gerdie's arm, stilling him, ceasing the croak and groan of his braces.

*"And with his touch of gold*
*Of gold!—*
*He was cursed with what his god foretold. . . ."*

Lyrics they knew well; their mother often sang about the Gold King as she milled about, and it had been one of the many lullabies she'd used to soothe them to sleep as children.

"Sounds like they're straight ahead," Gerdie said.

The sky was going dark now, stars beginning to burn bright against it. Now would be the time that wanderers ceased their traveling and began to set up camp. The warm summer air already smelled of wood fire.

As they drew closer and the songs grew louder, Wil began to recognize their accents. Overwhelmingly Southern Arrod, but others with various Eastern inflections. And some Brayshire.

Wil drew the voices in like air. Her stomach fluttered in that sick, dreamy way, both painful and longing.

Wil's mother had once upon a time wandered the world herself, with sand bejeweling the slender bones of her ankles. And even as a queen, she was wild in her billowing gowns, barefoot when she roamed the gardens, her fingertips callused, her skin bronzed by the sun. She kept secrets in her mouth like chocolates. With that mouth she had once smiled at a young king, and he swept her up and spun her in diamonds and made her his queen.

The princes gave little thought to the songs their mother hummed or who she had been before she was their mother. But Wil often felt that she was a wanderers' daughter. That if the king of Arrod had not been the one to steal her mother's heart, she would have been born out under the shimmering stars. She would have been lulled to sleep by the crackling of fire, atop a pillow of crisp grass and cool earth.

Gerdie caught her swooning and bumped her shoulder. "Maybe you should just run off with them."

"You could come with me," she replied. "I've seen the way you can alchemize glass and paperclips to look like diamonds and chains for Mother. I'm sure your skills would be quite profitable." She elevated her chin, proud of her idea. "We could be rich."

"We're already rich."

She narrowed her eyes. "All logic; no imagination. Can't you just play along for once?" But they were laughing now, both of their moods lifting the way they always seemed to when they were free of the castle.

The wanderers had set up their camp about a half mile from any neighboring towns, but already the camp was thrumming with people who had come to be wooed by the mysterious things for sale in the glowing tents. Scarves spun from silkbug strands, smooth stones purportedly capable of healing afflictions of the body and mind.

Gerdie averted his eyes from the vendors of miracle cures, the good humor fading from his face. He clenched his jaw. "What is it?" Wil said. "Are your legs hurting again? Is it too damp?"

"No." He snapped out of his thoughts. "I'm fine."

She tugged him onward. "Come on, then. The perfumes have to be this way. I can smell them."

They wove between dancing women and giggling, shrieking children. Some men were sitting cross-legged in a circle, whittling chunks of wood into toy trains and soldiers and stars.

Wil stopped before a caravan whose cracks and crevices were aglow with the light of the lantern inside. The tiny door swung open just as she'd raised her fist to knock.

A young woman stood before them, with honey-colored hair tied into a thick, burdening braid that rested on one shoulder and trailed past her waist. Her eyes were big and icy blue. Her fair skin was warmed by the lantern light. The smile she gave them was an embrace.

"I remember you from last year, wasn't it?" she said to Wil, in her wispy Brayshire accent. "You bought all those bottles of jesseray."

Wil felt warm at the idea that such a beautiful woman might remember her. "For my mother," she said.

The woman stepped aside to let them in, her slender arm

holding the door open as they ducked inside.

The caravan was small as a closet, and a silk cloth hung over the lantern, swathing the space in a pink glow. The walls were lined with shelves that housed hundreds of tiny glass bottles secured by leather straps.

In a corner was an elderly woman with silver hair pulled back into a tight bun, her eyes the same haunting blue as the young woman's. She was hunched over a mortar and pestle, grinding petals and oils, trickling them into a jar.

Gerdie studied the bottles with wary curiosity. His eyes watered, and Wil could tell he was trying to hold back a coughing fit. The rabid cacophony of smells enchanted Wil, but they only aggravated Gerdie's already-fragile lungs.

"You could wait outside," Wil whispered. He shook his head.

"How many bottles did you want this time, lovely?" the girl asked.

Wil raised the flap of her rawhide bag. "Four should be enough. One for each season."

The girl winked when the bottles and geldstuk exchanged hands. "Jesseray chooses whom it favors, you know. The scent changes when it touches the body," she said. "I bet your mother is very beautiful."

"Thank you," Wil said, mesmerized by the gleam of the bottles, the small music they made as they touched each other. She wrapped each one in cloth before tucking it away.

Not all of it was for her mother. Wil intended to keep one for herself, to spray it into the air sometimes and pretend she was someplace where wild jesseray blossoms grew in a smattering of colors.

Gerdie nudged her. It was just a subtle enough gesture to get her attention. She raised her eyes and realized that the old woman was staring at her. "I've seen you before," she said. Her voice sounded surprisingly young.

"Yes, Gram, she's come back for more of your perfume."

"No." With great difficulty, the old woman brought herself to her feet. She was scarcely taller than Wil, and when she leaned her face in close, Wil could smell the mint on her breath and skin. "When you were just a baby. Your mother brought you to me. She told me you were dying and she asked for my help."

Gerdie grabbed Wil's wrist. He tugged at her, but she was rooted there. "She did?"

"But you weren't dying," the old woman said. "You were marked, but not for death."

"Wil," Gerdie said. "Let's go."

Wil ignored him. "I was sick," she said. "When I was born."

"No." The old woman shook her head. "You were never sick. It was far worse than that."

All the smells and colors within the caravan suddenly took on a sinister persona.

"What was it?" Wil asked hoarsely.

"Darkness in your blood." The old woman's eyes flickered to Wil's chest, right where her scar lay hidden beneath the green bibbing of her dress. "There's something ugly in you. Something vicious."

"Grandma," the young woman cried, at the same time Gerdie pushed open the door.

"Enough." The fury in Gerdie's voice made Wil flinch. Stunned, she let him pull her back out into the sticky night air. "Can we go now?" he said, even as he was stomping to the outskirts of the camp, Wil following in a daze. "Do you have everything Papa wanted you to get?"

His biting tone only added to Wil's unease. Unconsciously she brought her palm between her breasts, feeling oddly exposed. Had the woman known about her birthmark?

"She was a marveler," Wil said, reasoning with herself. "She must have been."

"Wil, listen to me." Gerdie turned to her. "Marvelers are swindlers. Spells and curses are nonsense. Magic is a fairy tale. And Mother—she gives these things too much weight." Sadness in his voice at that last bit.

Wil stopped walking. The distant light from the camp set up by the wanderers still shone halos on her boots.

"But she knew." Her voice was small. "She knew about me."

"No." Gerdie's voice was stern. "She didn't. It's a trick. They say these things to anyone who will listen. If you'd stuck around a moment longer, she would have tried to sell you some magical potion to fix this 'darkness in your blood.'"

Wil rested her hand against her bag, feeling the bottles tucked safely away. Pieces of the world were contained in those bottles, diluted by drops of the sea. In the silence between breaths of wind, she could hear them whispering.

She couldn't help believing in what so many people who wandered the world described, despite her brother's logic. Despite her own logic.

No one knew for sure where the first marveler originated, but they existed the world over. They were especially prevalent in the West, where most travelers ventured, and in the East, the world's hub of electrical technology. Wil had heard of some people turning to them in Arrod, out of desperation—when a sick child was beyond the capabilities of medicine, for instance. But many, like Gerdie, considered marvelry a junk science.

"We still have a few hours, at least, before the party lets up," Gerdie said. He was trying to change the subject, but the placating softness of his tone irritated her.

"Fine," she said. "I'm hungry anyway." But she was lying. Her stomach was filled with perfumes and the old woman's words. The distant songs and giggles and murmurs of the camp had climbed under her skin, raising gooseflesh. She wanted to fall back into it. She wanted to run off into the world with the troupe and never, never return.

She began pacing for the Port Capital, whose electric street lanterns were shining in the distance, combating the stars.

There was a different kind of energy in the city. Maybe it would cleanse her of this dread and anticipation.

Without another word, they knew where to go.

There was a seasonal tavern that sat on the roof of what had once been an ancient church, but was now the Bank of the World. In the warmer seasons, when it was open, the tavern had the best view of the city and the water. Over the stone ledge, the clock still ticked and chimed the hour in unison with the towers.

When Wil was seven and Gerdie was eight, this place became a sort of sanctuary for them. After two years in the throes of his fever, Gerdie's lungs had finally strengthened enough for the crisp outdoor air. He was still staggering and falling over his braces, and one afternoon, Owen had taken him here, Wil tagging protectively along as she always did back then. Owen had knelt before Gerdie and met his eyes. "There's an elevator that will take you to the tavern," he said. "And there's a stairwell with five flights that leads to the same place. You pick how we get there."

It had taken more than an hour, but he'd done it, shoving Wil off when she tried to steady him. The next time was easier. And soon he was following Wil up the stone wall, relying heavily on his core and his arms, memorizing the footholds that saved him if he fumbled.

The tower resembled all the other buildings in the city, but it was alive. It welcomed them.

They had a table by the edge, where the ticking thrummed in the stone floor. But tonight, even the salty sea breeze couldn't clear the jesseray from Wil's lungs.

*There's something ugly in you. Something vicious.*

"Wil."

From Gerdie's tone, Wil knew that it was not his first attempt to get her attention. She blinked owlishly at him. "Hm?"

"You aren't eating."

She stared at the assortment of tiny fruit custards she'd ordered. "Guess I don't have an appetite after all."

"I don't know what it is about people who wander the world that they get in your head like this," he said. "Every time. You deal with crooks and cons by trade, and yet, because you want to join them, you hang on their every word."

"People who wander aren't necessarily cons," Wil said.

"Everyone is a con," Gerdie said.

Wil pointed her fork at him. "If everyone is a con, then nobody is."

"You know what I mean." Gerdie sighed. "Everyone is dishonest. We lie to our father. I don't tell him about the paralytics and poisons I put in weapons. You listen to street gossip and spy for Owen."

"That is different," Wil said, and scraped a forkful of baked raspberries, which she popped into her mouth defiantly. "Everything we do is for the good of our kingdom. Papa would do too much harm if he knew how powerful your weapons truly were;

he'd force you to mass-produce them in your cauldron, even if it killed you. He's too greedy, and bloodshed means nothing to him. And Owen uses my information to secretly build up foreign relations for when he's king."

They talked in low voices, despite being surrounded by mostly empty tables. Everyone in the kingdom would know Owen by the sight of him; their father had been priming him to follow in his footsteps from the time Owen could crawl.

But no one in the kingdom would recognize the three spares: Baren, who at twenty-three years old had already failed to live up to the king's hopes of making him his high guard, with his lack of combat skills and erratic temperament; Gerdie, who was only of any use to the king at his cauldron; and Wil, the daughter the king only regarded when he needed a spy. Rather than being seen, the spares were gossiped about.

"I just—" Gerdie frowned at her. "I worry about you."

He didn't have to finish the thought. Wil knew: he worried that she would become like their mother.

She bristled. "Where should we go next? We'll have a few hours."

"Let's just go home," Gerdie said. "Everyone will be in the ballroom. We can slip by in the shadows. I have work to get back to anyway."

Wil rested her chin on the backs of her interlaced fingers. "I can't wait to see these paralysis bullets you keep talking about."

"Hope you never have to use one," Gerdie said, but his eyes

flashed to match his excited grin. "But I am rather proud of them."

They descended the tower and wound their way through the crowd. The Port Capital was still thriving at this hour. Restaurants were turning on their electric lanterns, bars were opening, and along the city's edge, boats were lit up with strings of party lights. Wil was mindful not to stare at them. Not with Gerdie already scrutinizing her wanderlust.

Gerdie was the one to stop them walking. The portrait studio—a small storefront wedged between a toy shop and a shoemaker—had strung a new set of photos in its window. They were small, square cuts of shining paper that glinted in the moonlight, pinned by wooden clips to a length of twine.

The photographs were sepia, the subjects in each of them smiling cautiously, as though they'd been afraid the camera might steal their happiness away if they showed too much.

"What do you suppose it's like sitting for a photograph?" Wil asked.

"Tedious," Gerdie said. "I've heard it takes several seconds, and if you so much as blink, you'll ruin it."

"I wish I could have one of the small ones that they put in lockets," Wil said.

Gerdie looked away from the portraits to afford her a glance. "Of what?"

"Myself." She puffed her chest. "So that when I'm old, I'll remember what I used to look like."

He laughed. "That is the most conceited thing I've ever heard you say."

As they left the city behind them and headed into the thick of the trees, Wil forced her tone to be light. Maybe if she could convince her brother that she was no longer troubled by the old woman's words, it would be true. "What do you suppose Owen's bride will be like?"

She'd just gotten the words out, and in the next instant, an arm was wrapped against her throat, pinning her back against someone's massive chest. Someone's hot breath filled her ear, and the grasp tightened.

She dropped her weight, twisted right, and maneuvered her leg behind her assailant's, knocking him down with a kick to the back of his knee. She moved to punch while he was down, but he was on his feet again before she could land the blow.

In the ribbons of moonlight that bled down through the trees, Wil saw him: a gleaming bald head, sharp ears, and a cluster of muscles. Fear poisoned her rush of adrenaline.

The tallim vendor.

He came at her again, swinging for her chest. She ducked, and the flare of pain in her ribs caused her to hitch. She just managed to stumble out of the way and see the man punch the open air.

Beside her, the click of a gun. Gerdie fired a shot, and even in the darkness, his aim was perfect. The bullet tore through the man's upper arm. Gerdie always went for the arm. He didn't want to kill him. Though he had shot to incapacitate more than once, he had never killed anyone.

"Go." Wil shoved her brother toward a patch of darkness where the trees were thick. "He won't see where the shots are coming from," she said. But Gerdie knew what she meant—this was her fight, not his—and he stubbornly didn't move. He wasn't going to allow her to protect him.

He fired another shot, but he didn't know this man the way Wil did. This man was a freak of nature. She grabbed her dagger and twisted the hilt, but before she could slash him, he'd landed a punch to her fractured rib. He knew exactly where she was vulnerable, must have felt it crack that day when they'd fought.

All the air went out of her. She staggered back and then she was down on one knee, still clutching the hilt and sucking loud, hoarse breaths that didn't seem to fill her lungs. The pain filled her with the color red. Then blackness. Her head lolled.

A hand grabbed her by the wrist and ripped her to her feet. Gerdie. "Stay awake," he commanded, pushing her against a slender tree. She clung to the trunk and made herself breathe. Her bag fell from her shoulder, and, somewhere miles and miles away, Wil heard the bottles of jesseray perfume clattering together through their cloths.

By now the man understood that he would have to do away with the boy if he wanted his revenge on the girl. He clutched Gerdie's wrist in an iron grip and twisted, trying to wrest the gun from his hand. Gerdie was ready for it; he raised his arm and clutched the man's wrist with his free hand, twisting his hips in an effort to break free.

The man's grip only tightened. He moved for a punch to the face. Gerdie veered right, but he wasn't quick enough and took the blow to his temple. He staggered, his grip on his gun never waning. He kicked his right leg—his strongest side—using his braces to lock it straight and land a blow to the man's knee. That got him to slacken his grip. The full weight of bone and muscle and metal gave the kick a punishing force.

Before the man could come at Gerdie again, Wil swept low and slashed her dagger through the back of his calf, just above the line of his boot.

The man roared.

Gerdie stole the moment to fire another shot, this time to the man's clavicle, eliciting a grunt and a line of blood. The man punched Gerdie in the chest, knocking him to the ground. He turned on Wil. His knee came at her stomach so hard that when she blinked, she was on her back and staring straight up at the stars.

She was beyond whatever pain wracked her body. All she could feel was her own trembling. A sour taste in her mouth and burning in her throat told her that she had momentarily been unconscious, vomited.

Then the stars were obstructed by the man's silhouette.

"Think you can steal from me." The words came through

his teeth. Wil could see the shining white of them, and nothing else. Something was keeping her body from getting enough air. Something heavy pressed into her chest. A knee, she thought dazedly. When the man spoke again, all she heard was wind. Wind through trees. Wind filling her head, setting a flurry of gleaming insects in flight before her eyes.

And somewhere very, very far away, a gunshot. Her brother would be shooting to kill now, but with the man so close to her, she didn't know if Gerdie could get a clear shot without risking her life too.

Feebly, she clutched at the man's arms. She was trying to bring her hands to his face, to jam her thumbs in his eyes, but she didn't have the strength.

If she could get her legs out from under him, she might still have a chance. But her legs were gone. Disappeared. And the rest of her was following.

The man was going to kill her, she realized. She was going to die for a tin of tallim and a thousand geldstuk. Such useless little things.

"Wil . . ." Her brother's voice broke through the rushing wind for just a second. He sounded so frantic, like a hurricane was sucking him away.

*Run*, she wanted to say to him. *Mother can't lose us both.*

Then—Wil's eyes snapped open before she realized she'd closed them. The weight that had been killing her was gone—miraculously gone.

She gasped hungrily as air was granted passage back into her lungs. Realizing she was no longer under the man's grasp, she kicked herself backward and away from him.

He was crawling in the grass, retching.

Had Gerdie shot him in the lung? It was her best guess. He must have been desperate enough to go for the kill, she thought, as her body began to rematerialize from its numbness.

Then she saw her brother sitting stunned a couple of yards away, breathing hard, as though he'd been thrown there and had the wind knocked out of him. The gun was still in his slack hand, and he exchanged a bewildered look with Wil.

He didn't cause this.

Then what?

There was a crackling sound, like glass, and at first Wil thought she was hallucinating, that she was still not getting enough air, or that the feeble moonlight was playing tricks on her eyes. That was the only explanation when the vendor's hands, clutching the ground, turned to ruby-red glass. He turned his head to her accusingly, as though she were responsible (was she responsible?), and then his eyes became red glass, and his fat tongue, and his lips, and his neck. Blood leaked between the fine cracks as his skin broke like splintering wood and turned to stone.

It seemed like an eternity before it was through. At last, he fell onto his back, glimmering like precious stone, and dead. Worse than dead. Beyond it. Something that had been living moments earlier was now a thing that could never have been alive at all.

Wil felt something biting into her hands, and looked down to see that the grass beneath her had hardened into slivers of emerald. She heard her ragged gasps, felt the drum of her heartbeat, and knew by these things that she wasn't dreaming, or dead.

From east of the river, she could hear wanderers at their campfire singing about the cursed king with the golden touch.

# FOUR

"DON'T TOUCH ME," WIL CRIED when Gerdie began to crawl toward her. Somehow she knew that she would kill him if he did.

Her heart was throbbing on her tongue, in her ears, her chest. The stars were brighter, stabbing through the dark sky. Air was louder, the rustle of grass and leaves filling her, making her dizzy. Even her brother's face was unnaturally sharp and clear.

Then, gradually, the rush within her receded as a tide being coaxed from the shore back into the sea. Her breathing slowed. Her body stopped shuddering with the force of her heartbeat.

The pain in her ribs came back and a cry escaped her.

Gerdie reached for her again and she recoiled. "Don't."

"I need to feel if the break is worse," he insisted, his

unrelenting logic a strange comfort in this madness. "You could develop a clot."

"That's what you're worried about." The hysterical laugh that came out of her surely belonged to someone else. Sweat was beading her brow. But when she looked at her hands, her skin wasn't sickly or pale. It looked healthy, even more so than usual. Luminescent in the moonlight. She felt stronger than ever, invincible.

She forced her eyes to sweep the area until they landed on the man, lying several yards away on his back. His ruby-red eyes were staring at her even in death. Old blood dripped from the ruby's edges onto the grass.

The red stone had completely taken over his head, his hands, and much of his arms before it receded into his hairy, tanned skin. He must have died before he could change completely, Wil found herself thinking, as though this should make sense. The ruby stopped spreading when his heart stopped beating. Through his crystallized chest, she could see the dark shadow of his heart.

Her breaths came in short, panicked gasps. Her heart kicked up a fury in her chest.

Gentle hands removed the orange data goggles that were resting on the crown of her head; Gerdie fitted them over his own eyes, overlapping his monocle.

Using Wil's dagger, he cut the man's shirt to inspect Wil's gruesome handiwork. Wil made herself look. In the darkness, she could see organs, intestines, bones—all of it hardened into ruby.

"Look at that," Gerdie breathed, more to himself than to his sister. He pressed his hand to the man's chest. Through the ruby, the man's heart was visible, all its chambers and arteries etched in fine detail. All of it crystallized.

Her brother looked at her, and his eyes flitted down to one side, and she could tell that he was reading the data goggles, as though they were offering some explanation for what had happened to her. What she had done.

"Wil." She barely heard her brother calling for her. As she fought to catch her breath, more blades of grass hardened under her legs, her palms. This could not be real. She wanted to say those words out loud so that she could make them be true, but she couldn't bring herself to speak.

Dead. Ruby. Dead.

"Wil." Gerdie's voice was firm. She looked at him.

"Hold out your hand," he said.

When she did, Gerdie plucked a blade of grass and dropped it into her hand.

The change began immediately. The center hardened first, and then crept out to the edges, until the blade sat heavy in her palm.

Gerdie leaned close, and Wil could hear the quiet pitch of the data goggles churning out information about the gem. She saw her brother's eyes moving as he read. Once, then again. He blinked the data away and looked at her.

"That's pure emerald." He sounded frightened and amazed, and it was hard to tell which was more prominent. He began plucking the hardened grass around her, inspecting them the same way. "Real," he said. "All real."

"He's dead," Wil whispered. She was staring at the man again.

"Can you stand?"

"I—" She swallowed hard, nodded. "I think so."

"We're right by the river," he said. "If you can manage it, we should be able to drag him to the rapids. No one will find him there. He'll be pinned down by the water."

It was typical of her brother to focus on the details before dealing with the larger problem. This usually irritated her, but now she was grateful. Action allowed less time to panic.

Wil took a shaky breath and stood. "You take his shoulders. I'll get his feet." She didn't want to see the man's face, but as she hooked his boots under her arms she looked anyway. His ears and tongue and eyes were ruby.

The tip of his nose had also hardened into the gem, and despite himself, Gerdie leaned in for a closer look. The man's nostrils were the pink flesh of a man who'd had a few too many to drink, but that skin receded into a stone such as would be found encrusted in a debutante's ring. "Astounding," Gerdie marveled to himself.

"Could you not?" The sight was nauseating her.

They took one step, and the pain from her ribs shot up her spine. She gasped.

"Wil?"

"I'm fine." Only she wasn't. With a touch, she had done something nightmarish, something she already knew could never be undone. And as the strange exhilaration of this new power began to fade, her broken rib flared with new pain.

"Here." Gerdie's voice was gentle. He lowered the ruby corpse, its limbs splintering and crackling as they bent. There was still some muscle and sinew that hadn't crystallized. "We'll drag him. Do you think you can manage that?"

She nodded, feeling as though she were moving in slow motion.

Grunting but wordless, they ambled toward the river.

From within the man's boots there came a splintered sound like glass cracking apart and then its pieces rattling, and Wil knew that his feet had been affected too. She had killed this man. The crackle and creak of stone reminded her over and over.

She heard the chiming of the clock towers announcing midnight, and from that she knew that it had taken them more than half an hour to haul the man's body to the river.

When they at last reached the water's edge, Wil dropped to her knees, forcing Gerdie down with her as the man's weight hit the ground.

She doubled over the water and shuddered like she was

going to be sick, but nothing came.

The grass stuck to her sweaty palms. It wasn't turning to stone. What had changed?

Her pulse was slow. She felt sluggish and nauseous.

"I think it happens when my heart is beating fast," she mumbled. Her face in the river was a broken moon, the current tugging it off to one side.

"We have to get rid of him before someone finds him," Gerdie said, ever insistent on finishing the task at hand. "If we can get him in the water, the current will do the rest." His practical tone gave way to a moment of sympathy. "Come on. We're so close."

Wil forced herself to oblige. Together, they pushed the man forward. He hit the water with a hard splash. As Gerdie had promised, the current began drawing the man's body toward the rapids.

Wil watched until he was gone.

"The tallim," she said, after several long seconds. She turned to her brother, mind racing. "It spilled all over the floor that day I got it for you. It—I breathed it in. It was all over my hands. It must have been laced with something. That's why this is happening."

Gerdie positioned himself beside her, straightening his legs and struggling to find the least painful position. "The tallim wasn't laced with fillers," he said. "It was pure. I'd know. And I've gotten more than a lungful or two after tossing it into the cauldron."

"Then what?" Wil said. Her breathing was starting to grow rapid again. Something bit into her knees, and she jumped to her feet, startled. The grass where she'd been sitting had turned hard and glimmering.

By the time the clock towers struck one, they'd gathered all the bits of emerald grass. They wrapped them in cloth and buried them in Wil's bag. And then they began to walk home.

She did not walk close to her brother. The distance between them only added to the strangeness, only ignited her fear. This was not the first time their lives had been at risk. It was not the first time something frightening had happened, or strange. But they had always been able to hold each other up, fix the other's wounds.

A mere touch from her would kill him. She knew this. Not only because of what she had just seen, but because she could feel it. There was something deadly inside her. It had melted into her blood, become a part of her, and it buzzed like the energy generated by the mills.

Though her brother had not uttered a word of complaint, his limp hadn't gone unnoticed. A bruise was darkening his temple, half-covered by his waves of gold hair.

They had been walking in silence, but as the castle's stone wall began to appear in the distance, Gerdie said, "Are we going to talk about this?"

Wil rubbed her temple. "Maybe if we don't talk about it, it'll just go away."

"That was your first kill," Gerdie said.

Wil concentrated on breathing. Going into another panic would only summon this newfound horror. She could still see the ruby corpse rolling into the river.

"Hey," she said, trying to chase the thought away. "I'm sorry you got caught up in what happened back there. It wasn't your fight."

He looked at her for the first time since they'd gathered the emeralds.

"Yes it was. I get so mad at Papa, the way he uses us. The way he sends you out to do his bidding with no regard for the danger. But I'm no different." The frustration showed on his face. "You never tell me half of what happens. You hide what you're thinking so well, sometimes you even manage to hide it from yourself."

Wil didn't trust herself to reach out and grab his arm, so she said, "Stop." He turned, and they stood facing each other. "You aren't using me. I wanted you to have the tallim. I want you to have everything you need. Gerdie, Papa is trying to escalate this tension with the Southern Isles into a war. I don't know what it's going to mean, but I do know that the South doesn't have alchemists like you. *No one* can make the things that you do." She lowered her voice and leaned as close as she dared. "If it comes down to it, we can flee the kingdom. You, me, Mother, maybe Owen. We can overthrow Papa if we can't make him see reason."

Gerdie bristled, and she could see that he was flattered. "Your life isn't a price I'm willing to pay for my materials," he said. "That man was going to kill you. And you're the strongest person I've ever met."

"You haven't met very many people," she laughed.

He grudgingly smiled. But it didn't last long. "I'll figure out what's doing this to you. I will. In the meantime, you should lie low. No one can know about this."

They both gave in to the illusion that things were still the same. They still looked the same, at least.

They still had each other.

Neither of them was in any shape to attempt climbing the wall, and without a word passed between them, they walked for the iron gate, where two guards were stationed.

"Prince Gerhard," one of them said. "Princess Wilhelmina." From his breathless tone, Wil gathered that she looked worse than she felt. She rubbed at the dry blood crusted on the corner of her mouth.

The guards moved to help them, but Gerdie brushed them off. "We're fine," he said. "We got a little too enthusiastic at a boat party we attended. Everyone was taking turns diving over the edge. You won't tell our father, will you?"

"No, my lord. Of course I won't."

Of course he would. But Gerdie's lie was spoken so smoothly

that the king himself would believe it when the guards relayed it in the morning, and he'd think nothing of such benign antics.

They moved through the gate. When they'd walked past the oval garden, and the guards were out of sight, Wil's shoulders dropped. Her pace slowed. She felt as though her rib was splintering with every step, peppering her with stabs of pain, flashes of red before her eyes.

In the distance, the ballroom throbbed with light and music like a glowing heart in the western field.

Gerdie stopped to look at it.

Wil stood beside him, resisting her usual instinct to rest her elbow on his shoulder. The lights touched his face the way music touched ears. It crept inside him, made him restless. He looked at those distant bodies twirling across the windows the way that Wil looked at the sea.

"I hear princesses are wretched," Wil said in her most serious voice. "They pick things from their noses and hide them in their hair."

Gerdie's lips twitched, but he wouldn't allow himself to smile.

Eventually, they made their way to the darkened castle, empty aside from the guards who greeted them at the door.

Gerdie moved toward the servants' kitchen, which housed the door to his lab. "You're really going to work?" Wil frowned at him. "Now?"

He took the bag from her shoulder, careful not to touch her.

"I'm going to break down the emeralds. They pass for real with the data goggles, but there must be something else to them."

"I wish you'd sleep first," Wil said. She knew he hadn't been doing much of that.

"Yeah." He shrugged. "I wish for things too." He turned for his lab.

The stone stairwell that led to Wil's bedroom felt like a mile. She moved slowly, eyelids drooping. It wasn't the fight with the vendor, or even her injuries that made her limbs feel so heavy and her mind so fogged.

When she'd turned the man to stone, it was the most alive she'd ever felt, all her blood rushing through her extremities like the raging rapids. Her vision had been sharp, everything glowing before her. The feeling came again when she turned the grass into emeralds by the river. Exhilaration. Terror. *Life*, as though she had always been sleeping and was now finally awake.

And now that the feeling had passed, her blood was no longer rushing. It felt thick, sluggish. Her eyes were sore, her bones and muscles aching.

Whatever had changed in her was affecting her entire body. And in the morning, there would be such a thing as worry. In the morning, she would have to face what she had done. She had ended a man's life, and nearly lost her own, and put her brother at risk. She would have to face what had happened and what was happening to her, all of it.

But tonight, her mind had gone foggy and all of it felt far away. There was only her four-poster bed, netted with shimmering lace, and the warm, familiar sense that she was home, that she was safe now.

She let her dress fall to her ankles—green and lighter green, like the grass she had crystallized—and slipped into a nightgown. It was white. Like the blanket of snow that came each November, turning even the slums of the Port Capital into something empty and clean. She wanted to believe that this night could be so easily erased.

Just as she climbed into bed, there was a knock at her chamber door. "Wil?" Gerdie. "Can I come in?"

"Yes."

He was holding the stone mortar. She could smell the spring sprigs and mintlemint, and the spicy sweetness of estherpetals—the key ingredient in his sleep serum.

"For the pain," he said, as he sat on the edge of her bed.

Wil took the mortar into her hands and tilted it to her lips. She was not one for having her senses dulled by pain remedies, but her brother was a prodigy at mixing them, and she knew that she would awaken in the morning feeling restored, rather than in a persistent fog.

"Is it a dream serum?" she asked.

"No," Gerdie said. "I could mix you one if you'd like. I thought you might prefer a dreamless sleep."

"You know me so well."

"Do you feel any different?" he asked. "Does anything hurt? Are you dizzy?"

"No," Wil said. "Only tired."

Her brother narrowed his eyes, thinking. "Tired, or exhausted?"

"Should there be any difference?"

"Tired is one thing," Gerdie said. "But exhausted is how you'd feel after pushing a boulder up a hill."

"Oh," Wil said, settling back against her pillows. "Then yes. I'm exhausted."

The sleep serum was already beginning to work. The entire world felt like a distant star, winking almost imperceptibly in an endless universe of black.

Her brother didn't press for any more answers. At least not tonight. Tomorrow, they would both approach this with fervor, and the thought made Wil more exhausted still. She hoped, as her body grew warm with sleep, that by morning this would all have passed, even as she knew that this was just the beginning.

She closed her eyes and heard Gerdie still beside her. Looking at the clock and counting each breath she drew within a minute, she suspected, already analyzing her like something lying broken on his metal table.

For a moment, they were children again. He was small and burning with fever in a bed that threatened to swallow him. Wil was crawling up beside him, wiping his sweaty brow with her bare palm, telling him the story of the Gold King, and of the singing wolf, making up happier endings so he wouldn't have such troubled dreams.

This was the way it had always been between them. The world tried to destroy them, but they kept each other alive.

# FIVE

THE QUEEN AWOKE BEFORE DAWN with a sense that something had been stolen from her. Something that had been dropped into the sea.

This was not the first time she arose and haunted the castle at night, but her unrest was pointed this time; she knew that something was amiss.

She moved down the halls and looked in on each of her children. In the darkness at the threshold of their individual chambers she held her own breath to hear them breathe, the sounds reinforcing the beat of her heart.

There was Owen in his cavern of books, the electric lantern glowing at his bedside table, papers spread alongside his sleeping body. She moved to turn out the light, and kissed his crown of hair before she did. He was this nation's future king, but still a boy when he slept.

Then she looked in on Baren, the one who frightened her, snoring lightly in the blackness. Then Gerdie, who fretted and turned in his tangled sheets, his mind as busy as his cauldron even in sleep. His braces were propped against the wall by his bed, skeletal and waiting for soft flesh to give them life. It was a habit for her to touch his forehead, searching as ever for signs of illness. His cool skin against her hand was a relief.

Last was Wilhelmina, a heap of lace and ribbon at the heart of a white canopy bed. Her arm was strewn over the edge of the mattress, and even in the moonlight the queen could see the bruises staining her wrist. She went to such lengths to hide her perilous endeavors, this one, and the queen knew that it was for her sake.

Wil slept silent and still as death.

The window was open, and a warm breeze made the canopy linens rise and fall. The queen moved to close it. Her daughter was too much like her—in love with the free air and always wanting it to touch her, as though she might reach out and grab two fistfuls of stars and breathe in their scent like flowers.

Alone, the queen allowed herself to have the thought that was within her always. That her daughter was the thing she had wanted most in the world, the thing she'd fought death itself to have. After all those years of nervous compulsions and prayers and herbs and sons, she was granted her girl. And she loved her even more than the king, who was the flame in her chest, and the golden-haired sons who put the light in her eyes. It was a terrible joy and a terrible guilt—for she knew the dangers of loving anything in this world where things were too easily destroyed.

Her punishment for so greedily wanting a daughter was that she had been given one just like herself: a restless wanderer of a child who craved the world.

In the moonlight she could see Wil's face. In sleep, she was honest. There was no pretense painted on her skin like concealer. There was no softness to her expression. What was it she saw, in all that darkness? What trouble would greet her mind in the morning, before she laced herself into her dress and became a princess for her mother to see?

The queen swept her hand across Wil's brow and kissed her cheek. Once, twice, a third time, to keep the unrest in her heart at bay.

# SIX

THE ESTHERPETALS GAVE WIL A sleep that was mercifully free of dreams. She awoke with a sense that she had blinked and everything from the night before had just disappeared.

The mirror said otherwise. She sat at her dressing table and selected a pale pink lipstick to hide the cut on her bottom lip.

Covering the signs of battle was easy enough; she'd mastered that when her father first began sending her to the underground market, when she was ten. The king couldn't trust his men to acquire his illegal imports—every man would turn on his king for a price—and the daughter who looked nothing like royalty was his greatest resource.

For the king, having children had been a matter of strategy; he might have had a dozen more, if Wil's birth hadn't nearly been the death of the queen. Children could be primed into soldiers, and their loyalty was more easily earned—or so the king believed. He kept his children well guarded, an act which may have been mistaken for love if one hadn't met him. The guards, soldiers, and servants were well acquainted with the royal children, but most never left the castle proper, and those who did knew to keep all the castle's secrets quiet under penalty of death.

When Wil turned ten, the king impatiently thrust her into the world to do his bidding. Owen had been with her, but they were outnumbered two to one when they discovered the imported metal merely plated, and things went sour. "Stay alert and be everywhere," Owen had whispered, as they stood back-to-back, enemies closing them in. "Remember what I taught you."

She hadn't taken a single hit. Even so grossly outnumbered, Owen was too quick with his sword, and on his watch, no one touched her.

But by the time they made it back to the castle, an angry bruise was darkening his jaw.

"Here." Wil had taken his hands and pulled him onto the cushioned stool at her dressing table. Copying what her mother had taught her, she dabbed concealer over the mark and patted it down with powder. They looked nothing alike, as features went, but their skin was the same color—fair, turned golden by sun.

Owen sat patiently for all this and smirked when Wil stood back to admire her handiwork. "Thanks, Monster."

She'd been quite proud of herself, she remembered.

Now, she expertly traced the mark at her collarbone with concealer. She selected a brown dress with pink strings lacing the corseted waist, and capped sleeves with a ruffled trim that would cover the scrapes on her shoulder.

She even brushed her long hair and braided the top half of it into a dark crown around her head.

There. She looked the part of a princess again. Her mother would worry regardless—she was forever and brutally frightened that her children would be taken from her—but at least Wil wouldn't give her cause.

But before she descended the stairs for breakfast, she stood before the mirror at her dressing table, considering.

Odd that she still looked the same, she thought. Slight, unassuming. No one would see this monstrous thing inside her. The horrible thing she had done the night before. She could almost believe it hadn't happened.

She moved to the arched diamond-pane window and pushed it open. She reached out into the morning air and plucked an ivy leaf from one of the tendrils that grew along the stone. She held it in her palm.

There it sat, fleshy and green. She stroked it with her fingertip, curious. Nothing happened, and she began to wonder if last night had been a dream.

A noise in the hallway startled her. Baren's muffled voice as he shouted at some hapless servant who had crossed him.

She looked to the doorway and her heart began to pound. If her second-eldest brother was looking for a war this morning, she would be his target. He held a special disdain for her in particular. He always had.

The sudden shift of weight in her hand drew her eyes back to the ivy leaf. Keeping rhythm with the increasing beat of her heart, it had turned to emerald.

Wil walked to the breakfast table with deliberate slowness that could be mistaken for grace. She conjured memories of those dreadful comportment lessons, during which she would fritter hours of her precious time on this earth pacing the ballroom with a stack of dusty books on her head.

*Steady,* she told her heart.

In the dining room, a window of stained glass reached to three stories high, painting the morning light in a myriad of colors. It was a fractured mural of the world, as though someone had shattered a map and glued together what pieces could be saved. Dirigibles and gas balloons drifted over broken islands, sparkling octagons and triangles of a green and blue and gold ocean. Towers with windows full of light stretched over distant cityscapes. Ships rocked and drifted between them, never reaching their destinations.

The window was one of the few things in the castle that wasn't ancient. A wedding gift from the king to his queen. A piece of the world she so loved, a world she had chosen to leave behind when she fell in love with a young king and let him steal her away.

Beneath the window, at the far end of the dining table, the

king and queen sat side by side, like porcelain figurines.

All three of Wil's brothers were already seated, and from her father's impatient expression, they had been waiting for her to join them. Trays of toast and waffles beside bowls of softened butter, peanut butter, jam, and chocolate sprinkles sat untouched on the table. The tea had already been poured.

With an apologetic curtsy to her parents, she took her seat. She afforded Gerdie a glance from across the table. Though his hair was arranged into shiny blond waves and he was dressed in a neat, pressed, buttonned shirt, she could see how tired he was, and she knew that he had spent much of the night in his lab on her account.

Wil turned her attention to her mother, whose blue eyes were beaming with excitement. She was looking at Owen. "So," she said, as a trio of servants began laying covered dishes before them. "Now that we're all together, tell us who you've chosen as your bride."

"Ah—yes." Owen's voice drew everyone's attention. His cheeks were flushed, and Wil felt something like happiness persisting in her muddled heart. He looked utterly smitten.

"Her name is Addney," he said, slathering butter onto a slice of bread and then flattening sprinkles over it with the backside of his spoon.

"Oh yes, with those lovely dark eyes, and so tall," the queen said. "Not a princess but from an affluent family in Cannolay. She's quite a beauty, isn't she? Think of the children you'll have."

"Mother, please. We aren't quite there."

"It's a fine choice, and a wise one," King Hein said, as though Owen had ever truly had a choice. Of all the girls at the party, of course he had chosen one from the Southern Isles, as their father had wanted. He would spend the rest of his life here, because he was heir, and his days of wandering the world were ending.

A servant leaned past Wil to lay a platter of fruit on the table, and Wil flinched from her. The queen cast her a curious glance.

Baren sat slouched in his chair, rolling some imaginary piece of lint between his thumb and middle finger. Wil saw the brief, stabbing glare he cast at Owen.

No one regarded him.

Baren had grown up in the shadow of Arrod's heir. And though they resembled each other quite closely, he was not nearly so wise, or clever, or strong. When Gerdie and Wil were born, in rapid succession, Baren had expected them to take his place as the unwanted spares. Particularly Wil, the runt of a daughter at the end of a royal line, who had nearly killed the queen the day she was born.

Baren had been a terror for most of Wil's life. Wil supposed their contention began on the day that she was born. Growing up in Owen's shadow, Baren had never been a favorite of their father's. And then came Wil—a girl. A girl who should have been spinning in dresses and curling her hair. She was the only thing, Baren had thought, more useless than himself. The only one he could overpower. And yet she had surpassed him.

"Wilhelmina." The queen's gentle voice broke Wil out of a trance she didn't realize she'd fallen into.

"Yes, Mother?"

"You haven't touched your breakfast. Are you feeling all right?"

"Oh." She straightened her posture, forced a smile. "Yes. Sorry." She picked up her fork, using it to slice the toast in half. Sprinkles scattered across her plate. "So, Owen, when do we get to meet this bride of yours?"

"A September wedding will be fitting," the king answered.

"September is only next week," the queen lamented, the only one who could ever get away with questioning his authority. "Are you certain that's enough time?"

"I wish we had the luxury of time," the king said. "The sooner the better. Owen agrees with me."

Owen smiled. "Of course."

But Wil knew her brother. He had peripatetic blood. He breathed the open sea like air. And he was going to give it up for a girl with whom he'd danced for just one night.

The conversation turned to wedding plans, and Wil was grateful when the meal was over. Before her instructors could find her, she slipped through the castle gates. She did this with such certainty and purpose that the guards gave her polite nods.

Still nursing her injured rib, she took her time walking to the nomad camp.

Only to find wheel tracks in the mud, and the lingering scent of old fires in the damp morning air.

Gone. Already.

Her heart sank.

The sky rumbled with distant thunder. Had the approaching storm forced them to move on?

*There's something ugly in you. Something vicious.*

Wil stooped to brush her fingertips along the blades of grass. Her lashes fluttered and her vision sharpened, and she could taste the coming storm like coffee on her tongue. The world was at once frightening and fierce and so beautiful she couldn't stand it.

# SEVEN

IT RAINED FOR A WEEK straight. Summer was dying with fanfare—lightning filled the dreary castle walls, and thunder shook the windows.

Even in the rain, Wil ran barefoot through the oval garden until her adrenaline was rushing in her ears, and she experimented with the autumn leaves and used the data goggles to identify what she'd caused. The yellow maples turned to topaz, and sometimes the blades of grass were tourmalines. She swatted a fly and it fell to the ground with a hard thud, a tiny new amethyst.

She was fascinated to discover that some of the red leaves became rubies, when she was especially out of breath from her run, but other times they were garnet, when she was beginning to calm down.

And when she allowed herself to consider the man she had killed, she realized that she had seen him through a sheen of terror and violence, red like rage, not just his own against her, but her rage against him as well.

When she was finished, she always scoured the grass for blades of emeralds and then threw her handiwork into the rapids. In the evenings, she reported her findings to Gerdie, and together they pored through his books and potions looking for explanations.

They had concluded three things:

This power came out of her whenever her heart was racing.

It affected living things, but not objects.

It did not affect things that were dying, or already dead. When she touched the bowl of grapes in the servant's kitchen that had been long since plucked from their source, nothing happened. The same for the dead housefly she'd found on her window ledge.

In desperation, Gerdie mixed a potion from cacao powder, grayroot, and crushed arterleaves. "It keeps things from crystallizing in the cauldron. Maybe it will also keep you from crystallizing things," he'd said, wincing sympathetically as she drank the bitter liquid down.

But all it did was make her nauseous. She was sitting on the bench in his lab, chewing on ginger to ease her stomach. She slumped against the wall. "It isn't going away," she said. "Papa is going to find out, Gerdie. I can't refuse to run his errands.

He's going to send me into the market one day, and I'm going to turn some vendor into diamonds, and—"

"Papa is not going to find out." Gerdie's voice was firm. "He can't. We'll make this go away."

She looked at him. The potion had made her so sickly pale that her eyes appeared black against her skin. Her shoulders dropped. "How?"

"I don't know." He swallowed. "But I haven't met a challenge I can't solve yet."

"Do you think it's a curse?" she said. "Do you think what that woman said—"

"Stop that," Gerdie said. "There are no such things as curses. There's an explanation for this, and we'll find it. Crystals don't just appear magically in the earth; there's a scientific process. There's always a scientific process."

"Not this time," she muttered, swallowing the last of the ginger.

She had ignited his stubbornness with that. She saw it on his face, the way his chin jutted, one brow lowering. "Everything in the universe was thought to be magic once, before we came to understand it. We thought the stars were magic, but they aren't, are they? They're just hydrogen and helium and light traveling through space."

Wil closed her eyes in a long blink, not wanting to argue. It was senseless trying to counter her brother anyway. He remembered every word from every book he'd read, stored every thought he'd ever had, and he lived to call upon them.

And what was her argument anyway? She didn't have the words to explain this sudden change. It had been a week, and she was finding that her body craved the strange rush that moved through her when she turned things to stone. If she resisted for so much as a day, she felt weary, ill. She didn't merely possess this strange new power, she had realized with horror. She *needed* it.

She hadn't told her brother that part.

"I'm going to bed," she told him. "It's getting late. You should too." She nodded to his cauldron, currently bubbling with some new creation in progress. "There are more explosions when you operate that thing while you're sleep deprived."

He frowned at her, but didn't say anything as she stood and headed up the stairs.

From the grand entryway, Wil saw the faint orange light coming from the dining room. She followed it, and found Owen seated at his place at the table, papers spread out beside the light of an electric lantern.

"Hey," she said.

His elbow was on the table, his slender fingers bunched in his hair. He afforded her a fleeting glance. "Up late again, Little Monster?"

She knelt on the chair across from him and leaned over the table. "What are you doing?"

"Papa is gone until Monday, meeting with military forces in Southern Arrod, and I'm stuck signing off on some logistical stuff."

"Let me help. I can forge Papa's signature."

"Is that so?" He slid a blank sheet of paper and the ink and quill across the table. He watched as she wrote *King Hein of the Royal House of Heidle* in bold, elegant strokes.

"Very close," Owen said. "But see there? You added too much of a flourish to the *H*s. Your instructors taught you a more feminine technique."

"Story of my life," she muttered, and began again. If she left her upbringing entirely to her instructors, her life would be nothing but poise and billowing skirts, her brain puddling in her skull.

The queen was the one who insisted Wil learn all these gentle sensibilities and pretty things. It wasn't because she believed her daughter didn't have a mind, but because she feared the trouble that mind would cause her, Wil knew.

Wil did like pretty things. She liked dresses and braids and her silk pillows. But they were a disguise she wore, same as anything else.

Lightning filled the room, and Owen turned to look at the stained glass window and all its pieces of the world.

Wil followed his gaze. Those brief glances of the world were why Owen had chosen to work here. After the wedding, he wouldn't be traveling as much, if at all.

"I've heard rumors that Southern Arrod has telephones now," she said. "Is it true?"

"It is, in fact," Owen said. "They've run wires along street posts. Not that Papa will have anything to do with them."

"He'll have to, eventually," Wil said. "You can't stop technology."

Wil had heard of telephones for the better part of a decade. She had even seen one, once; it had been a prototype being carted around the port by a traveling salesman. The salesman's venture was wasted on Northern Arrod, though. King Hein was deeply untrusting of voices being carried through wires, as though a wire could break open and all his plans and secrets would be spilled out into the ether for anyone to hear.

Owen went back to his signatures. "You underestimate Papa's stoutness regarding these matters."

Wil knew that her father would never come to trust things like telephones; he would look past all the good they might have brought and find all the ways they left the kingdom vulnerable. Gerdie was like him in that way, relying on ancient sciences, and chemicals, herbs, and alchemy rather than machines.

"Fine then." She shrugged. "If the technology won't come to me, I'll go to it."

Owen smirked without raising his head. "When you're out exploring the world?"

"You'll still have me as your spy," she offered. "I'll be your eyes and ears in the world. It's only a matter of time before Papa sends me overseas anyway, now that I'm nearly sixteen and you'll be here more. Even Mother can't stop him."

He laughed. "Is that meant to put my mind at ease?"

Wil watched as he signed their father's name in swirling, elegant calligraphy. He didn't speak of the things that burdened him—he was like their father that way—but Wil could see it, especially in the way he sighed as he reached for a new stack of papers.

"I've noticed more guards than usual," Wil said. "New rotations, too."

Her brother smiled without looking up from his work. "Are they making it difficult for you to sneak off undetected?"

She sat back in her chair and folded her arms. "It would take more than a few extra guards."

"Just remember everything I taught you. Never leave this castle unarmed."

She bristled at his concern. "You don't have to worry. I'm not a child, you know."

He looked as though he had something to say to that, but he held back. Choosing battles was a talent of his.

"Owen?" she said, after a long silence. "Do you remember your first kill?"

"Fifteen years ago, in Brayshire," he said. "I was with Papa, and marauders tried to hijack a cargo ship bound for Grief, carrying medical supplies. The ship was accepting fares, and one of the hijackers was holding a child at knifepoint. So I shot him."

He said this with a nonchalant detachment that Wil might not have understood a week ago but understood now. If someone were to ask her about the man she had killed, she would speak of him the same way. Facts and reason. The rest frightened her too much to contend with.

Fifteen years ago. "You were much younger than I am now," she said, softly.

He glanced up from his paperwork and studied her. "Is there something you want to tell me?"

She opened her mouth to speak, and a boom shook the castle walls, much louder and angrier than the thunder. The smell of burned metal filled the air, and she was on her feet and through the servants' kitchen before she knew she had moved, Owen on her heels. She threw open the door to her brother's lab and was greeted by rolling plumes of black smoke. "Gerdie!"

She let Owen move past her, if only to eliminate the risk of touching him, and followed him into the darkness. At first she thought the blast had knocked out the electricity, but when she reached the bottom step, she realized the bulbs were merely covered in ash, damping much of the light.

Through the murk, she saw Gerdie's blond hair, his pale skin as he lay slumped on the ground.

Awful flashbacks of his childhood illness raced through her. The mornings she'd found him crumpled on the floor, convulsing, or worse, lying still as death.

"Gerdie!"

She stood on the bench and forced the small window open with the heel of her hand. It wasn't much, but it redirected some of the smoke, at least.

Owen was knelt before him, touching his face, the side of his neck, lifting his eyelid.

Wil hovered, afraid to get too close, fighting every instinct to help him up. Gerdie stirred and coughed, muttering something about shrapnel.

Owen sagged with relief. "We have to get you upstairs. You can't be breathing this in. Your lungs."

Nodding and coughing, Gerdie pulled himself up and let Owen help him hobble up the steps, Wil following and wringing her hands.

They made it all the way to Owen's chamber, none of them uttering a word until the doors to both his bedroom and the antechamber were closed. Walls in this castle had ears.

Gerdie collapsed into the desk chair. A thick trickle of blood dribbled from his forehead, and he took the cloth that Wil offered him and dabbed at it.

"You nearly took us all out with that one," Owen said. He was sitting on the edge of his bed, leaning forward. "Want to tell me just what the burning gods you were doing?"

"I was breaking down metals and crystals," he said. "I've developed this new potion that should be able to separate them, and I thought I could use the cauldron's heat, sort of like an oven—but—" He stopped speaking, but his mind was still turning out an explanation that wouldn't have made sense to anyone but him anyway.

"Okay." Owen rubbed his brows with his thumb and index

finger. He looked so tired. "The two of you need to tell me what's going on. The sneaking around. The secrecy. Wil, you're in that lab every waking second, if you're in this castle at all. And you ask me about my first kill, because why? You're just collecting stories?"

Gerdie and Wil exchanged a hesitant look, which did nothing to ease Owen's suspicions.

Then, making a decision, Wil removed the orange data goggles from the crown of her head. In her state of constant analysis, they had become a fixture there lately. She handed them to Owen.

Gerdie understood. He reached for the potted aloe plant on Owen's shelf. He tore away a prickly leaf and held it out.

Her pulse still thrumming from the rush of disclosing her secret, she let him drop it into her palm, and she held it up for Owen to see.

The hardening began to form at the blade's center, like a vein, and then it spread outward, until the entire thing was pure diamond.

"Burning gods," Owen breathed. He watched as, without touching him, Wil dropped it into his palm for his scrutiny.

He turned the diamond leaf in his palm and brought it close to the goggles over his eyes. His lips moved as he read the text, and then he looked at Wil.

"This is real."

She gripped at her nightgown, wresting the fabric anxiously

in her fingers; a rush was fluttering through her blood; she could taste the ash and scorched air all the way down in the lab from up here. "Yes."

Owen held the diamond up to the light, not quite believing. "How?"

Wil told him everything. The vendor she'd killed, what the old woman had said to her, all the things she had turned to precious stones, and Gerdie's attempts to cure her.

When she was through telling it, she leaned back against one of his bookshelves and folded her arms. She stared at the ground. "I didn't want to tell you. I thought maybe it was a fluke. A side effect from always handling those raw powders and chemicals I smuggle in, and that it would go away."

"But any chemicals she's handled, I have even more so," Gerdie spoke up. "And nothing has ever happened to me, aside from a few burns and dizzy spells."

"I think it's a curse," Wil said.

"Curses aren't real," Gerdie replied, irritated. This had become a common argument as of late.

"People don't just turn things into stone," she said. "When will you accept that not everything has a scientific—"

"Shut up, both of you," Owen snapped. He looked at Wil. "If Papa were to find out about this, I don't want to think about what that would mean. We're about to go to war, and the wealth this would generate—the *deaths* this would cause . . ." He trailed off. His face had gone pale.

It made Wil feel horribly guilty. She took a step toward him. "Owen, I—"

"You would never see the light of day again." He met her eyes. "I don't know what exactly he would plan for you, but you could forget about being sent out into the world. You could forget about leaving this castle. He would lock you up here where he could use you."

"Surely he wouldn't take it that far," Wil said. But her voice wavered.

"I know our father in a way that you never could," Owen said. "Either of you."

Wil stood dead center between her brothers, and she watched the way the diamond caught the light before Owen closed it in his fist. "You have to hide this," he said.

"I've been throwing them in the rapids—"

"Not just this. All of it." He drew a deep, steadying breath. After talk of war and being forced into marriage, this was the thing that shook his unshakable calm. "There's a marveler by the name of Pahn. He's the best the world has to offer. He's worked for King Zinil for decades. If anyone will know what this is, it's him."

"King Zinil?" Wil said. "I didn't think marvelry played much of a hand in the Southern kingdom."

"I don't think it does," Owen said. "But nonetheless, there's something about Pahn that the king finds useful."

"But hasn't the Southern Isles closed its borders?"

"He may not be there," Owen said. "He goes where he's needed. Often he goes into hiding—he has many enemies."

"What sort of enemies?" Wil asked.

"Marvelry is a controversial thing," Owen said. "Curses, spells, cures."

"A marveler?" Gerdie balked. "Burning gods, *that's* your solution? Why not a street magician?"

Owen gave him a cutting glare. "There's more to the world than what you've read in your texts. You may be a genius, but you don't know everything."

"How do I find him, then?" Wil said, before the argument between her brothers could mount.

"I don't know." Owen opened his palm, staring at the red marks his grasp on the diamond had dug into his skin.

Wil stared off, considering her options, but Owen read her mind. "If you ran off to find Pahn yourself, Papa would be suspicious. I'll see what I can find out. In the meantime—lie low."

# EIGHT

By the second week of September, the rain had given way to a gray sky and sepia plumage, and winds that smelled like fire and trees.

Owen and Addney were wed without any fanfare, beneath a trellis woven with bright autumn blossoms. She had a beauty befitting an heir's wife, the servants had murmured, with rich copper-brown skin, and long hair that swirled and curled at the edge like parchment held too close to the flame.

And so began the start of what would be a very long effort to merge two kingdoms.

The new house was still unfinished, and so Addney came to live in the castle. Wil would lie in bed and hear Addney and her brother whispering in the halls, laughing between kisses as they moved toward his chamber. And then the doors closed and there was silence, and Wil knew that some great change was underway.

For everyone but her.

Her sixteenth birthday was fast approaching, and she had made no strides in ridding herself of her power.

One dreary morning, she climbed out of bed and unbuttoned her nightgown. It fell from her body and pooled at her ankles, and she stood before the mirror wearing nothing but the data goggles.

She stared at the orange-tinted girl in that mirror. Her tangle of dark hair, dark-brown eyes, sharp chin. The same girl she had been on the thousands of mornings before this one.

Her eyes roved down to her shoulders, and her jutting collarbone, and the hollow of her throat.

Lying between her breasts was the white birthmark that seemed to grow with her, faint and gleaming against the light.

She stared for so long that the left lens of the data goggles produced scientific text about her heart.

She focused on the wall until the words disappeared. When her eyes returned to the mirror, she found her hips, and her thighs. She had always known every detail of herself—the parts of her that were strong, the parts that left her vulnerable in a fight, the parts that only she laid eyes upon, and the muscles that sat under her skin like a hard rope. The data goggles could tell her about her reproductive system. They could tell her about her ligaments and bones. But they could not tell her what had changed within her, if it was a curse, a punishment, or the herbs ingested or the prayers muttered during pregnancy by her superstitious mother.

*Something vicious.*

All the goggles could tell her was what the textbooks said, and she wished she were that simple.

Then she dressed, brushed her hair and twisted it into a knot at the nape of her neck. She spent extra time making herself presentable this morning, selecting a silk blouse the color of cream and a long red skirt bejeweled by diamond roses—both handmade in Brayshire, a gift from her father on one of his diplomatic missions.

After weeks without a word spoken between them, her father had requested a meeting with her in his throne room. It was a section of the castle set apart from the living quarters, and invitations were rare, even for the king's children.

For the first time in more than a year, Wil was greeted by her father's guards at the heavy oak doors of his throne room, and they pulled them open for her.

She walked the long velvet rug that led to her father's throne, her skin swathed in the light of ancient stained glass. Unlike the one in the dining room, these windows did not tell of pretty things. They were scenes from the centuries-old battle in which the Heidle legacy won the throne to Northern Arrod, and ultimately the half of the continent that would come to be known as Southern Arrod as well.

The window with the map of the world was her mother, but these battle scenes were decidedly her father. Somewhere, somehow, their two very different hearts convened. The love between the king and queen was one that Wil could never understand, but one that would be impossible for her to deny. She took an odd comfort in knowing that she and her brothers were not merely born to be soldiers for their father's cause, as he would have them believe. That there was something human in the world's most powerful king after all, something kind—and they were proof of it.

She stopped a perfect yard away from her father's feet where he sat on his throne, and she dipped into a dutiful curtsy. "You asked for me."

He dismissed the guards flanking him with a cant of his chin. Wil watched them go. Only after the doors were closed did her father lean forward. He studied her with something she could almost mistake for concern.

It made her uneasy. Had she betrayed something? Had he seen her in the gardens, turning things to stone? Noticed her rigid stride as her injuries slowly healed?

She stiffened her spine. "Is everything all right, Papa?"

"Have you had much opportunity to speak with Owen's new bride?"

"Not much," she said.

"She's the daughter of the most affluent family I could find in that cesspool Cannolay," the king said. "I would have preferred the princess herself. Would have been willing to wait until she was of marrying age. But King Zinil is beyond reasoning with."

The Southern Isles had only one princess, about whom very little was known, because the kings held their spares close to their chests like a hand of cards—so her father liked to say. Wil knew only that the Southern princess was fifteen years old, and that no one who claimed to have seen her could prove as much.

"Nevertheless," the king said, "I'd like you to keep an eye on Addney. Befriend her. Embrace her like a sister. Report back to me about anything you find suspicious."

She wanted to ask if he had a reason to suspect Owen's wife of treason. The thought that this woman might use her brother in some way, or worse, harm him, made her pulse quicken.

But she knew better than to question her father's orders.

She nodded. "Yes, Papa."

"Good." The king straightened in his chair. "I know I can rely on you."

That small bit of approval brought a smile to her lips, despite everything.

She left the throne room feeling hopeful. Befriending Addney was a small task. At the very least, a painless one. And her father trusted her. And trust led to overseas missions. He might even send her out to purchase something legal for once. She might be able to get a glimpse of the world and savor it, without being chased down dark alleys for the privilege.

Before succumbing to her morning lessons, she checked on Gerdie in his lab. In the interest of avoiding their father's suspicions, he had been working on the flexible armor their father had been pestering him for. The night before, Wil saw him hauling a box of old leather coats and silk gloves down from the attic. He'd nearly bitten her head off when she offered to help. The fatigue and frustration were making him into a beast, and she'd told him as much before storming off.

Because of his mounting irritability, she knocked before she entered this time.

"Gerdie? I'm just checking you're still alive down there." She rested her back against the door. "Mother will be sad if you blow yourself to bits the week before your seventeenth birthday. You know she's quite fond of you."

A long silence, and then his quiet reply, "Well, don't just stand there."

She descended the stairs and found him at his cauldron, his eyes bright, shoulders raised. He gave her a grin. "You're just in time. Here, I'll let you do the honors."

He handed her the pair of silver tongs he'd been holding.

Wil took them, blinking. He was actually letting her operate his cauldron? "You're in a good mood."

"Things just fell into place."

Following his instruction, she leaned away from the wisps of purple steam and lowered the tongs into the bubbling brew.

Something within the cauldron stirred, as though magnetically drawn to her, and when she lifted the tongs again, an object was pinched between them. It looked like liquid metal.

Carefully, she brought it to the stone table to cool. Purple liquid dripped down, sizzling when it hit the stone floor.

"What is it?" she asked. The thing she had extracted from the cauldron was still emitting too much steam for her to get a proper look.

Beside her, Gerdie was smiling. "Flexible armor," he said. "I've finally done it." He took the tongs and gently prodded the heap of liquid metal, until Wil could see that it was not liquid at all. Rather, it was some bizarre combination of steel and silk, malleable but shining.

It was a pair of gloves, long enough to reach the elbow.

"I'm still working on the full body armor that Papa wants," Gerdie said. "But these are for you."

Wil looked at him, understanding.

"Your power has its limits," Gerdie went on. "You said the grass doesn't change under your feet when you're wearing boots, right? So—"

"So, if I wear these, I'll finally be able to hold things without destroying them. . . ." Wil's voice trailed.

"I thought you'd sound happier," Gerdie said. "I know it's not a cure—yet—but it's something."

"I am happy," she said. How to explain? These gloves brought her the hope of being somewhat normal again, and she and hope had fallen into a cruel dance of wits as of late.

She smiled, but it didn't reach her eyes.

"What is it?" Gerdie said.

"I'm trying to lay the groundwork with Papa, so that he'll send me away," she said. "Maybe I'll be able to find Pahn while I'm out there. If I can get to him quickly, and be back in time, Papa won't ever have to know. I won't give him any reason to be suspicious."

Gerdie said nothing. He was biting back his argument against marvelers, and the notion of Wil venturing out into the world alone. They had both always known the day would come. She could never be happy living out a lifetime in one place.

When he did speak, all he said was, "Give me time to finish the paralysis bullets before you set off. I have a few other things in the queue as well. I'll make sure you're armed to the teeth. You'll be invincible."

Wil straightened her posture. "Maybe I already am."

By evening, the gloves had cooled, and Wil was left marveling at the way they fit. They were practically weightless, thin as a second skin. But when she tested a kitchen knife against them, the blade bent, leaving not so much as a scratch on the gleaming surface of the gloves.

It was highly impressive, Wil had to admit, even by Gerdie's scrupulous standards. And no doubt the metal and silk were infused with a myriad of powders and oils she'd retrieved for him.

Wil wore her gloves to the dinner table, and they caught the king's eye immediately.

"Progress on the flexible armor front," Wil told him, nodding to her brother. "I get to test the prototype."

"It looks like—is that silk?" the queen said, reaching out to sweep her fingertips over the knuckles.

Wil flinched before she could stop it. The concern in her mother's eyes cut through her, and she found it hard to breathe. She had never flinched away from her mother's touch, the youngest child and the only one still patient enough to accept her affections. Every day, she seemed to lose some small piece of her normal life to this thing. Someday there would be nothing left.

Wil was grateful for the small distraction when the servants brought in trays of food. Glazed chicken in a bed of orange shavings, carrots, asparagus and potatoes sprinkled with barley, tiny silver bowls of gravy and melted butter. Since the sudden emergence of her powers, Wil's appetite had been fickle, but she filled her plate regardless.

"Perhaps they will come in handy tonight," the king said. "A passenger ship arrived this afternoon from Brayshire. I've heard a rumor that there may be a Southern spy among them."

Owen spoke up immediately. "Papa, she isn't ready for that. She's never dealt with foreign spies, and if there is a spy, and he were to find out who she is, she would be taken hostage. Or—"

"Nonsense," the king said. "Rumors about the princess of

Arrod change like the tide, but not a single one of them has come close to the truth."

Wil knew what he meant by that. There were rumors that the princess of Arrod was attending prestigious boarding schools, or sailing the world, or locked away in a tower safe from the eyes of suitors. But these tales all had one thing in common: the princess of Arrod looked just like her parents and brothers, with their blue eyes and gold hair.

She did resemble the king a little, if one had a keen eye. So many of her expressions mirrored his, particularly when she was pensive or exasperated. But no one ever looked at her long enough to notice these things when she was beyond the castle wall, because she was quite good at making herself invisible.

The queen laid her hand on her husband's arm. As ever, her presence was gentle but strong. But Wil saw the way her lips quivered before she brought them to the king's ear and whispered something. It was a protest, Wil knew, for her mother would never argue with him where others could hear it.

The king leaned against her to listen, his eyes softening near imperceptibly, the way they always did for his queen. Whatever she said may have been enough to sway him. It usually was.

"Papa." Wil raised her voice, cutting off her mother's hushed words. "I'll do it."

She felt Owen's and Gerdie's cutting stares, but she kept her eyes on her father. He had never tasked her with anything this important before. Gaining intelligence on a foreign spy in a time of impending war would increase her worth to this king-dom by degrees. And if she could do this, soon he would be sending her out into the world for sure, months sooner than she'd anticipated. Then she could find Pahn and be rid of this power for good.

"Please," she said. "I want to do this for you. For Arrod."

Her father's proud expression was tarnished by her moth-er's paling complexion.

"Wouldn't you rather send me, Papa?" Baren spoke up. "I could wear a disguise—"

"Don't be a fool," the king said, with a flourish of his hand. "Your sister *is* a disguise. The most valuable one we have."

Without looking at him, Wil could feel Baren's eyes going dark and narrow. Another reminder that even she had a pur-pose.

After dinner, Gerdie moved to his laboratory and beckoned Wil to follow.

He stood over his worktable, twisting the hilt of her dagger apart so that he could refill it with sleep serum.

"Thanks," Wil said, affording a small bit of contrition in the wake of his obvious disapproval. She was running her fin-gertip along the open page of his notebook.

He glared at her. It was a look she had pretended to ignore throughout the duration of the meal, but now its edge was sharper.

"Whatever you want to say to me, just come out with it."

He sheathed the dagger and handed it back to her. "It wouldn't make a difference. You never listen."

"Is this an attempt to make me feel guilty?" Wil said. "Because I'm losing time even as we stand here. Lecture me after I've returned."

"I'll never understand the things that call to you," he said. "Becoming a wanderer. The water. Your incessant desire to make Papa value you. He's never going to, can't you see that? You are nothing to him. We are nothing to him."

Wil adjusted the sheath to her thigh, tugging it roughly into place. She did not look at him. She did not want him to see that he was right, and that the thing she so wanted was the thing she would never have, even as she pursued it.

"However Papa feels about my worth as a daughter doesn't matter," she said. "I don't need his love. I only need his trust. He'll use me as a spy—you've said so yourself. So I'll be the best spy. I'll be better than any of his men, and ten times more reliable because we share blood, and soon, he will send me out into the world."

"Out into the world for what purpose?" he pressed. "So you can employ magicians to cure you with potions made of bubbling soap and snake oil?"

She paced past him, toward the stairs. She was so angry, she pressed her lips tight to keep from saying any of a hundred things she would regret later. She was tired of her brother's logic, his lectures on the science of things. This was not a broken bone or a fractured collarbone or a fever carried over from a foreign land. He could not master it as he had so many other things. The thing that had overtaken her belonged to no one but her, and though she hated it, it was her possession. Only she had the right to speak to what it was, and what it could do, and how she could be rid of it.

"You don't know everything," was all that she said. She slammed the door behind her.

A short while later, Wil was making her way through the thick of the woods, wearing a pair of dark trousers and a gray tunic that had once belonged to Gerdie before he'd outgrown it. She had also helped herself to a pair of his platinum guns and a leather holster to go around her waist. On her way out, she had avoided her mother, who had begun tapping the walls and breathing in her compulsive numerical patterns.

Whenever the queen felt helpless, it compelled her to do things in multiples of threes and fives.

The queen believed that those numbers held the universe in balance somehow. That if she did not count correctly, if she did not step in time, some tragedy would befall her children. That when Owen set sail on one of his diplomatic affairs, the ship would never return and it would be because she hadn't shown that she loved him enough.

The bitter guilt of being the cause of her mother's worry followed her out into the chilly September night.

She had slipped down the halls and over the stone wall

before her mother could find her. She couldn't risk an embrace, the three inevitable kisses to her forehead.

Her father's source indicated that the ship's fares would be headed into a village five miles inland from the Port Capital—a small, bustling strip of taverns and hotels, mostly. Wil had been there before. Working class. Modest. Low crime, although the occasional rowdy sailor could raise trouble after a few too many at the tavern. And the taverns would be what she checked first.

There was a main road that led straight through, but, per her father's instructions, Wil took the roundabout way through the woods. The leaves were gleaming, slick with recent rain. She followed the sounds of the river eastward, and then walked alongside the water until she reached the rapids.

Here, alone in the darkness, her worry caught up with her.

There was a natural bridge in the form of a rock wall, under which the water passed on its way back to the sea. The water seemed angered by its presence, churning and hissing and pushing against it, producing a thick froth. And unless she wanted to swim in the frigid shallows and walk a mile out of her way, Wil had to cross that wall.

This was where she and Gerdie had hauled the dead vendor, and as the memory began to surface, Wil fought it back. She couldn't afford to allow him into her head now.

Another memory appeared in its place. She had crossed over these waters twice before—once to the other side, and once back—when she was a child and Baren had dared her. He had wanted her to fall in, and she'd known it. Here, the water wouldn't have merely drowned her. It would have devoured her. No one—not even the king and all his soldiers and guards—would have been able to recover her body.

That was why she'd accepted the dare. She wasn't going to disappear, no matter how much Baren wished it were so. The entire time she edged along, he'd shouted that she was the useless spare, that she should just let go. How proud she was to land on her feet before him.

How fitting that she was back here now, trying to prove her worth again.

She was ashamed of the time she wasted standing there now. Forcing herself into action, she removed one glove, then the other, folding them and stowing them in her rawhide bag.

She set one foot on the rock wall. It was rich with crevices, bits of mica winking at her like a thousand pairs of eyes in the starlight.

She hoisted herself up, and her fingers found something to hold on to. There. Not difficult. A child could do this.

The water spat at her boots.

"You're wind," she whispered. "You're everywhere."

She lifted herself higher, and imagined that she was floating above the river. Above the woods. The rapids were nothing from such a height. They were a babbling drunken argument on some noisy street—nothing that should matter to her.

A snapping sound ripped her back down to earth, and her

fingers tightened on the rock face. Her head whipped to the right. A figure was moving through the trees, strands of gold curls gleaming in the darkness.

Owen.

She charged forward with renewed fervor. She was nearly halfway across now—or so she told herself. Her heart was hurling itself against her chest like a violent prisoner in a cell, but her face didn't betray any of that. She couldn't show fear. She couldn't be afraid. Not if she wanted to be worth anything in her family.

"Monster," he called after her.

"Go away," she said.

She looked at him. His arms were at his sides, his shoulders lax. He was trying so hard not to press his authority on her. He was actually pleading. "Wil, please. Don't be an idiot."

When was the last time he'd called her by her name? When was the last time he'd said "please"—to anyone?

"I can't have you in my head right now," she said. She had to shout over the water. "I'm trying to concentrate."

"Let me talk to Papa about sending you overseas if that's what you want," he said. "You don't have to do this. King Zinil's spies are ruthless. Papa has threatened *war*. The entire South hates our family right now. If one of them found out who you are, you would be—" He was breathing hard, Wil realized. Something he'd just imagined had frightened him. "I wouldn't forgive myself."

She wanted to give in, if only to erase that horrified look from his face. But something refused to let her. That eight-year-old girl with gritted teeth and a fluttering stomach, fighting to prove her place as the scrawny daughter in a royal line.

"You don't have to protect me," she said.

He said something else, but she had willed herself not to hear it, and in the next instant he was climbing after her. She hastened her speed, hoisting her boots from foothold to foothold.

But she and Owen were matched wit for wit, stubborn heart for stubborn heart. He had always liked to tell her they were the same.

"Just listen," he said. They were both dead center now. Owen had no fear of this rock wall—he'd ventured it a hundred times, knew it like the back of his hand. He knew the entire kingdom, and so much of the world beyond. "Mother is beside herself. She pleaded with Papa, and he's coming to stop you."

"What?" Wil said, her fear lost to her anger. "You didn't try to stop him? How could you let him come after me like I'm a child?"

"Maybe he realized what he's asking of you," Owen said. "He treats you as though you're disposable—"

"That's why I have to do this," she cried, pressing her body close to the rock to maintain her concept of space. The action stirred a lingering pain in her healing rib. "You don't know what it's like to be a spare. You couldn't. Papa has always given you the world. The rest of us have to fight for glimpses of it."

The words hurt him, and she saw it on his face. Because she had just pitted herself against him, drawn a bold line that turned them into rivals. But she couldn't take them back. She had meant them. She went on, and Owen stayed stubbornly beside her.

She breathed through her frustration.

Her boot slipped on the drenched rock face. She heard herself scream before she could stop it, a sound that didn't even belong to her, a sound that held all the fear she'd been storing in her chest.

She couldn't regain her footing. Her vision was frenzied and moving fast, as though she were spiraling off the edge of the earth itself. For an awful moment she thought she had fallen completely, and she expected the water to fill her lungs.

But something was holding her.

"Breathe," Owen was telling her. He had her collar bunched in his fist, somehow managing not to touch her.

"Let go of me." Her voice was just another version of her scream. Shrill, foreign.

"It's okay," he was saying, calm for the both of them. "Lift your left leg; there's a foothold right by it. You've got this."

Her arms were burning, and she realized with dulled horror that her hands and Owen's grasp on her collar were the only things keeping her from certain death.

Tears stung her eyes, making further chaos of her vision.

Panic. She never panicked. "I'm not moving until you let go." She sobbed. Later she would curse herself for that sob, she made a note.

He released her collar, like he was agreeing to a hostage negotiation.

She held her breath for a beat, then drew it in through her nose, held it, let it go through her open mouth. She worked to draw her left leg up, relying on her core, ignoring the stabs of protest from her rib.

But if her mind was prepared to ignore that pain, her body wasn't. Her arms shook, fingers went numb, and when she fell away from the rock face, there wasn't even time for her to scream.

An arm wrapped around her waist, drawing her up from the water that sloshed greedily for her dangling feet. A force. Motion. And then she was lying on her side in the damp grass, shaking. New hunks of emerald bit at her through her clothes.

Owen was knelt beside her.

"No." Her voice was hoarse. "Owen, no." The next sob to leave her was a violent one. She pushed herself upright and then to her feet. She staggered back.

He stood to face her. For a moment they were the only things breathing in all the woods of Northern Arrod. He was twenty-five years old. And he was fifteen. And he was holding her over his shoulders to show her their kingdom. And he was pulling her up from the rapids. He was a million moments—an entire lifetime—all at once.

He was staring her down with that same defiance he'd always had. The persistent haughtiness of a someday king.

But they both saw the glint of diamond at his fingertip, and they knew that Arrod would never have him as its ruler.

# NINE

HE STOOD FOR AS LONG as his body would let him, as the clear, merciless diamond hardened the veins in his arms, and paralyzed his lungs, and eventually, inevitably, took his heart.

Wil caught him when his knees buckled and he fell forward, already dead. She stumbled to the ground with him in her arms.

Even his hair had succumbed to it, brittle strands of diamond flaking off into the gold.

Someone was saying his name. Screaming it.

Her throat was raw.

"What have you done?" Another voice came from the other side of the churning river. She saw her father, standing tall against the darkness, for once not flanked by his guards.

In a blink, her father was on their side of the river. Wil didn't even see him move.

He pulled Owen from her arms, cradling him in his lap. This must have been the way he'd held Owen when he was a child, Wil thought. She had never imagined Owen as a child. He had always been so proud, it never occurred to her that he had once been small. But here in death and moonlight, she saw that he was vulnerable. He had always been.

The king cupped his hands around the skin of Owen's face, which had been spared, save for the smooth diamond that had frozen at the curves of his cheeks and a glittering smattering of lashes.

He looked like something that had been unearthed from snow.

The king squeezed his eyes shut. "I should have killed you long ago," he told her. "And I still can't bring myself to do it."

Through her shock, Wil could hear in his voice that he had entertained the idea before. Did he know what she was capable of? Had he always? She was in no state to ask him. She was staring at Owen's chest, willing it to rise with a breath.

"Both of you died here tonight," the king said. "Leave this kingdom. If I see you again, I will slit your throat, like I should have on the day you were born."

Wil could not feel her legs, but somehow she began to move.

The kingdom of Arrod did not yet know what it had lost tonight, but the sky knew. Clouds churned like hands searching for something they had dropped in murky waters. The air rustled the leaves, making sobbing sounds.

Wil did not realize, until she found herself far beyond the river, how far she had run.

She stopped to catch her breath when her lungs began to burn and her vision roiled with bursts of darkness. And here, the quiet elegy of the woods gave way to distant laughter in the Port Capital, its towers muttering the hour in their language of bells and gears.

Eleven o'clock. At ten o'clock, Owen had been alive and thriving, the rich blue veins in his arms fed by the beating of his red heart.

Wil's own heart began to settle the longer she stood still, and through her haze she realized the injustice of this.

*Walk*, she told herself. If she lingered here between these trees even a moment longer, then she would never leave. She would lose her resolve and return pleading to her mother and crumple at her feet like a child. Her father would kill her for what she had done, but that wasn't the worst of it. The worst was that her mother would know. Wil would rather her mother believed she were dead than know the truth. It would destroy her.

But Gerdie—

"*Walk*." She said it aloud that time, and her legs obliged.

There would be no ships this late, but she had seen dirigibles take flight at all hours. The pilots kept erratic schedules, collecting fares to cover their own expenses as they flew wherever they needed to go.

She had been on dirigibles before, but only while they were grounded. Tonight, if she could find one that was departing, she would leave Northern Arrod for the first time in her life. There would be no coming back.

She didn't break stride even as she opened her bag to count her money. Two thousand geldstuk. Because Northern Arrod was the leading kingdom, its currency was accepted worldwide, though its value depended on foreign exchange rates. Air travel was cheaper than sea; this would be more than enough to get her out of the kingdom with money to spare.

There was only one dirigible taking passengers. It was smaller than the others, and parchment brown with an open-concept gondola. A man stood at its door, clean shaven with a warm but cocky grin that reminded Wil, distantly, of Owen. She didn't allow the thought to take root.

"Where are you headed?" she asked, her voice deceptively strong.

"Wanderer Country," the man said. It was another word for Brayshire. It had earned this nickname due to its status as a place of congregation for people wandering the world. "It's three hundred."

Mutely, Wil paid him and stepped past. The gondola was nearly empty. On the far side there was a group of four young people, chattering. Wil forced their voices away, until the words were as distant as the stars shining in the graying sky.

*Find Pahn,* she reminded herself. He was the only hope she had left now.

The floor of the dirigible was a sepia map of the world, embellished with sea creatures poking out of the waves and towering ghostly creatures trudging through the pine trees of the Western Isles.

It appeared to be hand-painted, and it was a map that Wil knew well. She'd found a version of it folded on a piece of parchment in her mother's things in the attic when she was a child.

There were no seats, only a long wooden railing that wrapped around the perimeter under the glassless windows. She clung to it and concentrated on breathing.

She did not immediately realize that they'd lifted off the ground, because all her organs were still set firmly down on Arrod soil. Her breath was down there too.

It took several moments for her to get her bearings, and when she did, she looked ahead and saw that the dirigible was rising higher and higher above the ocean.

Soon, she knew, her mother and brothers would hear that she was dead. She didn't know what her father would tell them—perhaps that she and Owen had been swallowed up by the rapids.

The dirigible rose up and up, and Wil made herself let go of that castle and all the things inside it. They were not hers.

The princess of Arrod was dead.

# TEN

THE QUEEN'S SCREAM SPLIT THE night in two.

Gerdie had been extracting a metal breastplate from his cauldron—his first attempt at this particular piece—but the shattering sound caused the vulnerable form to disintegrate.

By the time he reached the top step, he could hear more screams, though now they were softer and carried by sobs.

Strangely, he felt as though the heart had been scooped from his chest and the hollow spot had filled back up with blood.

The castle was dark. The only light came from the grand foyer, and as he moved toward it, he saw his mother crumpled on the floor, her nightgown spread around her like crushed petals. Baren stood beside her. The king stood before her, his head bowed, his expression blank.

"Mother?"

Baren and the king said nothing. But Baren's mouth rose into the beginnings of a smile, and in that moment, Gerdie knew.

His mother reached for him. He took slow steps toward her, his braces creaking in place of a heartbeat, and then he turned to his father.

Now that he was standing close, he could see that the king's eyes had grayed, and so had his face.

"Owen and Wilhelmina are gone," the king said.

The queen screamed again, and that time she grabbed Gerdie's hand in both of hers, pulling him down to her. He fell to his knees, rigid, numb, even as he felt her arms wrapping around him.

"Gone?" Gerdie heard himself say, his voice hollow and trailing.

"She was crossing the rock wall and she fell into the rapids," Baren said, as though he'd been waiting for his chance to speak. "Owen tried to save her, but he couldn't. They're both dead." The words were matter-of-fact, but there was no mistaking the pleasure he took in saying them.

*They're both dead.*

Gerdie's only immediate thought was of Wil's things. Of her sprawling chamber with all its shelves and drawers, its wardrobe packed full with clothes. She would be back to collect them. Someone with that many things in this world wouldn't simply leave. She wouldn't leave her books and her secrets. She wouldn't leave him.

They were not dead, he told himself. There was some mistake.

But if he couldn't believe his sister and brother were gone, the queen could. Her tears had dampened his sleeve. She was shaking.

"Come on," he told her softly, and he pulled her to her feet. All those nights as a child when he'd been carried up the stairs, now he was the one guiding his mother to her chamber. They took slow steps. He murmured that it would be all right, and she only sobbed.

*Owen and Wil aren't dead,* he wanted to tell her. The world would burn to its molten core before such a thing could be true. Not Owen, and certainly not Wil, both of whom were fit to outlive them all.

If they were gone, wouldn't he feel something? Anything? Wouldn't there be tears? Wouldn't he be on the floor and screaming too?

"Tell the king to summon all his guards," his mother murmured, as she crawled onto her bed and curled up.

His throat felt dry. "What for?"

"To find my children," she croaked. "I won't let them stay in that river. They need to be at peace."

Slowly, Gerdie began to understand. Owen and Wil *would* return home. But they wouldn't pull open the door and emerge from a rectangle of morning sun. They wouldn't be laughing, or conspiring in hushes. They would not open their books, or select an outfit from their silk hangers, or switch on their bed-side lanterns.

Though he fought it, though he would have done anything not to, he felt his heart beating again. He knew that he was still alive, and they were not.

# ELEVEN

THE WORLD WAS NOT AS large as it had once seemed.

Between Northern Arrod and Brayshire, there was an expanse of the North Sea turned black in the darkness of night. Somewhere over that expanse, consumed by the roaring September wind, Wil slumped against the railing of the dirigible and disappeared.

It was a dream of drowning in ink. Of silence. Of nothing. She had fallen into the rapids after all.

She was jolted awake in the morning when the dirigible touched down in Brayshire, where the harsh winds gave way to tepid air. Dawn painted the sky pink, and silhouetted against it were the shapes of a market square still sleeping. Everything was mobile—carts and tents. There were flowers blooming wild along dirt paths, trees that went on forever.

Brayshire: Wanderer Country.

She forced herself to stand. Even the fiery sunrise was dull, the world ashen and quiet.

*Find Pahn,* she reminded herself. The thought made her walk. *Find Pahn and cure this curse.* There was no other choice.

On the morning Wil was born—a cool October day splashed with color—she had been a frightening thing, so she'd been told. With thin, translucent skin and bones where babies were supposed to be healthy and fat. When Owen took his first look at her, to him she had resembled one of the monsters in his book of Western folklore. Undead creatures that crawled back up through the earth and demanded blood and souls. She balled her fists and let out a feeble roar of a cry, as though she meant to frighten him. He had only laughed. A future king, and a little monster in a lace-trimmed gown.

Now, stepping forward onto foreign land, Wil was born for the second time in her life, a different sort of monster. Or perhaps, the monster she was always destined to become.

A horrible feeling came all at once, after days and days of nothingness. After nights of dreamless sleep and weightless breaths that didn't feel like breathing at all. But on the last day of September, Wil awoke on the floor of her tent with a fistful of emerald grass digging into her skin.

It was scarcely dawn, the sky still hesitating to bloom.

Far in the distance, a train rent the world in two like the pull on a zipper. The ground shook.

She sat up, blinking at the bits of fractured green in her

palm. She did not remember dreaming anything that should have set her heart beating fast in her sleep, but that was no matter. She had been worrying about this day since she'd set foot on the dirigible, and her heart knew it.

Today was Gerdie's seventeenth birthday.

He would spend it mourning Owen. Mourning her. If he slept at all, he would awaken in a castle whose mirrors would be covered by black gossamer.

What would this do to his health? It had been a solid two years since he'd had a relapse that left him bedbound, but his Gray Fever hovered around him like an apparition, trying over and again to take him. For the first time, Wil wasn't there to be the thing that scared death away. She left Gerdie in that castle with Baren. Baren, who told Gerdie nature had selected him to die, and only their father's money and influence had saved him. Baren, who was now the heir to the world's most influential kingdom.

Because of her.

If her family thought she was dead, it would be less painful for them than the truth.

The funeral was long over by now. In Arrod, families wasted no time in their grieving. The first sunset after a death, each member of the family lit a candle and set it adrift on a length of wood. And when the water extinguished the last one, it meant the souls were at rest.

After that, the true mourning began. As Wil was out in the

world somewhere, she knew that her bed and Owen's had been covered in black gossamer. Addney had pinned an oleander to her dress, covering her heart to keep the memories of her beloved in place.

It had surely taken the queen all day to cover each mirror from the castle walls, but she would insist upon doing it herself—that was her place as the one who most believed in rituals. Barring reflections for the first month would keep her dead children at peace, so she wouldn't hear them screaming for her on windy nights.

There would be days and days of silence. Nothing but heartbeats and clock hands.

Heartsick and heavy, she dropped the gems into her rawhide bag, pulled on her gloves, and climbed from her tent.

Most of the people traveling through Wanderer Country were friendly, kind, and welcoming. Wil had kept her distance, saying little and smiling in lieu of conversation. Since her brother's death, smiles had become Wil's easiest lie. She could look human and whole by simply upturning her lips. No one could know that behind those lips were secrets, that they quivered with sobs when she was alone.

Most of Brayshire and its passing wanderers spoke Nearsh, and Wil only spoke when she needed to barter for food, and to try to learn about Pahn. Some had heard of him, while most insisted he was a myth. But no one knew how to get to him, or even what he looked like. The common rumor was that he was in King Zinil's mountain palace, and Wil hoped that wasn't true. The Southern Isles had completely closed off their borders in preparation for the potential war. No imports. No exports. No word.

South of Wanderer Country, there was Brayshire's capital city, called the Reeds. It had once been home to Brayshire's hierarchy before it was overthrown. In the absence of that hierarchy, the Reeds had become a sort of hub for artists and scholars. It was a half mile from here, and Wil knew that she would arrive just in time for the shops to open. If she got there before the rush of morning shoppers, she could sell the emeralds without drawing attention.

They hardly resembled grass, and she could pass them off as shards from a broken pendant. They would be worth a few silver pieces, at least. Fare for travel, once she had a solid lead on Pahn.

The walk cleared away the thought of the gloomy castle, if nothing else. She thought instead of Gerdie's sixteenth birthday last year, when they'd snuck onto a boat carrying a wedding party. It circled the Port Capital until well after midnight, and the party was so extravagant, the crowd so lavish and full, nobody knew that Wil and Gerdie were strangers to the newlyweds.

Gerdie had removed his monocle and hidden it in his pocket. He'd even found a girl to dance with, with long red hair that spun around her like a fire when she twirled.

Wil had found someone too. A tall boy with dark skin and a permanent grin. He'd wrapped her hair around his finger when their dance faded to a gentle sway. And then he'd kissed her—her first and only kiss—and it was so easy to get lost in it, to be someone else. He asked if he could see her again, and she told him that in the morning she would be on a boat headed east.

The lie had been as exhilarating as the kiss, because he had believed it.

Now, she tried to imagine her brother sneaking over the castle wall, losing himself in the Port Capital, away from the grieving castle. Maybe he could find some happiness, for a little while.

Maybe he didn't even believe she was dead. Maybe he sensed that she was alive. She would find a way to contact him, but not before she'd sought Pahn's help and she was rid of this curse. She didn't deserve to be near anyone she loved. Not while this awful thing was brewing inside her.

She arrived at the Reeds as the day began to brighten. Window shades were opening on storefronts like eyes and mouths.

At the heart of the market square, there was a jeweler. She'd been to him only once before, with a sapphire beetle with diamond flecks in its open wings. It looked exactly like a brooch, and she'd said she'd found it. No questions were asked—not in a land of people from all around the world who might have been anything from peddlers and swindlers to murderers and thieves. Or just a girl with a secret.

Little bells on the door handle chimed when she stepped inside. The old man at the counter brightened when he saw her.

Behind her, the cobbled square was all but empty, save for a few university students seeking out pastries and coffee and tea before their classes.

"If it isn't the girl who finds treasures," the man said. "What have you got for me today?"

She reached into her rawhide bag, counting each of the emerald blades to be sure she had them all, and then she laid them out. There they sat, the glass counter making it appear that they were floating over tiny hills of steel rings and glass beads.

The man blinked. "Emeralds this time."

"They're real," Wil said, and removed the orange data goggles from her head so that he could see for himself. But the man shook his head. That wouldn't be necessary.

"I suppose you found these as well?" He slid them around with his fingertip. "What peculiar shapes. I've never—"

The ground shook with the force of an explosion. The emeralds rattled.

Wil spun around to see that the windows were darkened by soot and ash.

"Marauders," the man gasped. "Come with me to the basement—we'll be safe there!"

"Mar—" The question was still on Wil's lips when the second explosion came. Through the grit on the windows she saw a burst of flame.

The man was shouting for her to follow him, to hide. But she ran for the door instead and threw it open. The calm market square was ravaged by orange and gray and red, fractured by screams and sobs.

When she looked over her shoulder, the man was gone, the steel door that presumably led to the basement pulled shut.

There were people on the ground—wanderers and students—but there were more than a dozen others, running through the melee, shouting in a sharp, hard language Wil didn't know. Marauders, Owen had told her, often invented their own tongue, so that their captives wouldn't be able to overthrow them.

They were well disguised, Wil realized, dressed in the local fashion of loose flowing tunics and trousers with belled hems and fitted thighs. She'd surely passed a few of them on her way into the square.

A scream drew her attention. Through the smoke, she saw a man hauling a girl to her feet. Her dark curls bounced frantically in her struggle, but she was no match. He had her back pinned to his chest.

Wil ran into the smoke, her mind playing out the possible scenarios in seconds. She wouldn't be able to touch either of them beyond her gloves or they'd be turned to stone, and so she'd have to find a way to slacken his grasp.

He didn't see her coming—he was too busy trying to take the girl. She was quite beautiful, Wil saw once she was closer, and he'd surely get a high price selling her to traffickers.

*Turn him to stone*. The thought came at once with startling clarity in the chaos. Her skin ached, her heart sped, and her brow dotted with sweat. The desire was primal. Wil forced it away. No time to be startled now.

She jammed the heel of her boot down on the man's foot, and she felt the toes break. He yelled, and in that half second he was stunned, Wil grabbed the girl's wrist with her steel gloves and pulled her away.

The girl disappeared beyond her periphery. The man was coming at Wil now, confused, angry. She dodged his clumsy attempt to grab her. He was big, but she learned in that single gesture that he wasn't skilled. Relied on brute strength and nothing more.

With her gloved hand, she landed a cross punch to his solar plexus. He staggered back and fell to the girl's feet. She let out a startled yelp.

"Go!" Wil told her. Why hadn't she fled by now? There was enough smoke and chaos for her to escape. The marauders were everywhere, but Wil couldn't focus. The world had become too bright and busy. Adrenaline was still running through her, making her arms tremble. She clenched her fists to steady them. *Turn him to stone,* her body was pleading. She was starved for it. She couldn't focus.

She turned for an alleyway and ran. If she could make it to the trees and out of sight, she could crystallize the grass instead.

But she didn't get far. Something hit her ankle, and the

world came up around her.

She flipped onto her back to face her assailant, and all she saw was a slender silhouette. Bright flashes throbbed across her vision. Had she hit her head?

There was barely time to form the thought before a white-hot pain lanced up her side. Then someone was trying to pull the rawhide bag that was crisscrossed over her chest.

She clung to it. There wasn't much in it—just some geldstuk and silver, and vials of sleep serum to refill her dagger—but she refused to let it go. It was a piece of her old life. It was hers.

She landed a kick to her assailant's stomach. The motion tore at her wound, and she screamed. Her fingers tightened around the rawhide strap.

Then another silhouette appeared, and the marauder's grip on her bag slackened. Wil touched a gloved hand to the searing pain at her side. It came up red with blood. It was going to rust, she thought dully, and tried to wipe it against her shirt.

Someone was crouched over her. A boy with dark eyes and black waves of hair whose fringes caught fire against the sun.

"Can you stand?" he asked her, in accented Nearsh. His voice was a million miles away.

"Yes," she said. But when she tried to move, the air itself had grown heavy and was sitting upon her chest. Breathing had become difficult.

Hands pressed against her wound. She saw blood on the sleeves of his long leather coat, and had the distant realization that it was hers.

"Don't," she started to say. She could feel her pulse thudding hard in her throat.

The boy reached under her back and her knees and lifted her up. Her head fell heavy in the hollow of his shoulder. She was going to kill him. She couldn't stop it. Everyone would see. But she could feel her body losing blood, and knew that she wouldn't live long enough to know what would happen next.

"You're going to be okay," the boy said, his voice low and soft against her ear. It soothed the frenzy of adrenaline buzzing electric in her veins.

And for one mad, feverish moment, she believed him.

# TWELVE

THE BOY DIDN'T DIE.

Over and again, waves of unconsciousness, heavy with dreams, tried to pull Wil into their depths. But she always fought her way back.

The autumn sky blurred overhead, white and gray with no trace of blue. And on the burned wind, she could smell something sweet and medicinal.

The boy was still carrying her, rushing her past the dark bloody chaos in the market square, and Wil wondered if she was dreaming, or dead. There was no way he should still be alive.

With her waning strength, she brought a hand to his face to be sure he was real. His jaw was sharp, but his skin was cool and soft. He looked at her. And then everything disappeared.

Stillness.

Something soft beneath her.

The sound of her own hard breathing magnified in her ears.

Voices—the boy's, with his Lavean accent, and a girl with a Brayshire accent.

Her eyelids were too heavy. Angry, hot flashes of pain stabbed at her hip, but focusing on the pain helped her return to consciousness. She could just make out a chandelier hanging from a wooden ceiling, its candles sleeping in a sunbeam. Everything was unfamiliar.

A vial was touched to her lips, and she flinched away.

"Can you hear me?" the boy said.

Wil moved her eyes to him. "Yes." Her voice was hoarse.

"I'm going to give you something for the pain," the boy said. "It's called morfin. It's going to put you out for a bit."

Morfin; a leaf that grew only in the tropics of the Southern Isles, and impossible to find even on the underground market, especially now that there was an export ban.

She should have fought him off, Wil knew. She couldn't afford to have her senses dulled any further. It was only pain, and she'd had worse. She had the fleeting thought that blood was spilling out of her, so much and so fast that her heart and bones would be carried off in the current of it. She felt heavy and numb.

The boy laid his hand on her forehead, and there was something comforting about the way his thumb smoothed her brow.

This time, when the vial was brought to her lips, she didn't fight it.

In her dream, she was under the rapids, and her lungs were full of water. Owen was still clinging to the rock face, trying to find her hand and pull her up. *Monster,* he called. He was crying, frantic. But she stayed out of reach. She refused to pull him down into such depths.

*It isn't safe where I am,* she told him. *You need to go on without me.*

The sound of calmer waters brought her back.

She opened her eyes, and in the far corner of the unfamiliar room, she saw the boy standing at a washbasin, scrubbing his hands. Something rich and herbal filled the air.

His sleeves were rolled to his shoulders, and slender black tattoos wrapped around his wrists and trailed to his biceps. The most intricate, elaborate rendering of vines and thorns and unfamiliar flowers and animals exploding into full bloom. Tattoos were a rite of passage in Southern culture, Wil knew. Even children had them, adding to them with each significant event in their lives—weddings, births, deaths, voyages.

When she was little, traveling through the Port Capital on Owen's shoulders, she used to watch the Lavean vendors loading and unloading cargo, their sleeves rolled up or their shirts removed. She regarded their tattoos as a sort of novel, telling a story in a language she wanted desperately to decipher. But she could never seem to find the beginning, or the ending. Maybe there wasn't one.

There was a tattoo at his throat, too, but most of it was covered by his high collar. All she could see were the tops of swirls, like the backs of creatures bobbing near the surface of the sea. Odd, Wil thought. He seemed to be deliberately hiding it.

She struggled to move. Her body was heavy. Her tongue felt like a lead weight in her mouth. But she managed to prop herself up onto her elbows.

She was lying on a mattress stuffed with down feathers. It was dark outside now. Candlelight flickered in the chandelier overhead, filling the room with warm dancing light.

Her arms were weighted, her mind hazy, vision blurring in and out. But she wasn't in pain.

The boy saw her fighting to sit up and moved to her side in an instant. "Hey now," he was saying. "Easy. You're going to pull at the stitches."

"Stitches?" Her voice felt far away.

He put his hands on her shoulders and eased her back down. "Marauder managed to land a pretty deep cut, but it didn't hit anything vital. Lucky day for your kidney, I'd say."

She blinked up at him, trying to understand what he was saying. *Focus,* she scolded herself.

"You stitched my wound?"

"I've had a lot of practice." He said this a bit haughtily, and the corner of his mouth rose, evoking a dimple on his cheek. "The hydronus oxide will keep infection away, and you aren't running a fever. All good signs."

"You—touched me?" She was back to wondering if she was truly awake.

Candlelight caught the amber of the boy's dark eyes. His face shifted from confusion to concern. "You should sleep more. You've lost a lot of blood."

This persistent exhaustion was beginning to frustrate her. "What happened?"

"What happened? You saved a girl from being snared by marauders and got stabbed for the trouble."

"I don't understand." Wil was talking more to herself than to him. "You carried me? And you're okay." She stared down at herself. She was still wearing her gloves, though they'd been wiped clean of her blood. Half her tunic had been cut away, exposing her raw hip and the black thread holding the wound shut like eyelids that had been sewn together.

"The morfin is making you delirious," the boy reasoned. "It'll wear off by morning."

The door on the adjacent wall creaked open. It was made of old, distressed wood with chipped gray paint, just like the ceiling and floor. Wil presumed this was an apartment in an old factory building; after the fall of Brayshire's hierarchy, much of its industrial complex had been renovated.

The girl from the market square stood in the doorway,

looking at her with pale blue eyes. "You're awake." Her voice was gentle, sweet.

Wil managed to push herself up onto her elbows again. "Where am I?"

"In my apartment, in Enow," the girl said, and offered a sympathetic smile. "I'm Hettie."

"Wil," Wil said, lowering herself back against the mattress after her head began to feel too heavy. "Thank you for letting me stay."

Hettie shook her head. "I should be thanking you. Marauders bombed half the market square. I don't know how many were wounded, or taken, and I—" Her trembling was all too apparent, even in Wil's muddled state. Hettie couldn't bring herself to finish what she was going to say. "Do you feel feverish?" She reached a hand for Wil's forehead, and Wil flinched away.

Beside her, the boy was watching her closely. Too closely.

"Some water, then," Hettie said with verve. "I'll be right back."

Wil looked at the boy; he was still watching her. "Why did you save me?"

"I run into fires, not from them," he said. "Like you."

"I was definitely running from that fire," she said.

He laughed. It was such an open, honest sound, and something about it made her feel better. "You landed a few good blows and saved a girl from certain torture first. That counts for something."

"I'm glad." Her lids fluttered as she tried to keep them open. "You still haven't told me your name."

"Loom," he said.

She closed her eyes. Only for a second, she told herself, as the waves pulled her under again.

# THIRTEEN

GERDIE TRIED TO APPLY REASON.

The pathophysiology of drowning went like this: two conscious people who slipped underwater would first hold their breath. They would understand that the air existed above the surface and would try to get to it. They would struggle and fight. This would use up the oxygen that was stored in their bodies, rendering them unconscious in thirty to sixty seconds.

Even if their hearts stopped beating, the damage done within those sixty seconds would not be irreversible. The brain would be key. Without air, its cells would begin to die by the third minute. One hundred and eighty seconds, the same amount of time it took to grind grayroot and arterleaves with a mortar and pestle, add serlot oil, and deposit the potion into a cauldron, which is what Gerdie had been doing when it happened.

After the fourth minute, survival with functional brain recovery was unlikely. By the tenth minute, all cells within the brain would have ceased functioning, and both of those people who had gone into the river—one trying to save the other—would be dead.

Death was final. He could not reach into his cauldron and find what he had lost. Could not fashion tallim powder and bits of broken glass and gears into an heir and a spare. There were no pieces left to fix.

Drowned.

It made no sense.

Each time he descended the stairs to his laboratory, he succumbed to a new habit of standing before the small window that leaked bleary light into the space. The bottom of the window frame was five feet two inches from the floor. His sister had been exactly that height, filling up the space perfectly when she stood there, as she often did, out of the way of his cauldron. The top of his own head came to the middle of the glass. An even five feet eight inches. He compulsively rerecorded his measurement daily, worried about growing even a fraction taller. Worried about moving farther from his memory of Wil, which existed without portraits, without so much as a recording of her voice. He had nothing of her but a room of lifeless trinkets, and the space between a window and a dusty floor.

Owen and Wil died on a Wednesday, and when Wednesday came around for the first time since their deaths, he forced himself to move. He couldn't bear that castle, with its black gossamer draped over the mirrors and beds and its persistent silence a moment longer.

It had even proved too much for Addney, who had taken to sleeping in the unfinished house where she and Owen had planned to live. She made herself scarce; Gerdie hadn't even seen any servants going out to tend to her needs. Only the queen herself would venture out there, morning and night, with trays of food, and sometimes one of Owen's books.

Climbing the stone wall was excruciating. The weather had been cold and damp, and that morning it had rained. His legs ached, and the pain radiated up his spine, charting a path that lanced through his brain and stabbed at his monocled eye. The vision in that eye was weaker today as well, partially blinded by the gleam of dampness everywhere, distorting everything like a camera lens that could not get its focus. But he didn't mind. This pain, at least, he could do something for. Brighter lighting would improve his vision. For his leg, there were stretches and tonics and salves. So many solutions—however temporary or weak they may be—that he couldn't believe he'd ever complained about them. He would give anything for all the hurt in life to be so fixable.

He knew that Wil had walked through the woods and climbed the rock wall over the rapids. He knew because she had told him that was her plan. But he was not half the climber his sister had been, so he crossed the river where it was calm and walked alongside it until he'd reached the spot where the water turned angry and violent.

He stared at it, taken all at once by his anger for this thing that had killed his brother and sister. Reason came back to him, this time uninvited. Their bodies were still pinned down there, it said. Even if he could go down and find them, he wouldn't recognize what he recovered. After a week underwater, the skin begins to peel away from tissue.

The queen had ordered men to recover the bodies. Part of Gerdie had hoped that they would be able to do it. If he could have seen them while they were still whole, he might have believed they were gone. But the task was impossible, and when the men returned empty-handed, the queen's scream was even worse than the first had been.

Still, now, he found himself looking for his sister's long hair, as though he'd see it fluttering like a flag, and he could grab on and pull her back up. And then—what?

When he awoke from his trance, he knelt in the grass and began to rummage for gemstones. For footprints. Torn beads from Owen's coat sleeves. Anything.

"You have to help me," he whispered to them both. "I have to know what happened. I can't live the rest of my life not knowing."

The queen, in her despair, believed the story the king told her, but she didn't know what Gerdie and Owen knew, about Wil's deadly new power. All week he'd thought of what Owen had said.

*I know our father in a way that you never could.*

"Did Papa kill you?" He'd thought it for days, but this was the first time he said the words aloud. He could almost expect to look up and see Wil knelt beside him, rolling her eyes, saying, "You're the genius. You figure it out."

"Have you taken to muttering like a madman?" The voice that called to him from across the rapids was real, and it startled Gerdie. Baren stood on the other side of the water, clutching the hilt of the sword at his hip. In only a week's time, he'd talked his way into becoming their father's high guard, his triumph a slap against the miserable silence within the castle.

Gerdie betrayed nothing. He forced back the threat of something awful and overwhelming that began to stir within him. The realization that Baren was all he had left. He would not let his brother see him in mourning. He went back to searching the grass.

"I don't know what you're looking for," Baren went on. "But you won't find anything. Papa said they never made it to the other side."

Gerdie tried to ignore him. He thought about the trade nations and the cluster of Eastern islands. He thought about the Ancient Sea and the undead apparitions of the West. He thought of all the places Owen had been, and that Wil had longed to see. He thought about boarding a ship and leaving for one of those places—any of them.

"They're dead, you know," Baren said. He hated being ignored more than anything. "You're not going to unearth them."

"Yes, I know."

"Do you?"

Gerdie looked up.

Baren's straight blond hair had gone dull in the past few days. His eyes were ringed with gray lines. Strange, he almost appeared to be stricken by grief, though he had every reason to be happy. He finally had what he wanted. He was the heir.

"Are you seeing ghosts?" Baren asked. "At night—wet footprints in the hall, and voices whispering."

Gerdie couldn't tell if his brother was being sincere. It was cruel if it was a trick, but it wouldn't be out of character. When Gerdie was ill, Baren loved to joke about a shadowed man roaming the gardens looking for a child's soul to steal.

But then he noticed Baren's hands. He clenched and unclenched his fists. Gerdie counted five times. It wasn't like Baren to be compulsive, but he did it two more times.

Gerdie stood. "No." His voice was guarded. "Ghosts aren't real, Baren."

"You don't know everything, not everything," Baren said.

The words lanced Gerdie's chest. Those had been Wil's final words to him, before she'd stomped up the stairs and out of his world forever. And she had been right.

"I've seen things," Baren went on.

"What things?" Gerdie asked, even as he knew he'd regret playing along.

"Our sister." Baren sounded nervous at that, as though Wil could be spying on them from the trees. "She comes to my room late at night, dripping water on the floor, her hair full of dead things. She sits in the chair by my bed and she doesn't let me sleep."

Gerdie knew this had to be a lie. If ghosts were real, Wil wouldn't bother with the likes of Baren. She wouldn't even go to their mother, he suspected, for fear of triggering her compulsions. She would go to him. She would rearrange his things, leave him clues she knew he could solve.

Even so, he asked, "What does she say?"

"Nothing. She either can't speak, or she won't. I suspect she won't. She wants me to suffer."

"Perhaps you can call it even, then," Gerdie said, dusting the grass from his trousers. He began walking for the calmer waters so he could cross, and Baren walked parallel to him.

"I thought you could talk to her for me," Baren said. "Make her leave."

"Why would I do that?"

"Because she'll listen to you," Baren insisted. "And Owen. Owen knows what I'm thinking, but *her*." He pulled at his hair. "She just stares and stares."

"Say her name," Gerdie said. He stopped, and they stood facing each other. "You've never liked saying it. How can I help you if you won't even say her name?"

Baren balked at that. He laughed, but it was a distracted sort, and his eyes stared past his brother. After a long silence, he said, "She wasn't even supposed to live, you know. Mother was in labor for days, screaming for *days*. A woman from a camp of wanderers came to see her. I remember her Brayshire accent. I heard her whisper to Mother, 'This child inside you is cursed. She'll cause you nothing but pain. You should let her drown in you.'"

Gerdie was breathless. "What did you say?"

"It's true," Baren said. "She's cursed. She's bad luck. You didn't see her when she was born, but I did. I knew." He shook his head. "Mother didn't listen. She never has when it came to her."

Gerdie's arms were trembling. It wasn't even anger. He couldn't manage anger. Was too dazed and broken. Wil was not there to say something to this. She was not anywhere. Even what was left in the rapids wasn't her anymore. It had been her, before she succumbed, before the water filled her lungs and her eyes and her hair. Now she only existed in words and in thoughts. And the words Baren had just said were too terrible.

Gerdie began walking at a faster clip. Baren kept up. "You know it's true," Baren went on.

Gerdie saw the vendor hardening into ruby, falling away and revealing Wil's stunned expression. He saw the old woman from the wanderers' camp.

*Darkness in your blood. There's something ugly in you. Something vicious.*

His breath came shallow and quick. The world felt dull.

"You know," Baren kept insisting. "She was supposed to die. A long time ago."

Gerdie's guns felt heavy in their holster. "Say that again, and I'll have to console Mother as she mourns a third child."

That silenced his brother, but it didn't stop him from keeping pace, even as Gerdie moved faster.

When he reached the calmer shallows, he steadied himself before crossing a trail of stones.

Wil could have crossed here. Why hadn't she crossed here?

# FOURTEEN

WIL DREAMED OF CASTLE WALLS and of her brothers. And then the king and queen, seated hand in hand before the stained glass window with a map of the world. They stared at Wil and never said a word. Behind them, glass dirigibles sailed over candied blue seas.

The king and queen were cold and strange, their faces darkened by shadow when Wil tried to get a better look at them. She could not find her mother's familiar smile, her father's strong eyes.

In her hazy half-sleep, Wil heard the bellowing of the university's clock tower, and remembered that she was far from home.

She counted five chimes. Her eyes opened, greeted by two candles left burning on the overhead chandelier, and the sound of cadenced breathing. She forced herself upright.

The haze of the morfin was waning, replaced by a dull pain.

The boy was sitting slumped in the corner across from her mattress, his chin tucked low, his dark lashes downcast, shoulders moving gently with each breath.

He was elegant in the low, flickering light. The lean muscles of his arms were traced in shadow. His strong jaw was slackened by sleep, giving him an unguarded gentleness.

Wil sat very still to watch him. She was sure that she was awake, and that he was alive. But how?

In the quiet and the calm, she began to feel the faint presence of hope. Maybe this dreadful thing inside her was gone. Maybe it had been a side effect of handling smuggled chemicals after all, and had at last worn off.

But a strange current in her blood brought her back to reality. It was a sensation with which she had become bitterly familiar. It had been a full day since she'd turned the grass to emerald now, and her entire body ached for it.

Carefully, she pulled herself to her feet, wincing as the pain ignited in her wound. She checked to be sure the holster was still at her hip, bearing the two guns Gerdie had given her the last time she saw him, and that her dagger was sheathed in one of her boots. She walked slowly past the boy and into another room that she presumed was the living area. In the darkness she could just make out Hettie's form lying asleep on a cushion. Beside that, a desk with a gas lamp and a stack of books. She was most likely a university student. Brayshire was the world's hub for art and music, and so many young people flocked here to pursue these things.

Beyond the apartment, there was a staircase that led to the alleyway outside. It was quiet now, the small city asleep and dreaming. The ground was mostly dirt, but Wil found a daisy sitting in a burst of dying grass. She removed one glove and reached for it.

Even before she'd finished plucking it from the ground, it had turned to solid diamond with an emerald stem, and her skin was awash from the sensation. Her heart thudded against her chest. With this went the distant hope that maybe her power had gone away after Loom survived it.

She was among the world's horrors, she thought. No different from the undead apparitions and monsters in the Western folklore. The apparitions stole skin and hearts because they wanted to be alive again, and turning things to stone made her feel the most alive she'd ever been. How long, she wondered, before this craving overtook her entirely? How long before she had crystallized every living thing in the world just to ease the pain?

She began walking to quell the adrenaline. Though she had never been to this part of town, it wasn't hard to find her way back to the market square. The smell of old fires still lingered long after the ashes had cooled.

There was still chaos to be dealt with come morning. Windows had been boarded, though all the buildings appeared to still be standing. Wil had never encountered marauders before; Owen told her they would never be so stupid as to attack the Port Capital, not with their father's aggressive police force. They preferred more remote regions, where they could cause a commotion, grab what they needed in the frenzy, and get away fast.

She had never thought to ask him if he'd encountered marauders himself. There were so many things she had never asked him. And though he was gone, the questions came, along with the persistent notion that she could still find him and ask them.

Her throat felt tight.

"Hey." A soft voice made her flinch. She turned to find Loom standing a mere yard away from her; she'd been so lost in her thoughts that she hadn't heard him approach—or he was just that stealthy. Those with the softest strides had the loudest secrets, her father often said.

"Hey," she said. "I wanted to see the damage."

"Looks like this place will be fine," Loom said. "Might take a little longer than normal to clean things up. Money is in smaller quantity out here. But I'm sure people will pull together."

"Have you been here long?" Wil asked. She knew from his accent that he had grown up in the Southern Isles.

He shrugged out of his leather coat and draped it over her shoulders. Only when she felt its warmth did she realize how chilly the night air was. Her blood still stained its sleeves, but it had been scrubbed dull.

She traced a fingertip over a faded red spot.

In the leather, she could smell the herbs that had filled her senses when he'd lifted her from the ground. She could smell winds and plants and the notion of some faraway land, and the war being waged there.

"I'm never anywhere for long," he said.

She raised her eyes to him. He was intricately designed; his bottom lip was too full and always pouting, as though he were the subject in a portrait whose artist had decided to be generous with it. And with each second that his mouth didn't move, she found herself increasingly curious about what he was thinking as he looked at her. The idea that he might be thinking about her gave her a strange rush. This boy, who had not only saved her life, but remained by her side through the night as she slept. There was no one left in the world to stay by her side.

"Why did you do it?" he said. "Why did you save a girl who was a stranger to you, when it wasn't your fight?"

"Because it *was* my fight," she said. "If someone like that man can see a person he wants and just sell them, and nothing is done about it, then the world is worse for it."

He gave a lopsided smile. Now that her mind was clear of the morfin's effects and she could truly focus on him, she saw the tragedy on his face, affixed to his skin just as surely as his tattoos.

"That's the kind of thinking that will get you killed," he said.

She shrugged. "I haven't been yet."

She turned to a charred storefront whose windows had been boarded, considering. Her father made no mention of marauders, didn't see them as a problem big enough to address. There was so much in the world that her father refused to see, but Owen had seen all of it. He wanted to fix all of it. And maybe he would have, but he was never going to be king. He was never going to be anything again, and it was all her fault.

The pain of that realization was a shard forever flowing through her blood, and she was always caught off guard when it stabbed at her.

Loom was watching her. He'd seen the change in her face.

"Northern Arrod, isn't it?" he said. "Your accent."

She pulled his jacket tighter around her as a gust of wind came through. "Yes."

"I've seen you around," he said. "You're the one who's been asking about Pahn."

She was no stranger to being invisible, but he had far surpassed her in that regard. She had never seen him. But he had seen her.

Wil didn't have to say anything. Her startled expression answered for her.

"What do you want with someone like that?" he said. "Haven't you heard that marvelers are swindlers and crooks?"

"What I hear doesn't have to be what I believe," Wil said, raising her chin. "And I believe he can help me."

Again she felt herself falling back under his scrutiny. Logic was pleading for her to get away, telling her that he was trouble, while something tragic drew her to him, something telling her that they were the same somehow.

"Pahn does not serve the public; he wants the world to think he's a myth," Loom pressed. "There's only one reason people seek him out, and it's because they're desperate."

Wil met his stare. "What does it matter?"

"I am trying to help you." The sudden urgency in Loom's voice startled her, breaking through the tenuous caution of strangers and giving the illusion of something familiar. "Whatever it is you think you need from him, you'd be wise to go somewhere else."

She saw Owen, hunched over the crystal aloe leaf, like the crystals that later filled his hair, his lungs, his heart. His lifeless blue eyes full of moonlight. The power that surged through her blood as she stood helpless.

"That's just it." When Wil spoke, she didn't recognize her own voice. "I have nowhere else to go."

Loom was studying her the way she studied vendors in the underground market, like he was waiting for her to betray something—anything—that might tell him who she really was. She feared what he would find, and for once, she was the one to look away.

"Hey." He reached, as though for her hand, but held the cuff of her coat sleeve instead. "Is it someone close to you? They're sick—is that it? Because there are some plants that can do amazing things. There's a ban on the Southern Isles, but I carry a lot of things with me."

Wil knew the wonders of Southern medicine. Her own father was trying to ravage the kingdom to take control of it all. It had saved her brother's life, and once she thought those plants could do anything, but not this time.

"I don't have anyone close to me," she said. She meant it to be one of her lies, but once the words had been spoken, she realized they were true. She pushed past him, toward the woods that bordered the market square.

He followed her, and their breathing grew shallow as she quickened her pace and he kept up. And then she broke into a run.

"Wait," he was saying. "Please just wait. You're still weak."

Against all reason, she stopped and swung around to face him. Her wound was aching and she suspected blood was beginning to leak past the stitches. She didn't want to let him see that he was right; her head felt light, her muscles aching.

"What do you want?"

He reached forward, concern in his eyes, and he cupped her cheek.

She tilted her head against his hand. His touch sent warmth through her blood, overpowering the wicked thing inside her. Still breathing hard, she said again, "What—"

Her heart kicked up a furious beat—in protest or in longing, she didn't know. She could hear him breathing, feel his fingers brush the length of her jaw and disappear in her hair.

He was still alive.

Insects buzzed and fluttered. "What is it?" he said, to her alarmed expression. "What's wrong?"

She felt that familiar rush. *No, no, no.* He was going to die in her arms, because she had been reckless.

But seconds passed, and when she heard the crackling of gems, his breath was still falling against her exposed throat.

"Hells," she heard him say, a moment before she turned her head and saw the branch of alber blossoms gleaming ruby against the darkness.

She ripped free of his grasp, her breath coming in panicked spurts no matter how she tried to keep calm.

She staggered back, and Loom advanced on her, the confusion in his eyes giving way to some sort of understanding. Now he knew why she was looking for Pahn.

Stupid. She was so stupid, letting herself give in to a moment of such recklessness—why had she given in? And now he could do anything with what he had just learned, this boy she didn't even know. This boy who should by all rights be her *enemy*, whose king would love nothing more than to see her family slaughtered.

He moved toward her again, and she knew what she had to do.

"I'm sorry," she said, and grabbed her dagger from its sheath and sliced a line across his forearm in one fluid motion.

A second later, his eyes went dull as the sleep serum overpowered him, and he collapsed.

# FIFTEEN

Wil ran for as long as her body would allow her, before the blood from her wounded side began to seep through the leather coat.

She knew that she had gone into the thick of the woods that bordered Brayshire, and judging by the sun's position as it began to rise, she had gone west. She tried to remember the maps that were posted throughout town. Cutting through the woods meant she'd reach the ocean in about five miles. Only a few hours' walk if she could keep going.

She slowed to a careful pace, lifting the flap of her bag as she went. Her tent was a lost cause now, left behind in the camp set up by the wanderers, but no matter. Everything else was here, including the branch of crystallized blossoms she'd grabbed in her haste. She pulled her data goggles onto her head and blinked once so that the time would appear in the lower right lens: 7:15.

It had been two hours. Two hours since she'd gotten too close to that boy. That strange, lovely boy with the deep sad eyes and tattoos he kept hidden like words that went unsaid.

Loom.

*Stop it,* she told herself. It would do no good to think of him. The mistake of falling into his touch had gotten her caught. He would be awake by now, and he would be in pursuit. Or worse, he could have told someone what she had done. He could have allies hidden somewhere in Brayshire, and they could be coming for her now.

Her knees threatened to buckle, and at last she relented when she reached a thin, babbling stream. She sat on a giant rock beside it, cringing as she shed her coat. The leather clung to her wound for a second before it fell away.

The stitches held. They were deftly placed, she noted, running her fingertips across their surface, but blood from the constant motion and adrenaline had seeped through.

With her gloved hand, she pulled at a tuft of thin feathery flowers growing wild among the fallen leaves. Spring sprigs. She rinsed a rock in the stream and used it to grind the flowers into a mushy white paste. It would help prevent infection, in a pinch. Gerdie had taught her that.

The paste was cool as she dabbed it over the blood, even soothing.

Breathing hard, she shed her torn, bloody tunic and began

shredding it into scraps to use as a makeshift bandage. If she was going to find a boat to take her out of the country, no captain would take a fare who was bleeding through her clothes. She couldn't imagine how she must have looked just then. Her bare stomach was pale as a root, her skin so wan it looked like a paper lantern devoid of light.

She bound her wound and pulled a fresh tunic from her bag. It was the only other piece of clothing she owned, loose fitting and made of red cotton, with baggy sleeves that tightened at the wrist, so that they belled out and looked full of wind. It had been slightly more expensive than the others for sale at the vendor's cart, but the gold-embroidered lions and thorns at the hem had reminded her of her dresses back home. The dresses she'd only worn to please her mother—the dresses she didn't know were a part of her identity until she'd been forced to leave them behind.

Her vision was blurring, exhaustion washing over her like a wave. "Focus," she whispered. "You're wind. You're everywhere."

But when she raised her eyes to the trees, she could not imagine herself hovering above them. She could not imagine the world beneath her, reduced to neat patches of land and sloping river lines. Instead, she saw her wardrobe full of dresses, so rich with colors. She saw herself as a little girl, spreading her hands and embracing those dresses, gathering them into her arms and falling into their softness, their silk, their smooth cool beads and ruffled hems.

She heard her brothers, their voices echoing down the

hallway and hitting every stone in the walls. She couldn't tell if they were laughing or calling for her. It didn't matter. Just for a little while, it didn't matter. They were safe, and the world had turned warm and soft.

She awoke with a start, the screech of a spawnling jolting her back into the woods, where the sun was now higher in the sky. She blinked into her data goggles: 10:15.

"Winds," she cursed.

Her side was not aching as much when she pulled herself to her feet, but that was little consolation, given how much time she had lost dozing in the middle of nowhere.

This time, as she walked, she was more mindful about not aggravating her stitches. But she did not slow her pace. Every snapped twig, every rustle of leaves against the mild wind felt like Loom following her.

It was highly unlikely, she tried to convince herself. If he was following her, these woods went on for miles in all directions. She would be long gone, on a ship out in the ocean, before he caught up.

The thought of him caused her heart to beat just a little faster.

Stupid, she told herself. Because of her carelessness, she had to flee the country. She forced herself to think about that instead.

Thanks to Loom, she knew, at least, that Pahn wasn't a myth. But either way, he wasn't here. He might be in the

Western Isles, she thought. It was a neutral territory with open borders, and from what Owen had told her, it was a good place to hide. Nothing exciting happened there. It was self-sufficient, with few imports and virtually no exports of note.

But more importantly, the people of the Western Isles were highly superstitious. Most shanty songs and fairy tales and folklore could be traced back to them. If Pahn wanted to blend in, he could do it in a place where everyone seemed to have a mysterious past.

Or, he might want to avoid a place like that altogether.

Frustration returned, and she tried to fight it away. If Pahn wasn't there, someone would know more about him, she told herself. Someone would have to.

It seemed like an eternity before she heard the water in the near distance. She could almost believe that she had wandered all the way back to Northern Arrod. The ocean sounded and smelled the same anywhere.

On this side of Brayshire was the Ancient Sea. It had featured prominently in her mother's tales from her life as a wanderer. "Do you know how it earned its name?" her mother had whispered one night, when Wil was a child, her lids heavy with sleep.

"A thousand years ago, countless soldiers died embattled in its waters. So many were lost at sea that the tides were red for days." The queen had played with Wil's hair, but her eyes were somewhere far, as though she wasn't telling the story to her daughter at all. She was whispering it into the walls, further filling the castle with her secrets. "The water is filled with ancient skeletons and spirits. Sailors claim to hear the spirits moaning on days when the winds are at their loudest. Some have claimed to hear voices of people they've lost."

A few yards later, Wil broke free of the woods and immediately found herself within a city. Flecks glimmered in white stone sidewalks that branched out like arteries in all directions. Shops and carts and roads. It was past noon now, and the sidewalks were full. Boats bobbed along the water's surface, tethered to their docks.

On the deck outside a seaside restaurant, a band was playing brass music that filled the streets with life. She allowed herself to be calmed by it. The songs were ships scattering out into the seas of her blood, and for just a few moments, for the first time since leaving home, she felt as though she was still alive.

While she had been worrying over what the boy had seen her do, the world had gone on, oblivious to any of it. She was no one here. She was normal. And finding a ride out of the country should be easy.

There was a dirigible docked on one far end of the shoreline, but it was already crowded. She opted to explore the smaller ships that lined the docks; they usually charged less than the larger ones, anyway.

"Are you looking for a ride?"

Wil turned to face the voice that had called to her. It belonged to a woman. Young, only a year or two older than Wil, and astonishingly beautiful. It was the kind of beauty that was sharp as a blade, sudden as an attack. Her copper-brown skin was shimmering under the bright sun; her hair was a contrast of darkness and light—streaked with glossy silver, as though it had been dyed, and true black. She had light-brown eyes framed by heavy lashes.

A tattoo coiled around the woman's lean upper arm, a serpent with jeweled eyes and tiny suns for scales. Above that, two moons in the sky of her skin, accented in shimmering silver, were overlapping; it was a popular Southern wedding ceremony tattoo, Wil knew from Owen's books. But if the woman was married, that spouse was nowhere in sight.

"Where are you headed?" Wil asked. The woman was standing before a modest ship, the kind commonly owned by families who might have room for the occasional fare. The shape of the deck was customized, just slightly longer than standard trade and passenger ships, which meant it was likely once owned by a royal family. The woman could have been from a royal family herself, but more commonly these ships were stolen, artfully repainted, and sold to the untrained customer; this was more likely the case. Wil saw the thin, reflective sheen of solar panels on the roof of its cabin and knew it was one of the more modern, digital models. Expensive and exclusive. She saw them often in Northern Arrod. Had even boarded a few larger ships when she and Gerdie snuck into parties.

"West," the woman said, and flashed a smile filled with shining white teeth. "Is that where you're going?"

"Yes," Wil said, doing her best not to betray the flare of pain in her side. "How much are you charging?"

From behind the young woman's legs, a little boy with long dark hair and light-brown eyes blinked curiously at Wil. The woman patted his head affectionately. "It's five hundred silver. This is my son. He won't be any trouble, will you, Ada?" The boy tilted his head up at her. Ada. The Lavean word for sun.

The woman held out her hand. "I'm Zay."

"Wil," Wil said. Something about Zay's breezy demeanor put her at ease. She followed her onto the ship, Ada hopping ahead of them.

The woman was undoubtedly Southern, and the ship had a rich aroma of plants and extracts that Wil couldn't identify.

Zay boasted about the ship, going on about its state-of-the-art navigation system, how it steered itself, all as she led Wil to her bunk. "Not much of a talker, are you?" Zay said. "That's okay. This is your bunk."

It was lavish for a ship's accommodations, with a lush down comforter and gold sheets. Wil didn't show her surprise, though. She sat on the edge of the bed, pretending it wasn't the softest mattress she had encountered since her days as a princess. "It's wonderful," Wil said. "Thank you."

"I'll give you privacy," Zay said. "There are some books in the drawer under the bed; help yourself to anything you like. We'll be leaving at the top of the hour." And then she closed the door.

It was not Wil's first time on a ship. She had been on dozens, but they stayed close to land if they left the port at all.

This was the first time she was going to actually set sail, though, and excitement stirred its way through her numbness. The wanderlust in her blood had always overpowered the royalty; though this ship was no castle, she felt as though she was home.

Above the bed, there was a small porthole, through which she could see endless water shimmering with pieces of sun. The world was so vast, a solution had to be out there somewhere. All she had to do was find it. She would start with Pahn, but if he eluded her, or if he couldn't help, or wouldn't, there would be another way. There had to be.

Before long, the ship pulled away from the docks.

Zay was standing at the railing when Wil found her, watching Brayshire get smaller in the distance. The ship moved fast—the land was already nearly out of sight.

"How many days will it take to get to the Western Isles?" Wil asked. Though this ship was smaller than the ones she'd boarded back home, its design was superior. She didn't feel as though they were moving at all.

"Hm?" Zay spun around to face her. Ada was at her heels, playing with a length of rope that had been tied into a sort of ragdoll. "I don't know. How long would it take to reach the Western Isles?"

In her confusion, it took Wil several seconds to realize that

Zay was not talking to her, but to someone who had come up onto the deck behind her. Someone who had moved so silently, she hadn't known anyone was there. Somehow, even before she turned around, she knew who it would be.

His skin had blanched just slightly, and his eyes were glassy—a side effect of the sleep serum. And the way those eyes looked at her had changed. Where once there had been curiosity, even intrigue, now there was impassiveness. A cut traced his forearm, the blood that lined it dark and dry.

Loom.

Her blood went cold.

"The Western Isles are two days by sea," he said. "But I don't see why it should matter. That isn't where we're going."

Wil took a step back, away from Loom. He was immune to her strange power, she knew that much, but she would fight him if she had to. Lean muscles, haughty stance. He would undoubtedly be a match, but he appeared a little unsteady; the sleep serum hadn't left his senses yet; his reflexes would be slow.

Zay might succumb to her powers and die instantly. But then again, she might not. If Loom was immune, there was a chance she would be as well. Something in their diets? Their genes, assuming they were family? She didn't know.

Her fists clenched inside her gloves. Zay would be easy to knock unconscious, Wil thought. She didn't have a fighter's stance and wouldn't see an attack coming. Loom might prove to be more of a challenge. He was more alert, as though he'd spent his life dodging arrows.

"Are you sure this is the right one?" Zay said, to Loom. "She doesn't look like much."

"It's her," Loom said. He was holding her bag, Wil realized, and he reached inside and pulled out a fistful of crystallized alber blossoms.

When Wil snatched the bag from his hand, he let her have it. No matter. The damage had already been done.

"Where are you taking me?" Wil didn't have to work hard to make her roiling anger sound like fear.

Zay looked at her as though she were a stain on her shoe. When Loom looked at her, though, some of that intrigue was back, although it was veiled now by suspicion, and something more sinister. "We're on a course for the Southern Isles," he said.

"That's impossible," Wil said. "It doesn't matter if the Southern Isles is your home; its borders are completely closed."

"Let me worry about that."

"Why the South? What do you want from me?"

"Let's talk belowdecks," Loom said. "There's a storm coming."

As though on cue, a rumble sounded, and the clear blue sky began to darken.

# SIXTEEN

THE HALLWAY BELOWDECKS WAS NARROW, Wil noted. Much too small for her to spread an arm straight out at her side. And Loom could barely clear the ceiling, which meant it was only a little more than six feet high. Zay brought up the lead, and Loom stayed close behind Wil.

She began running a list of attacks that could incapacitate two opponents in rapid succession in cramped quarters. She didn't know what sort of fighter Zay would be. Despite her ferocity, her bare arms didn't seem to have much muscle to them. Her stance was haughty and guarded, but not especially menacing.

Loom would be the true opponent, she suspected. He had been strong enough to carry her all the way to Hettie's apartment, and quickly at that, without getting winded.

She thought of what Owen had taught her about assessing opponents. What did Loom want from her, and how hard was he willing to fight her for it? He wouldn't kill her. She knew that. He needed her alive because her power meant something to him.

And Zay was hard to get a read on. She might be hiding her physical prowess.

They both stopped walking, pinning Wil between them.

"I have to disarm you," he said. "I'd prefer the easy way, but I'll leave that up to you."

"How kind." Wil spread her arms in a display of complicity. "You tended to my wound. You know where I keep them."

It was Zay, though, who raised the hem of Wil's tunic. Gerdie's twin platinum guns rested on either side of her hips, still fully loaded—his final parting gift before she'd left on their father's spy mission.

Zay whistled at the sight of them. Platinum guns weren't uncommon, but nothing Gerdie made was ever simple. The barrels were embellished with an etching of the Port Capital skyline—a perfect likeness he'd alchemized from a map dipped in coffee, which gave the engraving a sepia tint.

It was the sneer in Zay's eyes that awoke Wil's anger. The idea that this girl from an enemy kingdom was about to take something her brother had labored over. The only piece of Gerdie she had left.

Wil threw herself back, anticipating that Loom would catch

her. He did, and she wrapped her arms around his forearms, locking his elbows and pressing her back to his chest. Her right leg swung up and kicked Zay under the chin, hard. She was out before she hit the ground.

Loom broke free of her grasp and tried to grab her waist, but she spun out of reach, leaping over Zay's prone form.

Loom was fast, but she was faster. *Think,* she commanded herself. Gerdie had once wooed a captain's daughter into letting them see the control panel of a digital ship. It had been at the end of the hall. She sprinted for the door, Loom at her heels.

He grabbed her wrist, forcing her around to face him. She raised her arm, twisted free, and grabbed his fingers with her other hand. She was trying to break them, but he easily pulled away. She glanced behind her. The door was so close. When Loom reached for her again, she ducked low and evaded him by somersaulting for the door. She pulled it open, hurried inside, and slammed it shut behind her.

There was a latch that locked it from the inside, Wil recalled from her brief tour in the control room, to protect the captain in the event of a hostile takeover. There was a key that could open it from the outside, but only the captain and select crew-members would have it, and Wil hoped that somehow Loom wouldn't have one on him.

The other side of the door had gone unnervingly quiet, but there was no time to investigate why that was.

The button that activated the life raft was easy to spot. It had to be, in the event of an emergency, but especially a hijacking—these had grown common in Western waters, Owen had told her.

She pressed her palm to the glowing white button, and within seconds, a metal hatch had unfurled from the wall, revealing a rapidly inflating life raft.

Sounds from the other side of the door now. Zay's voice, the rattle of a key ring.

Wil jumped into the raft and jammed her palm against the red button on the wall beside it. The door began to close. Just before it entombed her in perfect, airtight darkness, Wil heard the door to the control panel burst open.

"She has to be in here." Zay's voice was dazed, but resolute. Wil was impressed she had come to so quickly.

"The raft," Loom said. And before Wil could hear the words he said next, the outer hatch of the compartment finally slid open, casting her raft out into open sea.

The wind had picked up and the waters were choppy. She grasped at the oars and began rowing for land. She had hoped to incapacitate Zay and Loom more indefinitely, but if they came after her now, she would have to shoot them. A tendon in the back of the ankle would be ideal, if she could manage it. But if they came at her from the water, she could go for the shoulders. They wouldn't be able to swim for her at any significant speed if they couldn't move their shoulders.

Though it hadn't been much time since she'd boarded the

ship, it had gone quite far from the port. Nervously, she glanced at the ship's deck, but there was no sign of either of them.

Land was far, but if she could keep rowing at this rate, she would reach it before she'd exhausted herself. Her gaze shifted from the shore to the ship. Loom and Zay had reached the control panel by the time she'd escaped, but they hadn't come after her yet.

*Why aren't they chasing me?*

Then the sharp sound of something bolting through the air. A clear, shimmering net enveloped her raft. Before she could react, there was a sharp tug, and she was underwater.

This was no ordinary net. The lower half of it dug through the raft with the force of the motion, shredding it to ribbons.

She could see the surface through the murk and gloom, but when she kicked toward it, the net snared her arms until she bled, and reeled her farther away.

*Don't panic,* she commanded herself. For a moment, she kept still, relaxing her muscles to slow her heart rate and store her energy.

Then, lungs burning, she unsheathed her dagger.

She tried sawing from several different angles, but the net was impenetrable. Unnatural. It had to be forged by alchemy.

Her vision was starting to tunnel. She couldn't tell if this sensation of rapidly moving was from the net being pulled, or some sort of hallucination.

She had been wrong about Loom. That was the only thought she had left. He was willing to kill her after all.

An eternity—or perhaps a second—later, her lungs came alive with a gasp.

There was air again.

The net hung from a rope on some sort of pulley that jutted from the side of the ship. Her vision returned with bright clarity.

Zay and Loom stood on the ship's deck now, two silhouettes against the cloudy sky, watching her. They were four yards away, Wil noted. Maybe five.

"I told you that wouldn't be enough to kill her," Zay told him. "See? She's fine."

*Fine.* Wil shoved the dagger back into its sheath; it was powerless here.

Underwater the net had been sharp and cutting, but when it was exposed to air, it became sticky and persistently clingy.

She hung helplessly amid the tatters of broken raft and drew deep, measured breaths, preparing her lung capacity in case they pulled her under again.

"You had to find the one creature in all of Northern Arrod who isn't as dumb as she looks," Zay complained to Loom. "This was supposed to be easy."

Loom didn't reply. Instead, he looked to Wil. She tried to read his expression, but it was blank. "Tell me your name," he said.

"You already know my name," she snapped. *Don't let him see your anger.* She focused on breathing.

"I know you Northern types," he said. "You like to give

your daughters long names with a flourish of syllables. Wil is an abbreviation if I've ever heard one."

She had to decide. Her name was a small compromise. If she conceded here, she could resist when he asked her something important.

"Wilhelmina." It felt strange to say. Only her mother ever called her that, and her father, if he bothered to refer to her at all.

"And?"

"And what?"

"Everyone has a last name. Tell me yours."

"I don't have one."

Heidle. Same as the king. Same as the queen and all the princes, including the dead one. It was an easy name to say. Winds knew she'd frittered away precious hours of her life writing it in clumsy calligraphy under the scrutiny of her instructors. She could see those infuriating curls and twists even now. Wilhelmina Heidle. But even if it killed her, she couldn't bring herself to confess, couldn't be that dead princess again.

"Tell me your name," Loom repeated.

She just stared at him.

"You could stay in there all day," he said. "I don't have anywhere pressing to be."

Winds, he was irritating. "I already told you, I don't have one. My mother traveled the world, and I've never met my father." It was partly true, which was more than he deserved.

"How are you able to turn things to stone?" Loom asked. "Were you cursed?"

"I don't know. That's why I'm trying to find Pahn."

"How can you not know how you turn things to stone?" Zay demanded.

"I just don't," Wil said. "The same way you don't know how to deflect a kick to the face."

Zay's fury was palpable. "Just throw her back in the water," she said.

Loom ignored that. "Where is your mother now?" he asked.

"I don't know."

"When exactly did this start?"

She didn't reply. If she told the truth, he might figure out that her powers had emerged shortly before the princess of Arrod died. She didn't want to take the chance. He was clearly perceptive. He had somehow anticipated that she'd be on a ship headed west and beaten her to it.

Zay said something that prompted an exasperated sigh from Loom, and they began to argue in Lavean murmurs that Wil couldn't hear at her distance. While their attention was off her, she studied her confinement. The spaces between the netting were diamond shaped, just big enough for a closed fist to pass through. There had to be a weak link in here somewhere. Some way for a captain to escape if he'd been held captive on his own ship. It was an old alchemist's trick that Gerdie had told her about. Any means to confine a prisoner had a hidden vulnerability so it couldn't be used against the one meant to use it.

She shifted her weight. At a glance, it would seem that she was trying to stretch her cramping limbs, but she worked at the diamonds of the rope with her boot, searching for an out.

She clutched the top of the net, where it gathered at the rope that held it in place. If she broke free, she could swim for shore. It wasn't very far; she could make it.

And then she found a weak length of net. Her boot kicked it apart. But rather than breaking the net, it severed it from the rope on the pulley, causing her to drop helplessly into the water.

The instant she went under, her body tried to kick itself to the surface, but the net ensnared her, cutting at her skin where she fought it.

No matter what she did, she was sinking.

Some dull, faraway part of her mind began to panic. No, she told herself. If there was one weak length, there had to be another nearby. But as she sank farther into the depths, she lost track of which end was which.

Everything was dark, too dark. Her lungs gave protest, forcing her to draw in water like a breath. For a moment, the pain of it woke her. She saw the daylight wobbling overhead, before it was blotted out by darkness.

# SEVENTEEN

*Monster . . .*

There was something in all that darkness of the Ancient Sea, calling to her. Something she thought had been lost to her forever.

*Listen to me, Monster—*

The calm filled her the way the water filled her. She knew that Owen was dead. She'd felt his last breath against her throat when she caught him. But even so, she knew somehow that he was not gone.

He was here.

She couldn't move, couldn't think, and only barely felt her brother's arm snaring her body and pulling her through the black.

She inhaled, knives shooting down her throat, shredding

her lungs. A hand was hitting her back, hard, forcing the water out so that air could find its way back in.

Bits of pale sky shone through her lashes. She heard herself retch and splutter, and under all that, a soft voice that said, "I've got you."

It was not Owen's voice. Delirium was replaced by clarity. The living voices replaced the dead. She opened her eyes and saw the ship. That vile, cursed thing, floating in the water before her.

Loom had an arm around her, his fist gripping the back of her shirt. She wanted to murder him.

His closeness infuriated her, and she tried to push him away, but as oxygen made its way back into her body she felt as though she was spinning in a riptide. He was watching her. She tried to glare at him, but had the sense that she looked more like she was going to pass out instead.

He was swimming for the ship now, and she resisted the instinct to rest her heavy head against his shoulder.

When they reached the rope ladder that hung over the side of the ship, she shoved him away and climbed onto the deck. Water dripped heavy off her clothes, her hair. Her gloves felt full with it.

Thin, hard drops of rain fell sparsely onto the deck. Loom had been right about a storm coming.

Zay was standing over her, arms crossed. The bruise on her chin greatly diminished the effect of her death glare.

Loom took Wil's elbow and tugged her to her feet. He opened his mouth to say something, but Wil reeled back and punched him in the jaw before he could. He staggered. When she came at him again with a kick, he caught her ankle and knocked her onto her back.

"Listen," he said, pinning her wrists. "I'm not going to hurt you."

She locked an arm around his elbow, slid a knee under his torso, and overtook him with a sweep, rolling him onto his back and straddling his waist.

He twisted his hips in an attempt to throw her off. She unsheathed her dagger in an instant and held it to his jugular.

He went still.

"What do you want from me?" she demanded.

There was a moment of bewilderment on his face before his guard went up again, and she reveled in it. He was clearly not used to getting bested, especially not from a runt like her. Her knees dug into his sides.

"All right," he snarled. "I'd been watching you for a while, trying to figure out where you got all those gems you kept trading." He blinked as a raindrop landed in his lashes. "When I saw the way you handled that marauder, I thought you must have been involved with the underground market. I wanted in."

"In?" Wil asked. "In illegal trade?"

"Yes." Wet hair shifted around his head, its own little sea of black waves. "You seemed to know what you were doing. And then, in the woods, when I discovered the truth—"

"None of this answers my question. What do you plan to do with a bunch of gemstones?"

"'A bunch of gemstones'? Ha. You Northern Arrod types have so much wealth to burn—"

She pressed the blade tighter to his skin. The arch of the dagger cradled the knob of his throat.

"That kind of wealth could save a kingdom," he went on.

"So what if it can?" Wil said. "Why should you be in charge of it?"

She was aware of Zay hovering somewhere behind her, but she didn't dare take her eyes from Loom. His breaths were shallow, revealing his vulnerability; Zay was some sort of ally—that much was clear—but he was the only fighter between them.

"I know you want to find Pahn," he said, through gritted teeth. "I can help you. I know where he's hiding out."

"You really do think I'm stupid," Wil said.

"It's the truth. I've had the immense displeasure of knowing him since I was a child. My father keeps Pahn under his thumb."

Wil narrowed her eyes. Her other hand was still pressed against his wrist, and she could feel his pulse through her glove. Rhythmic. Steady. If he was lying, he was good at disguising it.

Still, she couldn't be sure. She shifted the angle of her dagger. He swallowed hard, his skin flirting dangerously against the blade.

"Unbutton my collar," he told her.

"Loom," Zay hissed, "have you lost your mind?" She was speaking in Lavean. Wil didn't let on that she could speak the Southern Isles' language fluently. Most Northerners wouldn't bother unless they dealt in the ports, but her father had insisted that all his children speak the trade tongues.

But Loom ignored the words and kept his focus on Wil.

Still holding the dagger in place, with her other hand she undid the button at his collar and peeled away the fabric that had been obscuring his tattoos. She shifted the dagger to rest under his eye. He didn't move as she studied the marks. On the right side of his neck, black lines emerged from his hair, reaching around his throat like needle-thin flames. At a glance the lines seemed to swirl aimlessly, but up close she could see thin, detailed figures within them. Leaves and insects and columns of jagged branches that appeared to be choking him.

At the knob of his throat, there was a crown made of blades. She watched the way it glided with his skin when he inhaled deep. She had seen that crown before. It sat atop an anatomically correct heart impaled by blades that formed an X clean through it.

It wasn't merely a tattoo. It was the royal crest of the Southern Isles.

"High winds." She met his gaze, bewildered. "Did the king do that to you?"

"In a manner of speaking," Loom said. "He's my father."

For a second, she didn't believe him. But then she realized

that from the time she first saw him, she had recognized something about his sullen nature. The way he walked. Looked at her as though he was searching for something. But especially in the guarded way that he spoke, as though his bones had been splintered and were slowly healing into new shapes.

Hiding his royal lineage. She understood.

King Zinil of the Royal House of Raisius had never spoken of his children. He'd earned the title throughout the world as the Reclusive King, and even Wil's own family knew only that he had a son and a daughter, and barely anything beyond that.

"You can't return to the palace, can you?" she asked, easing up with the dagger a little. "He disowned you?"

Loom didn't deny it.

"But I don't understand. If the king disowned you, why would you want to help his kingdom?"

"A kingdom shouldn't be blamed for the actions of its king," he said. The words reminded her so much of something Owen would say that for a moment she was sure her heart had stopped beating.

"Banished or not," Loom went on, "those are still my people. They need someone, and my father is destroying the entire kingdom with his stubbornness and greed."

Maybe kings were not all that different.

Wil thought of her father. "It wouldn't stop the war that's coming," she said. "You can't expect to take on the wealthiest kingdom in the world. Even a ton of diamonds wouldn't grant you the allies for that."

"I don't need to take on the kingdom," Loom said, and there was a spark of excitement in his eyes. A sense of purpose. "I only need to kill its royal family."

Her throat went dry. He wanted to kill her family. Her father, her mother, her brothers—slaughtered. Gone. And he wanted her to help him.

What would he do if he knew that she was a Heidle? She remembered the look on Owen's face that night he'd come to stop her at the rapids. The terrible fear in his eyes.

*The entire South hates our family right now. If one of them found out who you are . . .*

Loom would never find out, she told herself. She scarcely looked the part of a princess. Without constant fussing, her hair fell wild, creeping out of braids and ponytails like the undead apparitions that stole across the Western moors. This side of her skin, there was her mother's restless blood, centuries of wanderers and believers of tall tales and magic. It was easy to abandon the princess of Arrod for dead.

She still had him vulnerable. She could kill him now and be done with it. Overpowering Zay would be no challenge, and then—what? Roll their bodies into the water and take his ship? Continue searching for Pahn amid clueless travelers? If Loom was telling the truth, then he might be the only one who could help her.

"I am willing to bet that your little trick got you banished from your family," Loom went on. "Am I right? They didn't want anything to do with you once they found out. You don't have to be alone. We can help each other."

"What do you think happens if you kill the royal family?" Wil said. "You'll just take over the throne? The king has advisers. He has a council. There are dozens fit to take over, and there's no promise they'll be any better than the Heidle family themselves. Northern Arrod has the world's leading alchemists. Your entire kingdom could be razed by explosives in a day."

"I will kill however many are necessary," Loom said.

Wil betrayed nothing. "I won't help you do that."

"Now can we throw her overboard?" Zay asked, this time in a language she knew Wil could understand.

Something cold swept across the back of Wil's neck, and before she could turn on Zay to see what she had done, her head filled with fog. She fought to keep her grip on her dagger, but from somewhere very far away, she heard the blade clatter against the deck.

# EIGHTEEN

It HAD BEEN TOO MANY days, and the castle was far too silent. Much as Baren's siblings had burdened him, their absence was more troubling. Silence was not the absence of presence—it was its own presence.

The morning that Baren met his sister for the first time, he had been eight years old. He followed his brother into their mother's chambers, and there she sat in a beam of light, pale and smiling, her hair tangled and sweaty. She was as beautiful as ever, and it stood to reason that any daughter of hers would inherit such beauty.

Only, his new sister wasn't beautiful. She was frightening. So pale her skin was like parchment paper concealing something uglier within her. He could see the hints of her bones. He could see fine purple lines in her cheeks, around her beady eyes.

Even the ever-cordial Owen scrunched his mouth at such a sight. "She looks like the undead monsters of the West."

The queen had laughed. "She does not."

"Can I hold her?" Owen asked.

The queen patted the space on the mattress beside her, and Owen climbed up, watching as the baby was transferred into his arms. He studied her face, carefully tracing her cheek, her bump of a nose, as though she were a broken bird he'd just found. "Hello, Monster."

"Don't you want to have a better look?" the queen asked Baren, who had backed against the wall.

"No," Baren said. He didn't need to look at his baby sister. He already saw how much his mother loved her. It was a different and more generous love than she had ever shown him. For that, he hated his sister more than he had ever hated anything, or ever would.

And now, not sixteen years later, the earth had opened up and water rushed through and pulled her under, and on her way down, she had pulled Owen with her. What would Owen have thought all those years ago, Baren wondered, if he knew the baby he held would grow to be the death of him?

But even though she was dead, Wil found her way back to the castle. She had been dead for six days the first time it happened. Baren was awoken in the still dark night by the sound of wet footsteps on the oak floor, getting closer. She sat in the chair by the window, where the waxing moon bathed her pale skin in blue, and she rocked the chair slowly forward and back.

Her hair was long and dark and dripping, and her eyes were as black as the empty space behind her. She was so real, even breathing—he thought—that he believed she had crawled her way out of the river, back to life, back to the world of beating hearts and blinking eyes.

She came back every night after that. She never spoke, only stared. He tried moving the chair, but the next night, she had dragged it back to the window. He broke the chair after that, grabbed it by its back and threw it against the wall until it was in splinters, which he then threw into the fireplace.

But it was no matter. The next night, when he awoke, Owen came to visit him instead. He stood over the bed, his perfect curls destroyed, tangled, and full of roots and river weeds. His blue eyes had gone dark, hemmed by deep gray bags that made him look dead.

"What do you want?" Baren finally asked. And Owen smiled. For a second, it was the kind, sweet smile that turned him into a boy. The smile the entire nation had loved. But then the smile spread, turned ugly. His lips parted and revealed blackened, rotted teeth. The smell of decay came from his mouth. He canted his head back and laughed, a sinister croak of a sound, so loud that Baren thought it would wake the entire castle. But no one came. No one heard it, and Baren knew that no one would ever believe him.

So Baren stopped sleeping. For two days, he staggered about the castle, swaying from wall to wall as though on a ship in stormy seas.

With no sense of direction, he opened the door to his brother's lab.

When he found himself halfway down the stairs, where the chemical smells and the scorched air began to reach him, Gerdie raised his head. And Baren saw his little brother for perhaps the first time. He saw how alike they looked, and he saw that they were the only Heidle children left with life in their eyes. He saw the expectation on his brother's face, the hope. And just as soon as that hope flared up, it was slaughtered and gone.

Baren realized what he had done. There was only one person who had ever barged into this place on a whim.

Gerdie looked back to his cauldron, as though embarrassed for having a thought so stupid as Wil being alive.

It didn't make sense, Baren thought. It didn't make sense that Wil would haunt him rather than the brother she had loved, the brother who would want to see her, even if she was dead, even if she was gruesome, even if she didn't speak.

"What do you want?" Gerdie's tone was dead. He sprinkled some gray powder into his cauldron and it flickered and flashed green, like lightning.

"You don't sleep for days sometimes," Baren said. His own voice sounded strange to him. "I know you can make potions to stay awake. As the heir, I'm ordering you to make one for me."

Gerdie looked up at him. "Last I checked, the heir doesn't give orders."

After two days of stumbling half-awake, Baren moved fast.

In a blink he had his brother pinned to the wall, a blade at his throat. Broken glass crunched under his feet, and some felled chemical hissed and fizzed against the stone. "You will take orders from me, little brother, or you will live to regret it."

There was no fear on Gerdie's face. There was nothing. Their sister had pulled him under the rapids as well. She was a curse, that girl, in life but especially in death.

Baren pressed the blade into his brother's flesh, and with a slight motion, a line of blood appeared.

Gerdie's eyes flicked to the blade. It was one he knew well. "If you're going to kill me with Owen's dagger, get on with it." His voice was low, and Baren's blood went cold at the sudden viciousness of it. "You want to be a king, and kings don't waste time threatening their prey. Do it. Add another ghost to your menagerie."

Baren shoved him, and his grasp on the hilt tightened. "Listen to me," he seethed. He could hear his own teeth grinding. "As long as I'm awake, the dead stay dead."

He saw something on his little brother's face. Concern? No. Concern was reserved for those he loved, dwindling though that population was. Curiosity.

"You think they're dead but they won't stay dead." Baren eased up on the blade but twisted his brother's shirt in his fist. "This castle is haunted, Gerhard, and they won't stop with me. They'll come for you eventually too."

"Let them come for me, then," Gerdie said. Despite his calm

tone, Baren could feel his brother's heart pounding against his fist.

"They aren't the same," Baren insisted. "They're wrong. They're evil."

Gerdie took a deep breath. He hadn't made a move yet to free himself. "Ghosts aren't real. If you're seeing Wil and Owen, it's just your own mind projecting your regrets."

Baren had considered this. He had considered everything. When his sister and brother came to visit him, he would stare at them, blood cold, skin clammy, until they went away. After, he would lie awake, questioning what he had seen. But there were no regrets.

"I'm glad they're dead—both of them," Baren said, at last causing his brother to wince. "I have no regrets."

"Then maybe," Gerdie began, slowly, "that's why you're the only one who's being haunted."

Gerdie hated himself for entertaining his brother's delusions. He hated himself for agreeing to keep vigil over Baren that night to prove that no ghosts would visit him.

But he was intrigued.

When Gerdie and Wil were children, Baren had taken great delight in tormenting them with his stories of apparitions come to take Gerdie's soul when his Gray Fever flared up. It didn't upset Gerdie so much as it infuriated Wil. Her eyes would go dark and her fists would clench, and she would thrum as though electric with her rage. Baren had fast learned that Gerdie was Wil's weakness, and the opposite was also true. If Gerdie found himself the victim of Baren's rage, Baren would snatch Wil by the wrist and dangle her from the open window, which was a game he could only play until Wil grew big enough to fight back, at which point he would barricade her door, or set one of her books on fire.

Even in death, Wil remained Gerdie's weakness. Wil was dead. Wil was gone. Gerdie had taken to saying those words in his head each morning to remind himself, and still it did nothing to convince him. It defied logic, but he felt that somewhere her lungs were still filling up with air.

This feeling, he had learned, was worse than accepting the truth.

Baren could still be preying on the bond he shared with his sister. But why? There was no sport in it now. Gerdie was more interested in this than in the notion of ghosts. So, after the sun had set and the castle was quiet, he went to his brother's chamber.

Baren was beginning to frighten him, truth be told. His eyes were lost in his gaunt face, their brightness gone. He was pale, almost sallow.

"What happened to your chair?" Gerdie asked, by way of greeting. When each of the royal children had been born, their father had commissioned rocking chairs from a carpenter in the city, with their names carved into the backing. Now Baren's chair lay splintered and charred in the fireplace.

If Baren had heard the question, he didn't acknowledge it. He hugged his arms—he looked so painfully thin—and drew back the rumpled blankets of his bed. "You'll see. They'll come."

Troubled though Baren was, it didn't take long for him to fall asleep. It was fitful. He muttered and stirred, his hair dark with sweat.

Once he was sure Baren wouldn't awaken, Gerdie eased Owen's dagger from his brother's sheath and tucked it into his own.

For hours, he sat on the floor at the foot of his brother's bed, a notebook resting against his thighs as he wrote formulas by the light of an electric lantern.

Somewhere within the bowels of the castle, a clock chimed the hour.

Odd, he thought. His mother had silenced every clock nearly a week ago. This was not among her superstitions; it was only that the castle had become so silent that the chiming made her flinch.

He listened to each of the four chimes, tracking the sound. It was coming from Wil's room. He was sure of it.

Each of the Heidle children had a chiming clock, and Wil had been terrible about remembering to wind hers, he recalled. But even if she had wound it right before she died, it would have stopped days ago. Had it been ticking all this time? Had he failed to hear it, hiding away in his laboratory whenever it marked the hour?

Gerdie whispered, "If you're really here, come and haunt me. Not him."

The only answer was the October wind, whistling as it crept through the latched window.

He didn't know when he drifted off to sleep, huddled over his notes. It was still dark when the creaking of a door startled him awake. Door, his mind emphasized too harshly. Not a ghost. A door.

"Gerhard?" his mother whispered. She moved to kneel before him. The battery in the lantern was dying, its light flickering and waning. "What are you doing in here?"

He wouldn't dare tell his mother the truth. Ever the insomniac, now she slept even less. She moved about the castle at all hours, fidgeting and counting and making sure the mirrors were covered—all to sate her wanderer's superstition that her children would come back to haunt them.

"I was worried about Baren," he said.

The queen offered a weak smile. It heartened her to believe that the estranged brothers were getting along, that smile said. But without Owen and without Wil, she was incomplete, and no small happiness could account for it.

"Come on," she said softly, and pulled him to his feet. "It's late and you should be in bed." She held his shoulders, and then she touched the side of his neck, where the blade had sliced him that afternoon. He had predicted that his mother would break down, that she would be too fragile to endure the loss of two children. But she had gotten stronger instead, and in his mother he had begun to see the free girl she had once been, before she was anyone's mother, or anyone's queen, when she had survived tragedies he would never know. He saw that side of her like bits of color refracted on the wall.

He wanted to ask her if she felt it too—that sense that Wil might walk through the door at any minute. That Owen still had something left to say. That there were no bodies to bury, and so there was a chance that none of this was real.

Without meaning to, without even realizing the words were in his head at all, he said, "I really thought they would come home."

# NINETEEN

Wil had no memory of blacking out, but when she came to, the storm outside had turned furious.

The ship lilted in one direction, and she clawed at the floor. It was cool and soft. Satin?

There was another jolt, and with it, she managed to open her eyes.

She was back in the cabin Zay had initially shown her to, lying on the bed. An electric lantern was swinging overhead, filling the space with dizzying shadows.

She rubbed a hand against her forehead. Her gloves were gone, and she sat up immediately at that. She patted at her hips, her thigh. The sheath and holsters were empty.

Her captors wouldn't be able to shoot her with the guns, at least. Her brother made all his guns with a trick trigger so his own weapons couldn't be used against him; it was so complex it had taken Wil several attempts to learn.

The gloves rested by her feet, a little rumpled, but upon inspection they weren't damaged. Loom must have searched them for hidden weapons.

She fitted her data goggles over her eyes. At least they hadn't taken this small piece of her old life from her after they'd rendered her unconscious. The goggles were harmless enough—a tourist trinket made of solar-powered glass and a leather strap. She blinked. The time glowed in the lower right lens. Midnight. It was a highly concentrated variant of sleep serum to have taken effect before she could put up a fight, and it lasted half as much time as more regulated doses used for a night's rest.

Loom must have anticipated that she'd be waking up, because the door to the cabin opened, and he stood at the threshold.

"I did offer to disarm you the easy way," he said, and closed the door behind him. He dragged the trunk from the corner of the room to her bedside and sat with an elbow resting on his knee. Wil had the fleeting thought that he could have locked her in the trunk instead, if he'd really wanted to incapacitate her. It was more than big enough.

Wil pushed herself upright. Her tongue felt like sandpaper, and her arms scarcely felt attached to her body. "Don't sell them," she said. "My weapons."

"I wouldn't," Loom said. "They're works of art. Where did you find them?"

She drew one knee to her chest, then the other, and extended each leg slowly, trying to shake free of the numbness. "They were gifts. If anything happens to them, you'll fast learn I don't need weapons to hurt you."

He canted his chin. "I already believe you about that. Who taught you to fight?"

"That was also a gift," she said.

When she was a child and ever sitting at an ailing Gerdie's bedside, Owen had worried for her. "Come on, Monster." He'd hoisted her up from the floor and carried her on his back. "Let's go to the oval garden. I'll show you how to shoot an arrow."

He'd only meant to distract her from her worries for a few hours, but she'd shown so much interest in learning to fight that it became a ritual of theirs. Something to look forward to. Short-range weapons, long-range, hand-to-hand combat, how to bridge a size disadvantage, evasion tactics. Their mother hadn't exactly approved.

The lantern light cast a warm glow on Loom's skin. But his face was colder than it had been before. Guarded.

This was not the boy who'd stood before her in the woods, all gentleness and wonder. That boy had been a mirage. A persistent one that she had been a fool to fall for—however briefly.

Now, he was wearing a loose-fitting cotton tunic, the unbuttoned collar revealing the royal tattoo that made him her enemy.

She stared at him. "What did you do to get banished from your own kingdom?"

"Does it matter?" he asked.

"I'm curious. Given your astonishing charm, it's a mystery that anyone would want to get rid of you."

He searched her eyes, matching her scrutiny. "I tried to kill my father." He stood. The waves rocked the ship, but his stance hardly wavered. "You must be hungry. I'll bring you something."

When Loom returned, it was with a dehydrated packaged sea ration. Wil had seen them for sale at ports in anticipation of long journeys. He tossed it to her. A brick wrapped in metallic airtight packaging. It was still sealed, but that didn't mean it hadn't been tampered with.

Wil turned it over in her hands, looking for puncture marks.

"Is the storm making you seasick?" Loom sat on the trunk again. Keeping guard, apparently. But there was no need for that, Wil thought. She wanted to escape, but the storm outside roiled the sea and she didn't have a death wish.

"No." She toyed with the packaging, but didn't open it.

"I got sick for years before I grew accustomed to ships," Loom said, arching an eyebrow. "I suppose you really are cut out for travel."

"What kind of net was that?" Wil asked.

"An alchemized combination of sepra and jellyfish tentacles, among other things," Loom said.

Jellyfish. Interesting. Sepra was a thin metal, cheap and fairly common. But Wil had never considered a living thing being used in alchemy. Gerdie had never mentioned it, at least.

"How did you cut through it?" Wil tentatively tore open the packaging of her sea ration. The smell of chemicals and something faintly like apples wafted out.

"Zay's jeweler's knife. It can cut through everything, even stone."

"Alchemized?" Wil asked, intrigued despite the madness of her situation. It gave her hope that a part of her was still the girl she had once been, scaling the castle wall and acquiring her brother's materials.

"Yes," Loom said. "By some old flame of her mother's in the East."

Wil set the ration down and positioned herself to sit on the edge of the bed. Loom was wary of her, but she could sense that some part of him was still susceptible to reason. "Loom," she said. "You must know that you can't buy alliances with gemstones. Particularly ones that are rare in the South. Think how many suspicions that would raise. King Hein in particular would find some way to get spies into the country to find out how you're doing it. Your people would be interrogated, tortured."

Loom's brows drew together at her words. He hadn't expected to be challenged on his politics, she supposed.

"You've never been to Cannolay," he finally said. "Or Messalin. Or any of the South's more impoverished cities at all. Have you?"

Wil shook her head.

"If you had, you'd know that my father deserves to be dethroned for what he's let his kingdom become. Fevers, disease, abject poverty—all because he refuses to form a single alliance with any of the trade nations. He's too proud, and while he lives in the famed mountain palace, his people are the ones suffering."

Wil thought of the rundown outskirts of the Port Capital in Northern Arrod. "I know—"

"No," Loom said. "Until you've seen it, you don't. You don't know anything about kings, but I come from one. I've stood beside him as he's destroyed his kingdom. I tried to kill him because there was no other way."

"You want to kill your father. You want to kill the Northern royals. Is that your only plan?" Wil fired back. "Because if that's all you've got, you aren't going to make a better king yourself."

"That's how kingdoms work!" he cried.

"Yes," Wil hissed. "And that's why they're such a mess."

"I didn't bring you along to be my adviser—"

"No. You 'brought me along' because you got overly zealous about something you know nothing about, and you are clinging to the idea that somehow I can fix your kingdom." She said her next words slowly. "I can't fix it."

"You don't even know what you're capable of," Loom muttered, looking to the tiny circular window. Water sloshed angrily against it.

The words cut deep, because Wil *did* know what she was capable of. She'd learned that night by the rapids. But she didn't say that. He had taken her hostage—for now—but he wouldn't truly have her. He wouldn't know a shred about who she was. Once they had reached solid land, she would be gone.

Still, there was some truth to what he said. She didn't know everything about her power. She didn't know where it had come from, or why he wasn't affected. If he was immune, perhaps others were as well.

She could see the tension in Loom's jaw when she looked at him. "Can you really take me to Pahn?"

"I can tell you where he is," Loom said. "But first, you have to help me. You have to see what the Southern Isles are like. I'm not asking you to kill my father and take the throne in his place. I'm just asking for a few diamonds, so I can acquire an ally to help me assassinate him."

"For how long?" Wil asked.

"It'll take us six days to get there," Loom said. "And then I only need a week to show you why I need your help. After that, I know you'll want to stay."

"And what makes you so sure of that?"

"Because you won't stand for injustices. I saw that in the market square."

Injustice. He was a fine one to speak of such things.

Outside, the winds were screaming. The water was filled with voices.

She'd heard Owen in the Ancient Sea; she was sure of it.

*What would you have me do?*

If she couldn't have him alive then she wanted a ghost, she wanted a chill, whispers in an angry sea. She wanted to know that he was somewhere. Anywhere. She had never believed in any sort of life after death, but now she understood why people did.

A flash of lightning was the only reply. If Gerdie were here now, he'd scold her for always being taken in by wild stories. He'd want her to come to a decision logically. Logic, she could do. She didn't have Owen's ghost to give her guidance, but she had been his sister for nearly sixteen years, and she had something better than a ghost. She had all the things he had taught her.

*You'll be the eyes of the kingdom when I'm on the throne.* That was what he'd said.

It had been years since anyone from Arrod entered the Southern Isles. A member of the royal family would be foolish to even attempt it. But Wil was the palace spy, banished or not. She had an opportunity that even Owen would have coveted.

"I'm not going to agree to anything." Wil sat back and folded her arms. "I'm not in the habit of bargaining with my captors."

Loom smirked. "Had many captors, have you?"

"There have been—attempts," Wil said. "But you're the first to manage this much success. You should feel special."

"I do, actually," Loom said.

She still hadn't ruled out the possibility of killing him if things got ugly.

Wanting to save a kingdom from its king, she understood—not that she could tell him so.

Though she knew his identity, she could sense there was more she had yet to learn. Things it would take more than a dagger to the throat to force out of him.

"Very well, then. Don't agree to anything." He stood. "I wouldn't bother trying to break the lock. Zay made it herself."

"She's an alchemist?" Wil asked.

"A jeweler," Loom said. He dug into the pocket of his cotton trousers and pulled out a handful of the rubies Wil had made from the alber blossoms. They were whittled down and made to look as though they'd fallen out of a setting.

Wil stared at them, surprised. This was the work of someone with care and patience; not what she had expected from Zay at all. "Who is she?" Wil asked. "Why is she helping you?"

Loom closed the gems in his fist and moved for the door. "Good night," was all he said.

# TWENTY

AFTER LOOM HAD GONE, WIL planned her next course of action. She didn't know at which port this ship would arrive, so planning an escape route was a matter to be contended with upon arrival. But she did know that Zay wouldn't risk touching her, and that Loom was immune somehow to her strange power. Unarmed, she would have to rely on raw wit and bare hands to fend him off. The element of surprise had always worked in her favor in such fights, and so she decided that she would work to earn his trust on this voyage, so that he wouldn't see it coming when she made her escape. Not too much trust, not all at once. That would arouse too much suspicion. She would be just amenable enough to make him believe she was considering his offer.

Remnants of the sleep serum lingered in her blood, and eventually she drifted off.

The night brought fitful dreams. Her mother's songs turned to wails of grief echoing between cavernous castle walls. The ocean storm drowned drifting funeral candles, disrupting the spirits of the dead, turning them ugly and vicious.

Wil fretted and thrashed, until the satin sheet was tangled around her legs.

She opened her eyes to complete darkness, so black and moonless she thought at first that she was still asleep. But then she heard the creak of the lantern swinging overhead. She rose to her knees on the mattress and reached for it. But turning the dial at its side did nothing. The power was out.

Her breath came in gasps. She had always hated the dark. It couldn't be trusted. There was forever a candle burning somewhere in the castle because darkness invited death, the queen would say. It was the reason people who wandered the world spent their nights dancing and drinking by firelight, sleeping at dawn. It would be too easy for death to slip in unnoticed and reach right through their skin to steal their life away.

But this darkness was loaded with something vile and strange. Thousands of feather-light legs were crawling down the walls, rushing at her. She swatted at them when they brushed her cheek. They spilled into her gloves, and frantically she pulled them off, threw them away. It made no difference. The legs still came. She clawed at them. Clawed until her hair turned wet with their blood.

She could hear the pounding of her heart. She stood,

grappling for the door. Locked. She pulled at the handle and felt along the frame, but it was smooth; the lock mechanism was on the outside. She kicked at it, pounded. She was too breathless to scream. She had not believed Loom could hate her this much, to lock her in a prison to be devoured by creatures that were filling up her sleeves and eyelashes.

The ship rocked sharply to one side, and she spilled to the floor. The creatures shrieked, their cry sounding suspiciously like the creak of the lantern. She drew her knees to her chest and made herself small. Morning would have to come, she told herself. There would be light again soon.

Over the sounds of the creatures and the wind, she heard something else. Footsteps running down the hall, and then her door coming open, spilling candlelight into the room.

"Wil?" Loom knelt on the ground before her. He was holding a lantern up between them, the orange glow sharpening the shadow of his jaw.

His skin was smooth, Wil noted. Nothing crawling on him. Nothing crawling anywhere. She inspected her hands. Nothing. She ran her fingers through her hair, tangled now from her struggle, but clean of any blood.

"Did you see something?" Loom asked. He was being oddly delicate with her. "When you woke up."

"I couldn't see anything," Wil said, the shakiness of her voice surprising her. "I heard something crawling."

She shivered.

"That brew of sleep serum can cause hallucinations some-times. It was probably aggravated by the storm." He was studying her again, and there was something in his expres-sion—guilt? He frowned. "Are you all right?"

Fine question to ask after he'd taken her hostage and locked her in the dark, she thought. "Why is the power out?" she asked. Her voice sounded steady that time, but her heart was still in her throat.

"I had to disable the lights to conserve energy for the steer-ing panel." He held his arm out against the wall to brace himself for the next jolt, sensing it a moment before it came. "The bat-tery in your lantern died out, and the dock wasn't feeding it any electricity to recharge."

Wil focused on his tattoos. Inky leaves with razor edges bloomed down the trellis of his veins. There was still the scab from where she'd cut him.

"You'll feel better if you eat something," he said. "The rations taste a bit like sand, but you get used to them. There are more in the galley."

"You're going to let me out of my prison cell?" Wil rose to her feet, using the wall to keep steady.

He regarded her with a flat gaze, as though to say he thought her assessment was dramatic. "If you want to try to swim away in this storm, I won't stop you. Just don't expect me to go in after you this time."

She stooped to recover her gloves from where she'd thrown

them. She didn't put them on, only straightened them and laid them gently across the bed. Though they'd scraped against the impenetrable net, there wasn't a single scuff to be found, and for just one second she thought to run down to the basement lab and tell her brother that these gloves were going to mean big things in the name of battle armor.

And then, worse than crawling creatures or dreary dreams, came the reminder of just how deeply she missed him.

*Find Pahn.*

All she had to do was humor Loom with this fool's errand until the ship arrived at port. She could escape and resume her search for Pahn. Pahn would have the answers, and then, only then, would she have any right to contact her brother. She would tell him everything—the whole hideous truth of what had happened that night she and Owen supposedly drowned.

She steeled herself. No good could come from Loom reading her vulnerability plain on her face.

Loom led her down the narrow hallway toward the galley. From behind a closed door, Ada was crying while Zay worked to soothe him with a Lavean lullaby. Her voice was low and sweet, even melodic.

By appearance, Zay was not much older than Wil, but she carried herself like the vendors Wil encountered in the underground market. Scheming, guarded, battle-worn. And yet, she knew how to use her youth and beauty to her advantage, playing the part of an innocent young ship captain looking for fares.

She wasn't much of a fighter, true, but her duplicity made her as treacherous as the choppy waters scarred by flashes of white lightning outside.

And there was her loyalty to Loom, as mysterious as it was admirable. Also something to worry about.

But Wil's wariness for Zay and Loom was mutual. Loom never turned his back to her once, even as he ushered her into the galley.

It was a small space, made smaller by the plants in metal baskets that were welded into the walls. Bright red leaves, purple vines, tiny speckled blossoms the likes of which she had never seen before. All of them were meticulously labeled in slanted calligraphy that reminded her of her own torturous hours of study.

Loom hooked the lantern to the ceiling. "Look at that," he said, picking up a small metal crate that rested on the counter. "I guess Zay found some fresh fruit at the port." He sat across from her at the small table bolted to the ground by the window. He looked at her as he pried open the lid. "Or will you crystallize these?"

She shook her head. "I can't. They've been off the tree for too long." Tentatively, she took an apple when he tilted the crate to her. She hadn't touched the ration, and now her stomach ached with hunger.

"So there are rules to your gift after all," Loom said, and bit into a pear.

Wil drew up a knee, watching him. His fingers were callused, knuckles marred by bruises and scars. His arms were covered by the loose sleeves of his tunic, and she remembered how those arms felt when he held her above the water—lean and solid as stone. The one-time heir to the Southern Isles had endured a lot. She believed that. Someone else, someone who hadn't grown up in a royal family of their own, wouldn't have.

Wil heard the rumors throughout Northern Arrod that the princes and princess of the Royal House of Heidle lived a life of excess and luxury. The princess with her long blond hair spent her days trying on dresses and flirting with servant boys. The princes had anything they desired and never had to work for it.

To belong to a royal family was to be a puppet whose image was mirrored onto thousands of tiny stages, each reflection dancing to a different tune as it suited the audience. But none of these images were the truth.

Making a decision, she said, "It isn't a gift."

Loom looked at her, inquisitive.

"What I have." She peeled a bit of apple skin with her thumb. "It isn't a gift. It's a curse."

"A curse is a very specific thing," Loom said. "It isn't just a means to describe bad fortune. Someone would have to place it on you."

"I know that." She couldn't help the defensiveness of her tone; she had been raised on her mother's tales and legends. "There was a woman who told me I have darkness in my blood.

Something ugly and vicious."

"Wanderers," Loom echoed, with a sneer. "How exhausting it must be for them, to think every star in the sky exists to affect the course of their little lives."

Wil bristled at that and bit into the apple.

"The world is filled with swindlers and cons," Loom went on. "Anyone will offer to cure what ails you for a price."

"I don't need you to tell me about the world."

"No?" He raised an eyebrow. Wil hated the elegance this gave his face. She hated that she found him so beautiful. "Because, while you don't exactly strike me as a fool, only a fool would turn to Pahn for help."

"You said yourself that your father uses him all the time," Wil said.

"Yes," Loom said. "My father, who is running his kingdom straight to the bottom of the sea, and who is the biggest fool I have ever known."

"Now I know where you get it from," Wil muttered into her next bite of apple.

She felt Loom's fury at that. "One doesn't have to be a king to make terrible decisions."

"What is that supposed to mean?"

"It means you're selfish—"

"Selfish?" Wil spluttered. "Selfish! You expect me to throw this power around to suit your needs and you don't know a thing about it."

"I'm trying to," he growled.

Trying. She hid her hands under the table. He made her so angry that she had started to tremble.

As though in solidarity, a hard wave smashed against the window, making her jump. She thought of her mother, tapping the stones in the castle walls in multiples of threes and fives, believing this would keep Owen and the king safe on their voyages. Wil would catch her, take her hands, and say, "Mother, let's go have some tea," or, "Tell me again about the Gold King"—anything to soothe her compulsions. But, whatever her mother was doing now, she was not wishing for her daughter's safety on this treacherous voyage. Her daughter was already dead.

Loom was watching her, trying to see just what it was that had caused that moment of pain in her eyes.

# TWENTY-ONE

ON THE SIXTH DAY OF October, the Southern Isles came into view. Wil was awake and lying backward on her bed so that she could watch them through her window.

Loom was under the unspoken impression that he could keep her here for a week. In one week exactly, she would turn sixteen. Loom had no way of knowing it, of course. Wil had nearly forgotten this herself.

She lowered her data goggles over her eyes, making everything orange. But through fog and distance, they could not tell her the names of any of the cities. The land was a faded purple mark against the sky, hardly real—markings an artist had tried to erase from a map.

The ship sailed alongside the isles without ever seeming to approach. Were they passing them entirely? Loom hadn't been forthcoming about his plans, given that he was banished. Zay even less so. Zay kept her distance except to glare and grumble.

Even as Wil tried to plot her course of escape, the sight of land was a relief. After a week of crystallizing the leaves of small plants, her body was restless, begging her for a greater release, and the strain had taken its toll on her stamina. In the last leg of the trip she'd been listless, fighting to stay awake, forcing down rations that tasted more and more like glue.

With each bite of rations and overripe fruit, she thought of the photographs of Lavean delicacies in Owen's encyclopedia. Roasted boar, seared gazelle, vegetables glazed in honey and clove oils, potatoes shredded, balled, and deep fried with herbs. She wished Loom could have packed something like that.

She had used meals to her advantage, though. Loom had begun to let down his guard, mistaking her weariness for amenability. Maybe he didn't trust her, but she could almost believe that he liked her, and that would make slipping away from him in a crowded port easier.

Watching the mountains through the fog, she was fantasizing about the South's indigenous plants. Large fronds and earthy tubers fat as organs; the relief of crystallizing them would make her shiver as it rolled through her blood like a wave. She hated it as much as she craved it.

To busy herself, she slipped into fresh clothes—a set of deep-violet satins marred by gold vines. The wide collar slumped to the side, revealing her shoulder no matter how many times she tried to fit it back in place. There were trousers to match, with a drawstring waist and legs that billowed out and buried her bare feet. The closet was filled with beautiful satin trousers and matching tops, embellished with gleaming threads. As the ship rocked, they fell against each other like empty bodies. Reds and yellows and a blue more brilliant than the sea itself.

Then she made her way onto the deck. After the hallucinations brought on by the sleep serum, Loom had stopped locking the door, which caused a heated argument between him and Zay that went on for nearly an hour, until the shouting awoke Ada. It surprised Wil how readily Loom came to her defense. She had never been a hostage before, but she would have imagined that captors were ruthless. Or at the very least cold and calculating. But Loom seemed as though he were probing for a reason to trust her.

Since then, Wil had taken to roaming the ship when she thought the parts she wanted to investigate were empty. She'd counted more than a dozen hidden compartments in the walls—all of them locked in some way she couldn't solve. She never found another lifeboat, but in the middle of the ocean an escape on a floating raft was just asking to die at sea. But it was nice to know the layout of his ship, so that she could steal it from him in her quest for Pahn, assuming she couldn't find another way out of the Southern port.

She made her way to the deck. In Northern Arrod, the air would be chilly and dry this time of year, but the Southern Isles were a land of perpetual burning hot summer, and the sunlight was so pure and bright that it was blinding in its cloudless sky. She gathered her hair and twisted it at the nape of her neck.

From out here, the islands were a bit more in focus, but the ship was still bypassing them.

"Beautiful," Loom said. "Aren't they?" He spoke with the wistfulness of a boy standing before the portrait of a dead lover.

She spun to face him. Her garments filled with air and then deflated against her skin.

"I like that color." He nodded to her outfit. "Suits you."

"I figured you wouldn't mind if I wore them," she said. "Have you kidnapped many girls? Is that why there are so many clothes in my cabin?"

He leaned against the railing beside her, unoffended by her slight. "They belonged to my sister. She'll never be seen outside the palace wearing the same thing more than once, so it's the task of some poor servant to lug a trunk of outfits everywhere she goes."

Wil lifted her wrist to study the sleeve. It overlapped her hand in a strangely elegant way. The fabric moved deftly as she twisted her arm one way and the other. The elusive Southern princess.

"But if you like any of her clothes, consider them yours," Loom said. "She won't be back to collect them."

"Do you ever think about them?" Wil said. "Your family."

He looked at her sidelong. "You ask a lot of questions for

someone who doesn't answer many of them."

She sighed and turned for the stairs. "Come get me when we've docked."

He snared her elbow, spinning her to face him. "I'll trade you," he said. "A question for a question."

She shook free of his grasp, but he was already letting go. "Fine."

"Do you ever think about your mother?" he said.

She searched him with her eyes, trying to find the menace of his intentions, but he only seemed interested. She didn't answer.

He leaned back against the railing and dropped his shoulders, like asking the question was a weight on him. "I was two when my mother died," he said. "That was fifteen years ago. I don't remember her at all. No sense letting myself miss her, really. I don't know what sort of person she was. Maybe she would be glad I'm banished from her kingdom."

He focused on the clean blue sky as though trying to throw the words into all that nothingness.

Wil didn't press him, though she was curious. So little was known about the Southern royals, even to her own father, and here she was close enough to touch one of them.

She lowered her data goggles as they got closer to land. *Landmass*, they read, followed by coordinates that answered none of her questions. "What is this place?"

Loom nodded to the horizon. "That's Messalin in the distance, about ten minutes by rowboat. The capital city of

Cannolay is further north—we passed it on the way—but we can't go there. My father has ordered for me to be killed upon sight. There's quite a bounty for my corpse, I hear." After a pause, he added, "Go on, you can say it."

She looked at him. "What?"

"I tried to kill my father. I deserve to have a bounty on my head."

Wil stared at the water. She thought she saw Owen sinking in the clear depths, his gold hair like fire around him, and she clutched at the railing to keep from diving in to save him.

"I wasn't going to say that," she murmured. She forced herself to look away from the water and stood up straight. "If we can't go to any of the ports, where are you taking us?"

"A palace," Loom said, and he seemed to indulge in annoying her with his vague details. Wil knew the Southern Isles to have only one palace, and there it was in the far distance, glittering against a mountainside, its windows shining like bits of sun as the ship sailed past.

Zay was doing the steering, Wil supposed. It wasn't long before they reached land, on an island of sand and boulders. From where Wil stood, it looked completely barren.

Perhaps this was all a trap, Wil thought, and Loom planned to imprison her here and use her powers as he pleased. She began scheming a way to overpower him and hijack the control room.

Loom hopped over the railing and began tying the ship to the bedraggled remains of an old dock.

Cautiously, she followed after him, watching his hands especially. He and Zay were quick with sleep serum. After Zay managed to put her out on the dock, Wil paid close attention and saw that they each kept pouches of powders and herbs sewn inside their sleeves. She could see the thin, nearly invisible threads that held them in place. Clever.

Loom walked beside her, keeping enough of a distance that she let herself look away from him for a moment and analyze her surroundings.

Several yards up from the shore, the sand faded to crushed stones, all of it glittering in the midmorning sun.

This place was not an island but a painting of an island. Something an artist had dreamed.

Her escape plan sank like a stone in her stomach.

The sea breeze had given way to warmth, and she shrugged the cloak from her shoulders and let it drape in the crook of her arm.

"Beautiful, isn't it?" Loom said.

"Yes," Wil said. Northern Arrod sat on the water, but its shore was all cityscapes and homes; there was no white sand to whisper under her feet like this. But she was already recalculating her escape route. The mainland was in the distance, too far away to swim. She could steal Loom's ship—the electric engines were fueled partly by sunlight, and there would be enough of that to get her to another port in neutral territory, where she could abandon it and be gone before Loom could catch up.

But this plan would take patience. Loom was beginning to warm to her, but he knew she could fight, and Zay's trust would be impossible to earn besides. They would be guarding that ship with their lives.

"A hundred years ago, the royal family lived here," Loom went on. "Before a great wind brought the tides up higher than the castle walls. My great-grandparents barely made it out with their lives. The castle was abandoned. The palace in Cannolay was built by the emperor of the Eastern Isles as a gift, to acknowledge their alliance."

Aside from some green peeking out in the crevices, there was nothing but stone and sand as far as Wil could see. She sat on a large rock and began unlacing her boots.

Loom was several yards ahead before he realized her absence and backtracked. "What are you doing?"

She slipped out of her boots. "Venture a guess." She tied the laces together, hung them over her shoulder, stood, and dusted the dirt from the violet satin. All else condemned, she loved the way the fabric felt on her bare hands. The fashions of the Southern Isles seemed to value comfort and function over form. The sea breeze filled the loose sleeves, offering reprieve from the punishing heat. The trouser legs were smooth and soft, but loose enough to offer adequate range of motion in a fight.

"You know . . ." He made a point of walking slower to keep up with her evasive pace. "It was mostly a silent journey out here. It's nice to hear your voice again."

Her chest swelled and dropped with a sigh. "Don't do that."

"What?"

"Play nice with me. We both know what this is. It's a hostage situation."

He chuckled. "It's clear to me you aren't hostage material."

Wil only looked at him in silence as she stood.

"We have more in common than you dare to admit, you know," he said.

"I have more in common with the king of Arrod than with you." She breezed past him.

"How are you able to walk barefoot on the stones like that? Isn't it painful?" There was concern in his voice.

She wasn't about to answer his question. In deceiving her, he had forfeited his right to get to know her. Her childhood spent barefoot climbing walls and trees, running to hide from her instructors. The years of calluses protecting her soles like armor. The family she still missed and loved, even if she had been cast out of it forever. The very same family Loom wanted to kill. She walked in silence.

The castle appeared to be made of sand at first.

In the distance it sparkled and shone, golden as the grains along the shore. But, as they trod closer, Wil could see that there was greenery on this island after all, in the form of weeds that snaked through the castle's stone walls. And the castle itself was not made of sand, but rather covered in it. Half buried in a dune, in fact, on the north side.

She had never seen such a thing. It was a relic. As though something divine had reached through the sky and planted it here in the sand and the stones for safekeeping.

They walked across an old drawbridge, its chains broken, forming a wooden mouth that was forever agape.

The castle doors, also wooden, were faded down to the bare boards. But Wil could see faint traces of etched patterns worn thin by the elements. She wanted to study them, but later when she was alone. She would not reward Loom with her interest in his broken castle.

Inside, the stone floors had been swept clean, but there were still traces of sand that had once filled this place. The island had tried to swallow it whole, but it stood proud come what may. With that, Wil was startled to realize that she liked this place.

She turned to Loom, her eyes dulled over. She thought that she was concealing herself, but from his gaze he seemed to recognize her sense of wonder. "Where do I sleep?" she asked.

"Anywhere you want. There are a dozen chambers up the stairs. It's never been outfitted for electricity, I'm afraid, but there's a water pump."

"You'll let me choose my own room? You'd grant that kindness to your prisoner?"

He didn't flinch at her biting tone. "You're not my prisoner, Wil. You're only here to help. Today we rest, and tomorrow we'll take a smaller boat to the mainland so you can see firsthand why I brought you here."

"I know why."

"No." His tone was eager. "Until you have seen Messalin, you don't know."

Wil knew Messalin in name only. It was a spot on a map in the atlas. She wanted to know what a tiny city in the outskirts of Cannolay meant in the grand scheme of the world, and she hated that Loom was the one to show her the things she'd wondered about as a child.

She wouldn't give him the satisfaction of knowing this. She moved for the staircase on the far end of the empty grand entryway, and turned when she felt him staring at her.

"What now?" she asked, gripping the banister with one hand.

"It's just—" He canted his head. "In those satins, in this castle, you look like royalty."

What game was he trying to play? They were enemies, through and through, and now that he had her on his island and the clock was ticking, he wanted to charm her into staying for his cause.

It was not going to work.

"I'm taking a very long nap," she said. "I haven't had a proper rest in a week. Wake me when it's time for dinner."

He bowed with a flourish. "Of course, Your Majesty."

She chose the last room at the end of the hall, with a large arched window that overlooked the ocean. The glass was filthy and cracked, but when she threw it open, the distant mountains of Cannolay were not visible. All she saw was that brilliantly bright sea.

It was a large chamber, and Wil could tell that it had once been beautiful. It was made of smooth white stone. The doorways and windows were trimmed by carved wood, painted a chipping aquamarine.

There was a fireplace with a wooden mantle that went up to the ceiling, with carvings of steerwolves stalking through heavy vines, painted over in that same chipped aquamarine.

And throughout the walls, vines snaked through the cracks, heart-shaped leaves twitching in the breeze through the open window.

The bed was large, the mattress stuffed with feathers. The bedding was orange, crisp and new. No way was it a survivor of some century-old flood. Someone had tended to it recently.

So this was where the banished prince lived. Quite nice, all things considered.

Wil listened at the door. Loom was in the kitchen, she'd guess by all the clattering.

She moved to the window. The sea breeze threw back her hair as she leaned forward to survey the structure. She counted the shelves and protruding bricks, charting her path, and then she began her descent.

She landed soundlessly in the sand. Her boots were slung over her shoulder, still tied at the laces. She wriggled into her gloves as she walked.

The sand erased her tracks, but the landscape provided little cover. There were no trees this close to the water. When the ship came into view, she crouched low behind a shallow dune, and watched.

Zay swan-dived off the deck and into the sea, bobbing to the surface with her face to the sun. Her hair was down now, floating around her like kelp. She dipped underwater again and then emerged at the shore. Trying to relieve herself from the punishing heat, Wil supposed.

Wil pressed herself more against the sand and stayed silent. After Zay stood and wrung the water from her hair, she walked several yards down the shoreline, to where a rowboat was bobbing on its rope. From there she extracted a fishing pole. Wil tensed, readying herself to run.

Zay climbed into the boat and rowed herself from the shore. She didn't go far. Only just enough to cast out a line. It made sense. Apart from rations, this island provided few meal options.

Wil had counted all thirty seconds it took Zay to row to her current spot. Keeping low, she crept toward the ship. She waded into the water, moving slowly to avoid making any sound, and then climbed the rope ladder that was draped over the ship's north-facing side, out of Zay's view.

Even as she made her way belowdecks, Wil didn't allow herself to breathe a sigh of relief. Never celebrate a victory until it's a victory, Owen had often said.

The engine was still running. It was nearly silent, its vibrations slight, but Wil could feel the rush of cool air blasting through the vent in the ceiling. Odd that Zay would leave it on, Wil thought. She didn't seem like the type who would forget.

For the second time on this sojourn, Wil found herself in the engine room. She closed the door and latched it—just in case.

She sat at the stool before the control panels and quickly did her best to learn what each one was for. The data goggles helped; because they were a port novelty, they had a comprehensive database of modern ships.

A digital screen showed her a detailed map of her coordinates. The nearest port was in Cannolay, the South's capital. But it was too close, Wil decided. Best to venture east, where she hadn't searched, and where Pahn was rumored to be.

She pressed her gloved palm to a glowing green button, and felt the rumble of the anchor retracting into the body of the ship.

"This will work," she muttered, grasping the wheel. It was shaped like an anchor. "This has to work." She bared her teeth, tugged at the wheel, and began to steer. Her stomach bubbled with nervous excitement. The ship lurched back from the shore. From one of the panel's screens, Wil watched Loom's island drawing back into the distance. She turned the wheel to face the horizon, and just that quickly, she was gone.

An hour passed before she felt confident with the controls. The ship did most of the work; she felt a kinship with it, as though they were partners that had escaped together.

She ran her palm across the length of the panel, smiling, then laughing.

"No one's following us now," Wil told the ship. All Zay and Loom had was that rowboat. Zay could row to the mainland, buy or steal a ship, Wil supposed, but there would be no catching up now.

A sound interrupted her thoughts. Small, soft, like a breath. Her blood went cold. She stood, pressed her ear to the door. The sound went on, shuffling. It couldn't be a person, she reasoned. A mouse? She hadn't seen any on the voyage out here, didn't even know if mice took up residence in ships.

Heart pounding, she opened the door just enough to peer out. What she saw was worse than a mouse. It was worse, even, than Zay wielding a blade—or wielding ten thousand blades and a hundred flaming torches.

The figure on the other side of the door smiled at her. A sweet, innocent smile that lit up his sleepy eyes.

Ada.

# TWENTY-TWO

"WHERE DID YOU COME FROM?" Wil asked, as though having an answer would somehow better her situation.

Ada was little more than two years old, small for his age, and very bright.

He'd been sucking on his finger, but he extracted it from his mouth with a wet plopping sound and pointed to the cabin beside him.

The ship lilted just slightly, and Ada staggered sideways but didn't fall. He was used to living at sea, had probably learned to walk here.

At least one of them was calm, Wil thought.

Ada walked forward, pushing the door open and inviting himself into the engine room. Wil jumped back to avoid touching him. And in that small gesture, a thousand new reasons plagued her. Ada was a child. Children needed to be cared for. Needed to be held, fed, changed. Ada was a crier at night— Wil knew this well—dependent upon his mother's singing and rocking him to sleep. Wil couldn't do any of these things, even though she thought she might be halfway decent at them under normal circumstances.

Even with her gloves, she wouldn't dare risk it. A simple brush of her skin and he'd be dead.

"Ada." Wil knelt before him. He fell to a seated position, playing with a length of rope he'd found on the floor. It was dyed green and vaguely resembled a bear made of knots and frays. "Do you know where your mother is?" She spoke in Lavean, even though she was fairly certain by his past responses and his time spent in port towns that he could understand Nearsh.

He shook his head. He was unconcerned, petting at the fray of the bear's paw.

"Do you know where your father is?" Desperately, Wil considered the idea that she could leave Ada with his father. Even if it meant returning to the Southern Isles, she stood a chance at avoiding Zay and Loom. She would likely have to abandon the ship, but there would be some other way out, surely.

Ada shook his head again, his dark hair spilling over his forehead.

"Is he in Messalin? Cannolay? Is he still alive?"

He only went on playing with the rope bear, not even bothering to look up.

"What about your grandparents?" Wil pressed.

Ada regarded her with a puckered, curious expression. His blank eyes said he'd never heard that word, much less considered the possibility that his mother might have parents of her own.

"Who else takes care of you?"

"Loom."

"There's no one else?"

Ada didn't answer, which was, in itself, an answer.

Somewhere in this exchange, Wil's adrenaline had died down. Now all she felt was resignation. "There's no one else," she echoed. Doubtless, Ada was a wanderer, but for all the people he had seen, he belonged only to one.

Ada crawled forward and tried to get into Wil's lap, and she moved away from him. "No," she said, sharply. "You can't do that. You can't ever do that."

She saw Zay in the fierce look Ada gave her just then. He had given her the gift of his trust and acceptance, and she had thrown it back at him. There weren't many left in the world who would accept a monster like her, and he seemed to know it.

She slumped forward, her fingers tangling in her hair. Ada had no one in the world, save his mother and Loom. She tried to think. There were sometimes orphanages near port towns, her brother had told her, to house the children so frequently abandoned during times of famine or war. And perhaps she could pay one of them to keep Ada safe—just for a little while, until she found Pahn and returned for him.

Ada dropped onto his side and let himself tumble with the rocking of the ship, breathing out a little giggle as the motion took him. Wil didn't know if he was too innocent to be wary of her, or if her week on this ship had made her an automatic presence in his tiny world, or if, for some inexplicable reason, he just liked her. But he couldn't have guessed at the plans she was trying to rationalize.

She hated herself for considering leaving him alone in an orphanage full of strangers, his mother nowhere to be seen. But as horrible as it would be for Ada, it would be even more so for Zay, who was a different thing entirely when she tended to her son. She would do anything to reach him. Swim the seas to have him back.

Even if Zay had poisoned her with her own sleep serum, even if she was brash and wholly unpleasant, Wil could take no pleasure in separating her from her child. In truth, she admired her ferocity. She imagined her own mother would have been the same way if she had raised her children as wanderers in such a treacherous world, rather than in a castle.

Wil lay on her stomach, chin propped by her gloved fist. "There must be some way I can return you unnoticed," she said. Ada didn't know what this meant, nor did he care, and Wil laughed at the fun he seemed to be having.

By nightfall, Wil had already begun steering for Loom's uncharted island. Ada was mercifully cooperative for most of the venture, especially when she sliced an apple into thin coins for him—something her nanny had done when Wil was small.

He stuck them to his cheeks, and covered his eyes with them, exhausting all the ways he could entertain himself before eating them. The ship was home to him, as was the sea, and Wil carried about entertaining him as though nothing was amiss.

It wasn't until sunset that Ada stood before the circular window in the control room and began to whimper. Maybe he thought his mother was out there buried in the waves, Wil supposed.

"Ada." She slid from the stool and knelt on the floor behind him. "Your mother is on the island waiting for you, and we'll be there soon."

He looked over his shoulder at her, tears pooling in the divot of his upper lip.

She thought of her own mother before she could brace herself for the weight of such sadness. And she began to hum—if only to drown the image out—one of her mother's old shanty songs. The humming turned to singing, about a man who turned everything he touched to gold, until it had destroyed him.

Ada's sobs faded away as he listened. After that, she sang the one about the singing wolf, and the boy whose heart had been stolen from him so that he'd grown up with a stone in his chest, always listening for its beating.

He didn't try to climb into her lap that time. He had accepted the distance that had to remain between them.

Somewhere in the fifth song, as the moon spread its broken light upon the dark sea, he drifted to sleep.

Wil reached forward and swept her gloved hand through his feathery hair, watching the way it fell back into place, as though he were too perfect a thing to be rumpled.

Though her castle had been full of children, she was the youngest one. She had never seen a child this small when they were sleeping, had never seen what a gift it was to be so young, in these quieter times when the eyelashes barely fluttered and the lips barely pursed, and all else was still. The sun had never burned his shoulders, and his hands didn't know the calluses a sword hilt would give them. His muscles had never ached after a long day. How long was this window exactly? Too small to be remembered, she supposed. Eventually he would grow to be like the rest of the world, when imperfection and scars and regrets became inevitable.

She had the fleeting thought that this calm could last forever, if only she could find a way to hold on to it. Maybe that was a thought mothers had.

Wil had never thought about being a mother herself. It had always been something faraway to decide upon, when she was older. There had always been too much that she wanted to do first. And now, nothing viable could grow in her cursed body anyway, even if she had all the time in the world. There was no faraway someday.

"You won't remember today," Wil whispered to him, as he tilted his face into her gloved palm. "But I want you to know that I will."

# TWENTY-THREE

WIL WOKE ADA ONCE THE island was in sight. Even in the darkness, she could see the broken castle like a scar against the night sky. It gave off no light. There were no signs of life on the island at all, and Wil wondered if Zay had gone to the mainland to find a boat. Maybe they'd already left. But then Wil saw the billowing of smoke from one of the castle's chimneys. Relief flooded her. Returning Ada to an empty island would have been an entirely different sort of problem.

She pressed the button that anchored the ship as they reached the shore. She had counted the twenty-five seconds it took for the anchor to retract. It would add to her escape time, but she could manage it if she moved fast.

Ada followed her like a loyal gosling, giddy to know that he was once again home. He'd made a little song out of the word *mama*, which she sang at a near whisper.

Ada didn't need help descending the ship's ladder—he'd been climbing that most of his life—and he bounded ahead of her, paddling easily through the shallow water and already running by the time he'd leaped onto the sand.

"Wait," she whispered, and he spun to face her.

"Ada, you know where home is, right?"

Bouncing and chewing on his finger, he pointed to the castle.

"Then run home," she told him. "Run really fast, okay? Don't stop for anything."

Whether Ada truly comprehended or whether he just happened to have the same idea, Wil couldn't be sure. Either way he raced for the castle.

He would be safe now, she knew. Her own fate was less certain until she could get out of here. She hoisted herself onto the ladder, climbing as fast as the shifting ropes would allow. She would only need a minute more, maybe less, and then she could be gone.

She ventured one last look after Ada, but he was already long gone.

She barely registered the searing, whistling breath of a sound, before the hurled dagger landed in her calf.

It tore easily through her flesh, grating the bone. Her spine went rigid with pain even before her mind could register it.

Someone was screaming. The stars spun, and her body hit the sea with a hard splash. Water rushed into her open mouth and she could taste her own blood in it as she pushed herself to the surface, reeling, hazy.

Arms scooped her up from the water, and she knew that it would be Loom even before she heard his breathy chuckle. "You're all right. I've got you."

She glared at him. "Seems to be your only goal in life these days, getting me." She wrested out of his arms, landing back in the shallows with a splash and trudging up onto the shore.

Dizzy, she sat at the water's edge and drew her leg up to inspect the damage.

The satin was already bled through, dripping from a tear in the fabric. The knife—or whatever had shredded her—was gone, leaving a fierce crescendo of pain in its stead.

She hooked her fingers into the tear at her pant leg and ripped it apart, trying to fashion it into a bandage. Her arms were trembling from a pain the rest of her couldn't seem to register, and she commanded herself to be steady.

"Here." Loom's voice, and then his hands taking over the task for her. She watched as he fashioned the scraps around the black wound. Watched, too, how the blood seeped through uninhibited, covering her skin and his.

His hands were slick with it, so dark, as though he'd reached into the night sky, and its innards had clung to his skin.

"I brought him back," Wil snapped. "You didn't have to throw a knife at me."

"I didn't," he said.

Zay emerged behind him. She was clutching Ada to her chest. Her eyes were ablaze, her lips pressed tight.

The night grew darker. She heard a strange, rough wind, and realized it was her own rapid and shallow breathing.

"Hey." Loom's voice was loud, and Wil realized that she was no longer on her feet and somehow the ground was under her back. Loom grasped her chin, searching her gaze. The image of him blurred and doubled. "Look at me," he demanded. But her eyes wouldn't focus.

He lifted her again. "Hells, Zay, she's bleeding out. You struck her artery."

"She struck mine," Zay replied.

Wil couldn't make out Loom's shouted response; it sounded underwater. She struggled to free herself from his grasp. "I can walk," she insisted. But her feet never seemed to reach the sand. The pair of them went on arguing, Zay's tone one of indifference, and Loom's of fury.

In a blink she was on the hard floor, beside a burning fire. She lay on her stomach, the wound at the back of her calf facing up. She pushed herself upright by her elbows and saw her own skin, pale as bone, as sweat and seawater splashed from her forehead in heavy drops. To stay conscious, she watched the bottles and pouches Loom wielded.

A liquid hissed when it touched her flesh, and with that sound she knew what he was planning. He was going to disinfect the wound, and then he was going to cauterize it.

Zay and Loom had been arguing, but their voices felt miles away, until Loom told her, "Just go away, then, if you're determined to be useless."

"Fine."

Ahead of them, Zay started up the stairs, petting Ada's hair, her kisses to the crown of his head making him cackle. "You smell like apples," she told him. She did not look back.

Wil wadded the cuff of her sleeve between her teeth. "Don't give me any warning before you do it."

He didn't warn her. He pressed the burning blade to her skin, and the cry Wil let out was not her own. It was the stunned wail her mother had made on the night she learned that her children were dead.

Several short, sharp compressions later, it was done. Loom tried to give her something for the pain, but she refused it. She hated the fog that had clouded her senses the last time. She hated how vulnerable it left her.

She was lolling though still conscious after her skin had been welded shut. The pain filled her vision with roiling stars, and she was certain that she had lost a few moments of herself, but the crescendo of it had passed, and eventually, she was able to pull herself upright and lean against the wall.

"Who is she to you?" she asked Loom, who was sitting across from her. The firelight burnished his skin, made his eyes as jeweled as the things she touched. He was so infuriatingly lovely.

"What are you talking about?" he said, and Wil realized he must have thought her delirious.

"Zay."

A smile melted some of the edge from his expression. "There isn't a word for what we are to each other. I should know. I speak quite a few languages."

Wil was breathing hard. She closed her eyes in a long blink. "Ada's lucky to have someone willing to throw knives on his behalf," she said.

"You brought him back unharmed," Loom said. "So she merely threw one of my knives. Not her jeweler's knife. That one would have gone clean through the bone. Really, I think she's starting to like you."

Wil laughed. It came out as little more than a breath. The room was turning blurry again. "I'm glad."

She must have lost consciousness, because the next thing she knew, she was being laid onto the satin sheets of a bed. The window was open from her earlier escape, the sound of the rustling sea taunting her with the freedom she'd had for a few precious hours. She would still be out there, if not for her nettling conscience, which she cursed just then. It was a weakness her father would have hated her for. He would be right. Zay and Loom had held her captive on that very ship against her will, and she owed them no loyalty. She could have kept Ada as their penance, shown them just what it meant to take someone away from their life.

But she had brought him back. Whole and happy and unharmed. She did not know whether this made her weaker than her captors, or stronger.

"Sleep on your stomach," Loom said. "It'll hurt less."

Her body sank into the softness of the mattress and her traitorous eyes felt heavy, but she didn't close them.

"That was an impressive escape, right up until you were thwarted by a two-year-old." He was fitting a thin sheet over her, leaving her leg uncovered. "Zay was set to steal a ship off the mainland to go after you, but I knew you'd bring him back."

"Are you an oracle as well as a prince?"

"No." He leaned over her and peeled the damp hair away from her face; his fingertips sweeping the back of her neck evoked a warm flutter in her chest. "I'm just observant."

He was gone for a few minutes, and when he returned he pressed a cold wet leaf to her forehead, and another to her cheek. They clung to her skin. "What is that?" Her voice felt too close, as though she'd spoken into her own skull.

"Lyster. It's for fevers."

"You know every plant, don't you?" She rested her cheek against her forearm. "Every root, every tree of this place."

"Yes." His voice was a warm song. "And every breath and every heartbeat too."

Without meaning to, she smiled. It was so quiet here, so calm. The satin glided against her with each menial shift.

When he stood to leave, she reached out and grabbed his wrist.

Just as there was something in her blood that made her deadly, there was something else that called to him, something that she could bury when her defenses were strong, but not tonight. Not while darkness burned away the edges of the world, and she could hear the absence of all that she'd lost, and she had never felt so alone.

Again she felt his fingers move through her hair.

Outside, the ocean shifted and rustled like millions of sheets of paper. She drifted to sleep, listening to their indecipherable stories.

The shrill cry of a gull woke her.

Wil opened her eyes to find that she'd spent the night facing the open window; the sky was cloudy and dark with a coming rain. Her head was cradled in her arms, and when she stretched, a stabbing pain cut her movement short. It shot up the length of her spine, down her arms, into her fingertips. It momentarily paralyzed her lungs, her heart.

Loom had made good on his promise not to give her anything for the pain, and now with some bitterness she wished she hadn't been so stubborn.

Laboriously, she looked over her shoulder at her leg. She was still wearing the torn and bloody trousers, severed at the knee on one side. A cloth was draped over the wound, fragrant with something sweet and minty that did nothing to mask the stench of burned flesh.

She braced herself and sat upright, drawing her knee to her chest. Metallic stars swam a funnel around her vision.

The cloth fell to the sheets, and she picked it up, inspecting it. She could identify the mintlemint by smell, and serlot oil with its sandy little seeds—common for mixing poultices and pastes—but the rest was foreign to her.

She made herself look at the wound, where the purpled shadow of Loom's dagger ran vertically down the back of her leg, like a seam on a doll. Loom had touched the blade to her skin in four rapid spurts, but each time had been in the exact same spot, and he had angled the blade along the grain, which would reduce the scarring greatly. She could see his attention to detail in that burning outline. Even Gerdie would be impressed, and he should know best; he had been tasked with repairing her all their lives.

"Morning." Loom was standing in the doorway, amusement in his slight smile. He held up a tray with an ornate crystal cup and a pitcher. "I thought you'd be thirsty."

"You left my window open," she mumbled, and pushed herself upright.

He put the glass in her hands. "You want to escape? Give it a try. I'll give you a five-minute head start."

"Chivalrous." She drank the water greedily, some of it spilling and dripping from her chin. She had never been so thirsty.

Loom sat on the edge of the mattress, just as the first rumble of thunder sounded outside. "How are you feeling?"

"Like I should be a day closer to finding Pahn instead of stuck here." She handed the emptied glass back to Loom.

He glanced at her leg, then to the cloth now lying on the

mattress beside it. "I predict you'll be up and back at it in no time. Which is a good thing, because we're going to Messalin tomorrow."

Wil stared at him. "It really means that much to you."

"I thought that should be obvious."

"No," Wil said. "Your kingdom, I mean. You really would do anything to try and save it."

He folded the cloth and set it on the nightstand. "That place—it's in my blood."

"It's in your father's blood, too," Wil pointed out, her tone gentle. "Maybe he's got his own plan for it."

"My father cares only for his pride," Loom said. "A kingdom is more than a mass of land. It's more than imports and exports. There are people living—dying—in the shadows of a mountain palace where my father spends his days giving orders to servants and grooming my sister to be just like him." He was talking faster now, as though the words were a flood he had been holding in. "I can't explain it; I know you're not from my world, that you should have no reason to care, but I *know* you'll understand if I can show you. I know it."

"Because you have a sense about me." Wil rested her elbow to the knee of her good leg, offering a sympathetic smile. "Even if I were exactly as you hoped and dreamed, I can't work miracles. I can't fix a kingdom. That sort of thing takes generations. Resources. Council. It will take more than just a banished prince and a girl with a curse."

Loom shrugged. "Prove me wrong, then."

"Suppose I do just that," Wil said. "Will you still take me to Pahn?"

"I always honor my word." After a beat, he offered his hand.

Wil stared at it a moment, and then she took it in hers, offering a firm shake to confirm their deal.

"You'll still take me at my word after I stole your ship?" Wil withdrew her hand, pretending she didn't want to savor the warmth of his grasp. It had been so long since she could touch any living thing without fear. She still didn't trust this odd immunity of Loom's, though every muscle within her remembered how it had felt when he scooped her out of the water. Even through the pain and the anger, even though his glibness had infuriated her, just knowing that someone could still touch her made her feel like she was still a part of this world. She was still human.

"It could have been a clean getaway," Loom said. "You could have turned Ada to diamond, then chopped him into bits and sold the shards to pay your way. That's what Zay kept screaming you would do."

"She really thought I would do that?"

"Try to understand, most people in her life have betrayed her. She can be . . . wary."

"Same could be said for you," Wil told him.

"I'm profusely wary," he said, though his easy grin spoke to the contrary. "Especially of you. And perhaps it will be my downfall, but I'm glad our paths crossed."

"Wish I could say the same," Wil mumbled, and averted her eyes so they wouldn't betray her lie.

It was quiet for a while, and then Loom said, "Wil?"

"Yes?"

"What is it, exactly, you are expecting Pahn to do for you?"

"I thought that was obvious. I want him to tell me why this is happening to me, and how to be rid of it." She studied his grim expression. "Don't tell me you're one of those who doesn't believe marvelers are legitimate."

"I don't need to believe anything," Loom said. "I have seen for myself and I know full well what marvelers can do. But— there will be a cost."

"I'll pay it."

His laugh was caustic. "You don't know what it will be."

Wil shook her head. "It doesn't matter." Whatever the cost, it wouldn't be more than what this curse had already cost her. Though she braced herself for it, the reminder of her family knocked her off guard. The way that Owen had stared at her as he died, as though he had always known he would one day give his life for hers. And her father casting her away. Her mother back at the castle covering the mirrors and whispering mourning songs. Gerdie, whom she could never face again unless she were fixed.

She raised her chin, hoping that Loom had not been able to read any of this on her face.

He didn't say another word.

# TWENTY-FOUR

FOR MOST OF THE DAY, Wil slept fitfully. She dreamed that she made it back to Arrod, and that she climbed the castle wall to enter through her bedroom window. Only all the windows had been replaced by mirrors draped in black gossamer, and the gossamer ensnared her until she was drowning.

The dead were not allowed to return.

By the time she managed to free herself from the tangles of her nightmare, it was evening. Her leg still ached, though it was more manageable.

Limping to keep her weight on her good leg, she made her way to the chamber's bath. She bathed carefully, and changed into the white satin tunic and trousers that were left folded by the sink, presumably by Loom.

She didn't bother with her gloves or her boots. With all the sand and stone, there was precious little out here to be her victim. For that reason alone, she liked this place. Not that she would say as much aloud.

The castle was quiet and still, and Wil was grateful there was no one to witness the pathetic way she hobbled down the steps, trying to keep her weight off her bad leg.

She found Loom by a fire he'd built along the shore, turning caught fish over the flames.

"Hey," he said, glancing as she positioned herself beside him. "I was going to come up in a little bit and see if you were hungry."

"Starved," she admitted. She had the vague recollection that he'd been to her room and set a plate of toast and fruit on the nightstand, but she'd been too tired to reach for it.

He handed her a plate of freshly cooked fish. The plate, like the glass from earlier, was finely etched crystal. "How's your leg? I'd tell you to stay off it, but I'd have better luck telling the clouds not to cover the sun."

"Healing nicely," Wil said. "You might have considered a career in medicine, rather than regicide."

He laughed. "Why not aspire toward both?"

After she'd eaten, Wil rolled her satin trousers up past her knees and lay back and let the fleeting sunlight touch her as it wished. She kept her knee bent to protect the healing flesh from the sand, but it didn't hurt nearly as much now.

"Land of eternal summers," Loom said, and lay beside her.

She shielded her eyes with her hand and glanced at him but said nothing.

"People used to travel to the Southern Isles for leisure," he went on. "It used to have many allies. The East, the ever-neutral West, and, yes, even the famously arrogant North. But my father is too proud for the good of his kingdom. Under his rule, the past two decades have seen us become hermits. Completely self-contained with growing poverty, all because he refuses for us to have any codependence. I used to think he just didn't see it, but he does."

Wil closed her eyes and angled her chin up toward the sunset. Shades of orange and red bloomed behind her eyelids. "Who can ever understand kings?" she muttered.

"This is going to be an ugly war," he said. "And your kingdom will have more kills to boast when it's through. I just hope it can end quickly."

*Your kingdom.*

"What is it?" Loom asked. Wil was sure that she had not let her face betray any of her worrying, but Loom was able to read her.

She heard him shift in the sand, most assuredly watching her. She draped her arm over her eyes, shielding them from the sun, and now, from him. "I think it's foolish of you to hang any hopes on me," she said. "I think that if you want to save your kingdom, you should come up with a better plan. One that employs logic and strength, not hope. Hope is not a weapon."

"Now I really wonder what your story is," Loom said. "If you think that hope isn't a weapon. Everything is a weapon."

"That's weak logic," Wil countered. "If everything were a weapon, we'd all be matched and the world would be a stalemate."

"Not everyone is strong," he said.

"I'm beginning to think you just like to argue." She sighed, arching her back in a stretch against the warm sand.

She heard footsteps shuffling toward them, Ada's contented giggling.

"Save any dinner for us?" Zay asked. Her presence sent a cold dread through Wil's blood. She didn't fear that Zay would harm her again—that knife throw had been justified, and doubtful such luck from an amateur fighter could be repeated. But no, it was something else. Wil was thinking of what Loom had told her, about Zay screaming that Wil might kill her son and sell the crystal shards of him to pay her way. She had believed herself a monster from the day she turned the vendor to ruby, and she had gone to such lengths to hide it, but Zay saw right through her.

Loom sat up, and Wil raised her arm from her eyes to watch him.

Zay grabbed at a tuft of his hair and kissed his forehead before dropping beside him. He clapped a hand around her shoulder and squeezed her against him. Their easy affection made Wil bristle.

"Ada." Zay patted her lap, and her little boy settled into the embrace. She gave him a hug so tight that he struggled to free himself, reaching for the plate. He was so used to being adored that he thought nothing of turning down affection; there was plenty of love for him to squander. Right now, he was only interested in food.

Zay didn't offer Wil a glance, but that lack of acknowledgment was also pointed, making it evident that she and Loom had come to some sort of understanding on this matter.

Under the relentless Southern heat, Loom eased out of his shirt, and Wil rolled her eyes away. She paid little mind to the conversation Zay and Loom lapsed into. They were speaking in Lavean now—something to do with witches and the mountain palace.

Wil scarcely cared what they had to say, until she heard the word Loom used to address Zay.

"I keep saying your temper will be the death of you one day, *ansuh*."

My wife.

She opened her eyes at that, and propped herself on her elbows.

And now she saw the proof on his upper left arm: two overlapping moons, accented in shimmering silver. A perfect match for Zay's.

Loom saw the recognition in her eyes. "Ah," he said. "I knew you spoke Lavean. I was wondering if you'd ever let on."

Her frustration only deepened at that.

"Then why"—she made her voice cool—"did you almost kiss me?"

Zay shoved Loom so hard he toppled sideways into the sand, prompting him to laugh.

Zay sneered at him, but then she laughed too. "Eternal hells. You really do have a lust for bad decisions," she said.

Neither of them seemed inclined to offer any sort of explanation, so Wil nodded to the toddler in Zay's lap and asked, "Is he yours, then?"

"Ada is nobody's but mine." Zay's jaw clenched.

"All right," Loom said to Zay. "You've had dinner. Isn't it about time for you to go someplace that isn't here?"

"Come on, Ada," Zay said. "Wouldn't want any of Loom's life choices to influence you." She rose to her feet, her son in tow, and left. But not before casting Wil a disdainful glower.

Once she was gone, Loom inched closer. In the fading light, his eyes seemed bigger and darker. But it was their sincerity that did Wil in over and again; the way he pleaded for her to believe every little word he said.

"It isn't what you think," he began. "Zay is the daughter of my father's high guard. As a reward for her father's loyalty, she was to be queen when I inherited the kingdom. We were promised to each other before we were born."

Wil eyed him skeptically. "But she has a child. He isn't yours?"

"He isn't," Loom said.

"But he must have a father," Wil said. "Where is he?"

"The father lives outside Cannolay, in Lamponay. The slums," Loom said. "He came to Zay's father and asked for her hand in marriage and was laughed from the palace. Instead, our wedding was pushed up. We had no choice in the matter. We pretended Ada was mine, for appearance's sake. But when I was exiled, my father wanted to keep him in the palace. So Zay told him the truth—that he was just a bastard. Given the bounty on my head, it would be unsafe for Ada if anyone believed he were my heir now."

Wil lay back and stared at the graying sky. "She wanted out of the palace that badly?"

"She never cared about being queen," he went on. "When I was banished from the kingdom, my father would have arranged for someone of her class to marry her and raise Ada as his own. But instead, she chose to follow me here. It's no sparkling palace in a mountainside, but it's home."

"Don't know why you bothered to keep it a secret," Wil said. "You could have just told me so."

"Says the girl who buries her own secrets deeper than the sand." His smile was warm in the dying embers of daylight. "Don't take anything snide she says to heart. Zay has had a difficult go of things. Life in a palace isn't as easy as you'd suspect."

"Oh no?" Wil raised an eyebrow. "It's not all dress

fittings and comportment?"

From Loom's hesitant expression, he couldn't decide if she was being serious. That made her smug. He couldn't draw everything out of her, after all.

# TWENTY-FIVE

THE NORTHERN KING'S ILLNESS CAME about all at once in the morning, and had turned dire by nightfall.

The state of him—sallow, perspiring, and groaning—only agitated Baren's fraying state. More than ever, he muttered about his ghosts, and began to adopt his mother's superstitions about warding away death and spirits.

Gerdie stood in his father's antechamber, silent and watching. He knew this was not Gray Fever. The pallor alone could tell him that much. It was possible his father had caught a virus that originated overseas. The only one to recently venture overseas had been Owen, and he hadn't mentioned any pandemics, but then, Owen was not always forthright about the things that troubled him.

His mother had not left his father's side. She had sent for

the doctor, which Gerdie found unsettling given his mother's distrust of modern medicine.

"I'm here, my love," the queen whispered. She held the king's hand in both of hers and pressed her face against his slack knuckles.

"Mother?" Gerdie ventured.

She turned her head, startled. "You shouldn't be in here, heart. It may be contagious."

With his traitorous immune system, Gerdie cared a great deal about avoiding contagions. He had read up on every illness; kept abreast of every epidemic; compulsively downed vitamins, never forgetting a dosage even when he might forget to sleep or eat. But he wasn't frightened of catching whatever his father had contracted. He knew somehow that his father was alone in whatever this was.

His mother didn't protest when he stepped closer, though.

"Have you eaten?" he asked. "Had some water, at least?"

As he stood over her, she raised her head and gave a wan smile. "I used to go days on nothing but sunlight and stars. Seems like a lifetime ago."

"I'll bring you something," he said.

"You aren't supposed to eat in a room where illness is present." Her voice was soft.

So many wanderers shared fears that revolved around rooms and windows and doors and mirrors. It was no wonder they often slept out under the open sky, Gerdie thought. It must have been exhausting being so afraid.

"Come outside, then." He touched her shoulder, and she laid her hand over his. "Please."

Only a month ago his family had been complete and unbreakable, and now there was nothing but empty beds draped with black gossamer, and his mother.

He didn't know how to say any of this. Owen had been the eloquent one. But the queen seemed to sense it. She rose from her vigil and called for a trio of servants to stay by the king's side. "We'll be in the oval garden," she told them. "Send for me if he wakes."

The oval garden was the queen's favorite place in the world. There were over a dozen gardens within the stone wall, but the oval garden was where the queen's thoughts had run wild. She plucked and planted whatever compelled her from one day to the next, and it was ever changing, and filled with all sorts of creatures.

Being here was like being in his mother's mind, Gerdie had often thought.

It was past midnight now. An odd hour for a picnic, but Gerdie suspected his mother needed to be out of the castle for a while.

They sat on the iron bench that overlooked the reflection pond, a basket of breads and cloth-covered dishes between them.

At last, the queen spoke. "The summer that we were first

married, your father and I used to sleep out here every night. Right there, where that cherry tree is now. It made me feel like I was still traveling the world, and it made him feel like he didn't have to be king."

"Papa didn't want to be king?" Gerdie asked. His father was always so immersed in his affairs, it was hard to imagine him as anything but the king. Gerdie had no concept of what having an actual father might have been like. A mother, brothers, a sister—these things he knew.

"He did." The queen canted her head as she spoke, trying to find the right words. "But it was a dark time for him. The throne is inherited, you know. His family was gone."

Gerdie knew this, of course. His grandparents had been murdered by a duplicitous guard who wanted the throne for himself. He knew only that his father had escaped. It wasn't something that was further discussed.

The dead had never mattered to him before now. What would be the use in thinking of them? But now, every day he thought about how long his own life might be. Owen and Wil would drown so many more times, in that vast expanse of years. In the children he might one day have whom they would not meet. In the changes they would not see, the songs they would not hear. In the portraits that were never taken.

"They did tend to take after me, didn't they?" the queen said. "I was so afraid that they would grow up and sail away, fall in love with the world and never come back."

"I worried too," Gerdie said. Somehow it was comforting to talk about his brother and sister aloud, as though they still existed. He almost blurted out the rest, about the vendor turning to ruby. But he couldn't bring himself to betray his sister's trust. He didn't want to ruin the memory his mother had of her. There would be no point. Wil was dead, and the thing they'd both tried so hard to solve had died with her.

Instead, he said, "I don't understand. What's so appealing about sleeping on the ground and sailing on ships?"

"The world speaks, and some of us can hear it," the queen said. "The shifting sand, the turning sea, the way the wind makes everything shake and flutter as though it's dancing full of secrets."

When Gerdie and Wil were small, Owen would sometimes sneak them off to the Port Capital with him. One and then the other, he would carry them on his shoulders. The three of them would tuck their hair into gray wool caps, and they would pretend to be nomads so that nobody would know who they really were. It was a game they played.

While Gerdie studied the mechanics of the ships and the structure of the buildings, and while he wondered at the cogs in the machines and the motion of the water mills, his brother and sister spoke easily with sailors and vendors, mimicking their accents flawlessly and pretending to be from anywhere but Arrod.

"I wish I felt it too."

The queen was about to say something, but the crunch and clatter of footsteps running over dried leaves silenced her. A servant emerged through the thickets, gasping. "Your Majesty," she blurted, dipping into a hasty curtsy. "It's the king. He's taken a turn for the worse."

The queen moved fast, her nightgown swimming around her. By the time Gerdie made it to his father's chamber, his mother was already by his side.

Gerdie froze at what he saw. The king was sprawled on the mattress soaked with sweat, thrashing, crying out like a child in pain. He wasn't conscious, Gerdie noted, but his lips were burbling with blood. In his vigil, he focused on the details, which led to no logical conclusions. After a while, those details panned out, giving way to larger details, which turned into questions. What would become of this kingdom if his father were to die? What would become of the war that already loomed like thunder across the water?

How was it possible that so much had befallen their family so quickly? He had never expected that the universe held a divine purpose for anyone within it, but this felt deliberate. First Owen and Wil, and now his father, all being pulled into a churning current of death. Without logic. Without explanation. There must have been a pattern he was missing.

He thought of Wil, which had become a compulsion since he'd lost her. He had argued when she called what happened to her a curse. But now he wondered.

The king was drowning in blood as he coughed it up.

Maybe they would all drown.

Servants ran to and from the room, carrying cloths and sloshing bowls, awaiting the queen's directive. The queen knelt by the bed, stroking the king's face, whispering something into his ear and then kissing the side of his head.

Baren moved to stand beside Gerdie. His eyes were glazed. "Papa will be dead by morning," Baren whispered. "The ghosts are killing him. They'll come for you next. Now do you believe me?"

# TWENTY-SIX

In the morning, Loom and Wil headed for Messalin. A topical salve had lessened the pain in her leg, but deep within her bones it still ached. She didn't let on. She didn't want to delay this hapless venture, and she didn't want Zay to have the satisfaction besides.

"Maybe you shouldn't speak," Loom said, as he led Wil to the tiny rowboat that bobbed along the shore.

"Excuse me?" She bypassed his extended hand and took a shaky step onto the boat.

"I don't mean it that way. I just think it would be better if you . . . didn't. At least, not in Messalin. Your pale skin won't give you away—you could be from Brayshire, or parts of the West. But your Northern accent is unmistakable. They'll only hear the voice of the enemy. It's dangerous."

Wil swept her long hair over one shoulder and gripped the edges of the boat as he used the oar to push them from land. "Suppose I talk like you," she said in Lavean, taking on her best impression of his accent.

He laughed. He was easier with his smiles out here, away from Wanderer Country. It was far too hot for his coat in the South's swampy heat, and he had covered his tattoos that morning with concealer Zay ground from cacao and sun oil. He was far less mysterious this way, Wil thought. Just a boy.

"That wasn't a terrible impression," he said.

"Well, what do you expect? I've had no one but you to listen to for the last week." She was still imitating his inflections, and her careful pace stole some of the edge from her words.

"Practice punctuating your syllables," he advised. "Up in Northern Arrod you let one word bleed into the next. Down here we enunciate."

"Noted."

As he rowed toward the mainland, she looked over her shoulder. Messalin was a dull scar on the horizon. She would never admit it to him, but she was excited to see what the Southern Isles were truly like, away from the sullen quarantine of Loom's castle.

"How much do you know about the royal family in Arrod?" Loom said, breaking her out of her reverie.

She shrugged. Her heart began to race.

"You know about the three princes, surely, and the

princess," Loom said.

Wil's grip on the edge of her seat tightened, and she willed their boat closer to its destination. "Yes," she said.

"And you know the heir and the princess drowned," Loom said, with the same detachment anyone would have when speaking of a distant kingdom. "The heir had married a woman from Cannolay. That right there was the first sign a war was imminent. He was forming an alliance. After his death, I wondered if she would return home, but she has proven to be a traitor."

"Does she have to be a traitor for not returning?" Wil said, in her own tongue again. "Maybe she just loved him."

"That isn't how political marriages work," Loom said. "Believe me. I know. Especially between different nations about to go to war. She was hoping to gain something from that alliance, as was the prince."

She forced herself to look at him. "Why are you telling me all this?"

"To give you an idea of the chatter you'll hear on the streets." He pushed the oars forward with extra force. "What's wrong?"

"Nothing."

"I've upset you."

She exhaled hard. "How long until we arrive?"

He stopped rowing, and the boat rocked helplessly at the whim of the waves.

"Tell me what I've done."

The mainland sat silent in the distance, still too far to swim for it. Loom would surely dive in after her, and she still didn't trust herself not to drown him for bringing her here.

"Just row."

"I want to understand," Loom said, his voice firm. She dared to look at him and his eyes were too serious, boring through her. If he gazed any harder, he would see through her skin, through her skull. He would see her memories and know what she had done.

"High winds." Wil grasped the oars. "I'll do it myself."

She was able to row at nearly twice his speed. She wondered what it was that suddenly made him so soft.

She could not figure him out. He resorted to dirty tactics to have his way, and then he seemed to care how she felt about it.

She didn't understand herself when she was around him, either.

He didn't try to recover the oars until they were so close that the sounds of city chatter could be heard. There was the smell of roasted boar and poultry, heavily spiced and coaxing an appetite out of her. It competed with the sea air. She didn't want to admit that she'd always been curious about Lavean food. She didn't tell Loom that she wanted to know everything about the world, every little piece of it, or that she had dreamed of coming here. Loom didn't deserve to know this. He didn't deserve to know anything about her.

"We'll want to head toward the mountains a bit," Loom

said. "There are children who will guard your boat from thieves if you pay them enough."

"How do you know the children won't steal your boat?" Wil asked. "Or sell it off?"

"Incentive," Loom said. "If they recognize you, and they do what's asked of them, they know you'll pay a higher price for their loyalty the next time."

As the boat jostled against the mainland, Wil felt a somber silence emanating out from the city, like a cloud eclipsing the sun.

The heat of late morning was magnified here, compounded by some persistent manmade smog that smelled of spices at one turn, and of something odious the next.

Wil recognized it all too well. During Gerdie's frequent childhood illnesses, a parade of doctors and herbalists trailed to his bedroom. Wil would hover, spying, in the halls. She would breathe in the mists and medicines and the palpable sick, like death had come but could not find entry.

Sweetness mingled with the fear and the loss.

Sickness, she knew. It was an old, uninvited friend.

Wil hadn't known what to expect of Messalin. In some regard, when she thought of new places, she always imagined that they would be a bit like her home. There would be gardens, and a clock tower to trill the passage of time. She expected, she realized with shame, traces of affluence.

Cannolay was affluent. She could see it sparkling in the distance, catching bits of the sun. But there would be none of that wealth here in Messalin. She climbed out of the boat, dodging a messy-haired young boy who offered up his hand, and tried to see the city that lay beyond a twist in the mountainside.

All she could make out from here was the flutter of faded sheets.

Loom struck a deal to ensure the boat's safety, and then he moved to Wil's side.

He leaned with his mouth close to her ear. His voice was a murmur that melted under her skin. "It isn't safe for me to spend too much time on the streets. Someone may recognize me." A cloak would only raise suspicions in this heat. "Stay near me. We're going to visit a friend."

The last friend she'd met had been his wife, and Wil was not put at ease.

"What do you need me to do?" Wil asked.

"Just watch," he said. "You think I'm going to exploit you, but I brought you all this way to make you see."

"I have a hard time believing that."

"I have faith in you," he said. "Once you've seen what I have, you'll do what you think is right."

*What* you *think is right,* she wanted to say.

After walking the short length of a dirt road, they found themselves at the heart of Messalin's city proper.

Loom had not prepared her for the volume of the crowd. The entire population of the Southern Isles must have flocked to this small market. He grabbed her wrist and tugged her deftly between bodies through makeshift passageways, ensuring she didn't so much as graze a shoulder.

Silver bangles sang from the wrists of women flitting past. Delicious meats lingered amid incense that burned to ward away sickness—Wil knew the latter firsthand.

They passed a vendor who was selling loaves of parmii, a sweet multigrain bread that Wil knew only from photos. Something about the sight of it comforted her, as though she had wandered into a page of Owen's atlas.

"How are you feeling?" Loom's breath disturbed the hair along her neck. "Anxious at all?"

"A little," she confessed. "Crowds don't bode well for me."

"I can give you something for the adrenaline if you'd like."

"No." She couldn't afford to have her senses dulled.

A moment later, she realized that she had wrapped her gloved arm around his, her body leaning into the safety that encompassed him. It was a tentative, wary closeness. She was still waiting for him to betray her, and she would be ready when he did.

For now, though, he provided an odd comfort.

The crowd relented as they walked on, and Wil at last felt as though she could breathe.

For the first time on this patch of land, there was grass, spreading up a hillside in brilliant luminescent green, dotted with strange gray blossoms that wrapped around lengths of rusted wire. The wires were bent into clumsy circles.

"What are those?" Wil asked. She was speaking Lavean in her best Southern accent.

It was safe to stop walking, for everyone passing by seemed to avoid the ground before this hillside.

"That's where the dead are buried," Loom said. "Those wires are passages for their souls to enter the afterlife. Only flowers the color of ash are permitted to grow there, to ward off any lingering spirits looking for color and life."

Wil had never heard of such a thing. If it was in any of the books in the castle, she had never found it. But then, many of the pages had been torn out because of her mother's superstitions, and it was very possible that they had been burned to ward off anything that made her uneasy.

It was so beautiful and sad, she thought. "Do you believe in it?" she asked.

"Your Northern Arrod is showing," he said. "Belief is not a luxury that gets contemplated here. When it comes to death, it simply is."

He started walking and she took a broad step to catch up. "But you must believe something."

"Whatever I do or don't believe isn't important."

It was the first time he seemed frightened of anything, and Wil was left to wonder. He stole touches from a girl whose heart could turn life to stone, and he navigated through that horrifying storm at sea without a batted lash, but a simple question about the afterlife and he was like a child afraid of the dark.

She decided it wasn't worth pursuing. Death traditions were a grim topic in a city that didn't need further help being grim.

Wil could see where it had once been pretty. Homes were carved out of the mountainside, against and atop one another, run over with flowers on vines.

Hanging from every cluster of mountain homes, and fluttering throughout the market, were cloth signs with hand-painted letters:

*Long Live King Zinil. Long Live the Royal House of Raisius.*

Loom said nothing about these. That musty scent of illness and incense lingered everywhere.

"How much farther?" she asked.

"Just at the end of this row here." He looked at her. Reflexively she returned his gaze and was stricken by the sight of him. He seemed wilted, all at once, and tired where just moments earlier he had been vibrant. Something about this place drained the blood from his cheeks.

He stopped walking and pulled her against a stone wall, away from foot traffic. "The woman's name is Rala. She's a cousin of Zay's. She's the most fitting example of why these isles need your help." He nodded to the mountains that climbed atop each other in the distance. "Any plant you can dream of is in those mountains. You could climb right up and take them. But these people, this kingdom—they don't have the resources to process them into medicines anymore. The king barely holds that power himself. It's right there, but it's useless unless we can afford the equipment."

"You've said as much before," Wil said, unnerved by his desperation. Even if she hated his methods in dragging her here, she wished that she could help in the way he believed she could. She wished it were possible without endangering her secret and putting her entire family at risk.

"But now I'm going to show you." He began walking again, and in a few strides they had arrived at a small house set apart from the others. It was carved in the mountainside and overrun with roots of competing trees. The door was ornately hand carved, painted bright green.

"Rala?" he called. When he opened the door, two small children darted past, chasing each other into the crowd and giggling.

Wil froze in place. There had already been something lingering in this city, but it was especially prevalent in this house. She would recognize it anywhere.

Gray Fever.

"Come on." Loom was already ahead of her, in that dark single room with its sounds of rattled breathing.

Wil forced herself past the curtain. It brushed against her bare forearm, a musty caress.

The room was small and cluttered, with one large bed that took up nearly half the space. There was a washbasin stuffed with clothes to indicate that many children lived here, but there was only one child alone in the bed.

There was a woman sitting beside the bed, dabbing at the child's damp face.

"Rala," Loom said again, gently. "I've brought someone for you to meet. This is Wil."

The woman's eyes fell on Wil.

Her heart was racing so much she felt that words alone could turn everyone on this isle to ruby. She meant to say hello but what came out was, "Steam will help with his breathing. Boil a pot of water and tent a blanket over it. An hour a day, if he can sit up for that long."

Rala offered the barest smile, first to her and then to Loom. "You've found a budding doctor, is that so? Does Zay approve?"

"Zay hates her," Loom said, and some of the tension lifted with his easy tone. "That's how I know she's good for me."

"I'm—not a doctor," Wil said. "But I know someone who lived through Gray Fever." She emphasized that word, *lived*. "It clung to him for a good two years or so, but he got better. There are all sorts of herbs you can try, and mint ground into a paste to open the air passages at night, but it's best if you boil them and have him breathe in the steam. And you'll want to give him lots of milk and eggs and organ meats, if you can. The riboflavin will help prevent vision loss."

Long after Gray Fever had diminished the vision in Gerdie's left eye, he'd researched everything about his illness, ever seeking answers for why things happened the way they did.

The Gray Fever had eaten away at the riboflavin in his body, weakening his cornea, causing it to thin and his vision to blur. Now whenever he feared a relapse, he drank a putrid cocktail of milk, eggs, and organ meats. Wil couldn't stand to be in the room when he downed it, but it did seem to work.

After she'd said the words, Wil noticed the eggshells discarded in a bowl at the foot of the bed, and she shrank back in embarrassment. Of course Rala would already know how to care for her child. Southern medicine had far more to offer than even the finest doctors in Arrod.

But Rala's smile was patient nonetheless when she said, "Almonds have proven more effective than organ meats—and more palatable."

"I'm sorry," Wil said. "I didn't mean—"

"You've managed to find one with a heart like yours," Rala interrupted, speaking to Loom.

Wil felt her face going hot in her embarrassment. But her gaze fell back onto the child.

Gray Fever wasn't highly contagious. It found the frail ones and sank its talons in. The other children were safe if their resistance was strong, but watching it take hold of someone they loved was its own affliction.

Looking at this sick child was like staring into the past. She wanted to go outside and pluck the gray flowers from the graves and turn them to diamonds.

"Wil isn't all I've found." Loom handed Rala a handful of

ruby alber blossoms that Zay had cut into gemstones.

"Bits of a necklace I found on a ship," Loom said. "But they're real. Wil, could you let her see your data goggles?"

Wil handed them over. At least he was asking this time.

"It will be more than enough for you to afford to bring the herbs you've collected to Cannolay and have them processed into medicines," he said.

Rala's eyes filled with tears. "Thank you."

She tried to recall the howling winds the night of the storm, tried to remember how real her brother's voice had sounded then. *Tell me what to do, Owen. Try to stop this war? Is it even possible?*

She looked at Loom. He crouched at the bedside and smoothed the child's fevered brow with his thumb. He may have lied to her in the past, but he couldn't fake this level of care. After years spent at a bedside in a room whose air was thick with death, she knew that devotion better than anyone.

This love he had for the kingdom changed him—or perhaps, Wil realized, she was seeing the real him for the first time. Here, he was not a scheming one-time prince. He was a king, in his own right, of broken things.

She cleared her throat. "We should go," she told him. "You said it wasn't safe to stay long."

He stood. Rala took his hands in gratitude. As they said their good-byes, Wil hugged her stomach and stepped outside. The sun had moved higher against the sky, candying it bright blue with its light. Bits of the city glinted with minerals in the mountain stone. It looked nothing like the forgotten outskirts of the Port Capital, and yet this place reminded Wil of home.

The homes in Messalin were falling into disrepair just like the homes in the Port Capital's outskirts. But their architecture was still lovingly upkept: carvings in doors and in the stone walls, not unlike Loom's tattoos, and fresh coats of paint over rotting frames and panes.

They made their way back to the boat in silence. Between alleyways and over hillsides, she could see the famed mountain palace keeping vigil high at the heart of Cannolay.

It was so close. She could run for it now, cut through the cemetery and climb the iron fence that bordered the Southern capital. Loom was fast, but she moved like water, and he wouldn't want to draw attention to himself. Once she was in Cannolay, there would be too much risk. Someone would recognize him and want to collect the bounty on his head. Sweat was already beginning to wash away the concealer over his tattoos, and he was tugging his collar to hide his inky crown.

From Cannolay, she could find some way out of here, surely. Hire a boat, or steal one. But then what? She was no closer to finding Pahn. Loom was the only one who knew where to find him, and besides that, he also knew about her power. There was no telling how else he might use it against her. No. She had given him her word, and she would keep it. She would play the part of an ally. But they were enemies, under all of it, and she needed to remember that.

Especially when she looked at him just then.

Though he should have been accustomed to the stifling heat, his face was flushed, his eyes glassy.

"Are you going to drop dead in the middle of the streets?"

He cut her a wicked smile. "And make things easy for you?"

"High winds forbid." He stumbled, and reflexively she snared his elbow. "Loom? What is it?"

He waved her off. "The heat. I've been away for a while. I've forgotten how stifling it can be."

Clearly a lie. Wil had lived her entire life in the far North, where it sometimes flurried in the summer, and this heat wasn't affecting her nearly as much.

Loom plodded onward and straightened his posture. "The Heir to the Royal House of Heidle was quite the celebrity," Loom said, and Wil felt her palms go slick with sweat inside her gloves. "I imagine you've met him?"

Wil shrugged. Her legs felt rubbery, going numb. She focused on the horizon.

"I met him once, a year ago," Loom went on. "It was in the Western Isles—neutral territory agreed upon by both parties, and he'd come to ask for my sister's hand in marriage."

Wil stalled at that. He'd met her brother. She remembered their surroundings and lowered her voice to a whisper. "He wanted to marry the princess?"

"I don't think it was his idea. He was his father's errand

boy, and so was I."

"What happened?" Her throat felt dry.

"I rejected his proposal on behalf of the family. I was carrying out my father's orders. My sister and I have never gotten along, but I'd sooner die than see her marry anyone from that vile Northern king's family. Who knows what would happen to her? King Hein would probably keep her trapped in his castle as leverage. Threaten to kill her if we don't meet his demands."

Wil couldn't argue this. It was exactly the sort of thing her father would do. But Owen—all this had happened a year ago. Wil tried to recall her brother's ventures out into the world, but half the time he didn't tell her where he was going, much less what he was doing, no matter how she'd nettled him. She did know her father had wanted a marriage alliance with the Southern princess, but she hadn't known the steps he took to make it happen.

Loom went on. "As a show of good faith, Prince Owen had arrived in the Western Isles without reinforcements. That night, my father ordered that he be assassinated in his bed. Ten men crept into the prince's bedroom. None crept back out."

"He killed the assassins?"

"All of them. I saw the slaughter myself in the morning. By the looks of it, they never stood a chance. Blood on the ceiling. He was long gone by then. King Hein never tried to negotiate with us again. Any promises to open trade lines between our kingdoms became an impossibility. King Hein refuses to negotiate.

He wants all or nothing, and he tried to use my sister—a child at the time—to establish a direct line to my family."

She remembered now. It was a cold September over a year ago when Owen returned. He'd ruffled her sloppy ponytail as he passed her on the castle steps, and then he'd gone straight to his chamber and locked the doors. Nobody saw him for days. It had annoyed her when her knocks went unanswered.

Wil felt her heart sinking. She felt nauseous and weak. She was well aware of the horrors her father wrought as king. She knew that he had done his share to cause this devastation in the South, and within his own kingdom too.

But Owen—she knew Owen. She knew his heart. Over and again, she and Gerdie had readily betrayed their father for him, because he was going to be a good king, a just king.

Maybe there was no such thing. Owen must have known this, and it must have been a lonely realization. She felt a glimpse of that loneliness now, and it threatened to destroy her.

*Oh, Owen. I wish you'd told me.*

Loom narrowed his eyes at her, and Wil threw her defenses back up.

"And you went along with the assassination plan?" Wil said.

"I didn't have much choice in the matter," Loom said. "I was just following orders. Such is the life of an heir." He said it with mock tragedy.

Wil said, "If there are more people in the Isles like Rala,

people who know you, who would trust you, why not start your own army to overthrow your father?"

He laughed, and it irritated Wil how condescending it sounded. "It wouldn't be as easy as it sounds." They were back to the shoreline now. Loom paid the boy who had guarded the small rowboat, and Wil waited in tense silence. Once they were back out on the water, away from spying ears, Loom went on. "I need to buy alliances. Then kill the Northern royals. That's the only way I'll be able to redeem myself to my father. Once I have his trust and stand to inherit the kingdom again, I'll kill him. Successfully this time."

Wil steeled herself. *You're wind*, she reminded herself. *You are everywhere.* She forced her mind out of this tiny rowboat. She saw her castle with its remaining princes, its king and queen. Her father was not always a reasonable man, but the Southern Isles had things he wanted. He would be open to negotiations. Baren was the heir, and her father had seen his efforts wasted on that one; he struggled where Owen had excelled; he wasn't clever, nor was he reasonable, nor would his cocky demeanor make him any good at foreign relations. Her father would be open to communicating directly.

"You don't have to kill them." She spoke slowly, trying to feign detachment from the situation. "After I've gone to find Pahn, I think you should head to Northern Arrod. Talk to the king. It can be mutually beneficial."

Loom shook his head. Sweat made the satin cling to his

skin. His eyes were languid. He looked so tired, and Wil began to wonder if he'd caught something, but what contagion could be floating around Messalin that would affect him this quickly? Not Gray Fever; he appeared far too healthy to be vulnerable, and anyway it wouldn't come on so suddenly. Whatever it was, he seemed determined to ignore it. "You don't understand kings. Killing them is the only way to stop all this war."

"Killing to stop the killing?" Wil said.

"The Northern king is already killing us," Loom pressed. "He hijacked all our trade ships, did you know that? He released the captains but kept the wares for himself, and he refuses to trade until we give him our entire kingdom. Wil, he's exiled us. Our hospitals are falling apart. We're dying, and if he continues to breathe, all he needs to do is wait until we're too weak to fight at all, and take us over."

Wil knew that what he was saying was true, and still she refused to let him know it. Her family was not to blame for her father's actions. Where Loom saw cold murderers, she saw a genius boy in his lab, a woman who sang her children to sleep, an heir who had wanted to change things, who had died to spare her life. "You would murder an entire royal line in the name of peace." Wil folded her arms. "Sure, makes a lot of sense."

"In the grand scheme of a greater good, their lives are nothing," Loom said.

Wil barely knew what happened next. In a blink, she had taken him by the collar and hurled him into the water. He fell with a loud splash, and she was grasping the edges of the boat, trying to steady its violent rocking.

He bobbled up to the surface, spitting water. "Has it ever been suggested to you that you have a problem controlling your impulses?"

Jaw clenched, Wil grabbed the oars and propelled herself toward the island. He was struggling to keep up with her, but it was no use for all her fury as she rowed.

He disappeared under the water, and when he didn't surface, she considered going after him. She scolded herself for having the thought. No. Let him drown. He deserved it, after everything.

Seconds went by. "Burning gods," she cursed, and stilled the oars.

Before she could decide whether or not to go after him, his arm hooked over the side of the boat. Loom hoisted himself above the surface, gasping. Something was very wrong; she had seen him swim farther than this without effort before, but now he looked as though he could barely stay conscious.

"I didn't realize you were such a fan of the royal family," he gasped.

She glared at him as he struggled back onto the boat. They traveled the rest of the way in silence.

Zay was sitting on the beach, rubbing a frothy salve on Ada's arms to protect his skin against the sun. When she saw the boat approaching, she stood and waded into the water to pull it ashore.

"You were gone too long," she accused Loom, by way of greeting. "How was Rala?"

"The same," Loom said, accepting her help guiding him onto the sand. He stumbled. "She asked after you and Ada, of course."

Zay rubbed her fingertips against his neck, smudging the sweaty concealer. "Too long," she said again. She cast a disdainful glance at Wil.

Zay was stunning in the daylight and all her fury, Wil thought, as she sat uneasy under her scrutiny. Her skin was shimmering with sweat; her haphazard hair was gathered high atop her head.

But where Zay had nothing but contempt for Wil, her little boy had fascination. He stood at the water's edge watching her disembark from the rickety boat, and reached for the long curtain of Wil's hair as it fell before her.

"No, no, Ada," Zay said, catching his outstretched hand. "Don't touch the witch; she'll turn you into a rock, and I will be very sad. I'll have to strangle her with the boat ties to have my revenge."

Wil narrowed her eyes. "It sounds like you've already written the novel."

"I'm hardly the only one who fantasizes about strangling your kind with boat ties," Zay said coolly. "The fact that you're a witch has nothing to do with it."

"Enough." Loom's voice startled both girls, freezing them still. He turned on Zay. "You don't talk to her like that."

Shock washed over Zay's eyes like a shadow. The shock quickly turned to anger, and she folded her arms. "You're out of your head right now, *ansoh*."

She was right, Wil thought. He pressed his palm to his temple, wincing. He sucked a breath through his teeth, and something within Wil lurched. She touched his forehead. Burning hot. "You need to rest," she said. "You can't die on me." He raised his eyes to her. "Not until you've fulfilled your end of our bargain," she added.

Zay let out an indignant huff and tugged Loom by the wrist. "There are some lyster leaves back at the castle. Let's get your fever down." She didn't seem surprised by the state of him at all.

"What's wrong with him?" Wil started to follow them, but Zay stopped her with a glare.

"He'll be fine."

"He doesn't look—"

"Zay's right," Loom interrupted. "I don't do well in this heat. I'll feel better by tonight."

Only he wasn't. He didn't come from his room even after the sun had gone down. Zay hovered in his doorway keeping constant vigil, as though she thought Wil would try to kill him in his sleep.

Wil wouldn't, but it suited her just fine if they thought so.

# TWENTY-SEVEN

THE BREEZE ROLLED THROUGH THE open window, salty and cool.

Loom lay on his stomach, chin on his overlapped arms, and he sighed in tandem with the gently turning sea. For hours he had coasted in a half-sleep of sullen dreams, but now he was awake.

Zay was sitting cross-legged on the bed beside him, and she pressed a cold cloth to the back of his neck. She touched her hand to his forehead. "Your fever is finally breaking. How are you feeling?"

He tilted his face to her. "You don't have to dote on me."

She scoffed. "Don't pretend not to need me. Without me you'd sail right off the edge of the world."

"Only if I were in pursuit of something worthy of the fall," he said.

"Like a certain Northern girl with a pretty face and a fistful of raw diamonds?"

Loom glanced sidelong at her, smirking. "You think she's pretty?"

Zay doused a fresh cloth in a bowl of lyster-infused water. She wrung it out and gently dabbed at his bare shoulders, which were still pink with fever. "I worry about what's happening to you since you met that girl. You used to have more sense."

He closed his eyes. "You want to talk to me about sense, *ansuh*?"

She straightened her spine, wielding the majesty to rival any queen. "What is that supposed to mean?"

"You don't want to have this conversation with me."

"On the contrary," she said. "I want to know what you're so smug about."

He sat up to face her, and the wet cloth fell to the blankets with a dull sound. "I said nothing of your sense," he began, "when you were fifteen and you snuck out of the palace walls after midnight to be with a man leagues below your class. Again and again. I said nothing of your sense when he got you pregnant. I was the one you screamed curses at as you brought Ada into the world. I say nothing of your sense even now, when you row out to Lamponay, slum of the Southern Isles, to continue your affair with the man who doesn't even ask about his son, a man who will never deserve either of you."

At that, Zay's eyes burned defiant. "I have told him not to

worry about Ada," she said. "Ada belongs only to me."

"Yes, and he listens to you, and I know that drives you mad. He doesn't even love his son enough to fight for him," Loom said. "I don't save you from yourself, Zaylin. Even when someone should."

"That girl could kill you," Zay whispered, seething. "You don't know who or *what* she is. You don't know where she came from, or what else she can do."

"She isn't dangerous," Loom said. "I can't explain it, but I just—know somehow that she won't hurt me. She isn't the evil thing you make her out to be."

"There's something off and you know it," Zay said. "She's hiding something."

"Find me someone who isn't."

She laid her hand to his heart, pressing down hard to feel it beating. "You are in very deep waters, my dearest one."

He laid his hand over hers, and his fingers curled, holding on. "I know."

Her eyes softened at the pain on his face. "I want you to have all the things that make you happy in this world," she said, giving his chest a shove. "But I won't let anything hurt you. I will kill that girl if she tries."

# TWENTY-EIGHT

WIL COULDN'T LIE STILL.

Since her banishment, she had slept on patches of dirt and in unfamiliar beds and on ships that jostled through the night. She had slept through the murmurs and the lovemaking and the eternal music of Wanderer Country. She had slept through nightmares that turned life to stone in her hands.

But she could not sleep in the silence of this castle. At night there was nothing but blackness, not even a ghost to stir the air.

Loom, visibly unwell, had gone to bed before sunset. And Zay had stolen herself and her child away to dote over him, which had suited Wil just fine at the time. But now she would have preferred even Zay's scowling jabs to this nothingness.

She had promised herself that she wouldn't think of home. The memories did not bring her company, and the absence of the castle's life and noise made the night air that much cooler.

She tried not to worry for her brother, choosing instead to console herself by thinking of his determination. True, she had warded away death when he was ill, but he had been the one to so relentlessly claw his way back every time. His life was precious to him because he had fought for it.

He would be okay without her. Wil had to believe that.

Yet, still, when she closed her eyes, she saw him crumpled in grief on the floor of his lab. She saw his cauldron overrun with webs and dust. He had no one now. He was all alone with that genius mind of his, which fast took him to dark places when there was no one to reel him back.

Wil kicked away the satin and got out of bed. She couldn't stay here. She needed stars.

She moved quickly through the castle, barefoot and without her gloves. That freedom was the greatest luxury this abandoned island could offer.

When she reached the water's edge, she pressed herself against the sand and stared at the night sky, freckled with stars and all different shades of blue twisting into each other.

In the distance, she could see the dark shadow of Messalin, asleep across the water. Beyond that, Cannolay sat higher and brighter, with lights that never ceased.

Wil didn't let herself think about who was awake in that city, and what attacks they might be planning against her kingdom. She positioned herself so that the city was no longer in view, and there was nothing but the stars to see.

She lay like that for nearly an hour, trying unconsciously to sync her breaths to the rolling of the waves.

"Couldn't sleep?" Loom's voice. She opened her eyes and saw him standing silver and lean under the electric moon.

"No." She propped herself by her elbows, watching as he sat beside her. "How are you feeling?"

He smiled. It was a tired, sincere smile, and for once his face was not guarded by his relentless pretenses. "Nice of you to care."

"Habit, I suppose," Wil said. All her life, she'd had someone to look out for.

"I gathered as much." Loom's sincerity was the same now as it had been in Messalin, and Wil's heart beat faster. She sat up, straightening her posture in an attempt to regain control of her body.

"Was it true?" Loom asked. "Did you really know someone with Gray Fever who lived?"

She hesitated. When she met Loom, it had been through a haze of grief and flame. From that melee emerged a stranger within herself—a girl with no past, who was ruthless and cold, who wanted this once-prince to suffer for what he had done to her. For what he wanted to do to her family.

But she was tired of that stranger. She was tired of being trapped in that fog of mourning. She wanted to tell him something true, some small piece that could make her human in his presence. Maybe he didn't deserve it, after what he'd done to her, but she owed it to herself.

At last, she said, "My brother." Her voice was soft. "I hadn't thought there was any hope for him. He hadn't opened his eyes for days. Even his skin and his hair smelled of death: like the dirt after a long rain."

Loom canted his head. In his eyes, she saw gratitude burning as brightly as the moon reflected. "You have a brother." Knowing she had told him something true, and because she had wanted to, he savored it. He knew something about her now.

She averted her gaze and touched the back of her hand to his forehead. His fever had gone down considerably, but she could still feel the lingering warmth of it, especially now against the cool night air. He leaned into her touch the same moment she withdrew.

"I can tell that you care about him," Loom said. "From the way that you spoke about him to Rala. Your eyes changed, like I was looking at a memory of you projected."

She stared past him, to the ocean that unfurled like blankets made of deep blue ink. She was afraid to look at him, afraid of what else he'd be able to read.

"What is that like?" he asked.

"What?" Wil asked.

"Trying to protect him."

It was her turn to read his expression. The once-prince of the Southern Isles had only one sibling. A sister who was as elusive to the world as he was. She answered his question as a means of asking him a question of her own.

"Like a planet orbiting the sun," she said. "Just the way it always was."

Loom nodded to Wil's outfit: silver satin trousers and a top to match, embellished with purple dragonflies with dragon scales. The clothes belonged to the princess, Wil knew, but Loom regarded them as though his sister were suddenly present.

"I was two when my mother died," he said. "That was fifteen years ago. I don't remember her at all. Maybe you've heard that royals don't have portraits taken, so I have no way to memorialize her. Nothing but a handkerchief that I'm told she would dampen to soothe my fevers."

Wil knew all about royal families and their fear of portraits. It was one of the few things upon which all the world leaders had agreed for centuries; revealing portraits and photographs of royal children was a safety risk, opening royal families up to kidnapping for negotiations and revenge.

She would never see Owen again, not even as fading colors on a canvas.

Loom went on. "She died just hours after bringing my sister into the world. I can't see her face, but I can still see the servants running from her bed with bloody sheets in their arms as I hid under her dressing table."

"That's awful," Wil said.

He smiled caustically. "My sister tells her enemies, 'I killed my own dear mother; think what I'd do to you.'"

It sounded like something Baren might say, Wil thought,

could he boast such a thing.

She thought of the look on Loom's face after he'd picked her up from the sidewalk in the melee. Her blood on his shirt. His kindness.

"What's her name?" she asked.

"Her name is Espel."

"Like the root?"

Loom smiled. "You've heard of the world's deadliest poison root? That's impressive."

Gerdie had been coveting that poison for years, wanting to use it in his weapons, but it was impossible to find. Extracted in small quantities, sanctioned only by the Southern king. Never exported.

"My father said she was a warrior from birth," Loom went on. "But for a girl to become a warrior, she would have to work that much harder to be feared."

"So he named her after a poison?"

"Not simply a poison," Loom said. "A poison that many have died to acquire."

Wil rubbed the satin between her thumb and index finger. There had only been two girls to wear this garment, and both of them had killed their blood.

"I was afforded the finest instructors and trainers when I was young," he said. "But my father saw to Espel's upbringing himself. He taught her how to poison a blade. He taught her how to kill an enemy before her approach was announced. I think it's because he's always feared her. She had already killed his wife. He wanted her loyalty so that she wouldn't send him to the same fate."

"Would she?" Wil asked.

"If it served her, perhaps," Loom said. "I don't know."

"Would he kill her?" Wil couldn't help her morbid interest.

"No," Loom said with certainty. "He treasures her. She's his legacy."

Wil considered this.

"What about you?" Loom asked. "Where do you come from?"

"Northern Arrod. You already knew that."

"Yes. But I suppose I was asking for you to tell me your story."

"I don't have one."

"The girl who turns things to stone doesn't have a story." The wild playfulness in his eyes made her pulse quicken. "Will you at least tell me how you're able to control it?"

"Control? I have no control over it at all. I'll kill anyone that touches me."

"Not me," Loom said.

"No," Wil said. "Not you. Although I'm not sure why that is."

"Maybe it doesn't affect people," Loom suggested. "Maybe it's just plants."

Wil betrayed nothing. "It affects people."

Loom was quiet for a while. Then he said, "I was given a sword from the time I could walk. My father prefers them to arrows and guns. He says blades require the most skill. He wanted my sister and me to be able to kill anyone who might harm us. He said the world was our enemy."

She looked at him.

"The day I turned ten," he continued, "my father received a passenger boat containing orphans from various countries in the Eastern Isles, but mostly Grief. A plague had swept through the country and there was no shortage of displaced children. Some were my age, most were older. There were at least twenty of them.

"My father called for Espel and me to come down to the southernmost garden. It was summer, and a hundred and fifteen degrees. He took away our swords and our daggers, and he handed them to the orphans. One at a time, he ordered us to fight them with our bare hands, while they tried to use our own weapons against us. 'Fight to the death,' he told us. 'Kill them before they can draw your blood.'

"We killed them as fast as we could," Loom said. "I wish I could say it was a fair fight, but most of them were fatigued by the heat, starving from the journey, and frightened. Eventually, my sister met her match in a little girl who didn't look like much, but turned out to have a hell of a lot of fire in her. She had Espel on the ground in seconds, and she would have killed my sister if my father didn't intervene.

"He pulled the girl up by her wrist, and he laughed and patted her shoulder, and he said, 'Congratulations. You are now the captain of my daughter's guard.'"

"What about you?" Wil said. "Who became captain of your guard?"

Loom smiled, and it was the saddest smile Wil had ever seen. "None of them. I haven't met my match yet."

If Loom had told this story to some other girl, she might not have believed him. She might have laughed and told him he ought to become a novelist, and surely no father would make his children do something so bloody and terrible. But Wil was the daughter of the Northern king, and she believed every word.

She reached across the sand and put her hand over his.

"You don't have to tell me your story," he said. "Not now, at least. But if you ever choose to tell me, I won't judge you for any of it. I'm in no position to."

She could feel the tentativeness in his fist under her hand. She could feel that he wanted to hold on to her in some way. When she looked at him in the moonlight, she could see the boy who had been forced to kill. She could see a prince.

Like her, there were things he wouldn't say aloud. It wasn't that he wanted to keep them secret, but rather that he wanted to keep them from drawing breath and devouring him alive.

"Does that frighten you?" Loom asked.

"No," Wil said.

More than a thousand children died the same winter Gerdie caught Gray Fever. Wil didn't know this until several years later, when Owen told her. In Wil, Owen saw a bit of himself, and as she got older, he began unveiling more of the kingdom's darkest secrets to prepare her for what being a Heidle meant. What their legacy truly was. "Papa ordered chemists to sell a medication to families with sick children that year," he'd said. "It was carried in shops and among street peddlers alike. But it was poison, Wil. He knew that the sick weren't going to get better, and so he killed them off, to stop it from spreading."

The words had sickened her, not only because of what they meant, but also because she didn't doubt it. She had seen her father's disregard for anyone who could not be of use to him. She hated the way her father had looked at Gerdie when he was at his most ill, as though his value would be determined by whether he could be fixed.

That was why she had always been so hard on Gerdie to stop talking about his aches and pains unless she was certain their father or Baren wouldn't overhear him.

"It's impossible to frighten me," Wil told Loom. "I'm a monster, didn't you know?"

"No, you aren't," he said. "I have met monsters."

Loom thought the truths of his own kingdom would frighten her, but they didn't. She was already well versed in the cruelty of kings. He saw that when he looked at her now, and when he reached to touch her face, it was with a fragile sort of curiosity. His fingertips asked what his lips didn't. *Who are you? Where did you come from?*

She held her breath when his thumb traced her bottom lip.

In that deft little motion, he was nearly coaxing her secrets out of her. They began replaying in her mind. The first time she held a sword in her child hands, how with that first clumsy swing of the blade her eyes widened in astonishment, a secret power blooming open in her ribs. The dirigibles coasting in the stained glass window. The king who loved his children only because he loved the queen who gave them to him. The vendor pinning her down, crushing the life out of her. The distant whooshing of her brother's bullets. Then that same power tumbling and breaking free. The crackle of gemstone.

Loom drew back.

His face changed. He was no longer looking at her, but at something behind her. The wonder in his face turned to horror.

She looked over her shoulder, and saw the faraway city of Cannolay, engulfed in flames.

# TWENTY-NINE

DARKLEAD.

So this was what her brother's alchemized weapon could do.

Wil stood frozen on the shore, her face alight with the blaze of distant fire. She couldn't feel her lungs, yet she heard each breath outside herself.

Gerdie. He was the only one who knew how to use his horrid invention.

But he wouldn't have done this. Not of his own volition.

Superimposed over the faraway flames, she conjured images of her brother shackled in his basement, coerced by their father, possibly even tortured, and lost in his grief.

He was all alone. What was their father doing to him? It was her job to protect him, and she couldn't. She was so far away, she may as well have been watching this unfold from the stars.

Somewhere in the castle, her father was flanked by counselors and plans, and he had ordered this. Even she hadn't thought he would go this far so quickly. Had Owen tried to tell her?

"Wil!" Loom skidded to a stop at her side. "Are you all right?"

"Of course I am. I'm all the way over here. But the mainland—"

"We have to go to Cannolay," Loom said. "We have to help."

"You aren't going anywhere near that place, you idiot," Zay cried. "What use are you to anyone when you drop dead on its shores?"

"Now isn't the time to—"

"You already pressed your luck today. You're staying here. I'll go."

"I'll go with you," Wil said.

Zay was already running for the rowboat, but she stopped to look over her shoulder. "What's it to you?"

Someone in that burning city would have to know what had happened. She hoped. Maybe the attack had come with word—news, a threat, something—from Northern Arrod.

"You dragged me out here because you wanted my help," she said. "So do you want my help or don't you?"

Zay's eyes turned suspicious. She had always been wary of Wil, disdainful of anyone with Nearsh blood in general, but ever since the night Wil had returned Ada, all of this became tainted with curiosity. Zay didn't know what to make of Wil any more than Wil knew what to make of her.

Wil ran to catch up to her, and Loom snared her elbow, spinning her to face him. Tiny burning cities in his eyes. "You don't have to do this," he said.

"I want to."

He was searching her face, reading her in that way of his.

He was so close, and her blood rushed from her heart in rivers that all seemed to lead to him, pushing her closer, tempting her to touch him. She could smell the streets of Messalin in his hair, with its graves and gray flowers. She could taste his love for all of it on her tongue, like a kiss.

His full, parted lips were heavy with the weight of her name. He drew a breath to say it.

She broke free of his grasp before he could. Her heart beat with lethal force. "I have to go," she said, turned, and ran up a sand dune to catch up to Zay.

Zay rowed furiously. Wil twisted her hair at the nape of her neck to get it out of her way. Her eyes never left the burning capital once.

They were halfway across the water when Wil said, "It's not going to help, is it? All the diamonds and rubies in the world couldn't fix this."

Zay turned to look at the ashes billowing up into the night sky. "He would have been a good king," she said. "I'm not just saying that because I would have been his queen. He loves this stupid kingdom more than anyone can." She shook her head, pulling herself out of a trance. "It's going to be bloody. I hope you're not squeamish."

From here, Wil could smell the smoke from Cannolay. The scorched skin. Burned hair. All of it wafting across the watery divide.

Owen had told her about an explosion he'd seen in a small country in the East. Nothing so big as this. It had all seemed so far away then. A dark paragraph in a fairy tale, as she lay in the cool grass and asked him to tell her something she didn't know about the world. Owen had never been one to shield her from the truth, not even when she was small.

She gritted her teeth against a wave of pain at her core. It wasn't really the inevitable carnage, or even the worry, and it certainly wasn't the gentle rocking of the sea. Something was changing in her, pushing from the underside of her ribs, trying to splinter her bones to burst free. Something new that wasn't there before.

It had all started when she met Loom, the only living thing in the world she knew to be immune to her touch.

Zay picked up on her uneasiness. "I've got smelling salts if you faint." Her voice was only a little bit taunting.

"I'm fine."

"I'll destroy you, you know," Zay said. "If you hurt him. So I hope you're not planning something."

This was meant to scare her, Wil supposed. But the sentiment made Zay seem less menacing. More sincere. Though Zay was married to Loom, and though that marriage was merely political, she loved him in a way that ran as deep as bone marrow. The way that Wil loved her brothers—the one living, and the one dead—enough to row into a city that was burning against the black sky.

"I understand," she said.

"Yes. I somehow believe that you do." Zay narrowed her eyes, suspicious. "You know, there's something about you I never noticed before, but the shadows really catch it now."

Wil looked at her. "What?"

"I saw the queen of Arrod once, when I was a little girl. She had a distinct chin and soft cheeks, a lot like yours. You look like her. Has anyone ever told you that?"

Wil would have given anything just then to see her mother's face. She didn't know that she ever would again.

"No," she said, and it was the truth. She studied Zay for any sign that this was a trick, but the thought of the queen already seemed gone from Zay's mind when she looked over her shoulder at the city burning in the distance.

The lights of Cannolay were that much closer now. They had to pass Messalin to reach the capital, and they stayed in the dark waters away from the lights' reach. It would be so easy to disappear forever in the darkness here. Even the moon's glow no longer touched them.

When they finally reached Cannolay, it was far from any buildings, but the smoke had thickened the air nonetheless.

The boat crashed into the rocks, and once they were on

their feet, Zay dragged it ashore. "Try not to talk to anyone," Zay said. "Last thing I need is someone overhearing your accent and gutting us up on a laundry line. Your kind isn't exactly welcome here. Especially now."

Silence would be more welcome than conversation, Wil thought, and followed Zay into the darkness.

It was a wonder that the Southern Isles were so well known for their medicinal plants. Wil had only been here a short while, but in that time she'd seen little more than dirt, sand, and rocks.

The rocks crested after what seemed to be an eternity of climbing, and all at once the city came into view.

Zay raised her head into a breeze that moved the wild hair from her cheeks. "See down there?" She nodded into the blackness. "It's the Red River. They call it that because the minerals along the bottom look like rust. It's a main water source. If there's going to be another attack, it'll likely hit there."

Zay was just like Loom, Wil thought. She still cared for this city, even after it had cast her away. She was still eager to climb these rocks in the veil of moonlight and offer what small salvation she could give.

"Zay?" Wil stood beside her. "Something happened to Loom when we went to Messalin, didn't it? Something about that place makes him ill."

"I'm surprised he didn't tell you. You make the secrets spill from his tongue the way that gems spill from your fingertips."

"So I was right then. What is it about that place?"

Zay shook her head, began climbing down. "That's something you'll have to take up with him. I'm not in the business of divulging secrets."

They moved in darkness down the embankment, and by the time they'd reached the bottom, Wil could hear the gentle rush of water.

"Watch where you step down here," Zay said as they reached the ground. "There's a lot of vegetation. Try not to crystallize anything. Most of these are medicinal and they're of more use to people as they are."

Wil couldn't watch anything; it was so dark that she could scarcely make out Zay's form in the moonlight.

"Stop." A voice came booming across the darkness, and Zay went rigid.

"What?" Wil whispered. "Who is that?"

"The king's finest." She grabbed Wil's gloved hand. "Come on." She took off running for the embankment, Wil keeping even pace.

Wil's heart was racing and she ambled in the blackness, trying not to touch Zay with her bare skin, which was a challenge until they reached the jagged rocks and Zay at last released her hand.

"Under the command of King Zinil of the Royal House of Raisius, you are ordered to stop!" The voice was accompanied by the clatter of swords.

"Don't say a word," Zay whispered fiercely. There was no

panic in her voice, but somehow Wil knew that Zay was fright-ened. The way she also knew that they had been caught.

The commotion of swords and footfalls was as close as her next breath. Wil felt a strong hand grasp her arm and move to tear her away from the rocks.

She closed her eyes to the inevitable crackle of skin turning to stone.

# THIRTY

THIS WAS THE FIRST TIME Wil heard one of her victims cry out. He was fighting it, she realized, his muscles bulging, jaw clenched. He had probably been fighting all his life. But the most seasoned warrior in the world was no match for this. The persistent ruby did not negotiate, did not argue, and within seconds the man was dead.

Torchlight filled the temperate air, and all the guards ran and fell to a stop before the one who had been unfortunate enough to grab her. She could feel their horror and their trepidation, heavy as the humid air. They didn't know what she was, but all at once they knew she wasn't human.

Wil was not even horrified by the sight of his ruby eyes with their raised pinpricks of irises. Not even sickened. He looked just as she expected, glimmering brilliantly in the light of the moon. Her skin bloomed with gooseflesh. She could taste the froth of the sea water churning on the shore.

Zay was pulling her back onto the wall by the gloved arm. Wil snapped back to attention. She tore her eyes away from the dead man and hurried up the rocks. Another kill. Owen flashed through her mind, the way he'd slaughtered the assassins that came to kill him. It wasn't cruel if it was necessary. That's what he would tell her.

She moved fast. If there was one thing in the world her muscles would never forget, it was climbing walls.

There was the sound of something cutting through the air, then the wet sound of steel burrowing into flesh. Zay cried in pain, small rocks crumbling away from her as her grip slackened.

There was no time to inspect the damage. Wil extended her gloved hand and was just able to grab her by the sleeve. "Come on. I can pull you the rest of the way."

Zay wrenched herself out of her grasp. The rocks under her feet were red with blood. "Leave. They won't kill me. Take the boat back."

"No. Take my hand."

"You really are useless," Zay seethed.

The guards were coming out of their stupor and had begun climbing after them. As one of them grabbed Wil by the hair, someone called out, "Harm her and I'll castrate you myself." It was a girl's voice.

The guards had already gotten Zay. She was slung over one of their shoulders, hissing mad, blood pouring from her right ankle.

The guard who had Wil was afraid to touch her, wisely so, and continued to tug on her hair like he was reining a horse. Before this curse, she would have been able to fight him off her, but now to touch meant to kill, and she restrained herself.

They were shrouded in a dome of torchlight now. At the center was the ruby soldier, his hands formed into claws, his mouth frozen in a defiant snarl.

Wil waited for the guilt to come, but it didn't. She felt nothing for this man she had destroyed.

At the heart of the guards stood a single girl, small in stature, perhaps younger than Wil. The lean muscles in her arms cast shadows against the dancing flame. A slender silver tattoo trailed down her left arm, glimmering in the warm brown of her skin. It was of some scaled, fanged creature whose teeth clamped around her wrist.

Without bothering to look, the girl reached out and plucked the dagger embedded in Zay's ankle, and Zay screamed.

The girl wiped the blade against her thigh, leaving red streaks on the sapphire blue satin of her short trousers, before returning the dagger to its holster at her hip. There were more blades of various sizes resting in a strap across her chest. Dotted along her left hip were vials of liquid in bright colors. Poisons, no doubt. Perhaps they weren't all lethal, but meant to incapacitate.

The girl raised her focus to Wil. There was something familiar in her dark amber eyes, and Wil knew immediately that this was the girl whose clothes she had been wearing. The intensity of her gaze. Unmistakable. When she cocked her head, Wil could see another tattoo wrapped around her throat, in silver ink rather than black. The pattern was familiar—thorny vines bearing the Southern royal crest of a heart impaled by blades.

This was Espel. Loom's sister.

Zay let out a moan. Her head was lolling as she hung over the guard's shoulder, and Wil feared she would die. She was scarcely conscious when the guard dropped her onto the sand.

Wil wanted to go to her and stop the bleeding. But there were guards surrounding her, and a princess with many knives and precision aim was staring her down.

"Hells," Espel said, as she looked at Wil's gloves and then at her face. "What are you?"

"I heard her speak, Your Highness. She's from the North." A girl in a silver satin robe emerged from the shadows beyond the torchlight. She was tall and slender, and her eyes were cold like her voice. Her accent told Wil that Lavean wasn't her first language—she was from one of the Eastern countries. If her accent hadn't given her away, her tawny skin and black hair would have. She maintained a protective stance, hand on the hilt of her sword. Could this be the princess's guard from Loom's story? The traumatized orphan who had been handed a weapon and told to fight for her life all those years ago?

Espel gave no indication she was listening. She reached over her shoulder, and Wil expected her to draw yet another knife, but she only pulled the long rope of her hair away from her neck, letting the breeze cool her skin. She was sweating, dark stains of it marring her satin tunic. She smelled of a city on fire.

She nodded at the gasping heap that was Zay. "Someone tend to the Traitor's wife. I want her alive." She waved her arm over the length of the ruby corpse. "And break this into pieces and get it into a sack. I don't want anyone to be seen carrying gemstones back to the palace."

The guards, with bewildered eyes, set about this task of shattering the ruby, stomping the arms with their boots and removing his clothes.

Wil's own bones ached at the sound.

Espel's gaze had yet to leave Wil.

She had a sharp chin, but a soft face. Her cheeks were round and smooth, her eyes dark and eerily kind the way that Loom's eyes were kind; perhaps they did not know to whom they belonged. She so resembled her brother. What had it been like for them, Wil wondered, to grow up alongside each other, looking so much alike and yet being raised as enemies? The boy with all his secrets, determined to save his kingdom, and the girl who was lauded for killing her mother.

Wil had thought, when Loom first told her of Espel, that it couldn't possibly be an infant's fault what happened to her mother. Now, watching the shiver of excitement that rose through the princess as the severed ruby hand caught the torchlight, she wasn't so sure.

"She must be a marveler, Your Highness," the girl said.

Running would not end well, Wil knew. She could escape the guards, but not a thrown knife. And Espel's blades were coated in something. Zay had gone unconscious.

The gemstones grated against each other as the guards threw them into a burlap sack; they moved hastily, as though touching the crystallized limbs would subject them to the same fate.

Espel canted her head. "If you came here with the Traitor's wife, that means the Traitor sent you."

Wil didn't have a chance to reply. The girl in the silver robe moved like an apparition, her sleeves moving about her like cursive being scrawled against the dark sky. Her long black hair was tied into a braid that disappeared under her robe.

Something swept across the backs of Wil's ankles, knocking her to the sand.

The girl in the silver robe was knelt beside her, a length of chain in her hands. She stretched it across Wil's throat, pinning her in place.

Wil did not attempt to move. Her heart had other ideas, beating against her chest and trying to be free of her prone body. She focused on breathing. *Don't struggle,* she told herself. She knew that she did not have the advantage now. Escape would have to come later, and in order to escape later, she would need to survive this.

*You're everywhere,* she reminded herself. She couldn't move, but she could observe. Guards had finished packaging the severed body and were scouring the sand for remnants. There was nothing around them. The city was a solid ten minutes by foot, Wil remembered, and in a state of chaos. Nobody would be coming here, except for a princess and her guard who had been out looking for invaders.

For all the years Wil had spent learning to fight, her only lesson on surviving a hostage situation had come from her father. He never explained how he knew so much on the matter, but she remembered his eyes as he sat in his throne, studying her the way a sculptor would regard something he'd decided to glaze to perfection when it would be easier to throw it into the fire. He had not expected his daughter to be of any use to him, yet somehow she had redeemed herself, and he wanted to protect her.

"First things first," he had said, "speak in questions. Give your captor a reason to be intrigued by you."

"The Traitor." Wil echoed the words of Espel, who stood over her. "You mean your brother, don't you?"

Espel's face morphed into a sweet smile. A child's smile, with a wicked gleam, as small and as sharp as the glints of fire in her eyes. "When a snake slithers free of its egg, does it call anyone its sister?"

She crouched beside Wil and traced a finger along the length of her steel glove.

"Your Highness." The girl in the silver robe's tone was pleading. Espel ignored her and lifted Wil's hand in both of her own, probing the palm and each finger, as though they could provide an explanation.

The chain tightened across Wil's throat.

The look on Espel's face just then was an echo of her brother's. Her lips were pursed curiously, her lashes burdening her eyes. It was a cruel trick of the light that she could have all his mannerisms and nothing else. She was his image reflected in a window, vague and fading. A familiar stranger.

It was a cruel trick, also, that Espel's face made Wil miss Loom. Made her wish he were standing in his sister's place now. He should be here while the kingdom he so loved was burning.

"Shackle her wrists," Espel told the guards. "The gloves will protect you. But if you harm her, I'll make sure you die nonetheless."

It took the guards several minutes to work out just what to do with a prisoner whose touch would turn them to stone. The girl in the silver robe never eased up on the chain for a second, even after the guards had shackled Wil's wrists to her ankles, leaving her painfully arched. They laid her on a piece of driftwood barely wide enough to hold her, and two of the men hoisted her up.

It was a luxury compared to Zay, who was slung, unconscious

and bleeding, over a guard's shoulder. Wil listened hard to make sure she was still breathing.

"We'll move through the mountain's channel and head straight for the dungeons," the girl in the silver robe was ordering them. "Put out those torches. No one is to see us."

Once the last torch was extinguished, the darkness was near absolute. Wil could just barely make out the city in the far distance, billowing with smoke against a starry and oblivious sky. She took in what details she could. They were walking alongside a mountain.

Wil conjured up a memory of her brother's atlas. The cities surrounding Cannolay all ran parallel to pieces of one large mountain that peaked in Cannolay and formed the palace itself. Messalin was to the east of where they had arrived at the shore, and they were moving in the opposite direction, which meant they were being taken to the palace. And for a moment, just a moment, they rounded a corner and she saw it in the distance. The palace was a beacon. Its lights burned on into the night, unafraid as it kept watch over its city. It sloped up toward the sky on the face of a mountain, all stone that had been smoothed into spires and columns, each window and archway trimmed in marble and gold.

Loom had said the palace was a gift from the emperor of the East a hundred years ago, and that appeared to be true. The palace, while a perfect extension of Cannolay's mountains, also bore carved statues and patterns on its pillars that resembled the things Wil had seen in Owen's books. She couldn't help but let the horror of her situation subside as she stared at it. No photo could do it justice. Its face burned bright against the night sky like a star carved of stone.

Then the stars were blotted out, and the air went damp and sour. For a moment, Wil could almost believe that she had lost consciousness—her body was already numb from her restraints—but then a guard lit another torch, and she realized that they were inside a narrow channel carved into the mountain.

It was quiet now, save for the shuffling of boots. The girl in the silver robe headed the party, while Espel kept up the rear. The princess said nothing, but Wil could feel her eyes boring into her. Curious. Conniving.

Wil tried to keep track of the distance by counting the strides of the guards, but there were too many of them, and the sounds of their boots all blurred together.

Eventually, the ceiling grew lower. It was cold and Wil had begun to shiver. She could see her breath. Quite a contrast to the South's perpetual warmth.

The clinking of metal. Her chains were undone, and she was tossed unceremoniously to the ground. Her legs were numb, the muscles in her arms trembling. Zay was dropped beside her, and instinctively Wil scrambled out of reach so that they would not touch.

In the torchlight, Zay's brow was furrowed and sweaty, her cheeks red with fever.

Wil didn't have time to notice that she and Zay were in a prison cell before she heard the iron bars slam shut behind her. The guards and the princess and the girl in the silver robe continued on down the path, taking the light with them, leaving Wil and Zay in the dark bowels of the mountain cave.

# THIRTY-ONE

"Zay?" Wil whispered into the blackness.

It had been more than an hour, Wil was certain. It felt like an eternity. Maybe it was even morning outside.

Already she had paced the length of their tiny cell a dozen times, fumbling for something amid the iron bars and rock walls to manipulate for an escape. But there was nothing. Wil felt each bar and could not even find the lock.

Zay's raspy, erratic breaths gave away her location in the tiny space. Wil knelt beside her, tentatively reaching a gloved hand and finding her ankle. In the darkness, Wil had managed to tear away her sleeve and fashion it into a bandage to staunch the bleeding. It seemed to have worked. But she could do nothing for whatever poison had coated the blade.

"Zay," she said again, pleading. "You have to wake up."

Silence, followed by a low groan. Zay murmured something

that sounded like "Ada." And then she said it again, gasping. "Ada? They've taken him."

"No," Wil said. "Ada is fine. But we haven't been so fortunate." She could tell by Zay's stupor that Zay had been subject to a hallucinatory sleep serum, much like the one Wil had experienced on the ship. And it had homed in on Zay's one real fear.

"I think we're in the palace dungeon," Wil said. "Is that possible? Is there a dungeon?"

"There are several." Zay's breathing was labored, and she sucked air through her teeth as she moved her wounded leg. "How long was I out?"

"I'm not sure," Wil said. She wished she had even a fraction of Gerdie's genius. He would have found some way to keep track of the minutes. Timed the drips of condensation and crafted them into seconds—something. But all Wil could decipher was the distance between the rock walls and the iron bars.

Zay murmured something about ships and drowning, and then she went silent and still again.

"No." Wil shoved Zay's shoulder with her gloved hand. "Stay with me."

Nothing.

Wil paced the length of the cell again. Twenty iron bars. Three stone walls. A cell approximately wide enough for two people of her height to lie flat. All she could do was count. Numbers and little lengths and breaths that all added up to nothing.

She sat in the dirt again. No sense exhausting herself trying to find a way out.

She tried to be like the wind, to be everywhere, observe everything. But even the wind would never find her here.

"Torture." Her father's voice came back into her head, and just like that she was back in her memory of standing before him in the throne room. She was dressed like a princess, her hair pinned and neat, her spine straight.

"They'll weaken you so that you'll be easier to manipulate."

She had paid such close attention. She had imagined herself hanging upside down. Drowning. Having her nails plucked from their beds. She imagined fire, blood, shouting.

But she hadn't imagined silence and blackness, and now it all made sense. Princess Espel threw her down here to weaken her resolve. She would be back; it was only a matter of time.

Wil closed her eyes. She thought of the oval garden in the summer. She thought of how it buzzed, and how the trees were lungs that sighed as she ran through the paths they lined. She conjured up each map in Owen's atlas and sorted all the countries and kingdoms alphabetically, and then in the order of their founding. She whispered their capital cities aloud.

She thought of Loom. Or rather, he came to her head uninvited, the way he always seemed to. He would know by now that something had gone wrong.

She felt that odd pain in her core again. Something churning.

"Southern Arrod," she whispered. "Northern Arrod. Brayshire. Cannolay—"

There was a sound somewhere far to the left of her cell. And then a flickering orange glow as the torch was brought closer.

Wil sat up. She could just make out Zay's limp form now; her lips twitched, trying to form words as she dreamed; her face was coated in sweat.

Footsteps were approaching as the light drew nearer. Wil worked to keep her face neutral and her breathing calm.

Princess Espel stood over her, on the other side of the iron bars. Her chin was canted, and she held something behind her back with both hands. All her daggers and vials jangled like bracelets and beads.

The girl in the silver robe stood behind her, glowering, torch in hand. The silver ink in Espel's tattoos caught the light, like fragments of a secret language being decoded one letter at a time.

She regarded Wil with a gaze that was curious and cold. Then she tossed the thing she had been holding. It slipped between the iron bars and landed at Wil's feet.

It was the ruby heart of the guard Wil had killed, all its arteries and veins etched into its surface, the edges jagged from where they'd been broken apart from the rest of him.

"What are you?" Espel said at last.

Wil didn't reply. If she was to survive this situation, she needed to be whatever her captor needed her to be, and she wasn't yet sure what that was.

"The Traitor sent you to destroy me," Espel said.

"He doesn't send me anywhere," Wil said. "Your brother may have a lot of ideas for how this kingdom could be saved, but he's an abysmal planner."

Espel's lips raised into something not quite a smile. "Boys," she mused. "Do you have any experience with brothers?"

"Yes," Wil said. "Quite a lot." She kept her voice and her face neutral, but she began to hope that she was making progress with this elusive princess who stood to inherit her dying kingdom, and who was kept so well hidden she was more legend than girl. Stripped of her guards, and with nothing but stone and torchlight behind her, she was still just a child.

"And your brother," Espel went on. "Is he greedy like the Traitor? Would he try to behead a king in that king's bed to claim the throne?"

"Yes," Wil said, because that was just the sort of thing Baren would do.

"And what does your brother make of this?" Espel nodded to the ruby heart, which cast red shadows on the wall of Wil's cell, like the blood of her unwitting victims.

Baren was unaware of Wil's power. But even so, she knew that if he had seen for himself what she was capable of, his opinion of her would be the same as it had always been. "He says that I'm a curse who was never meant to be born."

"Your Highness," the girl in the silver robe began. "I do not think you should speak so freely with the prisoner—"

"I did not ask for your council, Masalee," Espel snapped. "You are here to hold my torch, and that is all. If you cannot be silent, a sconce can replace you."

The girl in the silver robe broke the distance between them in one fluid stride. "As your high guard, I cannot leave your vicinity, under the orders of the king." There was an edge to the words.

Espel's eyes were focused dead ahead. "I see. You fear my father more than you do me."

"There's no fear, Your Highness. There is only my duty to ensure the safety of my future queen." Her eyes flashed to Wil.

Espel drew a long breath through her nose. "Your insubordination will be dealt with later. Once again."

Masalee's expression was unreadable, and she took a step back.

Compared to Loom's description, Espel's composure was a surprise. Baren had been the terror of Wil's own castle, but his demands from the servants could be heard echoing down the halls.

Espel looked at Zay, and her expression turned to one of annoyance. "I suppose you should do something," she told Masalee. "I want her fit to stand by morning."

Masalee set the torch in a sconce and moved forward. She looked at Wil, and her jaw clenched.

She rested her palm to one of the bars, and under her touch the iron burned orange. The outline of hinges appeared briefly, and Masalee was able to open the bars like a door.

A marveler. Wil had heard only rumors of what marvelry could do; it was a skill that had originated in the East and slowly made its way around the world. But marvelers were a secretive lot. She had probably met dozens of them in the Port Capital and never known it.

If Gerdie were here, she'd shove him and grin like a fool. *See that? I told you so.* She could see his astonishment. She could see his sage eyes trying to draw logic from the absence of logic.

The thought disappeared as the bars slammed shut again.

Wil watched as Masalee knelt beside Zay, her robe gathering around her like a pond made of moonlight. She gracefully undid the binding on Zay's ankle as though she were peeling away the ribbon on a package. The skin was angry and swollen where the knife had entered it, and the old wound on Wil's own calf throbbed at the sight of it.

Wil tried to hide her fascination as she watched. Masalee rested her hands over the wound and blood stained her fingers. There was no flourish to it. No fanfare. She had the placid concentration of a doctor suturing a wound and who had done it a thousand times before. The shredded flesh reached for itself, like teeth in a mouth slowly closing.

Then the wound was gone, leaving crusted blood in the shape of it.

Zay's brow furrowed in her sleep. Something troubling was happening in that head of hers, but at least the red from her fever seemed to be fading.

"Come," Espel said, reaching for Wil's gloved hand. "I take it these are meant to contain your power."

Instinctively Wil's hand rose to meet hers, this strange and fierce girl who was just barely her height. Espel called Wil's ability a power, but she had a power of her own, a pull that commanded compliance.

Wil stood to approach her.

At once Espel seemed less menacing. Though something dangerous lurked ever in her eyes, she regarded Wil like a curiosity. She ran her fingertips up and down the length of the steel glove, marveling. "You're from the North and you've wandered into enemy territory unprotected," Espel said. "You're quite brave, aren't you? Even if it was a stupid thing to do." She raised her eyes from the gloves to Wil. "Why?"

"To help in the aftermath of the attack." Wil decided honesty was her only defense.

Espel's fingertips returned to the steel glove's palm. It was a strange dance, two girls from warring nations, stripped of their pretenses, trying to measure the threat before them.

Wil could still feel Loom's absence, but it was not so menacing now. It was a dull pain in her stomach, where smooth skin had grown over her wound and created a pale scar. She felt tethered between the estranged siblings, as though they were each pulling her in different directions and refusing to let go.

"I apologize for the band of brutes that greeted you when you arrived," Espel said, still holding Wil's steel hand as they walked. "My father insists I take them with me at night. Rather useless if you ask me, the lot of them."

Striding alongside Espel, Wil's heart thudded so clumsily and with such force she was certain the princess could hear it.

"What should I do with her, Your Highness?" Masalee's interruption seemed pointed.

Espel sighed through her nose, considering the options as though contemplating an assortment of pastries. "The night-lace from the blade should put her out until morning. I'll deal with her then." Espel turned back to Wil, her eyes gleaming. "Have you ever seen a palace before? You probably haven't. The royals in Northern Arrod are quite stingy; they've got that high wall so that nobody can see their castle. But, even if you had, you've never seen one like this."

Espel squeezed her hand before letting go. "It's the greatest palace in the world," she said. "It's indestructible. Marvelers from all over the world have blessed it."

"Your Highness." Masalee stood, and her head moved just slightly in Wil's direction and then back. A question.

"Masalee. Show our guest to the opal chamber," Espel said, at once bored and toneless. "Be sure no one sees you. Use the channels." Only Wil caught the way Masalee's eyes darkened with—something. Disappointment?

No.

In the fleeting light of the torch, it looked very much like longing.

# THIRTY-TWO

THEY MOVED THROUGH NARROW PASSAGES carved from stone. Servants' channels, Wil guessed. There were a few in her own castle, and she and Gerdie had used them in their games.

The opal chamber was rightly named. The marble floors shimmered and gleamed, a different color each way the light touched them. The far wall was raw mountainside, carved into an elaborate headboard much like the stained glass scenes at the broken castle—animals in the foliage carrying mangled prey in their jaws, amid carved blossoms and vines.

Wil could feel the hatred emanating from the princess's guard like a summer fog. In the bright light of the opal chamber, Masalee's elegant face was filled with disdain. She offered no explanation, giving Wil only a bitter laugh when she took in the state of her damp clothes and limp hair.

Wil had never felt so scrutinized in her life.

When Masalee left, Wil deflated with a sigh.

Loom would soon notice that she and Zay weren't coming back, if he hadn't already. He wouldn't be able to come after her, not with the bounty on his head. Zay was no good in her state. Wil would have to find a way to get both of them out of here.

Though she was desperate to get to Pahn, she couldn't resist the rare opportunity to see the famed mountain palace, of uncovering its secrets. Maybe she could learn something that would help her family, would end this war.

In the stillness of this large and empty room, the enormity of the night's events finally reached her. She could see the guard she had killed as clearly as if he were still before her. All ruby, even his hair, even his forearms. This was a first. Usually her victim would die before they had completely crystallized.

But this time, the ruby had spread fast. By the time he was dead, there had not been an inch of skin left to the guard.

She was getting stronger. Her body thrummed with the electric energy of it, even now. When she caught her reflection in the dressing mirror, her skin seemed brighter, her eyes a deeper brown.

It was an especially hot night, and the air was heavy.

Through a pair of glass double doors there was a stone balcony just wide enough for her to step out on and gaze at the city.

It was all cloaked in blackness, including most of the palace itself. Wil strained her eyes and tried to see across the water to the distant island with its broken castle. Loom was there, worrying. She knew it. Just as she felt his presence, she also felt his absence. Felt every wave of water that rolled between them. Felt the anxious air leaving his lungs and filling the soundless night.

She felt the distance just as fiercely as she'd felt his thumb grazing her lip.

There was a sound within her temporary quarters, and she spun on her heel just in time to see the one of the heavy carved doors opening.

Espel stood, backlit by the sconces in the hall. Her small frame did nothing to fill the gaping doorway, but something about her was arresting even so. She wore a white linen gown that ruffled and rolled around her feet like the sea bursting over rocks.

When she met Wil's eyes, her stoic expression turned to a sweet smile. "It's a great view, usually. The flecks in the stone catch the sunlight and it's like the air is on fire all day."

Espel advanced until she was beside Wil on the balcony, a hairsbreadth from touching Wil's arm.

"I suppose the Traitor has told you I eat live baby goats for breakfast, or that I bathe in the blood of my enemies," Espel said, stretching her arms out over the ledge. "We've never gotten on well. I'm sure you know what a trial brothers can be. Always so desperate to be the Important One." She sighed and turned onto her back, hanging upside down over the railing to look at the stars splayed above them.

Espel's demeanor turned serious. "What do you make of your king's handiwork?"

"I don't have a king anymore." The words were easy for Wil to say because they were the truth.

"Perhaps not," Espel said. "But what you do have is an extraordinary power." She stood upright. "I'd like to know more about it. Come and take a walk with me." The breezy invitation was not a question.

Wil kept even pace with Espel, and the moment they stepped into the hallway, Masalee emerged from the shadows between the sconces. "Your Highness."

"Oh," Espel said, as though inspecting something she'd stepped in. "Bring us some tea. We'll be in the Star Garden."

Wil saw the muscles go rigid under Masalee's robe. "I can summon a servant, Your Highness."

"If I had wanted a servant, I'd have told a servant to do it," Espel went on, and began walking again. Masalee kept pace behind her.

"The entire palace overlooks the Ancient Sea," Espel said. "You can hear the tides from every room. Do you know how it earned its name?"

"For the soldiers who died in battle," Wil said.

Espel noticed the change in her. "What do you think about that?"

"What I think is that the sea makes us delirious," Wil said.

"We look to it to find the things we've lost."

Espel tilted her head, but said nothing. Wil supposed the origin of names was important to a girl who had been named for something so deadly. Did the name define her, or merely suit the fire with which she was born?

They moved down a labyrinthine set of hallways where flimsy candles danced halfway up to menacing ceilings. The faint etchings in the mountain walls told stories of love and violence and corpses, of fiery ships succumbing to watery graves.

"I suspect your mind is as powerful as your hands," Espel said at last. "It would be a shame for a girl with your ability to have a dull brain. So many girls allow themselves to be bleeding idiots because that's what's expected of them. Dress like a girl. Walk like one. Eat like one. Desire the things a girl should desire, and nothing more—but how can that be called desire, if it's dictated?"

Wil was frightened by how much she agreed. She had not expected to have so much in common with a princess who boasted of killing her mother.

They reached a pair of massive doors made of pale wood. Its carvings were of plants that resembled the tattoos snaking up Espel's wrist as she reached for the handle. In the flickering firelight, the fanged creature appeared to be biting into her wrist. The lines were slender and gleamed with bits of silver.

The door opened with a frightful groan, and the warm night air rolled into the palace.

Wil marveled at what she saw.

There was a garden that sat atop a mountain plane, overlooking the city and sea. There appeared to be nothing separating the garden's edge from the sky, but Wil could make out a silver gleam in the air, just faintly. She had never seen an electrical dome up close before, but she had read that they were invisible and only air could pass through them. They repelled weapons and generated backup energy from the sun so that cutting their electricity wouldn't disable them.

Espel led them out onto a pathway of raw mountain stone. "Stay put," she ordered Masalee.

The starlight was a bright beacon out here. The world was still and calm.

Chemical smoke still lingered on the air, a bitter reminder that peace was an illusion. Still, the flowers were unaware of any bloodshed. The blossoms were varying shades of silver and white, like the stars themselves.

Espel spun on her heel and faced Wil, stopping her short. "So then. Tell me about your power."

"It began earlier this year," Wil said, the truth spilling from her like blood from a wound. "It happens when there's adrenaline, but not when I'm calm."

"Are you calm now?" Espel said.

"No." Despite her outward composure, Wil could feel her heart beating staccato in her chest.

"What can you transform?"

"Anything living."

Wil waited for Espel to demand another display of her powers. But after staring ponderingly at the blossoms around them, Espel said, "How long were you in the company of the Traitor?"

Wil hesitated.

"No harm is going to come to him at my hand, believe me," Espel said, reading her expression easily. "He wouldn't be stupid enough to come back here, and I have no interest in chasing him through the slums besides."

"It's been weeks now," Wil said. "We met at a camp."

"And he brought you to the South with a plan of some sort," Espel said, falling gracefully onto an iron bench. She crossed one leg atop the other and canted her head just slightly in invitation. Wil sat beside her.

Espel wasn't afraid to get close. There were mere inches separating her from certain death against Wil's skin. The princess glanced to her guard, who was rigid in the doorway, a hand at the hilt of her sword.

The sword wouldn't do anything, Wil thought. The crystal would overtake the princess's body in the time it would take her guard to cross the space between them. Though Wil would still be left an easy target.

The princess didn't ask very many questions about Wil's past. She didn't care about her brothers or her upbringing, or even her Northern Arrod accent. She was interested only in Wil's power—when it started and how it worked. Everything.

When Espel was content with her answers, she turned her head and stared out at her kingdom that was devastated but unbroken by the zealous king's attack. "You should sleep," she told Wil. "Tomorrow you'll meet the king."

Tomorrow, she thought, she would find out what had happened to her family and discover some way out of the palace. She would find Zay, and they would return to the broken castle that lay hidden across the sea, where even the starlight couldn't find it.

The palace itself smelled faintly of incense and mists. But the night breeze through the open window carried the charred, chemical smell of the darklead.

# THIRTY-THREE

THE COLD STEEL OF A blade against her throat was what made Wil open her eyes.

She didn't dare move.

The only light came from the sconces flickering in the hallway.

This was it, she thought. Espel had discovered she was King Hein's daughter. She was going to try to murder her in exchange for the lives lost in the darklead explosion and be done with it. Or worse, spirit her off by knifepoint to a dungeon in the bowels of this mountain palace and bleed her powers dry.

A face moved close to hers, the breathing hot in her ear. But it wasn't Espel's voice that whispered to her. "I'm not afraid of you." Masalee. "I've killed seventeen men to keep my place as the princess's guard, and I won't think twice about killing you, too."

Wil's heart was pounding in her chest, but the princess's guard had managed to immobilize her without their skin touching.

"I don't know where you've come from, or what you have planned, but if you mean any harm to Her Highness, I will be the first to find out. I'll hang you from the market square by your intestines for all of Cannolay to see. So we're clear."

Wil didn't speak. Her head moved in the barest nod. She understood.

The blade pressed against her skin. A single motion and it would slice her open. Masalee moved over her, and Wil could just make out the gleam in her eyes. Then she withdrew her sword and melted back into the darkness.

# THIRTY-FOUR

WHEN WIL CLOSED HER EYES again, she didn't sleep for a long time. Though her body lay between foreign satins, her mind braved the night-dark waters back to Northern Arrod.

She saw a memory of Gerdie, nine years old, his face serious as he knelt over her. She lay in the grass, gasping. Tears blurred her vision and pain muddled her head.

"Look at me," he ordered her.

Behind him was the stone wall, slick with a recent rain, and the smear her jeweled shoe had made in a patch of moss as she fell from several feet up. Those stupid, glittering shoes her mother insisted she wear instead of her brother's boots.

Gerdie ran his fingertips along her shoulder, and her body quaked from the pain of it. Her brother bit his lip, as though her pain had shot up his arm and stabbed at him too.

He stood, and for a panicked moment she thought he was going to leave her to go look for help, but he only broke a branch off a tree and knelt beside her again. "Bite down on this," he said. "We'll go on three."

He only counted to one. With a hard push, he forced her shoulder back into its socket.

The branch did nothing to muffle her scream. She kicked and writhed.

"Shh, shh," he said in a rush, and pressed his palm to her forehead. Only then did she realize that he was shaking too. "It's all over now. It's all right."

It was the first time he would repair her. It wouldn't be the last. There were plenty of breaks and bruises and bleeding gashes awaiting her in the years to come. So many that they no longer frightened her. In addition to his alchemy, he would go on to develop a prowess for medicine, his sister another complex thing for him to solve.

He stayed beside her for more than an hour, long after the ringing in her ears had faded, and the sweat dried from her brow, and the violent pain became a dull throb.

"I've been reading about alchemized glass," he told her. "There's this kind called phoenix glass. You could shatter it to dust, but with a little water and heat, it'll come back together again, stronger than it was before."

She rolled her head to the side and looked at him. His eyes were bright, wise beyond what the rest of his child face could convey.

"We're just royal spares, Wil. We won't inherit the kingdom or serve on Papa's guard. It's like we're made of leftover pieces." He bent his knee, and the braces on his leg creaked loudly, as they always did when the weather was damp. "I'm all copper and hinges, and you're that indestructible glass. When we fall apart we know how to put ourselves back together. No one else will do it."

As the sun rose, a servant entered Wil's temporary quarters and laid an outfit for her on the divan beside the changing screen. Wil pretended to be asleep. When the door groaned shut, she opened her eyes.

The day's first light stretched across the marble floor, and Wil gave up on the idea of getting any more sleep. She drew a bath, and as she sank into the tepid water, she worked to remain composed.

No one knew her identity, she told herself. She had wanted to be a spy all her life, and now here was her chance. She had the elusive Southern princess at arm's length.

Most importantly, the king and the princess would be receiving word from the North following this attack. Some sort of demand, or threat. Something that would indicate just what was happening in the castle.

She needed to know that her brother was safe. If he was in danger, then Pahn would wait. Loom would wait. She would find a way home, though it would break her mother's heart, though her father would kill her for it. She would find him and get him somewhere safe, where his mind and his skills couldn't be tortured out of him for the king's gain.

After the water had gone cold, she tied her damp hair into a figure eight and dressed in the linens laid out for her. It was surprisingly light for such a long gown, off white, sleeveless, and entirely unassuming.

It would be easy to flee in this, Wil thought. No one would suspect that she'd come out of the palace. She could blend right in with the crowd and disappear.

She forced herself to put on her gloves, despite the stifling heat. The silk and steel were malleable, but they didn't allow for much air.

After she'd gotten dressed, she moved to the balcony, hoping the fresh air might rejuvenate her and give her strength for whatever awaited. But if the night had been humid, the morning was worse.

She worried about Zay. Wherever she was, she surely didn't have the luxury of a balcony. Was she locked in a sweltering basement? Hanging upside down in a wardrobe? She needed to get to her before something awful happened—if nothing had already.

As though someone were reading her thoughts, one of the heavy doors was pushed open.

There stood Espel in a ray of light, eyes blazing. Her long hair was drawn over one shoulder, tied tightly with a length of satin that blossomed out into the shape of a lily. She wore purple satin trousers and a tunic, and across her chest and around her waist were her vials and blades, poisons shimmering in rich hues.

Masalee was a step behind her, her eyes focused ahead, her hand on her hilt.

"I'm glad you're awake," Espel said to Wil. "You have to be up with the sun if you want to see my father. He's quite busy." She nodded to the orange goggles fixed atop Wil's head. "You should remove those. They clash."

Wil hesitated. They were the only piece of Owen she had left. But offending the princess would ruin her chances of learning anything about Northern Arrod's attack. Mournfully, she removed them from her crown, setting aside the dead for the sake of the living.

"They'll be perfectly safe, I assure you," Espel said. "The servants know better than to disturb anything when they turn down the beds. Come, my father will be waiting."

It seemed as though they walked for hours, and when Espel pulled back a heavy door at the end of a dark corridor, she expected a throne room like her father's in her own castle. Instead she got sunlight, hitting the white sand and temporarily blinding her. They stepped outside and onto a beach along the ocean's edge.

A small crowd was gathered, all of them dressed uniformly in blue and white or red and gold linen—servants and guards.

At the water's edge stood a man with skin darkened and

weathered by sun. And at his side stood a taller and leaner man, a sword at his hip and light-brown eyes. Wil stifled a gasp. He was Zay's father; he had to be—she looked just like him. And that meant the man he was guarding so closely was King Zinil.

He did not seem so frightening, she thought, as she imagined the guard's sword slicing through his chest.

"I haven't told him about you yet." Espel's whisper pulled Wil from her thoughts. "I wanted him to see for himself, after the morning trials."

Morning trials? Wil didn't dare to ask. But she didn't have to. The doors were pushed open again, and one of the servants raised a large brass funnel and blew into it, creating a fearsome sound that surely carried throughout the entire kingdom.

"Bring out the offender!" The king's voice was deep and frightening. Wil was studying his face, trying to find any resemblance to Loom. But there was nothing. He was hardly a man at all. He was more of a statue, with soulless eyes and a beard that clung to the square angles of his jaw. Tattoos wove down his arms and around his throat in patterns similar to those of each of his children. Loom hid his tattoos when he was in public, because King Zinil had turned them into a mark of exile. He would immediately be identified, maybe even killed as a traitor. But Wil had noticed that Loom wore those tattoos proudly when they were alone. She supposed they still meant something to him.

From down the hallway, there was the creaking of wheels.

Servants were dragging out a guillotine; they struggled to carry it across the sand once they'd left the marble floor of the palace.

Wil's palms were sweating in her gloves. She was about to witness an execution. She was not unaware that these took place, but when her own father conducted them, it was privately and without fanfare. He took no pleasure in it. She and her brothers had never seen one up close, all except for Owen, who had the burden of learning everything a king had to know.

"Let go of me! I can walk without being dragged."

Wil nearly toppled back against Masalee's menacing form. She knew that voice. Zay.

No.

Their eyes met, and for an instant Zay stopped struggling against the two guards who had her arms and were holding her an inch above the ground. Her face was stoic and unafraid. There was no pleading glance and certainly no tears. There was nothing but a girl who knew she was about to die.

"Zaylin Lassiv," the king pressed in his commanding voice. "You were offered salvation when your husband was banished, but you chose to remain married to a traitor, thereby becoming a traitor yourself." Some of the servants averted their eyes. Wil could see which ones knew her, cared for her. "The terms of your banishment state that due to your association with a traitor, you are to be executed should you ever return to this palace."

"I didn't return to your palace," Zay fired off. "I returned to a bleeding river three miles away. I was dragged here drugged and unconscious by your heir."

"Don't make it worse, you stupid girl," one of the servants standing beside Wil whispered. She sounded like she was holding back tears.

Espel cocked an eyebrow and watched her father the way children in the market would watch a marionette show.

"My daughter was guarding her kingdom," the king said, unfazed by Zay's insubordination. "She perceived a threat and determined a course of action."

"What threat?" Zay snarled. "I was unarmed! I couldn't have been a threat even if I'd wanted to."

"My daughter informed me that you did in fact have a most unconventional weapon."

The king had no interest in further arguing with a dead girl. He looked to his guard, the man with the light-brown eyes. Like Masalee, he also wore a silver robe. Wil supposed this was an honor reserved for high guards. "Set her down and carry through when I give the command," the king said.

The king's guard stepped forward. He held Zay's wrists for a second. Only a second, and then he pulled her forward. She stumbled, and she didn't fight as he led her to the guillotine.

When they stopped walking, she stood in his shadow and looked at him. Her lip trembled, and the fire left her eyes. "Father."

He put his hands on her shoulders and pushed her onto the plank.

She was shaking, or maybe it was just the wind fluttering her clothes as he laid her on her stomach and fitted her neck into the divot.

Frantically, Wil looked through the crowd for something she could do. Turning the king to stone wasn't an option. Masalee or Espel would hurl a dagger at her before she'd made it to him, and even if she did manage to take him out, there were dozens of guards who still had her surrounded. It would be her neck under the blade next.

She turned to Espel, who was toying with the collar of her tunic, her eyes wild with intrigue. At last Wil saw what Loom had described.

*I have met monsters.*

"We'll put her head in a box and send it to the Traitor," Espel said, coming to the idea the way a poet comes to a verse. She was staring at the blade as it caught the glare from the rising sun. "A shame to let all that lovely hair of hers go to waste. Masalee, talk to a servant about fashioning it into a wig."

"Yes, Your Highness."

There was the sound of metal slicing through the air, and Wil felt the breath leave her body. The king hadn't given the order, but Zay's father was so eager to be done with it that he had dropped the blade already.

Wil looked to the guillotine, though she knew the horror

waiting there was something she could never take back.

But the blade was still suspended high in the air and Zay still had her head to show for it. Even she seemed surprised by this, and she raised her head just as the sound of metal ripped over her a second time.

The king's guard stumbled back. Blood dripped from daggers lodged in either of his arms. The crowd gasped and shrieked and scattered.

The next blade hit the king in the left shoulder. His guard was immobilized and there was no one else willing to give their life to shield him.

Espel growled and ran into the clearing. "Show yourself, you coward! You traitor!"

Masalee hovered around her like a shark circling prey, her eyes darting in all directions as she tried to anticipate the next attack.

Zay saw her opening and jumped to her feet. Wil ran to her.

Another dagger ripped through the air, and Wil's stomach lurched as she heard it land in flesh. "Who's doing this?"

"Who do you think?" Zay said. Her grip was like iron on Wil's wrist.

Wil raised her eyes to the stone overhang, two stories up. There was Loom, his skin gleaming bright, his stance broad, unbreakable, beautiful in its defiance. He raised his arm, and another blade shot from his hand like a shard of sunlight.

Something pulled at Zay and she let out a cry as she was

ripped away from Wil's side. Her father pinned her to the sand, his knee on her stomach, one of the fallen daggers brandished in his fist. "I won't betray my king for you, girl," he said through gritted teeth.

Zay tried to kick at him, but her eyes were pleading. "Father," she said. Her voice took on a gentler, plaintive tone. "Father."

He silenced her with a slash to her cheek. A red gash appeared, clean and straight, and then began to bleed.

Wil knocked him away with a clean kick to his temple. He fell away, mystified with pain, and covered his ears to stop the ringing.

Zay only stared at him, astonished.

Wil grabbed her with a gloved hand and tore her to her feet. "We have to run. Now. Come on."

Nodding, Zay stumbled after her. She wiped at her face, smearing blood across her cheek.

Someone grabbed Wil's wrist, and instinctively she twisted free.

"Don't let them escape," Espel was shouting to the kingsmen. "If you hurt her, I'll have your heads! I'll have your families' heads!"

Wil dodged another arm that tried to snare her, and with her gloved hands she shoved Zay forward. Zay stumbled, dazed, and Wil wondered if the blade that cut her had been poisoned. But no, that wasn't illness or fatigue in her eyes. It was astonishment. Shame. Hurt.

Espel came running for them, Masalee at her heels, a rush of fury.

Another blade shot across the divide and sliced the back of Espel's ankle. Wil heard the tendon tear, and the princess was down in a pile of bloody sand, gritting her teeth, screaming. Masalee knelt beside her. "Your Highness!"

"Get them." Espel's voice was strained. But Masalee, stubbornly loyal, wouldn't leave her side. She was tearing the fabric of her sleeve to make a bandage even as Espel hit and shoved her.

Wil and Zay raced across the sand that reduced their speed by half and made it into the city square. There should have been a wall of guards to stop them, but King Zinil's ego had dictated that they be present for Zay's execution. He wanted them to witness what happened to his perceived traitors. He wanted them to see that he would have a father kill his own child.

They raced past vendors and down an alleyway, stopping at last to catch their breath.

Zay doubled forward and dry heaved.

Wil rubbed circles on her back with her gloved hand, and for once Zay didn't spurn her closeness. She spat and shuddered and let out something like a sob.

"Zay . . ." Wil began and then trailed off. What could she possibly say to comfort her? That she understood? That she feared her own father would have done the same if she ever returned home? That she still, knowing that, loved him so much that she wished she could cut his memory out of her heart and bleed him away?

Zay stood and brushed Wil away from her. "Loom will catch up to us at Rala's house. I'm sure that's where he left Ada. There's no one else he trusts. Must have figured out we were captured when we didn't come back. And we've witnessed enough morning executions for him to know what was going to go down." She shook her head.

Nothing more was spoken after that. Zay trudged onward with her head high, but her gaze was on something that only she could see. Some memory of a time when the arms that had shoved her onto the guillotine had held her.

When they left the alleyway, they blended easily into the crowd. No one had the luxury of knowing what went on in the palace. They didn't know that Zay had nearly lost her head, or that Wil was set to become the princess's new plaything.

"Rala?" Zay stepped inside the house, and Wil lingered in the doorway. This place still smelled of Gray Fever and the death it brought.

"Ada?" Zay called, and the boy stirred on a blanket on the floor where he'd been dozing. "Ada!" She swept him into her arms and clung to him like the world itself might come to take him away. He giggled and buried his hands under her hair.

Wil backed away from the door and out into the sunlight, away from the quiet and the sick.

A hand brushed her bare forearm and she jumped.

"Miss me?" Loom's voice was cocky as ever, but when Wil turned to face him, her eyes grew wide with alarm.

He hadn't bothered to conceal his tattoos, he must have been in such a rush, and a sweaty sheen coated his face, which had turned a purpled shade of pale. His eyes were sunken, the bones in his cheeks pronounced, his lips quivering and bleeding. His skin looked as though it could slide from his bones.

"Don't stare at me that way. I can't look as bad as all that," he said.

He fell forward, and Wil wrapped an arm around his back, shifting his weight against her shoulder. "I've got you," she said.

She touched his forehead and then his cheeks. Dangerously hot. "We have to go," she called to Zay. "Now."

"Hells," Zay muttered at the sight of him. But her false anger didn't mask her fear. She put an arm around his waist and together she and Wil hauled him toward the outskirts. His head swayed and dipped and darted back up as he tried to remain conscious.

"You know better than to get that close to the palace," Zay said. "Are you listening to me? Wake up!"

He drew a sharp breath and rolled his hazy eyes in her direction. "But if I'd let them take your head, my dear wife, how would you be able to yell at me?"

"Idiot." She kissed his cheek. "That's what you are."

His knees buckled.

"What is this?" Wil demanded, hoisting him back up. "What's happening to him?"

"Curse," Loom muttered. His lids were heavy.

"What curse?" Wil asked.

"I told you, no good can come from meeting Pahn."

"Hells," Zay swore. Blood stained the back of her hand, her cheek, her collar. "We don't have time for this. We need to get you home so I can figure out how to undo this."

"Can't go back there." Loom's breaths were becoming more labored with each step. "That's the first place the king will look for us. They'll kill us now, you know that—kill us and take Wil." He looked at Wil, desperation lighting his tired features. "If you're brought back to that palace, you'll never escape again. For as long as Espel has her way she'll—she'll—"

"Shh," Wil said. "That won't happen. Just save your strength."

It was with great difficulty that they managed to drag Loom over the rock embankment.

A few yards from the water, with his modest ship in sight, he collapsed into an unconscious heap of fevered skin and dead limbs.

Zay swore and knelt beside him. Ada mimicked the gesture and dropped down next to her. Her cheek hovered over Loom's parted lips. "Still breathing, but he won't be for long if he stays here. Help me lift him onto the ship." She hoisted him by the shoulders and Wil grabbed his feet.

Loom let out a feeble groan as they laid him on the deck of the ship. Zay doubled forward to rest her forehead against his. His hair was gathered in her fist. "I'll fix this," she whispered. "Hang on, *ansoh*." My husband.

Zay ran for the stairs, dragging Ada by the hand. "Take care of him while I steer us out of here." She looked over her shoulder at Wil, and her eyes were misty and red. "You keep him alive."

She was gone, and seconds later the boat was moving.

"Loom?" Wil undid the buttons of his sweaty tunic, hoping the cool sea air might bring some relief. His arms fell heavy against the deck as they came from their sleeves. Lifeless. "Open your eyes," she demanded. "If you think I'm going to let you die now after everything you've gotten us into, you truly don't know the first thing about me."

His lashes twitched, and she saw his eyes again, glassy but comprehending. "Good." Her shoulders dropped. "That's good. I'm going to go belowdecks and find some lyster to cool your fever."

"Sharp memory," he rasped. His eyes rolled back as they closed. "It's in the kitchen. You have to get the leaves wet."

She was gone and back in seconds, the potted lyster plant in one hand and a canteen in the other. She plucked a leaf in her gloved fingers, doused it, and pressed it against his forehead.

He looked at her, his chest heaving as he breathed. "How could you ever believe you were a monster?" he whispered.

She pressed another leaf to the side of his neck. "Is this helping at all?"

He nodded, then let out a strangled sound and gagged up a mouthful of frothy white vomit.

"Winds." Her voice was frustrated. She had tended to enough sickness in her life to know that this was the work of something cruelly unnatural. Something that even her genius brother wouldn't find in one of his books. She turned him onto his side as he coughed and shuddered. *Don't lose it,* she was telling herself. *You can't lose it now.*

"Loom, stay with me. Tell me what we're dealing with. Tell me what to do."

She put his head in her lap and applied more leaves to his fevered skin.

He squinted at her, blinded by the sunlight. "It's a curse. There's nothing to do."

"Curse," she echoed. "What curse? What are you saying?"

"After all I've demanded from you, you deserve to know." He closed his eyes and then forced himself back awake. "It was a year ago that I tried to murder my father. After that, he ordered Pahn to curse me so that I could never inherit the throne under any circumstances. I enter the palace walls, I die. My heart will stop beating and there will be nothing—no doctor or herb or machine—that can revive me."

"But—" Wil's voice caught. "You didn't even go inside the palace, and you're away from it now. So you should be getting better, right?"

He laughed, a low, creaky sound and shuddered with pain. "I got too close. The damage is done."

She laid another lyster leaf against the side of his neck, and one to his forehead. He sighed with relief at their coolness, but his skin was still sallow and hot. His eyes were all pupil.

"It's meant to be a reminder," he murmured. "A reminder that my home can never love me the way that I love it."

"Why don't you just let it go?" She was desperate to keep him conscious. "You don't have to be king. The burden's been lifted."

"No," he whispered. "Those hunks of land, those people who are sick and dying and afraid—they need me."

"You won't be able to rule any kingdoms if you're dead." She reached for another leaf, and he caught her hand, and pressed it hard against his heart. He wanted her to feel it beating under his skin, steady and stubborn as the rest of him. And she did.

"I'm not dead." His voice was fading, even as he fought to look at her. "And that is my kingdom."

# THIRTY-FIVE

THE MAINLAND GLITTERED IN THE distance as they sailed away, its mountain palace reaching skyward like a beacon of power. There were no ships trailing after them. There were no guards in pursuit; no king calling for Loom's head. They didn't have to, for they all knew that the curse had done its work. The banished prince was going to die.

Loom was lost in an unreachable sleep by the time the mountain palace disappeared from view. He didn't stir even as Wil and Zay carried him to his bunk.

After they'd laid him atop his sheets, Zay knelt down and pushed the sweaty hair from his face. "I love you, you idiot," she whispered, and kissed his temple. He shifted with a quiet groan.

Wil's jealousy was sudden and stinging. It wasn't just the

gesture, but the certainty of it. Zay knew this boy. Knew all his secrets, the lies he told and why he told them. She had known him when they were both small and innocent, before he became this banished, breaking, and unbreakable prince. When she said that she loved him, it was the truth, because for each other they withheld nothing.

Wil was not sure she was capable of loving anyone in such a way. Love itself was not a word she was accustomed to hearing in the castle where she grew up. It had seemed like such a small thing to Wil anyway. Just a word. So what was this feeling in her stomach at the sound of it?

"Where are we taking him?" she asked. "Do you know a healer who can help him?"

Zay stood from Loom's bedside and placed her hands on her hips. "You should be happy now," she said. "We're taking him to your precious Pahn. He's the only one who can undo this."

Pahn. "He'll help?" Wil asked eagerly. "Loom made it sound as though they were enemies."

"Loom is well beyond the capabilities of a healer," Zay said. "Pahn is the only choice we have." She touched the back of her hand to Loom's forehead. "I have to go set our course. You stay with him. Use the lyster to keep his fever down."

She couldn't be out of the room fast enough. Down the hall, the door to the control room slammed shut.

Wil turned to Loom, who was gasping and spent. After

everything, his suffering would be the thing that brought her to Pahn.

"This is your own fault," she said, though she knew that he was beyond hearing her. It was the truth. If he hadn't stolen her away to do his bidding, none of this would have happened, and she would have found her own way to Pahn.

She would not allow herself to feel guilty for his misery or the stroke of good fortune it had just granted her. She would not feel guilty for being the daughter of his kingdom's enemy, or for hiding it from him. He did not deserve her secrets, she told herself. After what he'd done to her, he barely deserved her kindness.

Still, kept vigil at Loom's bedside for hours, until the day gave way to a dark, placid night. Thoughts of Pahn were lost as she labored to soothe Loom. He murmured and thrashed. His skin burned hot, but sweat no longer beaded his face, which frightened her. It meant that his fever refused to break.

As he slept, Wil told him her mother's tales that she'd picked up in her travels. She told him of the Singing Wolf and the Gold King. She told him that he was foolish to have returned to that mountain palace, knowing it could be the death of him.

And in the silence of Loom's sleep, she began to wonder if she would still be on this ship if it weren't headed straight for Pahn, or if she would have left him to search for Pahn herself. She wondered if Loom meant more to her than simply a means to be rid of this curse.

"Our families want to kill each other, and maybe one of them will succeed," she told him. She doused her fingertip with water and traced it along his lower lip. Reflexively, he drank it. "We're enemies, you and me. You just don't know it."

Down the hall, Zay was singing Ada to sleep, and then the ship fell silent for a while.

"Hey." Zay's voice was hushed as she appeared in the doorway. "How is he?"

"I don't know." Wil studied him. His skin was a tarp draped loosely over his bones. "So far he's kept water down. If all goes well, I can mash one of the rations into a paste so he's getting something in his stomach."

"You're good at this bedside manner thing, aren't you?" Zay said. "Never would have expected it, given your violent streak."

Wil was only violent when she was being threatened, and these two had been a constant threat. But she didn't say that. "He doesn't seem to be in pain, at least," she said. "I'll do what I can, but I'm no marveler."

Zay frowned worriedly at him.

"Come outside with me." Zay held up the bottle that was in her hand. "The night air will do us both some good. He's not going anywhere."

Wil felt guilty leaving his side, but Zay was right. The tiny cabin was heavy with sickness; she was beginning to lose her mind in there.

When they stepped onto the deck, it was illuminated by starlight. The sky was perfect and clear, no clouds or land to be seen. Zay took a drink from the bottle, cringing as she swallowed and then offering it up to Wil.

Wil took a swig. She'd had spirits before—sparkling champagne and ciders during the celebrations she and Gerdie snuck their way into, and sometimes shots of a sharp amber liquid to help with the pain when a bone needed to be set. This liquid, though, burned even more harshly than that.

"You the praying type?" Zay asked, taking the bottle.

"No," Wil said.

Zay laughed. "You're all rich up north. Rich people don't need gods."

"Didn't you grow up in a palace?" Wil said.

"Well, I wasn't born there." Zay took another swig. "Nothing in that palace was ever mine."

Still, Wil supposed Zay was right. Her own father never seemed to have use for any gods, only his council, and her mother found religion in compulsions and superstitions. Owen found it in the freedom of the open world, and Gerdie in the science of things. There was no talk of blaming their misfortunes on gods, or turning to them for mercy. Wil had not felt the presence of any gods when Owen died; the only thing with them that night had been the stars, and the spitting river water, and her curse.

"I think I can get us there in less than a week," Zay said.

"The Northern waters will be closed around Arrod, so we have to keep as far east as we can, which will add another day."

"The lyster isn't doing very much for his fever," Wil said. "It's like his body is trying to heal, but the curse won't let it."

"I'll figure something out." Zay tried to sound assured. "There are dozens of plants and potions all over this ship."

Wil had more questions, but she knew she would not like the answers. How much worse was Loom going to get? What if the marveler couldn't help? Or wouldn't?

For a while, the only sound was of the water cresting against the sides of the boat. There were no cities out here, no insects buzzing in grass. The world itself could have ended and they wouldn't know it.

Wil lay back against the deck, and her blood fell to the rhythm of the waves. She didn't tell Zay just why she was so experienced in bedside manner. But she was thinking about it then.

Gerdie called to her on nights when he feared his illness would wrap around him like black wings and consume him.

Zay was the first one to break the silence between them. "When Ada was born, Loom heard me screaming and broke through the locked door to get to me." She laughed. "The midwife and three servants tried to push him from the room; they said that any man who saw his wife in such a state would never find her attractive again. He drew his sword and promised to behead anyone who stood between us."

She lay back against the deck. "This curse won't stop me. I'll beat down any door and take down anyone who stands in my path to save him."

Wil rolled onto her side to face her. "Will the king be out looking for us?"

Zay shook her head. "Not for Loom, no. He probably expects him to already be dead, and in a time of war he can't afford to spare any men to go chasing after him."

"What about Espel?"

"There's no telling what that one will do," Zay said.

"She seemed—almost normal at times," Wil said. "Not at all what I expected."

"She wasn't allowed to act sweet when she was a kid," Zay said. "When she was three or four years old, I remember she came in from the garden after a walk with her nanny, with a flower tucked in her hair. The king told her to remove it, and when she refused, he drew his sword and cut the entire chunk of hair right off her head, flower and all. That day, he dismissed her nanny. It was all combat training after that."

"So she did have a soul, once," Wil said.

"She has a soul. It's just a rotten one," Zay said. "Loom has similar stories from his own childhood, and he didn't turn out like her. Nothing like her."

"Perhaps it's different for girls," Wil said. "'We're told who we're meant to be, and we strive to be just that, even if we know it isn't right. Love is used as a weapon against us. When we don't do as we're told, it gets taken away, and when we do, it's returned again like a treasured doll."

"It sounds like you speak from experience," Zay said.

"You may think I'm a witch, but I was human once. Before all this."

"You've just made me feel as though I have something in common with the princess of the Southern Isles, and that exceeds human ability," Zay said. "You're a strange thing. But one day I'll figure you out."

"If you do, maybe you can clue me in."

Zay laughed. A loud, uninhibited sound that carried right up to the stars and across the endless waters.

"Have they always been pitted against each other?" Wil asked.

"I was too young to remember the queen dying in child-birth," Zay said. "But everyone in the palace said that her death broke the king. And here he was left with the last thing she could give him. I suppose Espel just frightened him." She shrugged. "Loom and Espel knew how to be what was expected of them. They were rivals. They had no choice in the matter. But Loom thought he could get through to her. Maybe he still does, though I can't imagine why. I've never heard her say a kind word to him in her life."

"He didn't aim to kill when he threw his dagger," Wil said. "He only wounded her enough to stop her, but he had a clear shot at her heart. He could have ensured right then that she would never be queen."

Zay tipped the bottle toward Wil in a salute. "Nothing gets by you." Her smile was sad. "I never had siblings. Maybe there's something about his loyalty I just don't understand."

Wil thought of Baren. If throwing a dagger at his heart could somehow bring Owen back, she would do it. She would mourn Baren the way she mourned the rabbits the cooks skinned and drained for supper. A sacrifice could not be a tragedy. "He must see some good in her," Wil said.

"Yeah, well, I worry his loyalty will be the death of him." Zay stood, tugging her hair loose from its bun. It fell around her like a tangled black flame with flashes of silver. "I can be loyal too," she said, turning for the stairs.

The silence of the sea at night was more fearsome than the storms they'd encountered on their way to the Southern Isles.

It was late, and the lantern was dim as it swayed over Loom, pulling at the sharp angles of his face. For some time now Wil had been fighting the haze of sleep, not wanting to return to her own bunk. Not wanting to leave the quiet, steady rasp of Loom's breathing. Aside from the occasional whir as Zay strained the engine, his was the only sign of life.

Eventually, exhausted, she grabbed the comforter from her cabin and made a nest of it on the floor by Loom's bed. He thrashed in his sleep, muttering fragments of Lavean in his fever. He turned onto his stomach, and sighed, and went quiet again.

Wil strained her ears to listen to him breathing, until she

fell into a fitful half-sleep of her own. She had kept bedside vigil before, and she had mastered the practice of listening to what was around her, even in sleep. She was distantly aware of footsteps, and then the lantern being dimmed to conserve energy, and gentle voices.

"Hey," Zay murmured. "How are you feeling?"

"Never better." Loom's voice was strained.

"Why is there a black tunic covering the porthole?" Zay asked.

"Wil put it there. I'm not entirely sure why."

"Sit up. You need to drink something."

"You're worrying too much," he said. "You get that from your mother."

"I know what you're doing," she said, "and it isn't going to work. You can't make me angry."

"Isn't that your default personality?"

"Get some sleep, you rotten brat. I'll check on you again in a bit."

"Hey." Loom's voice softened. "I don't suppose you were able to find your mother while you were in the palace."

Zay was quiet for several seconds. There was the sound of blankets rustling. "A servant was able to get to me while I was being held in the dungeon. She told me that my mother fled the kingdom shortly after you and I left."

"Would she have gone back to Grief?" Loom asked.

"I don't think so. My father would know to look for her there." Another pause, and when Zay spoke again, it was with difficulty. "She'll be fine. She knows how to navigate the world, and she's clever."

"You get that from your mother too," Loom said.

It didn't surprise Wil to know that Zay was adept at navigating the world. Wil had sensed this about her the moment she first saw her, at the port in Brayshire. That was what had made her beauty so striking, Wil supposed: the ease with which Zay moved through the world, as though she had conquered it.

"Go easy in the control room, will you?" Loom's words were beginning to slur in his fatigue. "I hear the way you're straining the engine to go faster than it's meant to. You won't improve our situation if the ship breaks down out here."

He was asleep as soon as the words were spoken.

Wil felt Zay's shadow lingering over her. Zay made no secret of her suspicions, but even as she lay under her glare, Wil knew that Zay would hold her temper for Loom's sake. There was a balance, held in place by his fragile state, and everyone on the ship was at the mercy of this curse.

For days, there was no land in sight. Loom bobbed to the surface of consciousness on occasion, and sometimes Wil could even persuade him to have some broth, or a bite of the stale ration bars from the kitchen. She read aloud to him from the books under the bed, and even when he slept, he moved his lips to the lines he knew by heart.

After she'd finished the chapter, while Loom slept, Wil laid the open book on the bed beside him and reached for the lyster plant. The leaf turned to emerald even before she'd finished plucking it from its branch. Pain shot from her stomach to her throat and she pursed her lips to hold back a cry.

Somewhere, buried in the pain, there came relief. She had gone too long without releasing her power, lost as she'd been at sea and in her thoughts.

Loom's hand reached out and touched her cheek. His sleeves were rolled to the shoulders, and she could see his marriage tattoo. The silver outline was fading, as though the black of the moons was absorbing it.

She forced a smile when he opened his eyes and looked at her. "I thought you were asleep."

"I dreamed that something was coming for you." His eyes were the most alert they'd been since the curse took hold of him.

"No one is coming for me."

"Not now," he said. "Years ago. Decades ago."

"Decades ago, I didn't exist and neither did you. Maybe we need to get some more food in you. Do you think you can hold it down?"

"Don't mollify me," he said. "Just listen. I dreamed there was a king. He had been studying dark marveler arts. He wanted to destroy something. He wanted to destroy you."

She smirked. "If he wants to claw his way out of the grave, he's welcome to try."

"Pity the king," he said. The humor drained from his face. With his current pallor, the look he gave her was all the more frightening. "Wil, marvelers don't fight fair. I'm proof of that. But I won't die. I refuse to let my father be that happy."

"Let's make him livid, then, and get you back into fighting shape," Wil said. "Zay thinks she can get us to the marveler by end of tomorrow."

"I hope she isn't killing the engine. She drives this thing like hellfire when she's in one of her moods," Loom said.

She picked up the book, and he put his hand over her wrist, stilling her. "Don't read that story. I've already read that one a hundred times."

"When I was little, I loved the story about the Gold King," she said. "Do you know it?"

"The fairy tale?" Loom asked. "Everything he touched turned to gold."

"Yes," Wil said. "But it isn't just a fairy tale. There's some history to it. Some several hundred years ago, a man set out to try and turn ordinary metals into gold, and that's how alchemy originated: the art of taking materials and reconfiguring them into something else."

"Did he do it?" Loom asked. "Did he make real gold?"

"It's widely speculated and no one knows for sure," Wil said. "But I doubt it. I think he just made something that resembled gold. I've seen glass cut and made to look like very convincing diamonds using alchemy, but it's still glass. There are plenty of theories, though. One is that he managed to really make gold. It made him rich, but the gods of the high winds disliked his greed and cursed him with the golden touch. Since then, so it goes, alchemy has been limited to fusing and repurposing objects but never changing their core materials."

Loom touched her chin, tentatively, as though she might draw another blade and hold it to his throat if he overstepped. "You know a lot about alchemy."

That was Gerdie's doing, but she didn't say that.

In his feverish state, he had wrested away from the sheets, and now Wil noticed the tattoos that bloomed across his arms and collar, coming to frame his bare and unmarked chest. The two moons overlapping on his left arm were also set apart from the others, as though none of the other patterns could dare to touch something so sacred.

Even Wil didn't feel right touching them, and had avoided those moons as she tended to his fever. They did not belong to her. She had heard of Lavean wedding tattoos, but hadn't been prepared for the power they implied, like a tangible presence on his skin.

Loom followed her gaze, and then looked at Wil again with brows raised. He was inviting her to ask questions, but she didn't. She had no right. And besides, she told herself, what did it matter that he was married?

It didn't matter. She would repeat those words until she believed them.

"Tell me about you," he said. He was holding the leaf in his other hand, bobbing it through his fingers.

There was a catch in her voice. "What do you want to know?"

"I want to know about your family," he said. "Your mother. Your brother. Did they abandon you once your power came out?"

She saw her mother collapsing into wails at the news of her children's deaths. She saw Gerdie locking himself in his lab, furiously poring over his cauldron, his mind ever busy, desperate to think rather than feel, rather than accept what he had lost.

She saw the flames in Cannolay.

"There's nothing for me to tell."

"I don't believe that for a minute," Loom said.

"Is this supposed to be a story or an interrogation?"

"A bit of both," he said, in that presumptuous way he clearly thought was charming.

She narrowed her eyes. "I didn't ask to be a part of your sojourn, Loom Raisius. You tricked me into coming along, and now I'm here, and, I might add, this morning I changed your sheets after you got sick on them. Some of it got in my hair. You can ask your questions, but I don't owe you any answers." She stood.

Who was this boy? This boy who had swooped into her life and never seemed to be far from her thoughts. He was a pin in a map, the paper spinning in place, never taking her anywhere. Somehow their destinies had become tangled, and Wil couldn't help thinking she was to blame for failing to get away from him. For not wanting to get away from him now.

"Wait," Loom said. "Don't go."

"I'm not going anywhere. We're trapped in the middle of the bleeding ocean. You should sleep. Try not to dream about any more murderous corpses."

"It wasn't a—"

She was already out the door.

# THIRTY-SIX

Up north in the Eastern Sea, between Arrod and the Eastern Isles, there was a cluster of small countries.

Owen had once told her that this was a good place to disappear. Many of the countries were ancient and impoverished, always overlooked in times of war and rarely frequented by vendors.

But as the country named Grief appeared in the distance, Wil found it to be beautiful. The boats were lined up along the marina, slender and white like fragile bones, backlit by the setting pink sun. The hills were a violently bright shade of green.

It was Wil's sixteenth birthday today, a fact that had nearly gone forgotten now that she no longer had her data goggles to remind her of the date. Time itself had drowned in all that open sea. For just a moment, she stood there with her secret. After days of anticipating Pahn and tending to Loom and cautiously befriending Zay, her mind traveled back to the castle. What was Gerdie doing? Was he safe? Was he thinking of her? He held dates and hours in his head like insects in a great web, and he surely hadn't forgotten.

The brutal sound of coughing carried up the stairs, jarring Wil from her thoughts, and she ran to check on Loom. He, at least, she could do something for.

He was sitting up when she found him, his face skeletal, the sheen gone from his skin. He looked nothing like the boy he'd been just days before.

"We're here now," Wil said, and sat on the bed beside him and doused a lyster leaf for his forehead. "You just have to hang on for a bit longer."

He slouched forward and rested his brow against her shoulder, murmuring her name as though the sound of it brought relief.

She could smell his hair. Like the dirt after a long rain.

# THIRTY-SEVEN

ZAY WAS GONE FOR HOURS. She took Ada with her. Maybe she thought that a small child would elicit some sympathy from this illustrious marveler. Or perhaps she just didn't trust him in Wil's care. Loom was in no condition to watch after him.

Wil sat beside him, mopping his brow. His fever kept breaking, but it returned with a fury every time. She thought he was sleeping, but as she pressed a cool leaf to his forehead, he caught her wrist. There was fight in his eyes, which were made amber by the late afternoon sun.

For a moment, she saw the child he must have been in that mountain palace, with a dead mother and a little sister he wasn't allowed to love, who wasn't allowed to love him. How lonely it must have been, she thought.

"Hey," she said. "How are you feeling?" The tenderness

of her voice surprised her, as though they were old friends, as though they were anything to each other at all. "More dreams of evil kings come to steal me away?"

He shook his head against the pillow. "No." His voice was a whisper. "No dreams. Just thoughts."

"Oh?" She brought a spoonful of water to his lips, and he drank it obligingly. He probably didn't want it, but after many bedside arguments he had learned not to fight her on these small, necessary things.

"I was thinking of the day I saw you in the market square," he said. "The way you moved, this blur of fight and blood and muscle. There had been a rip in the blue sky and you broke through it. You just appeared, and the world changed."

An ache in her chest. Blood pushing her veins toward him as roots through the earth seeking out a means to survive.

"You're delirious," she said.

"I don't want for us to be enemies," he said.

"What do you want us to be, then?"

"Honest with each other." He closed his eyes, and even as sleep tried to pull him back under, he fought it.

"Loom?" She hesitated. "I'm sorry for what's happening to your kingdom. The explosion, the war—all of it." Her voice was soft. "You can't know how sorry I am."

"It isn't your fault," he murmured, and his fingers wove between hers. "I've never hated the North the way much of my kingdom does. I don't blame the Nearsh people for this."

Wil knew the words he didn't say: that he blamed the Northern royals. He blamed the king and queen and all their children.

Was it true? She tried to imagine what it would be like for her in the castle now. Baren as heir, manipulating the guards to enforce his bidding. Gerdie sweating over his cauldron. And her, the one whose features betrayed no royal beauty at all, sneaking into the underground market of the Port Capital to play spy and gather tools that could be fashioned into weapons.

Maybe not, she tried to reason. Maybe she and Gerdie would have fled by now, and the queen as well, if she could be persuaded to leave her husband.

None of this mattered to Loom. If he knew who she really was, if he knew whose blood went through her veins, he'd have thrown her overboard by now.

Soon, footsteps filled the hallway, and men appeared in the doorway holding a gurney fashioned from wooden posts and burlap.

There were three of them. Two held the gurney while a third rolled Loom's prone body onto it. He groaned but didn't open his eyes.

"What are you doing?" Wil said. "Where are you taking him?"

"To Pahn, where did you think?" Zay was standing in the doorway with her arms crossed. "I had to convince him that a banished prince who tested his limits was still worth saving, and he sent his apprentices to collect him."

The men moved up the stairs, hoisting the gurney between them. Wil followed, Zay a step beside her carrying Ada. It was after dark now, and the carriage was the only thing to see. Its windows were illuminated by the electric white glow therein.

Several months back, Owen returned from a sojourn and described the electric carriages that were beginning to appear like crops in technologically advanced cities. Their own father was still resistant to them, and unwilling to dig into the coffers to pave the roads to accommodate them besides.

The machine before her was still unlike anything Wil had been able to imagine from her brother's stories. It was tall, with slender wheels that came nearly to her shoulders. She could feel its loud thrum in her legs and in her teeth, as though she were an appliance to be charged as well.

She couldn't help admiring the thing, even as the men hoisted Loom unceremoniously onto the backseat and folded the gurney. Zay followed after him, and then came Wil at a cautious distance. The inside of the carriage was spacious, the seat upholstered with tufted black velvet. Wil ran her palm against the fabric wonderingly.

If Loom were awake, he'd be all too eager to explain how the carriage worked. He loved explaining things, as though the world itself were a gift he was presenting to her.

Wil reached for his wrist to feel his pulse. Steady, if faint. One of his fingers twitched at the touch of her steel glove. A thick blue vein in his wrist sat at the center of a slender tattoo of a steerwolf's head, canted and howling; its scruff receded into thorny vines.

His body was a collection of little stories, inky vignettes all connected by one long vine that ran through each of them. What did they mean? Had he wanted them, or were they obligations? Did he wear them the way she wore her own illusions? Had they hurt?

She traced a crease in his palm. She wanted to know these stories. She wanted to know all his stories.

The ride was silent. Zay held Loom's head in her lap and wound his hair around her fingers as she stared on. A flash of light darting past the window revealed the worry on Zay's face. Wil was taken aback by how vulnerable she looked.

The electric thrum of the carriage was loud in the night.

They drove into a city that was hardwired with burning blue bulbs of light along the streets. Wires dripped down the sides of buildings like rain. Lights and life poured from windows and open doors. Bright signs advertised gambling huts and all-night dining. In the distance, peppered throughout the city Wil could see slender stars spinning, their metal faces gleaming on the electric lights; she wondered at what they were. She was in awe of all of it, but she couldn't focus on the surroundings. Loom's breathing had taken on a slow rattle with frighteningly long pauses in between.

They drove beyond the lights of the city and down a hilly

dirt road, and Wil thought of Zay walking all this way with Ada in tow.

The carriage stopped in a field with nothing but trees. No—Wil could make out the faint outline of a staircase lit by lanterns with artificial flames. Also electrical, she presumed.

The men got out of the carriage and unfolded the gurney.

When Wil stepped outside, the chill in the air struck her all at once. In her earlier frenzied state she had not bothered to notice that they were no longer in the land of eternal summer, and that this was November in the North.

Zay moved beside her, hugging her arms, shaking but not entirely from the cold.

"Why haven't they said anything to us?" Wil whispered.

"They aren't allowed to speak until they've completed their apprenticeship and become marvelers. They've vowed to do all he asks of them without question."

"How long will that be?"

"Years, usually."

Hoisting the gurney between them, the men began their trek up the stairs, and Wil and Zay followed. Ada had fallen asleep, and Zay carried him to her chest like he was no burden to bear.

Wil stopped counting after the fiftieth step. She strained her ears to listen for Loom's breathing instead. As long as he was breathing, he could be saved, she told herself.

Honest with each other. Had he meant that?

They had moved beyond the treetops, and the city lights

were like radioactive stars in the distance.

At the top step, there was a small wooden cottage, its windows glowing faintly in the dark. One of the men waved them inside.

The warmth of the fireplace melted the cold from Wil's skin.

The men laid the gurney by the fire, not stopping to savor a moment of the warmth for themselves before they disappeared down a dark corridor.

Wil's heart lurched, too wary for hope. "Do you trust Pahn?"

"You'd do well to never trust marvelers," Zay said. "But they'll do anything for a price."

"Price?" Wil asked.

"Ah, she returns as promised!" A man emerged from the corridor, his arms outstretched. "The rebel Zaylin, ripe from the sea but still lovely as ever." His dark eyes darted to Loom and back to her. "And I see you've brought the patient."

Something about his voice made Wil's skin itch. He was a small man, a hairsbreadth taller than she was, and frail, with leathery, tawny skin and a long white braid trailing down his bony back. Here he was: her only hope of being rid of this curse. And now, of saving Loom.

He advanced on Loom, staring at his limp form as though he was a tattered rug in need of repair. "It's bad," Pahn said, "but the fact that he survived the journey is impressive."

Maybe she had once again warded away death, Wil began to think.

"You can heal him," Zay insisted. "You said you could heal him if his heart was still beating." The way that Zay spoke Nearsh was beautiful, heavily accented and confident, to go with her proud stance and defiant incline of her chin. It was the first time Wil heard a hint of pleading in her voice.

"I can heal him and risk incurring the wrath of the Southern king. I'm not a street magician; my services aren't free."

"As I've said, I can pay you." Zay spoke through gritted teeth.

"I believe you promised something I've never seen before. Forgive my skepticism, Zaylin, you hardly have a reputation for being honest, and at my age I have seen it all."

Zay set Ada by the fire, and he curled up contentedly in his sleep. She turned to Wil. "Take off your gloves."

Wil understood at once. She was the price.

The marveler laughed. "I'm nothing like those letches from your palace; I have no interest in young girls."

"I don't want you to have sex with her, you deviant." Zay paced forward and yanked the glove from Wil's right hand. She plucked a leaf from the weeds growing through the wall and dropped it in Wil's palm.

It hardened to emerald immediately, and at that the marveler's brows rose. "Well then," he said to Wil. "Where did you come from?"

Wil steeled herself against his stare. "Can you heal him? I thought curses couldn't be undone."

"Anything can be undone," the marveler said. "But I will not be undoing his curse; that would be breaking a vow with King Zinil, which I intend to honor. I would simply be healing him."

"Then heal him." Zay's vocie was tight, but it was out of fear, not anger. Wil had spent enough time around her now to know the difference.

"Follow me," Pahn said, and opened the door, letting in the cold air.

Wil went after him, casting a pointed glare at Zay. "If you were going to barter with my curse, you could have clued me in."

"I wasn't sure that you would do it."

"Of course I"—Loom muttered something in his troubled dreams—"Of course I would have." She stepped out into the night air, pulling the door shut behind her.

Pahn's lantern did little to light the way. They walked between the trees and away from the tiny cottage, Wil cursing Zay in her thoughts the entire time. If this strange man tried to kill her, her revenge would be swift and fierce.

"This tree," he said, coming to a stop, "is over one thousand years old. It's been here longer than this city. Longer than there have been humans in this country to build this city. The roots snake all the way down this hill and under the streets. They jut out of sidewalks and in the grass."

He held the lantern up, illuminating the bony angles of his

aged face. And then he brought the light to the tree. It was thick as a room of a house, wrapped in its own branches and vines.

"Most of the leaves have fallen off for the winter," Wil said. "I can't change anything that's already dead."

"I don't want you to change the leaves, girl. I want you to turn this tree into stone."

"The entire tree?" Wil said, bewildered. "You want me to ruin something that's a thousand years old?"

"If you can." The marveler took a step back, waving his arm in invitation. "Please."

"And you'll heal Loom?"

"I will give him medicine, that is the agreement," he said. "And I always honor my agreements."

Her heart was already beating fast, and she stepped forward and laid her hand against the trunk.

She closed her eyes and thought of her mother when she was calm and her hair and face were full of light. Of the singed air after a cauldron explosion, the determination of Gerdie's brilliance palpable as a breath.

She thought of home, and the tree turned to stone.

The release was greater than she cared to admit. All week on the ship, she'd plucked leaves from Loom's many plants, creating bits of emerald or ruby. But it hadn't been enough. And now she felt as though her body had been filled with broken bones that were fitting back into place and smoothing over, stronger than ever.

She let out a shuddering breath and opened her eyes.

The tree was gleaming in the moonlight—red and green and diamond, all braided into each other. She could see more clearly through the night's darkness. She could smell the dying days of autumn in the air, could taste the snow waiting to fall like dancers waiting in the wings of their stage.

Pahn looked on in silence for a while, and then he said, "I must ask the name of the girl who could do such a thing."

"I'm Wil," she said.

For the first time since her arrival, he smiled genuinely. "I am called Pahn."

She knew this, but she didn't let on. Didn't let him know how desperately she needed his help with things beyond Loom's health. She suspected seeming too eager would only raise the price.

Pahn pressed his palm to the crystallized trunk. His brows drew together with concentration, and then, like a rapidly spreading moss, the tree was covered over with bark.

Wil worked to contain her shock. "You can undo it?" Her mind spun with the possibilities. The tree was whole again, alive again. So perhaps this curse could be undone after all. Living things could be brought back.

"Nothing as grand as that," Pahn said. "It's merely an illusion."

Wil hated herself for hoping.

They returned to the cottage. The silent men carried Loom's

limp body to a room with a cot and a flickering chandelier and little else. His lips were pale. Even his tattoos seemed to be fading with him, as though he were a figure being erased from a painting.

Pahn knelt beside him and pressed down on Loom's forehead so hard that his head canted back and his mouth opened.

"What have you gotten yourself into, you foolish child?" Pahn said.

Wil stood in the corner, her fingers flexing anxiously in their gloves. The smell of death was overwhelming now that crystallizing the tree had awoken her senses. She could hear Loom's rasped breaths like a sheet of paper being crinkled by her ear. She could hear, also, Zay's incoherent whispers, pleas with the gods burning in the stars. Wil could taste Zay's fear on her tongue.

After Zay's attempted execution, she had spent days at sea, caring for Ada and trying to keep Loom alive. She held on to hope and to perseverance, and to her sanity. But no one held on to her.

"I'll need the grindings," Pahn said to one of his silent men. The man left and returned with a cup of something that looked like bark shavings, while another brought a mug that emitted steam and smelled of spices.

Wil found all of it nauseating—the fear, the smells, the presence of death waiting to pluck the soul from Loom's pallid skin.

Pahn tore open Loom's tunic with a jagged blade and peeled

it from his body. The tattoos that snaked around Loom's arms ended where his chest began, and in that smooth unmarred skin Wil could see the boy he might have been, if he hadn't been marked a prince, if he hadn't been ordered to kill as a child. She saw his vulnerabilities laid bare.

Pahn mixed the shavings with the herbal water, creating a paste so burning hot that it emitted steam even as he spread it across Loom's chest. But if it was painful, Loom was beyond feeling it.

The marveler stood, bits of paste still clinging to his fingers. "That's it. If the boy is meant to live, he'll live."

"That's all you can do?" Zay said. "After everything? I could have done that."

"Look at him," Pahn said. "He is barely clinging to life. You should have brought him to me sooner."

"There are no airships leaving the South." Zay clenched her jaw. "All we had was our ship. I can't control the length of the ocean."

"Nor can I," Pahn said. "I have fulfilled my end of the bargain." He nodded to Wil. "You, I am greatly interested in. Follow me."

"I'm not leaving him," Wil said. No matter what had happened between them, he'd never left her side when she needed him to stay, his touch reminding her that she was still a part of the living.

"Very well," Pahn said. He gestured to the floor. "Do sit.

We'll talk here." He nodded to Zay. "I believe your child is waking up. Talk to one of my men about feeding him."

Zay went, but not before stooping by Loom's bedside and whispering something as she smoothed the hair from his face.

Once she was gone, Pahn sat before Wil and said, "I'd like you to tell me about this power of yours."

"I'd love to," Wil said. "But the truth is that I don't know. I assume it's a curse of some sort."

Pahn sat back, considering. "Curses cannot cause prosperity such as diamonds," he said. "Wealth, immortality—all of that is impossible."

"So then it isn't a curse?"

"I didn't say that. This would make more sense if you turned things to ordinary stone or toads or worms—things like that. But you create something beautiful and prosperous. Tell me, are there any exceptions to this power? Anything that isn't affected? A particular plant, perhaps."

"Loom," Wil said.

Pahn looked to Loom and back to her. "There are two types of curses," he said. "Loom's curse was cast. It was a punishment for his own wrongdoing. This is the most ethical sort. But there is another. A curse can be inherited."

"Inherited?" Wil said. "You mean that I was born with it? Why would someone want to curse me before I was born?"

"As I said, it's less than ethical," Pahn said. "It's a dirty affair that most marvelers would have nothing to do with, birth curses. But there is a way to know for sure. Do you have any strange scars? Distinguishing marks?"

Wil's blood was cold. "Yes," she said. "But it's just a birthmark."

"Like an incision, and white in color, on your chest?"

Wil's fist instinctively curled over her chest. "Yes."

"There's a mark on your heart," Pahn said. "Someone wanted you to have a life of suffering. Someone wanted to punish you."

"Punish me for what?" she cried. "What could I have done to anger anyone before I was born?"

Pahn shook his head slowly. "That, I do not know. Assuming the marveler is still alive, you would have to find the one who cast it and ask."

"But you can undo it, can't you?" Wil said. "I've already crystallized most of that tree. That alone could build a kingdom."

"I have no interest in building kingdoms, girl. And even if I did, birth curses cannot be undone."

"There has to be some way," Wil said. "Please."

"I could remove your heart, but I doubt you'd find that a preferable solution." His brows rose. "But I can tell you why Loom isn't affected. Though yours was inherited and his was cast, you both have cursed hearts. You are forgotten. Throwaways. Left to live your days in the outskirts of the world."

Wil's mind was spinning. "I don't understand."

Pahn leaned toward her. "Just as beauty attracts beauty, cursed souls are also drawn to each other. It's an illusion, to keep your kind in the world's shadows."

"I . . ."

On the cot, Loom broke apart from the bottomless well of his dark dreams, and opened his eyes. He let out a pained groan, and his lips moved in the shape of her name, though no sound came out, and then he was gone again.

She looked to Pahn. "You're saying that everything I may feel for him, and that he may feel for me . . . is a lie? Because we're cursed?"

"I've seen this sort of attraction thousands of times, and it's very common," Pahn said. "But your particular curse is truly the most interesting I've seen, and I once met a boy who thought he was a salamander when the moon was full."

It made sense. It explained this pull she felt toward Loom, like a little boat rising helplessly with the swell of a wave.

"There is another extract I can give the boy to be sure he lives," Pahn said. "But it's in short supply and hard to come by, therefore expensive. I will use it, but in exchange, I must ask you to do something for me. I'll give you one month to oblige, and if you don't return, I'll take your absence as a refusal and I'll stop his heart for good."

Wil forced strength into her voice. "What do you want me to do?"

# THIRTY-EIGHT

THE SNOW BEGAN LATE IN the night and was still falling by morning.

Wil had been lying awake since before dawn. She watched the sky begin to pale through the single window in the small room. All night it had rattled and let a chill in through its crevices.

Sometime in the night, when exhaustion took hold, she lay on the edge of Loom's cot, turned away from him. Just as she had begun to fall asleep, Loom shifted in his sleep and wrapped his arm around her waist, drawing her in with a silent sigh that filled her hair.

It was hours later and she had barely moved, afraid that she might disturb him. His breathing was light and even. His forehead pressed to the back of her neck was cool, no longer drenched with perspiration.

He was going to live. Now that the sun was rising, Wil was sure of it. Pahn had kept his word, and it was time for her to do the same.

For now, though, she let herself linger in his presence, let his breaths disappear under her tunic and rustle the fine hairs at the nape of her neck. In this quiet place, she could close her fingers around his and hold their joined hands over the mark of her curse on her chest. She could imagine what it was to be loved, to be safe.

Because soon, she knew, there would be the new day bright with snow. There would be two cursed hearts who were drawn to each other only because that was a part of their curse: forgotten things signaling out to other forgotten things.

None of this was real. She knew that. She and Loom could not be honest with each other, as he had hoped, because this curse wouldn't allow them to ever know what might have been if they had met with normal hearts.

Still, as she sank against him and ignored the light of morning that crept over their bodies, this felt like the truth.

She bowed her head and kissed the back of his hand, just to know how it might have felt to love him. Her lips lingered on his skin. She wasn't prepared for how deceptively right it felt.

For a moment in time, this was their kingdom. Just as the world had cast them out, the world was not welcome here.

Then she forced herself to stand. The absence of his body touched her like a cold wind.

Loom's fist tightened in the empty space where she'd been,

and he opened his eyes. "Wil?"

"Hey." She knelt beside him. "You lived through the night after all."

"I told you. I refuse to let my father be happy."

He cupped his hand against the side of her throat, and she leaned into the touch as he traced his thumb along the line of her jaw.

It was so good to see the life in his eyes again. All that mischief and tragedy he showed her, as though she were worthy of his trust.

"How do you feel?"

"Like Zay owes me. I told her it was too dangerous for you two to enter the city at night. Nearly cost her head."

"Don't be too hard on her," Wil said. "She was the one who thought to bring you to Pahn."

He pushed himself upright, testing his strength. "So what was it? What was the trade for my health? I know Pahn doesn't work for free."

"We can talk about that later. What's important is that you're well."

His gaze fell flat. "Tell me it wasn't you."

"We were low on options." She sat on the edge of the bed, and he wrapped a blanket around her; she was accustomed to the cold, but he wasn't. "He wanted me to crystallize an ancient tree."

"What for?"

"If I didn't do it, he was going to let you die. I didn't ask

389

beyond that." She rose to her feet. "I'm going to bring you some breakfast."

"I can get it myself if—"

"No." The word came out too fast and too loud. "No. Please, just rest."

She shed the blanket from her shoulders and moved for the door, but he grabbed her shirt and reeled her back. She fell against his chest, and at the warmth of his lips against her ear, she closed her eyes.

He smelled of strange ground roots and the oil the marveler had forced down his throat to make him well again. That musty presence of death still lingered, though, warning her that this wasn't over.

She thought he would kiss her, but instead when his lips moved it was with a warning. "We can't stay here," he whispered. He grabbed her chin and brought her face up to meet his. She loved the way he touched her—so eager and so gentle. "You may not have dealt with marvelers, but I have. We have to leave this place. Today. He has something planned for that tree and for you, and it's best we don't stay to find out."

Wil studied his face. His dark, serious eyes, the stern line of his lips. "Will you at least eat something first? You've barely held down anything for a week, and all of this will be for nothing if you collapse from hunger."

He pressed his fingertips against her throat, to where her heart was beating fast.

She kissed him. It was a still kiss, her lips pressed unmoving against his. It did not feel like an illusion; it did not feel like a curse; it felt as natural as the grass beneath her bare feet so long ago when she was free.

His lips moved against hers. "I love you," he said.

She held her breath.

She didn't want to respond. Saying anything at all in the throes of this curse would be a lie. She didn't know how love should feel, and as she considered this, she thought of everything that had rushed into her head the moment Loom called Zay his wife. With that revelation, she had presumed that Ada was their child. She had imagined Loom looking at Zay the way he had looked at her before she crystallized the alber blossoms in Brayshire. Had imagined his hand trailing the length of Zay's hip, the wicked smile on Zay's lips before she must have kissed him.

She had felt flustered and heartsick and jealous.

Now, Loom tucked her hair behind her shoulder, his fingertips sweeping her throat. Again she felt flustered, and heartsick, and jealous—not of Zay this time, but of the girl Loom believed she was. Again, she felt that his love did not belong to her. Even so, she wanted to pluck those lovely words up from the earth—fat and healthy and dripping with their roots—and keep them.

She sensed his expectancy. He had told her he loved her, and he was waiting for her to respond.

But she couldn't. The curse and all its lies of love were not the only deception at play. She was the daughter of his enemy. Her brother had alchemized the weapon that tore his city ablaze. Love her? Of course he didn't. If he knew the truth about her, there would be weapons drawn. He would want her dead.

"I have to go," she blurted. "Stay here. Please, just stay here."

She was gone before he could utter a word of protest.

Wil found Zay by the fire, eating from a bowl of rice topped with steamed vegetables and slices of boiled egg. Ada was beside her, contentedly biting into a pear.

"How is he?" Zay asked. "I checked in on him in the night. If I had known those grindings would work that well—"

"It wasn't the grindings," Wil said. Loom's words were still buzzing inside her. She wondered if they showed on her skin, made her brighter somehow. She sat across from Zay and leaned close, her voice hushed. "Pahn made him drink some extract, and that's when he started to improve."

Zay paled. "What did he ask for in return?"

"You can't tell Loom."

"What did you do?" Zay's voice was tight.

"Pahn wants me to return to my home and discover the origin of my curse. He says that the answer lies in my family lineage. I need to find the name of the marveler who cursed me and bring it to him in a month's time."

"What happens if you don't?"

Wil bunched the fabric of her trousers in her fists. Her posture was rigid. "Loom will die."

For a moment Zay was too bewildered to speak. She blinked furiously. "I may have despised you from the start, but until this moment I never thought you were stupid."

"He was going to die." Wil's voice was steady. "You saw him. I couldn't sit back doing nothing."

Zay shook her head. "Loom won't let you be indebted to Pahn for his sake."

"It's done," Wil said. "I have to leave. Tonight. One of the silent men will bring me to the port. The Arrod borders are closed to Southern ships, but the East is still an ally."

Zay bit her lip and looked to the closed door that led to Loom's bed.

"Look at me," Wil said. "I will come back in time. You have to keep him here. Don't let him do anything stupid."

She laughed bitterly. "I'm his wife, not a weaver of miracles." She hesitated. "I'll do what I can. But if you don't return, you'll have me to deal with. I am far worse than any curses you may encounter, and there will be nowhere you go that I can't find you."

"Yes," Wil said. "I know." She stood and pulled the steel gloves from her belt.

Wil avoided Loom for the rest of the morning, but eventually he found her, as ever. Now she knew why he was so good at sensing her presence. And, as she listened for it, she realized that she could sense him too.

She was sitting at the edge of the cliff that overlooked the city. Even without hearing his footsteps, she knew that he was coming, his nearness like a touch, snaking around her throat, her wrists, soft and warm against the chilly air.

She didn't move, letting the feeling tumble through her.

He sat beside her, and both of them stared at the faraway electric lights winking against the cloudy gloom. "I was wondering where you'd gone off to," he said. "Aren't you too cold?"

At last, she looked at him. His cheeks were pinched pink by the frigid wind. "I'm never cold," she said. This weather made her think of home, of the draft that crept in around the castle windows during the winter, hissing a tiny symphony as the snow danced in time.

Loom nodded to the city, strung together by electrical wires in the distance, like the vine that connected all his tattoos. "Is Arrod like this?"

"No," Wil said. "The electricity comes from the water mills, but we don't have nearly as many buildings, or roads built for automobiles. You can smell the ocean and the rivers from anywhere." She smiled, remembering the Port Capital. "We still use carriage horses. A bit dated, I know."

"Cannolay is more dated, I assure you." Loom laughed.

Her fond memories of home darkened as she thought of her father. He was the one resistant to things like automobiles and telephones. But he had no qualms about using an alchemized bomb on the Southern Isles. Why?

"It's all wind energy here," Loom said. "There's plenty of it at this altitude." He nodded to a tower far in the distance, billowing gray clouds. "That's where digital panels for dirigibles and ships are manufactured and then sold around the world."

"That's what those spinning stars are," she said. "They harness the wind. Am I right?"

"Wind turbines," Loom affirmed.

Wil marveled at how fascinating the world was, even in her grief. Water and air and sun could feed life to so many things.

"Listen," Loom said, "Wil. You're under no obligation to help me. I asked for two weeks, and you gave them to me. You have no reason to grant me one last favor, but still I have to ask."

"What is it?" she said.

"Whatever Pahn has promised you, don't do it. Don't rid yourself of this power."

She drew back at that. "Why in the world not? It's made me into a monster."

"No," he said, startling her when he took her hand. The life in his touch. The energy. But it wasn't her curse that drew her to him in that moment. It was his arm, wrapping around her and bringing her in. "It hasn't," he said against her mouth, and then kissed her.

She let herself fall—foolishly, selfishly, knowing all the while that what it ignited in her was a lie.

This was not like her first kiss, when she and the boy from the party had been curious strangers who meant nothing to each other. With Loom, it felt so certain, as though they had lived a hundred lives before, and found their way to each other in all of them. As though they were always meant to end up here: this boy who had murdered and stolen, and this girl made of secrets and lies, their cursed hearts pounding.

He brought his mouth to her ear and murmured in Lavean, "Tell me something true."

She felt herself weakening at the words, and she forced herself to stay alert, to resist the thing telling her to grab his face in her hands and kiss him again.

"What?" she said.

He kissed the side of her throat, and she sat taller as the sensation rolled up her spine like a wave. "I want to know something about you," he said. "Anything."

She put her hands on his shoulders. She meant to push him away, but her fingers only tightened. Just for a little while, she reasoned. Tonight she would be gone on a ship bound for Northern Arrod, and the distance would clear her head. What did a few moments matter now?

"I'm not what you think," she said.

He laughed into her neck, and she felt the smooth perfect row of his teeth against her skin. "I've never known what to think."

"I just—" Her fingers moved through his hair. It was damp and heavy; he must have bathed recently. Gone, too, was the smell of herbs, of death and all the desperate attempts to ward it off. He was whole again. Alive again.

She forced herself to push him away. The air was colder, the sky grayer. His puzzled expression was almost too much to bear.

"I'm sorry," he said. "I thought you wanted me to—"

"You should rest," she said.

He was watching her with that wary skepticism again, silently asking for an explanation, as though she could be trusted to tell him the truth. It was odd that someone with so little cause to trust anyone placed so much trust in her, Wil thought.

She thought of how she had felt in the boat, rowing away from Messalin. How she could smell the city on him, could feel his love for it emanating. It had startled her. It still did. She had never doubted that love was real, and now he looked at her the same way.

Could that be a symptom of the curse? Could any curse be that strong?

"You're bleeding." Loom brushed his fingertips under her nose, and when he held them up, they were dark with blood. She coughed and more erupted from her mouth. The earlier strange pain in her core returned, and she grimaced.

"Look at me." Loom's words were almost lost in a shrill whine that made everything bright white. He grabbed her face in his hands, but where his touch had soothed her moments earlier, now it ignited the pain that shot through her limbs.

Then, as Loom pulled her against his chest, the pain stopped. Clarity returned like clouds parting, and she could smell her blood on his coat, feel it dampening her mouth and nostrils.

"Wil," he said gently. "Wil, turn around. Look what you've done."

She looked over her shoulder and followed his gaze. All the grass where she'd been sitting was shimmering—a tiny valley of gold.

The pain was gone, but she felt as though she had just heaved a mountain off her body. She reached out and plucked one of the blades. A residual shiver ran through her.

"Has that ever happened before?" He touched her forehead, inspecting her.

She rubbed the back of her hand across her mouth, wiping the blood away. "No. It's never been gold."

It had never hurt like that either, as though her bones were splintering under the weight of her own power. But she recognized that pain; she had begun to feel it, just faintly, that night on the beach with Loom.

She looked from the gold to him. It was him. It had to be. Thinking of him made her turn things to gold. But, no, it had to run deeper than that; this hadn't happened in all the time she'd spent with him. What was different now?

The look of concern on Loom's face surprised her. "How do you feel?" His voice sounded far away, and then very close.

"Fine," she said. "I think it's over."

Loom crawled forward in the grass and began plucking the

golden blades from the dirt. "We have to hide these," he said. "I don't want to think about what Pahn would do to you if he saw this."

The sudden rush of the wind felt too cold, filled with the earthy smell of decaying leaves. When she moved to gather the gold, she could taste metal on her tongue.

Loom was staring at her. "I've never seen your eyes look like that."

"Do I look sick?" Wil studied her palms, filled with blades of hardened grass. Her skin was bronzed, as though she'd spent a summer in the sun.

"No," he said. "You're so . . . bright."

"It'll pass," she said, and even as the words came out she could feel herself returning to normal. Her new normal, anyway.

They walked deep into the woods and buried the gold beneath some dirt that hadn't yet frozen in the cold.

On the walk back to Pahn's cabin, he kept studying her, sneaking glances he must have thought were inconspicuous. She pulled her collar up higher. Flutters of pain and something wonderful moved within her, like trapped birds with razors for wings.

# THIRTY-NINE

SHORTLY BEFORE THE SUN WENT down, Loom retreated to bed and fell into a deep sleep.

Wil stood in the doorway, arms crossed, watching him. Despite the sudden fatigue, he seemed well. There was still color in his face, and his breathing was clear and even.

She didn't know how long she stood there delaying the inevitable before Zay came up beside her and prodded her in the hip with something. "Here," she said. "I thought you'd want these back." She was holding Wil's sheathed dagger in one hand and the holster containing her guns in the other. "Couldn't figure out how to shoot the guns anyway. I hope you don't mind I borrowed some of the sleep serum to put in his food. I figured it'd be easier for you to sneak off if he was out cold."

"Thank you," Wil said. The words were too small to

convey her gratitude, but Zay didn't seem the type for sentimental good-byes.

When she fitted the holster and sheath back in place, a bit of the old Northern princess came awake. Wil had spent so much time burying that girl, she was struck by how much she missed her.

"Don't get yourself killed," Zay said.

"Take care of him," Wil said. "Tell him—tell him I'll come back."

Wil descended the steps that led away from Pahn's home, and as soon as her feet touched the ground, the staircase disappeared entirely. She spun to find herself staring at a jagged mountain that did not hint at human presence. This was how he hid from the world, doubtless because he had made his share of enemies.

Hiding, Wil understood. Her own father was a master at it. He hid his children in plain sight too.

She understood that marvelers were beyond her understanding, and that it was foolish to trust them. But business was not about trust. Owen had taught her that. Pahn looked at her and he saw something to be gained. She saw the same in him.

It was mid-October and the ports were bare. The silent men left Wil with a pouch containing just enough coins for a ship to take her to Northern Arrod and back. Pahn had even given her a suede coat that was trimmed with gray wolf fur, and he had carried on as though she should be indebted to his great kindness for bestowing such a gift.

It did protect against the chill, she supposed.

There was only one ship headed west for Northern Arrod, loaded mostly with crates of silks and buttons. There were few passengers, all likely of Arrod descent, Wil noted, all going home. No one else was interested in entering a country in a time of war.

Wil clung to the railing as the captain shouted orders to his men somewhere behind her.

And then they were moving. The afternoon sun was high. The water glimmered so sharply that she could almost believe that the sea was filled with diamonds. But this time the diamonds had no power over her. She couldn't be stopped. The ship sliced clean through them.

# ACKNOWLEDGMENTS

This story has been years in the making, and an insurmountable debt of gratitude is owed to the people who have been along for the ride during those years. Thanks as always to my family for all of their love and for believing in me.

No thanks will ever be enough for my lovely, lovely friend Aprilynne Pike, who heard my original idea for this story and whose advice turned that story into what it is now. Huge thanks are also due to Beth Revis, who made me actually sit down and write it. This story also would not exist without the support and encouragement of Laini Taylor, whose late-night chats served as a means to procrastinate and whose encouragement served as a motivator to stop procrastinating. Enormous and cake-filled thanks to Sabaa Tahir, whose friendship and encouragement and support, I should mention, are worth far more than a handful of words.

Thank you to everyone who has been willing to hear my ideas over the years and offer their feedback: Harry Lam, who knows All The Things. Renée Ahdieh, who is the standard to which all prose in the world should be held. Leigh Bardugo, whose characters have broken my heart but whose kind words have taped it back together. Ann Aguirre, who knows how to write a fight scene like the best of them and who helped me equip Wil with the skills that shaped who she is. The talented and amazing Samantha Shannon—thank you so much for everything. Laura Bickle, Aimée Carter, Sangu Mandanna, Maureen Willmann, and Christine Munger, for their kindness and support in this endeavor. Cindy Pon, my friend since way back when, for only getting more wonderful each year. Jodi Meadows, who has been such a source of encouragement. CJ Redwine, my gem of a friend, for picking up the pieces and gluing me back together so many times.

Thank you to Deb Frattini, whom I first met as a petrified undergrad applying to colleges. Thank you for keeping my first essay in your desk, and thank you for still reading the things I send you.

Thank you to Randi Oomens, who read this as an early draft and whose notes are the reason so many of these characters are as strong as they are. Thank you to Sona Charaipotra, Natasha Razi, and Tara Sim, for your genius, wisdom, time, experience, and insights. I can never put into words how much your efforts to make these characters and this world shine has meant to me.

Thanks as ever to my otherworldly agent, Barbara Poelle, for still being as enthusiastic and believing in me just as much now as when we first signed nearly a decade ago. I would never be on this journey if not for you.

Thank you to my editor, Kristin Rens, for believing in this story from the start, and for championing it through ten billion rewrites and revisions. Thank you to the entire team at Balzer + Bray for their hard work, creative genius, patience, love, and generosity of time and spirit, and for giving this story a place in the world.

Last but never least, thank you to my readers for following my stories for all these years, or for just now cracking open one of their spines. I wouldn't be here without all of your support and love. An extra-, extraspecial thank-you to those who preordered this book and sent such kind notes of encouragement:

Jessey
Bement,
Domini
Bigham, Lissa
Bilyk-Pring, Amber
Bird, David Bock, Jillian
Brown, Tam Chronin, Andrea
Churchill, Desirae Cisneros, Joni
Collison, Jennie Cresswell, Tiffanie
Dang, Hannah Davies, Heather DeFilippis,
Julia DeLeon, Denise Doyle, Jenn Edwards,
Deena Edwards, Sabrina Ekstein, Amy Israel Felker,
Steph Fidis, Marcy Funderburk, Angelique Melanie Geyer,
Maddie Wilkinson Gurr, Caitlin Haines, Melissa Hardy,
Sabrina Heuschkel, Raelynn N Jacobe, Scarlett Kail, Kimberly
Kosydor, Shari Linn, Ros A Lynn, Nicole Maria, Matin
Matinez, Eleni McKnight, Marissa Maurer, Stephanie
Michelle, Hanna Müller, Ashleigh Nave, Jenn
Neuberger, M Andrew Patterson, Jessica
Porter, Rachel Rowlands, Tracy Russell,
Aneesa Suleman, Anni Holladay
Thompson, Michelle Trego,
Maura Trice, Kaitlyn
Weiler, Kat Weltha,
Heidy White,
Elizabeth
Whitmire